SCHOOL
SPIRITS

SCHOOL SPIRITS

RACHEL HAWKINS

HYPERION
NEW YORK

First Edition
1 3 5 7 9 10 8 6 4 2
G475-5664-5-13060
Printed in the United States of America

Library of Congress Cataloging-in-Publication Data
Hawkins, Rachel, 1979–
    School spirits / Rachel Hawkins.—First edition.
        pages cm
    Summary: Fifteen-year-old Izzy, whose family has fought monsters for centuries, investigates a series of hauntings at her new high school.
    ISBN 978-1-4231-4849-4
    [1. Supernatural—Fiction. 2. Monsters—Fiction. 3. Magic—Fiction. 4. High schools—Fiction. 5. Schools—Fiction.] I. Title.
    PZ7.H313525Sc 2013
    [Fic]—dc22   2012046402

Reinforced binding

Visit www.un-requiredreading.com

For Katie, the closest thing to a sister I have

CHAPTER 1

Killing a vampire is actually a lot easier than you'd think. I know movies and TV make it look really hard, like if you don't hit the right spot, it won't work. But the truth is, those are just rumors spread by vampire hunters to make themselves seem tougher. If everyone knew how easy it actually is to kill a vamp, there wouldn't be so many movies and TV shows and stuff. All it takes is a wooden stake and enough pressure to send it through the chest cavity. Doesn't really matter if you hit the heart or not.

See? So easy.

But capturing a vampire? Yeah, that's a little bit tougher.

"Just. Hold. Still," I mumbled around the tiny flashlight in my mouth. I was straddling the vamp's chest, my right hand holding a stake poised over his heart, my left clutching the little piece of paper with the ritual on it.

"Release me, mortal!" the vampire cried, but his voice broke on the last word, kind of ruining the dramatic effect. "My brothers will be here soon, and we will bathe in your blood."

I spit out the miniflashlight, and it landed on the hardwood floor with a clink. Pressing the stake closer, I leaned over him. "Nice try. We've been watching you for a week. You're working this town solo. No nest in sight."

"Nest" is what vampires call both their houses and the group of fellow vampires who are basically their roommates. I thought it was a pretty dorky name, but then, a lot about vampires is dorky.

This one was especially bad. Not only was he rocking the gelled hair, he'd moved into the one creepy, pseudo-Victorian mansion in town. He might as well have hung a neon sign blaring, HERE THERE BE VAMPIRE. All of his furniture was red velvet and heavy wood, and when I'd busted in earlier, he was in the middle of writing in a journal while a pretty blond girl sat near the fireplace.

She'd bolted when she saw me, and I was already cringing, thinking of how Mom would react to there being a witness.

The vampire, who was going by the name of Pascal, but was probably really a Brad or a Jason, twisted underneath me, but I was firmly seated. One of the perks of being a Brannick is that we're stronger than your average person. It also didn't hurt that this vamp was pretty small. When I'd wrestled him to the floor, I noticed that he was only a few inches taller than me, and most of that was his hair.

Sighing, I squinted at the piece of paper again. It was only a few words in Latin, but getting them right was important, and I'd never done this ritual by myself before.

That thought sent a bolt of pain through my chest, one I did my best to ignore.

Underneath me, "Pascal" stopped struggling. Tilting his head to the side, he watched me with his dark eyes. "Who is Finley?"

My grip tightened on the stake. "What?"

Pascal was still studying me, upper lip curling over his fangs. "Your head. It's full of that name. Finley, Finley, Finley."

Oh, freaking great. Vampires are a pain in the butt when they're just your garden-variety bloodsucker, but a few of them have extra powers. Low-level mind reading, telekinesis, that kind of thing. Apparently Pascal was one of the special ones.

"Get out of my head," I snarled at him, renewing my focus on the sheet of paper. *"Vado—"* I started, but then Pascal interrupted with, "She's your sister. Finley."

Hearing my sister's name from this . . . this *thing's* lips made the pain in my chest even worse, but at least no tears stung my eyes. I can't think of anything more pathetic than crying in front of a vampire.

Besides, if it were Finley here, if I was the one who was missing, she wouldn't have let a vamp, much less a vamp called *Pascal*, get to her. So I scowled down at him and pressed the stake hard enough to just break the skin.

Pascal drew in a hissing breath, but he never took his eyes off my face. "Nearly a year. That's how long this Finley has been gone. How long you've been working alone. How long you've felt like it was all your fau—"

"Vado tergum," I said, dropping the piece of paper and laying my free hand flat against his sternum.

Pascal's gaze fell to my hand and he went even paler. "What is that?" he asked, his voice high with fear and pain. "What are you doing?"

"It's better than getting staked," I told him, but as the smell of burning cloth filled the air, I wasn't so sure.

"You're a Brannick!" he shrieked. "Brannicks don't do *magic*! What the hell is this?"

I kept up a steady stream of Latin, but *What the hell is this* was a totally valid question. The Brannicks had spent millennia staking vamps and shooting werewolves with silver-tipped arrows (and later, with solid silver bullets). We'd burned witches and enslaved Fae, and basically

4

became what monsters told scary stories about.

But things were different now. For starters, there were no more Brannicks besides me and my mom. Rather than hunt the Creatures of the Night, we worked for the Council that governed them. And they didn't call themselves monsters; they went by the much more civilized term "Prodigium." So the Brannicks were now more or less Prodigium cops. If one of their kind got out of hand, we tracked them, captured them, and did a ritual that sent them directly to the Council, who would then decide their punishment.

Yeah, it was a lot harder than just staking a vampire or shooting a werewolf, but the truce between Brannicks and Prodigium was a good thing. Besides, our cousin, Sophie, was a Prodigium, and set to be Head of the Council someday. It was either make peace or suffer some majorly awkward family holidays.

The ritual was nearly finished, the air around Pascal starting to shimmer slightly, when he suddenly shouted, "The boy in the mirror!"

Surprised, I sat back a little. "What did you just say?"

Pascal's chest was heaving up and down, and his skin had gone from ivory to gray. "That's what you're afraid of," he panted. "That he had something to do with Finley's vanishing."

My mouth had gone dry, and, blinking at him, I

shook my head. "No—" I started to say, only to realize too late that my hand had slipped off his chest.

Taking advantage of my distraction, Pascal gave another twist, this one stronger than the others, and managed to free one of his arms from beneath my knees. I was already ducking the blow, but the back of his hand caught me across the temple, sending me sprawling.

My head cracked against an end table, and stars spun in my vision. There was a blur of motion—vampires may not be that strong, but they *can* be fast—and Pascal was up the stairs and gone.

Sitting up, I winced as I touched my temple. Luckily, there was no blood, but a lump was already forming, and I glared at the staircase. My stake had rolled under the table, and I picked it up, curling my fingers around the wood. The Council may prefer for us to send monsters to them, but staking a vamp in self-defense? They'd be okay with that.

Probably.

I carefully made my way up the stairs, stake raised at shoulder level. The wall was lined with those tacky globe lamps—seriously, vampires are the worst—and a twinkling caught my eye.

Glancing down, I saw that I was covered in a fine layer of shimmery silver. Oh, *gross*. He was one of those body-glitter-wearing jerks. Now I was even more embarrassed that I'd let Pascal get inside my head, that I'd dropped my guard long enough for him to get away from me. If he got out of the house . . .

My fingernails dug into the stake. No. I was not letting that happen.

The landing was covered in burgundy carpet that muffled my footsteps. Directly across from me was a large mirror in a heavy gilt frame, and in it, I looked a lot less like a bad-ass vampire slayer and a lot more like a scared teenage girl.

My skin was nearly as papery white as Pascal's, a sharp contrast against the bright red of my braid.

Swallowing hard, I did my best to calm my hammering heart and racing mind. There was one thing vampires and Brannicks had in common: a few of us had special powers. Pascal's was reading minds, and mine—in addition to the strength and quick healing that came with being a Brannick—was sensing Prodigium. And right now, my Spidey senses were telling me Pascal had gone to the right.

I took one step in that direction.

On the one hand, my detection skills were dead on. On the other, I'd expected Pascal to be cowering behind a door or trying to open a window and get out. What I hadn't expected was for him to suddenly come barreling out of the darkness and slam into me.

We flew back onto the landing, crashing to the floor. I felt the stake tumble from my fingers, and with a grunt, tried to ram my knee up into Pascal's stomach. But this time, Pascal had the advantage—he was faster than me, and he'd caught me by surprise. He dodged my knee like it was nothing, and his fingers sank into my hair, jerking my head hard to the side and exposing my neck.

He was smiling, lips deep pink against the stark white of his fangs, and his eyes were black pools. Despite the stupid hair and the silly name and the flowing white shirt, he looked every bit the terrifying monster.

And when he ducked his head and I felt the sharp sting of his fangs piercing my skin, my scream was high and thin. This couldn't be happening. I couldn't go out like this, drained of blood by a dorky vampire calling himself *Pascal*.

A gray circle began to fill my vision, and I was so cold, colder than I'd ever been in my entire life. Then, from above me, there was a flash of silver, a glimpse of bright copper, and suddenly, Pascal was the one screaming. His body fell off of mine, and I raised a trembling hand to my neck, the rush of blood hot against my freezing skin.

Blinking rapidly to clear my vision, I scooted backward on the carpet, watching as the redheaded woman all in black dropped a knee in the middle of Pascal's chest, one hand pushing a bright silver amulet against his cheek.

Her other hand reached back and pulled a stake from the belt around her waist.

The stake swung down, and there was a sound almost like the popping of a bubble, and Pascal vanished in a surprisingly tiny cloud of dust and ash.

Head still swimming, I looked at the woman as she turned back to me.

Even though I knew it was impossible, I heard myself ask, "Finn?"

But the woman who strode over to me wasn't my sister.

"You okay?" Mom asked.

I pressed my palm tighter to the holes in my neck and nodded. "Yeah," I replied. Using the wall to brace myself, I went to stand up. As I did, my eyes skated over my mom, noticing that even though she'd been right on top of Pascal, she'd somehow managed to avoid getting even one speck of glitter on her.

"Of course," I muttered, and then the carpet was rushing up to meet me as I passed out at Mom's feet.

CHAPTER 2

The lights in our kitchen were too harsh. My eyes ached in the fluorescent glare, and my head was pounding. It didn't help that we'd taken an Itineris home. That was a type of magic portal, and they were located at posts all over the world. Problem was, like most things involving magic, there was a catch. While an Itineris made traveling a lot more convenient, it was also really rough on your body. I guess getting bent and twisted through the space-time continuum isn't exactly good for you.

The concoction in front of me finally seemed cool enough to drink, so I choked it down. It tasted like pine trees smell, but the ache in my head disappeared almost immediately. Across from me, Mom turned her coffee mug around and around in her hands. Her mouth was set in a hard line.

"He was a young vamp," she said at last, and I fought the urge to lower my head to the table.

"Yes," I replied, hand reaching up to touch the little puncture marks just under my jaw. Thanks to Mom's "tea," they were already starting to close, but they still hurt.

"He should have been no issue at all for you, Isolde," she continued, her gaze still on her mug. "I would never have sent you in there alone if I'd thought you couldn't handle it."

My hand dropped back to the table. "I could handle it."

Mom looked at the bite on my neck and raised her eyebrows. When she was younger, my mom had been beautiful. And even now there was something about the strong lines of her face that made people look twice at her. Her eyes were the same dark green as mine and Finley's, but there was a hardness that neither I nor my sister had.

"I mean, I *was* handling it," I mumbled. "But he was one of those mind-reading ones, and he . . . he got inside my head—"

"Then you should have shoved him right the heck out," Mom fired back, and I wondered what felt worse, the vampire bite or the guilt.

With a sigh, Mom dropped her head and rubbed her

eyes. "I'm sorry, Iz. I know you did the best you could."

But your best wasn't good enough.

Mom didn't have to say the words. I felt them hanging between us in the kitchen. There were a lot of words filling up the space between me and Mom these days. My sister's name was probably the biggest. Nearly a year ago, Finley disappeared on a case in New Orleans. It had been a totally routine job—just a coven of Dark Witches selling some particularly nasty spells to humans. We'd gone together, but at the last minute, Finley had told me to wait in the car while she dealt with the witches herself.

I could still see her standing under the streetlight, red hair so bright it almost hurt to look at. "I got this one, Iz," she'd told me before nodding at the book in my lap. "Finish your chapter." A dimple had appeared in her cheek when she grinned. "I know you're dying to."

I had been. The heroine had just been kidnapped by pirates, so things were clearly about to get awesome. And it had seemed like such an easy job, and Finley had swaggered off toward the coven's house with such confidence that I hadn't worried, not really. Not until I'd sat in the car for over an hour and Finley still hadn't come out. Not until I'd walked into the house and found it completely empty, the smell of smoke and sulfur heavy in the air, Finley's weapon belt on the floor in front of a sagging sofa.

Mom and I looked for her for six months. Six months of tracking down leads and sleeping in motel rooms and researching other cases like Finley's, and it all led nowhere. My sister was just . . . gone.

And then one day, Mom had just packed up our things and announced we were going home. "We have a job to do," she'd said. "Brannicks hunt monsters. It's what we do, and what we need to get back to. Finley would want that."

That had been the last time Mom had said Finley's name.

Now Mom sat across the table from me, and her coffee mug turned, turned, turned.

"Maybe we should take it easy for a while," she said at last. "Let you go on a few more missions with me, get your legs back under you."

Finley had been doing solo missions since she was fourteen. I was almost sixteen now, and this had been the first time Mom had let me out in the field by myself. I really didn't want it to be the *last* time, too.

I shoved my own mug. "Mom, I can do this. I just . . . Look, the vamp, he could read my mind, and I wasn't ready for that. But now I know! And I can be better on my guard next time."

Mom lifted her gaze from the table. "What did he see?"

I knew what she meant. Picking at the Formica table-top, I shrugged. "I thought about Finn for a sec. He . . . saw that, I guess. It just distracted me."

I didn't add the bit about how Pascal had mentioned the boy in the mirror. Bringing up Finn was going to bother Mom enough.

Just like I'd thought, her eyes suddenly seemed a million miles away. "Okay," she said gruffly, her chair shrieking on the linoleum as she shoved it back and stood. "Well, just . . . just go to bed. We'll think about our next move tomorrow."

Deep parentheses bracketed Mom's mouth, and her shoulders seemed more slumped than they had been just a few moments ago. As she passed my chair, for just a moment, Mom laid a hand on my head. "I'm glad you're okay," she murmured. And then, with a ruffle of my hair, she was gone.

Sighing, I picked up my cup and swirled the dregs of tea still left in it. Every bone in my body ached to go upstairs, take a shower, and crawl into my bunk.

But there was something I had to do first.

Our house wasn't much. A few bedrooms, a tiny kitchen, and a bathroom that hadn't been updated since the 1960s. Once upon a time, it had been the Brannick family compound. Back when there had been more

Brannicks. Now it was just a house surrounded by thick woods. But there was one room that really set it apart from your normal home.

We had a War Room.

It sounded cooler than it actually was. It was really just an extra bedroom stuffed with a bunch of boxes, a large round table, and a mirror.

It was the mirror I walked to now, yanking off the heavy canvas cover. Inside the glass, a warlock stared back at me.

His name was Torin, and he looked a couple years older than me, maybe eighteen or so. But since he'd gotten trapped in the mirror back in 1583, he was technically over four hundred years old.

"Isolde!" he called happily, leaning back, his hands on the table. "To what do I owe this lovely visit?" It was always bizarre watching Torin. Trapped in the mirror, he appeared to be sitting at the table in the middle of the War Room. But the actual table was empty. Even though I'd seen the phenomenon my whole life, I still caught myself glancing back and forth, as though Torin would magically appear on our side of the glass.

The thought made my head hurt all over again. In his own time, Torin had been an extremely powerful dark warlock. No one knew what spell he was attempting when he'd trapped himself inside the mirror, but one of my ancestors, Avis Brannick, had found him and taken responsibility for him.

The fact that Torin made the occasional prophecy had probably had something to do with that. His ability to see the future had come in handy for a few Brannicks over the years; easier to fight a witch or a faerie when you know what it's going to do.

But I hadn't come to have my fortune told. Climbing up onto the table, I crossed my legs and propped my chin in my hand. "I got bitten by a vampire tonight."

Frowning, Torin leaned forward. "Oh," he said, once his eyes settled on the bite mark. "So you did. That . . . What is the word you use?"

I couldn't help but smile a little as I rolled my eyes. "Sucks."

Torin nodded. "Even so." He mimicked my pose, ruby pinkie ring flashing in the dim light. Shaggy blond hair fell over his forehead, and when he smiled at me, his teeth were just the slightest bit crooked. "Tell me the whole story."

So I did, the way I always had, ever since I was old enough to go with Mom and Finley on missions. There was something . . . I don't know, relaxing about telling the story to Torin. I knew he wasn't looking for all the flaws in my mission, all the places where I had zigged when I should have zagged.

Unlike Mom, Torin didn't frown through the entire thing. Instead, he chuckled when I described Pascal's lair, grimaced when I mentioned the body glitter, and raised his eyebrows when I talked about chasing the vamp up the stairs.

"But you're all right. And you lived to fight another day."

Sighing, I pulled my braid over my shoulder, fiddling with the ends of my hair. "Yeah, but if Mom hadn't come in . . . She thinks I shouldn't be doing jobs on my own. Which, I mean, I should. This one got a little out of hand, but if she'd just trust me a little more—"

"If she had trusted you completely, she wouldn't have followed you, which means she wouldn't have burst in when she did," Torin said, lifting his shoulders. "And you, my lovely Isolde, would either be exsanguinated on what I can only guess was truly dreadful carpet, or the bride of the undead." He narrowed his eyes. "Neither fate suits you. Or me, for that matter."

His words seemed to lodge somewhere in my chest, but I shook them off. Torin had been a part of my life for, well, all of my life. When Mom and Finley had gone out on missions, he had kept me company. And after Finley disappeared, he was the only one I could talk to about my sister. Which is why that niggling suspicion, the one Pascal had picked up on, bothered me so much.

"Your mum is simply worried about you," Torin said, pulling me out of my thoughts. "She's lost one daughter. I'm sure the idea of losing another is particularly hellish for her."

"I know," I said, the guilt returning with a vengeance. What if I'd gotten myself killed tonight, all because I let one stupid vamp mess with my mind? Where would Mom have been then?

I tugged the rubber band off the end of my braid and started unraveling the strands. A thin layer of vampire ash rose from them. Ugh. Apparently I'd been closer to Pascal than I'd thought.

Wrinkling my nose with disgust, I hopped off the table. "Okay. Shower, bed. Thanks for the debriefing."

Torin made a little flourish with his hand, lace cuff falling back from his wrist. "Any time, Isolde."

I was nearly to the door before I turned back. "Torin, you . . ." I trailed off, not sure how to finish. Finally I took a deep breath and said, a little too fast, "You swear you don't know anything about Finn, right?"

I'd asked it before, the night Finley disappeared. Other than her belt, there'd been no sign of my sister in that rickety house. But there had been a mirror. A big one with a thick wooden frame, carved cherubs grinning at me. And while it could've been a trick of the light, I could've sworn that the glass had glowed slightly.

But I'd been beyond freaked out that night, confused, upset. I couldn't be sure what I'd seen, really.

In his mirror, Torin came up close to the glass. "No, Isolde," he said, his voice surprisingly gentle. "I do not know where your sister is."

"Right." I ran a hand through my hair, blowing out a long breath. "Right. Okay." Reaching out, I flicked off the switch.

From out of the darkness, Torin added, "Besides, Finley was never of much interest to me. She isn't the Brannick who will set me free, after all, is she?"

It was a wonder I could speak given how tight my throat had gone. "That's never going to happen, Torin. I may be nicer to you than my mom or Finn, but you'll be chatting with my *grandkids* from that mirror."

Torin only laughed. "I've seen what I've seen. The time will come when you will finally let me out of this cursed glass prison. But until then, go wash that vampire out of your hair and get a good rest. You and Aislinn will be taking quite the journey tomorrow."

"Where are we going?" I demanded. "What did you see?"

But there was no answer.

CHAPTER 3

When I woke up the next morning, Mom was already dressed and waiting for me at the kitchen table. She frowned at my tank top and pajama pants and pointed back up the stairs. "Get dressed. We're leaving in five minutes."

"Leaving?" The clock said it was just a little past six. Apparently Torin had been right. I rubbed the sleep from my eyes. "Where are we going?"

But Mom just said, "And now it's four minutes. Go."

There wasn't much to the bedroom Finley and I had shared. A bunk bed—Finn had claimed the top—a dresser, a battered desk, and a mirror. Finley's clothes were still folded in the drawers, and almost without thinking, I grabbed one of her black sweatshirts, tugging it over my tank top. I traded my flannel pants for jeans (my own, since Finn had been taller than me), and added a scuffed pair of black boots.

Jogging back downstairs, I twisted my hair into a sloppy braid over one shoulder. Hopefully, wherever we were going didn't have a dress code.

Mom was just outside the front door, and when I appeared at her side, she didn't say anything, merely jerked her head toward the woods surrounding the compound. Years ago, all the Brannicks had lived in this secluded spot deep in the woods of northern Tennessee. There were still outbuildings and training yards to accommodate at least a hundred people, but I'd never seen the place that full. By the time I was old enough to remember, the only Brannicks left were me, Mom, and Finn.

The woods were full of noise that morning, from the cracking of branches under our feet to the birds singing, but Mom didn't say anything and I didn't ask any questions.

Nearly a mile into the trees, we came to the Itineris. To anyone walking by—not that many people ever just "walked by" in these woods—the portal wouldn't have looked like anything but a small opening in a bunch of branches. They wouldn't even know it was there unless they accidentally stepped into it.

Which would probably be fatal since the Itineris was

too intense for humans. We could only use it because we had some residual magic in our blood.

Mom held out her hand to me, and I took it, ducking under the branches and stepping into the Itineris.

One of the weirdest things about using the Itineris is how it feels. There's no rushing wind or sense of motion, but a crippling, sickening pressure, as though the weight of the whole universe is pressing down on you.

Suddenly, we were standing on a paved road.

Well, Mom was standing. I was on my knees, gasping. The portal was always rough on me.

Mom helped me to my feet, but that was clearly all the TLC I was going to get. As soon as I was steady, she started walking down the road.

"Where are we?" I asked, following.

"Alabama," she replied.

I didn't ask what part of Alabama, but between the sand and the slight tang of salt on the wind, I guessed we were somewhere near the beach. We hadn't been walking long when we came across a path of crushed shells. Mom turned onto it, her boots crunching and sounding too loud in the quiet.

At the end of the driveway was a small, one-story house that actually looked a little bit like our place. An ancient Jeep was parked just by the front porch, and several sets of wind chimes twisted in the breeze.

★ ★ ★

The screen door creaked open, and a woman stepped out, squinting down the drive at us. She seemed to be about ten years or so older than my mom, and her dark blond hair, shot through with gray, was piled on top of her head in a messy knot. Her arms, bare in a black tank top, were pale and flabby. Roughly a dozen necklaces and pendants hung around her neck, and she held a coffee cup in her right hand. "Ash?" she asked, frowning at us.

"Maya," Mom returned. She gestured at me. "Mind if me and Izzy come in for a bit?"

Maya glanced over, seeming to notice me for the first time. I raised my hand in a tiny wave. "Hi."

Maya didn't wave back, but sighed and said, "Too early in the morning for Brannicks." Then she turned and walked back into the house.

I dug a little hole in the shells with the tip of my boot. "Does that mean we should go?"

To my surprise, Mom just chuckled. "No. If Maya hadn't wanted us here, trust me, she would have let us know."

"Who is she?" I asked, but Mom didn't answer; just trudged up the steps and into the house.

And after a long moment, I followed.

The house wasn't quite as spartan as our place, but it still wasn't what anyone would call homey. No pictures lined the walls, although Maya did have one of those crazy cat clocks, the swinging tail marking off seconds, its eyes darting back and forth like it was watching for something. The only other things of note were a sagging couch covered in an ugly orange-and-brown plaid and a crooked coffee table. But that wasn't what had me freezing in the doorway. Instead of magazines or heavy books, the coffee table was covered in . . . feet. Not human feet— at least I didn't *see* any—but half a dozen chickens' feet, several of those rabbit's foot key chains, and a brown, furry paw. Char marks dotted the table's scarred surface, and there was a cracked leather book lying open facedown, its pages wrinkled. Everything about it screamed magic, but I hadn't sensed anything when we came in, so I didn't think Maya could be Prodigium. Maybe she was just a . . . taxidermist or something. Mom had made some weird friends over the years.

And she must've been here before, because she didn't even blink at the bizarre collection. But she did lean in and whisper, "Don't say anything until I tell you to, okay? And don't take anything Maya gives you to drink."

I tried very hard not to gulp. "Got it."

Sure enough, Maya came out of the kitchen holding three mugs, steam rising off of them. Even across the room, the smell turned my stomach. Still, Mom accepted two cups before sitting on the couch. I sat next to her as

Maya took a seat on the floor in front of the coffee table. She was wearing a long skirt, and it jangled softly when she moved, as though there were bells hidden in its folds.

"So you're Izzy," she said, blowing the top of her drink. "Your mama brought Finley here plenty of times, but she always said you were too young to go out on jobs. How old are you now, thirteen?"

I had always looked younger than I was. "I'll be sixteen next month," I told her, and she gave a low whistle. "My, my, time is flying. When I first met you, Ash, Izzy was what? Five? Maybe six? It was right after her daddy died, and—"

"We didn't come here to chat, Maya," Mom broke in. "I wanted to go through the file."

Maya rolled her big blue eyes. "That's it? You could've e-mailed, you know. You didn't have to hike all the way out here for that kind of thing. I thought at the very least you wanted another locator spell. See if we'd have any luck finding your girl this time."

CHAPTER 4

With that, she rose to her feet and went back into the kitchen. While she pulled things out of cabinets and drawers, I leaned closer to Mom. "A locator spell? For Finn?"

"Hush, Izzy." She said it calmly, but her shoulders were stiff, and she was bouncing one foot up and down.

"She's a *witch*?" I hissed. "You went to a witch looking for Finn and you never told me?"

"It was none of your business." Mom's voice was sharper now, her hands digging into her thighs, and I jerked my head back like she had slapped me. To be honest, I kind of felt like she had.

Then Mom sighed and leaned closer to me, her voice softer as she said, "Iz."

I shook my head, biting off anything else I wanted to

ask about Finn. Instead, I said, "I couldn't feel her. Maya. And I can always sense witches."

"I'm a *hedge* witch," Maya said, coming back into the living room holding a folder overflowing with paper despite all the rubber bands wrapped around it. "Which is why your mother is insulting me greatly by using me to gather this sort of stuff." She waved the folder a little, and few Post-it notes fell out.

"What's in there?" I asked, and Maya sighed, pulling the rubber bands off the folder.

"Articles, weird things that popped up on the Internet . . . Basically, I keep an eye out for any news story that seems to involve the supernatural."

I turned to Mom. "This is how you find cases?"

Mom had never looked sheepish in her life, I was willing to bet, but something really close to that expression crossed her face now. "Not always. But sometimes it makes sense to . . . outsource."

I knew Mom had friends who helped her out on cases from time to time. There was the guy who got her the boat when she had to find those killer mermaids, and we always seemed to have plenty of money that came from some mysterious source. But a middle-aged lady in the middle of nowhere collecting articles about possible supernatural happenings? That seemed kind of . . . lame.

As Maya sat down in front of the coffee table, I pulled

the sleeves of my shirt over my hands and asked, "What's a hedge witch?"

Clearing all the feet away, Maya opened the folder. "The kind of witches you're used to are born that way. What is that stupid word they have for themselves?"

"Prodigium," Mom and I answered in unison.

"Right, well, Prodigium come into their powers at what, twelve? Thirteen? And they can just do magic. No wands, no spell books necessary unless they're trying to do the super-dark crap. Point is, it's an inborn ability." Maya began paging through the papers. Some were newspaper articles with big garish headlines. I spotted one that blared, SEA MONSTER SPOTTED AT NEW ENGLAND RESORT!

"Now, it strikes me that this is incredibly unfair," Maya continued. A pair of glasses dangled from a beaded chain around her neck, and she picked them up, balancing them on the end of her nose as she continued to scan the papers. An article that seemed to be about crop circles drifted to the carpet.

"Why should some people be born gods while the rest of us poor mortals have to struggle through the mud of humanity, trying—"

"Enough, Maya." Mom turned to me. "A hedge witch is someone who can do magic, but they've learned it from books. And their abilities are severely limited compared to natural witches."

"I resent the term *hedge witch*," Maya said with a haughty lift of her shoulders. "What I do is every bit as natural as what fancy Latin witches can do. If anything, hedge magic is more elegant."

I glanced at the little pile of feet on the carpet and bit back a sarcastic comment.

"Ah," Maya said at last, pulling out a large piece of paper. "Here's the one I was looking for. Caught my eye because it happened so close by."

She handed it to Mom, and I leaned so that I could read it over her shoulder. It was a photocopy of a newspaper piece. There was a grainy photo of a stretcher being pulled out of a large brick building, police tape everywhere. The caption read, STILL NO LEADS IN ATTACK ON POPULAR TEACHER.

"What happened?" I tapped the picture.

"Was just a few months ago," Maya said. "I remember it because that town in Mississippi was close enough to here that it made the local news. The science teacher was found nearly dead from a blow to the head."

"Okay, well, that seems awful but not necessarily supernatural," I said, but Mom shook her head. Pointing to a section of the article, she said, "Read this part. 'Police are particularly baffled as David Snyder was found in a room *locked from the inside*.' No witnesses, no fingerprints. And he swears he was alone in the room."

I read all of that, but I still didn't get it. "It's creepy, but it still isn't all that Brannick-y."

Mom looked up at me, the corners of her mouth turning down. "Unless it's a haunting."

Digging my fingers into the couch cushions, I tried very hard not to roll my eyes. "Mom, come on. A *ghost* case?"

As far as Supernatural Threats went, ghosts were way down there at the bottom of the list. For the most part, they just floated around and creeped people out, and they were ridiculously easy to banish.

But Mom actually smiled. "This sounds perfect, Iz. Exactly the kind of case you could tackle by yourself, get your confidence back—"

Now I couldn't keep the petulance out of my voice. "Mom, ghosts jobs are nothing. They're . . . they're like Brannick training wheels."

"Tell that to Mr. Snyder," Maya muttered, and Mom nodded.

"If this is a haunting, it's a potentially dangerous one. We owe it to the students of"—she squinted at the paper—"Mary Evans High to keep them safe."

Flipping my braid over my shoulder, I sank deeper into the couch. "I know, but—" I sat up straight. "Wait, this happened at a high school?"

Mom had always gone out of her way to avoid jobs that happened at schools. She'd never said why, but

I'd guessed it had to do with me and Finn and Mom not wanting us to get any ideas about a "regular life." That's why we'd always been homeschooled, although I doubt many kids had to write an essay on *The Hammer of Witches* as their midterm. And sure, a few years ago, I'd kind of . . . not longed for it, exactly, but I'd thought high school had a certain exotic appeal. But that was when I was just a kid.

Whatever was on that piece of newspaper suddenly became very interesting to Mom, and dread began to settle in my stomach. "Mom, is this . . . am I going to have to go to this high school?"

Mom didn't look up. "It would be the best way for you to do the necessary reconnaissance work. And it might be good for you." Her mouth tightened into a firm line, and I knew that whatever came out of her mouth next, it would be a command, not a request. "This is the case for us right now, Isolde. The case we need."

When Mom used that voice, there was no arguing. It was the same tone she used to get me to put in an extra hour on the training field.

The same tone she used the day she'd said we were done looking for Finley.

"Yes, ma'am," I said, hoping I didn't sound sullen. But . . . high school. Regular high school, with . . . with . . . Yeah, I had no idea what that would actually entail, other than a vague notion of school dances and lockers. And while our cabin in the woods may not be much, it was home.

"The town is only about fifty miles from here," Maya offered. "I could ride with y'all, show you around." She narrowed her eyes at Mom. "And I'm assuming you have ways of finding a place once you get there."

"I'll make some calls," Mom said tersely.

"We won't need a *place*," I insisted, rising to my feet. "*Places* are for jobs that are more than chasing down Casper."

Mom began gathering the pieces of paper. A few caught her eye, and she folded them carefully, putting them in the pocket of her jacket. "Enough, Iz."

She stood up and said to Maya, "We'll need to go home, get a few things first. We'll drive down next week."

I frowned at that. We had a car, but it was not the most reliable thing, and as much as I loathed Itineris travel, it was a lot faster.

While Mom and Maya made plans, I sat back on the couch, the newspaper article in my hand. I knew I should have been more concerned about the guy being pulled out on a stretcher, but my gaze kept going again and again to the big brick building behind him. Mary Evans High.

A shiver went through me, and I was pretty sure it had nothing to do with any ghost.

CHAPTER 5

"**I**'m so glad you could finally join me, Isolde," Torin said, smiling as he crossed a large gilded room. He was wearing a fancy suit of emerald-green velvet rather than his usual outfit of black pants and white shirt, so I knew I was dreaming.

Again.

"I told you, no dreams," I said, but he just shrugged.

"Yes, but that was ages ago."

"It was two weeks ago," I countered, even as I took the golden goblet he offered me. My hand glittered with rings, and the dress I was wearing was so heavy I wanted to sit down. "And if memory serves, I've been telling you to cut out the dream-walking thing for the past five years." I smoothed my skirt. "Why can I never wear my regular clothes?"

Torin sipped his own drink. "My world, my dress code. Besides, you look lovely."

There were never any mirrors in these dreams, so I had to take his word for it.

"Was this your house?" I asked. Liveried servants lined one wall, holding trays with more goblets. Music was playing somewhere nearby, but I couldn't quite pin down the song.

"Free me, and you can see for yourself."

Scowling, I handed him back his cup. "That's never happening. No matter how many times you invade my dreams to play dress-up."

He took my hand in his, and I was surprised by how warm his skin was. Torin had never touched me in these dreams before. "I'm simply trying to show you that I'm not all bad. That freeing me will not unleash some sort of plague onto the world. This is all I want," he said, nodding at the room. "My old life back."

I jerked my hand from his. "Your 'old life' ended nearly half a millennia ago. This"—I waved a bejeweled hand— "doesn't exist anymore. Outside of rap videos, at least."

Torin leaned against the wall with an extravagant sigh. "You make me sad, Isolde."

"And you bug me. Now get out of here and let me dream about . . . I don't know, whatever it is normal teenage girls dream about."

Turning his head, Torin studied me. His eyes were green, like mine, but whereas mine were shot through with gray, his had flecks of gold, like a cat's. Or maybe they were just reflecting all the gilded crap in the room. "Do you even know how to be a normal teenage girl?"

I backed up, wobbling in my brocade dress. "I guess I'll figure it out, won't I?"

His grin was slow and lazy. "Indeed. And speaking of—"

The room began to fade, and another voice said, "Here you go."

Something landed in my lap, jolting me out of sleep.

Mom was sliding into the driver's seat of the car, and I rubbed my eyes. That's right. I wasn't in a sixteenth-century ballroom. I was in the parking lot of a Walmart. I felt the dream curling around me, but I shook it off as I sat up, inspecting the bag Mom had tossed at me.

"I got everything they had that was set in high school," she told me, starting the car.

Reaching into the bag, I pulled out several boxed sets of TV shows. I held up one, making a face. "Um, Mom, unless regular high school involves me having to avenge the murder of my boyfriend's identical twin who turns out to actually *be* my boyfriend, I don't think this is going to be a huge help."

"Better than nothing."

The car sputtered and lurched as Mom turned onto the highway, and I fought the urge to ask why we couldn't have gotten a new car for this job.

Mom had managed to find us a tiny rental house in the tiny town of Ideal, Mississippi. Maybe the town founders had called it "Ideal" as a joke. Other than a few strip malls and neighborhood after neighborhood of houses exactly like ours, Ideal didn't have that much to offer.

Except for a high school that may or may not have a major-league haunting going on.

We pulled into the driveway of our house. Like the house on either side of it, it was covered in beige vinyl siding, and while it was definitely a step up from the cabin, it was still depressing.

I helped Mom lug the rest of her purchases in, and was about to head up to my room to watch my brand-new TV shows on my brand-new television when Mom stopped me.

"Should we . . . Do you want to go back and get you some new clothes? I didn't even think about that."

My entire wardrobe consisted of black jeans, black T-shirts, and a selection of hoodies. Those were black, too, except for the pink one Finn had once gotten me as a joke. "I'll be fine," I told her. I'd seen enough kids to know that, while I wouldn't exactly be a supermodel, I wouldn't look like a total freak, either.

Mom nodded. "Okay. What about your cover story? Should we go over that one more time?"

I just barely managed to keep from rolling my eyes. We'd been over my cover story at least half a dozen times on the drive from Tennessee to Alabama, and then again on the drive from Maya's to here. I could have recited it in my sleep. The gist of it was that I was Izzy Brannick—Mom let me use my real name since this was my first time doing a case solo—and I was from Tennessee. My mom had taken a job in the next town over, but we moved to Ideal because the schools were better. Short, simple, sweet.

Still, I repeated it to Mom. When I was done, she seemed satisfied, although I had a feeling I'd have to do it again before school tomorrow. "Anything else you want to talk about?" Mom asked, and I shook my head.

"You good for the rest of the night?" Mom was already glancing down the stairs.

"Sure," I told her. "Go . . . do your thing."

Mom's "thing" was locking herself in the spare bedroom and poring over books and journals and weird magical documents. I wasn't sure if she was searching for something that would help us on this case or just boning up on her General Monster Research. And there was that little part of me that wondered if she was looking for clues about Finn, but I never asked. I didn't even know where any of that stuff had come from. It had just started show-ing up at the house right after we moved in last week. From more of Mom's "friends," I guessed.

Once I was in my room, I sorted through the DVDs, trying to decide which one to watch first. The one with the girl who falls in love with an alien sounded the most interesting, but I figured it, like the *Secret Twin Murder Show*, wouldn't be that useful. So in the end, I picked the show about the poor girl who transfers to the rich-kid high school, *Ivy Springs*.

The cover was pretty boring, but by episode three, I was so into it that I didn't even notice Torin in my mir-ror until he cleared his throat. Frowning, I reached out and clicked pause right before Everton, the rich boy, told Leslie, our impoverished heroine, that he had feelings for her. "What?" I snapped at Torin.

"Just checking in on you. You could be a little thank-ful, you know. Getting out of my own mirror requires considerable power on my part."

"First of all, no, it doesn't," I countered. "You zip in and out of those things all the time. And secondly, I would be thankful if I wanted to talk to you, but I don't, so I'm not." I had too much on my plate right now to deal with Torin. Especially since I was still irritated about the dream invasion.

"That is unkind," Torin sniffed. In the mirror, he

was sitting on my bed. Mom had let me pick out a new bedspread yesterday, but I'd been so overwhelmed by all the patterns and the flowers and the pop stars that I'd ended up picking a plain green blanket that looked almost identical to the covers I'd left behind.

Ignoring Torin, I started the show up again. Everton confessed his love, Leslie swooned, and just as they were about to kiss, Torin piped up, "Those two seem insipid."

I shot a look at him. "Shut up."

"I mean it. And doesn't that lad have another girl? This can really only end badly for everyone involved."

In spite of myself, I smiled a little. "I guess I should get used to this kind of drama."

Torin smiled back. "Certainly scarier than staking vampires, isn't it?"

I wondered what it said about me that watching a teen soap opera with a four-hundred-year-old warlock felt, well . . . normal.

"I don't know why I'm doing all of this," I said, not taking my eyes off the screen. "Or why Mom is going to all this trouble. If there's a ghost here—and I kind of doubt it—it won't require my going to this school for, like, months or renting a house. We could just get in, get out—"

"Isolde, do not be so dense." In the mirror, Torin

was leaning back on his hands, ankles crossed. "Your moving here has nothing to do with any ghost. Granted, there's a chance a haunting is happening at Betty Crocker High—"

"Mary Evans," I corrected, but he blew a hank of blond hair out of his eyes and shrugged.

"But clearly, Aislinn's true motivation here is to let you experience a taste of regular human life. She's gruff and difficult, that woman, so of course she'd rather die than tell you, 'Oh, Isolde, guilt over your sister's disappearance has left me swimming in a veritable sea of angst—'"

"Stop it." Standing up, I flipped off the television and turned to face Torin. "Just . . . if you can't help with Finley, then don't talk about her, okay?"

Torin pursed his lips slightly, tilting his head and studying me. Then he said, "I did not mean to offend. I simply wanted to make sure you understood why you're really here, Isolde. This isn't about hunting a ghost. It's about your mum trying to do something for you that she never did for your sister."

Snorting, I headed for the door. "Mom doesn't think like that."

"I've known her longer than you have," Torin called, and I froze, hand on the doorknob. I'd never really thought of it like that, but yeah, Torin had been in our family for centuries. He'd seen Mom grow up. Had known my grandmother, my great-grandmother, all the Brannicks stretching back to the sixteenth century.

Leaning forward, Torin gave his best sheepish smile. "Now, can we please stop quarreling and finish this program? I really do want to see what fresh hell is unleashed next."

I hesitated, and Torin clasped his hands on his knees, sitting up straight. "I promise to behave."

Somehow, I doubted that, but to be honest, I really wanted to see how that episode went. So I settled back on the floor and turned the TV on. Leslie and Everton kissed, his girlfriend found out, and the episode ended with Leslie running down the street in tears while some seriously whiny music wailed in the background.

"Well," Torin said as the credits began to roll, "take heart, Isolde. At least a ghost will be less terrifying than *that*."

CHAPTER 6

The next morning, I woke up before my alarm. It wasn't like I'd never thought about the first day of school before. I remembered going into stores with Mom and Finn, passing all those displays of pencils and binders and backpacks, and wondering what it must be like to live that kind of life. But I'd never thought that would be my life.

I was still brooding when I headed downstairs and into the kitchen. Mom was already there, and from the look of things, she'd been busy.

"Do you expect me to eat . . . all of this?" I stared at the kitchen table, which was practically buckling under the weight of all the food. Pancakes, bacon, eggs, a fruit bowl, an entire loaf of toast, and . . .

"Is that actual gruel?" I asked, pointing to a pot.

"Grits," Mom answered, wiping her hands on a dish towel stuck in her waistband. "And no," she continued, "you don't have to eat all of it. I just . . . I want you to start your day off right."

I grabbed a plate and some bacon. "Mom, you didn't make this much food the day Finn and I chased our first werewolf. I'm pretty sure today will be less challenging than that." I was trying to joke, but Mom frowned.

"I don't think I ever made you girls any food. Finn could make mac and cheese by the time she was four, and you were using a microwave by that age. I should've cooked more."

I stared at her. "Mom, we were fine. And I happen to like SpaghettiOs. Especially the kind with the meatballs. Finn used to give me the meatballs out of her bowl, and—"

I hate crying. The tears, the snot, the red face. All of it. But what I really hate is when crying sneaks up on you unexpectedly. So I looked down at my plate and shoved a piece of bacon into my mouth, hoping that would stop the sob that was welling up in my throat.

You need these meatballs more than I do, Junior. You're so skinny, a shifter is gonna pick his teeth with you one day.

Mom had turned back to the sink. "Hurry up before you miss your bus," she said, and I could've imagined it, but her voice sounded a little watery, too.

The bacon might as well have been made of cardboard for as much as I tasted it, but I got it down. "Right. Okay. Well. I, uh, guess I'll go wait for the bus."

Mom turned. "Do you want me to wait with you?"

I did. A lot. Why was hunting monsters *less scary* than waiting by a freaking stop sign in the suburbs? But I shrugged. "No, don't worry about it. I think I can handle standing on a corner by myself for ten minutes."

The parentheses deepened around her mouth. "Don't get smart."

"I wasn't! I . . ." Sighing, I shouldered my backpack. It was the same one I used to take when Finn and I would patrol, but this time there were no crossbows or vials of holy water. Just notebooks and two packs of pens.

"I'll be home after three," I told Mom.

"Okay," she replied. "Remember, main thing today is just to start getting yourself situated. Head down—"

"Eyes open," I finished for her. That might as well have been the Brannick family motto.

Mom gave a sharp nod. "Right. We'll talk when you get home. And . . ."

She walked over and, to my surprise, gave me a hug. "Have a good day, Iz."

I hugged her back, closing my eyes and breathing in the safe, familiar smell of Mom. Brannicks aren't huggers, and I couldn't remember the last time Mom had wrapped her arms around me. "I will."

The kitchen was right off the main hallway leading to the front door. The old owners of the house had put up a little shelf with hooks, a box for keys, and a tiny mirror to, I don't know, check your lipstick before you went out or whatever. I snagged my black jacket from one of the hooks, and as I did, caught a flash of movement.

Torin.

In the mirror, he leaned against the wall behind me. "Nervous?" he asked, grinning.

Glancing down the hall toward the kitchen, I leaned in closer and whispered, "No."

His grin got bigger. "Yes, you are. You're a Brannick, a Queen Among Women, and you're scared of going to school. When, really, it's the school that should be scared of you."

He said it like that was something to be proud of. Mom was still banging pans, water running in the sink, but I kept my voice as low as I could. "What the heck does that mean?"

"Like I said," Torin replied, "you're a Brannick. Not only have you been trained to dispose of the most powerful creatures this world has ever known, you've been bred to be an effective killer. Over one thousand years of genetics, all coming together to form Isolde Brannick, a deadly weapon."

I stared at him. "Torin, is . . . is this your idea of a pep talk?"

His brow wrinkled. "A what? I am simply trying to make you feel more confident about your day by giving you a small speech on your many virtues."

Adjusting my bag on my shoulder, I poked at the glass. "That's a pep talk, then. Except yours isn't really helping." Now Torin was leaning back against the wall, his arms folded over his chest. "I actually felt it was going quite well, and I hadn't even gotten to the part where I declare you a tiger sent to matriculate among kittens."

In the kitchen, the water shut off. I glared at Torin. "I'm not a *tiger*," I hissed. He gave one of his elegant shrugs as Mom called, "Iz?"

She stepped out of the kitchen, but by then, Torin had already vanished from the mirror.

"Yeah?" I replied, hoping I sounded casual.

"Just . . . be careful today, okay?"

It was such a weird thing for her to say. I mean, it was a perfectly normal thing for regular moms to say, but not for *mine*. And for a second, I wondered if I actually could be the sort of person who had a mom who told her to "be careful." The kind who rode buses and whose mom cooked breakfast.

Then she added, "Lie low. And remember your cover."

The bus ride ended up being easier than I'd thought. I snagged a seat by myself and spent the twenty-minute ride watching the boring streets of Ideal flash by and trying to tell myself that I'd faced off with werewolves and demons, for heaven's sake. Not one other kid on this bus had done that. So how tough could it be navigating high school? All I had to do was go into the main office, hand the secretary my (fake) paperwork, get a schedule, and then . . . go to class. Mom and I had agreed I shouldn't start asking questions about the attack on the science teacher too quickly, but I could definitely keep my ear to the ground.

I'd studied a map of the school last night, but that didn't prepare me for the crush of people and confusing warren of hallways and stairs and classrooms as I walked through the giant double doors. It was so . . . *loud*. To my left, a group of girls shrieked and laughed about something, while just in front of me, two boys were shouting at each other, earbuds jammed firmly in their ears.

Pushing my shoulders back, I tried to move with the same sense of purpose that everyone else seemed to have, but that wasn't really helpful since I didn't actually know where I was going. I wandered down one hallway, only to have to double back when it dead-ended in a row of lockers. Then I thought I'd found the main office, but that was actually the attendance office.

"The main office is in the east wing," the harried attendance lady had told me, and I'd nodded and mumbled, "Thanks," like I knew where the heck the east wing was.

Well, other than east, obviously.

By the time I found the main office, it was nearly time for first period, and the secretary hardly looked at my papers. "Here," she said, shoving a folder at me. "Schedule and list of extracurricular activities. Now get moving before third bell."

Third bell? There hadn't even been one so far.

At that moment, a harsh buzzing filled the air, and as I stepped out into the corridor, kids suddenly began to sprint for the staircases and other hallways. Pressing myself against the wall, I struggled to open the folder and not get run over. As I did, I kept up a running monologue with myself. *Oh my God, chill out. Your heart is going a million miles an hour over a bunch of kids? You fight monsters. Get a hold of yourself, Brannick.*

And I'd almost managed to do that when a boy nearly a foot taller than me collided with my shoulder, sending the folder spinning out of my hands, papers scattering everywhere.

My muscles tensed, and before I could stop it, my

hand had darted out to . . . I don't know, grab the guy, or punch him, or who knew what. Thank God he'd already moved too far past me, and my hand just flopped harmlessly in midair.

Taking a deep breath, I tried to calm down. The last thing I needed was to let my instincts take over before I'd even set foot in my first class. I knelt down and started to pick up my papers.

"Hey, you okay?"

A boy about my age stood in front of me. Sandy brown hair fell in his eyes, which, I noticed, were dark brown. "Just, uh, dropped some stuff."

Crouching down, the boy gathered up my schedule and list of school clubs while I fished the map out from under the water fountain. "You must be new," he said, and my head shot up.

"How did you know?"

"Um, the folder saying 'NEW STUDENT' kind of gave it away."

Oh, right. Now that he mentioned it, that was scrawled across the top. "Ah," I said, unsure of what else to say.

"And according to this," he continued, brandishing my schedule, "you and I have first period English together. Come on, I'll walk you."

As I followed him, the boy adjusted his dark green

backpack covered in various badges that read things like, "Rusted Nail," and "The Filthy Monkeys." I figured either those were bands, or this kid was in the weirdest Boy Scout troop ever.

"I'm Adam," he threw over his shoulder. When I just nodded, he stopped. "I'm assuming you have a name, too."

"Oh. Yeah. Izzy. My name is Izzy."

Adam inclined his head. "Well, nice to meet you, Izzy."

There was another bell, the second one, and I heard doors begin to close. "Is that—" I started, but Adam waved a hand. "You're new and I was showing you around and being a good citizen. We're good. So." Still walking, he held up the list of extracurricular activities. "Have you picked which of our fine organizations to join yet?"

I took the paper back. "Seeing as how I've been here all of five minutes, no. And besides, I'm not much of a joiner."

"Fair enough," he said amiably, leading me up a staircase. "But hey, at least you know if you get a sudden urge to be part of a chess club, or a lacrosse team, or a ghost-hunting society, you'll have the option."

I froze on the fifth step. "A what?"

Adam turned, shoving a handful of hair out of

his eyes. "Lacrosse? It's this sport with sticks, and—"

"Not that," I said, scanning the list. "Do you have a ghost-hunting group?" And sure enough, there it was on the list, the Paranormal Management Society. Trying to hide my glee, I folded the paper up and shoved it into my back pocket with a nonchalant shrug. "I mean . . . that's just weird."

Adam snorted and started climbing the stairs again. "That's one word for it. The chick that runs it, Romy Hayden, is a total wack job. Which you'll see since she's in English with us. And speaking of"—he stopped in front of a door and gave a bow—"here we are."

CHAPTER 7

By the time we walked into class, everyone was already in their desks, and I felt thirty pairs of eyes suddenly land on me.

It was not the best feeling.

"This is Izzy," Adam announced to the teacher. According to my schedule, she was Mrs. Steele, and Adam was right: she didn't seem put out by our lateness. "Welcome to Mary Evans High, Izzy," she said to me. "Why don't you take a seat near the front for today. Romy, can you move over one desk?"

I spun around, wanting to catch sight of this girl. It wasn't like I thought her little ghost-hunters club would actually be that useful. Every once and a while, groups like that spring up somewhere in the country, and they have a really bad tendency to result in a high body count.

Nothing more dangerous than civilians who think they can track Prodigium, Mom had said a few years ago after she'd had to go clean up after one of those groups. "Kids read a few books, watch a couple of stupid TV shows, and get in over their heads before they know what's happened."

But still, if I was looking for a vengeful ghost, this was a start, and a heck of a lot better one than I'd thought I'd get.

A tall Asian girl got out of one of the desks in the first row, and I realized I'd seen her on the bus. It would've been hard to miss her. Next to my all-black ensemble she was a riot of color. Her jeans were bright red, and her white T-shirt had two rainbows splashed across it, with the words DOUBLE RAINBOW ALL THE WAY written in electric-blue bubble letters. A hat that same vivid blue was yanked low on her head, and the frames of her glasses were neon purple. When got up, I noticed she was wearing red Converse sneakers.

As she sagged into the other desk, she flipped up the dark lenses of her sunglasses, revealing regular glass underneath. "Enjoy that desk. It's one of my favorites."

I didn't know what to say to that. Mom said to get close to people, find stuff out. Investigate. What she'd neglected to mention was how. Should I introduce myself to Romy now? Use the cover story? Or was that too much too soon?

Luckily, I was literally saved by the bell. It trilled, and Mrs. Steele started handing out work sheets. I spent the next fifty minutes using words like "inscrutable" in a sentence. When class ended, Romy bolted for the door, so I didn't have to practice my cover story after all.

Next up was P.E., the one class I wasn't that worried about. Mom had had me and Finn running at least six miles a day basically since we could walk. Besides, in all the TV shows Mom had gotten me, people usually just spent P.E. talking under the bleachers, or meeting up with their secret boyfriends. Since I didn't have anyone to talk to, or a boyfriend, secret or otherwise, I figured I had this.

Or I would have if I'd been able to find the gym. It took me a while to figure out that the gym was actually an entirely separate building, slightly downhill from the school itself. And once I finally got there, I realized there was one thing I didn't have: a uniform. Everyone else was coming out of the locker rooms in these awful gray shirt/shorts combos with MEHS scrawled across the chest.

The coach, a tubby guy who was about my mom's age, looked me up and down and barked, "You! Why aren't you dressed out?"

Before I could answer, a voice called, "She's new, duh."

It was Romy. Dressed all in gray, she seemed smaller than she had earlier. The coach frowned at her. "Attitude!"

"Sorry," she said, sounding anything but. Then she turned to me. "He basically shouts everything. You'll get used to it."

And then, to prove her point, the coach yelled, "Okay, you over here!" He waved at my half of the gym, "You're Team A, rest of you are Team B. Opposite sides, let's go!"

Groaning, Romy pushed her glasses up her nose.

"Teams for what?" I asked as the kids next to us began heading for the nearest wall.

"Effing dodgeball," she said with a long sigh.

Dodgeball. Right. I'd heard of that. And it seemed kind of self-explanatory. Clearly, there'd be balls. And then we'd . . . dodge.

Sure enough, the coach began placing a line of red rubber balls between our two "teams."

"I swear to God, if my glasses get broken again, I'm suing this crappy school," Romy muttered darkly under her breath. When she caught me looking at her, she added, "Twice last year. Two pairs." She raised her voice, her eyes fixed on the coach's back. "This game is barbaric!" she called.

"Zip it, Hayden," the coach replied with the air of

someone who had said those three words many, many times.

Romy scowled but stepped into line. I stepped next to her, tugging at the hem of my hoodie.

"What's your name?" Romy asked. A tiny dimple flashed in one cheek. "I mean, in my head, you'll always be The Girl Who Took My Desk, but that's kind of an awkward thing to call you all the time."

"Izzy."

"Ah, a fellow holder of a cutesy name. So you're new?"

I nodded, but before I could say anything else, the coach blew his whistle. At the sound, several kids darted forward and grabbed the rubber balls. Before the whistle had even faded, a tall boy on the other side of the gym took aim at Romy and threw.

The ball didn't hit her glasses at least, but it did slam into her forearm with a meaty smack. Romy winced, rubbing the red mark already forming on her skin. As the tall boy laughed and high-fived one of his friends, Romy called out, "Yeah, nice one, Ben. You took out a ninety-pound myopic chick. Congratulations on your masculinity!" With that, she trudged over to the bleachers.

Out of the corner of my eye, I caught a ball zooming at me, but I jerked back so that it sailed harmlessly by. Okay. I could do this. It was actually kind of similar to a training exercise Mom used to make me and Finley do. That involved dodging a much heavier ball made of leather, but the principle was the same. It was one of Mom's favorite training exercises because it combined both strength and agility. Finley had always been better than me at the strength part, but agile? That I could do.

By now, kids were getting hit all over the place, and soon there were only five of us on our side of the gym, and six on the other side. One of those was the tall boy, Ben, who had hit Romy. I guess some girls would've thought he was cute, but all I could see was "psychotic jerk who goes out of his way to hit girls."

His gaze locked with mine, and one corner of his mouth lifted in a smirk. Rearing back on one leg, like he was pitching a baseball, Ben hurled a red rubber ball directly at me. He threw it so hard that I actually staggered back a step when I caught it. But I did catch it. Ben's smirk turned into a frown, I guess because he'd been looking forward to seeing me sprawled across the gym floor.

"Too bad, buddy," I muttered under my breath. And with that, I threw the ball back at him.

I meant to hit him in the arm, the same place he'd hit Romy. I didn't mean for it to hurt—okay, so maybe I meant for it to hurt a *little* bit—but the second the ball was out of my hands I knew I'd thrown it too hard. The ball we trained with back home was made of boiled leather. It was heavy and required some real heft to get it through the air. This ball was rubber, but I'd put the same amount of force behind it.

It hit Ben's shoulder and sent him skidding across the hardwood, his sneakers shrieking as he slid. Arms pinwheeling, he stumbled back against the far wall of the gym before finally collapsing in a heap.

For a second, everything was deadly quiet. Then the coach's shrill whistle pierced the air. "You!" he barked, letting the whistle fall from his lips. "New girl! What's your name?"

I was suddenly very aware of everyone in the gym staring at me. Crap.

Straightening my shoulders, I faced the coach. "Izzy Brannick."

"Okay, Izzy Brannick, do you wanna tell me why you just knocked McCrary here on his butt?"

Confused, I glanced over at Ben. One of his friends was helping him up. His face was pale, and when the other boy touched his shoulder, Ben winced.

"I was just . . . playing the game," I replied, and this time there was a little waver in my voice.

"He was *out*," the coach said, and when I just stared at him, he shook his head. "You caught his throw. So he was already out. There was no need to throw the ball at him, and certainly no need to—" He broke off to look at Ben, and his eyes went wide. "Dear God, did you *dislocate his shoulder?*"

Ben did look a little . . . crooked.

"I didn't mean to," I said, but the coach wasn't listening. "Get him to the nurse's office," he called to the boy beside Ben. Then his gaze swung back to me. "And you. You . . . just go run some laps. Until the end of the period."

"Seriously, it was an accident—" I said, but Coach Lewis just pointed at the double doors. "FOOTBALL FIELD. LAPS."

I heard a few giggles, and Romy was squinting at me, but basically everyone else in the gym was watching me with a combination of dislike and fear. Suddenly I saw myself through their eyes—all in black, my hair scraped back from my face—and I wondered how "fitting in" had ever seemed possible.

CHAPTER 8

The football field was right behind the gym, just down the hill. In addition to the running track circling it, the field also boasted several sets of rickety-looking bleachers. I jogged down the steps to the track, my breath coming out in small white clouds. My cheeks were still so hot, I was surprised they didn't steam in the cold air.

The sun was bright overhead, and I realized with a start that it was only around nine in the morning. Not even lunch and I'd already nearly killed someone. What had Torin said about me going to a regular school? That I was a tiger and they were kittens? I didn't feel much like a tiger, and that Ben kid hadn't looked like a kitten, but still. He was the one going to the nurse's office, and I was the one being punished.

Not that this was real punishment, I guess. Running, I could do.

The track around the football field wasn't even a real track. It was more like a well-worn path, the packed dirt showing through the brown, dry grass. Glad I'd chosen sneakers instead of boots (although I was pretty quick in those, too), I set off.

The February air knifed through my lungs, every breath burning. But with each thump of my sneakers against the track, I started to feel a little more . . . okay, so "normal" probably isn't the greatest word, but less crappy at least. Mom always said that exercise was the best cure for everything. Finn and I knew a mission hadn't gone well when Mom came back to the compound and spent a few hours on the training field.

Man, what I wouldn't have given for that field now. A couple of laps around a lame high school track was one thing, but kicking the heck out of a dummy or flinging some throwing stars would've felt a lot more satisfying.

Picking up my speed, I rounded the corner, and suddenly felt like someone was watching me. I glanced up, and sure enough, there was a guy in the bleachers. I only caught a few details as I jogged past—wavy black hair, sunglasses, something weird about his jacket—and when he lifted one hand to wave at me, I ignored him.

He was still there when I went around the second time, but now he was standing up, hands shoved into his pockets, shoulders up against the cold. "Weirdo," I muttered. Okay, so maybe the girl who had just laid out a guy with a dodgeball had no room to talk, but still. Even *I* knew it wasn't socially acceptable to stare at people.

I pulled my hoodie up and kept running, faster now, and when I made the lap the third time, the bleachers were empty. Awesome. Maybe Watcher Dude had found some other girl to creep on.

Lowering my eyes back to the track, I wondered just how many laps I was supposed to do. The coach had just said "some." Was that a set number that everyone else who went to high school already knew? Did that mean I had to run until the end of P.E.? And would I even be able to hear the bell out—

Suddenly, a pair of shiny black shoes came into view directly in front of me. Watcher Dude was standing in the middle of the track. He didn't move as I darted to the side, my sneakers skidding on the dirt as I slowed down.

Breathing hard, I whirled around to face him. "The heck?" I panted.

He took off his sunglasses, and as he hooked them in the collar of his shirt, I noticed that the arms were bright aqua. His eyes were nearly the same shade of blue as he squinted at me. "Is someone trying to murder you?"

"What?"

Shrugging, he put his hands in the pockets of his jacket. The other boys I'd seen at Mary Evans High were wearing pullover fleeces or North Face jackets, like Adam. This guy was wearing a navy peacoat, and there was a gray scarf twisted into a complicated knot at his throat.

"I've just never seen anyone run that . . . determinedly," he said. "So I assumed someone must be chasing you." With an exaggerated lean, he peered down the track. "But that doesn't seem to be the case. So why were you running?"

"Coach Lewis told me to."

His eyebrows went up. "Ah. So you're being punished for something. Coach Lewis is not the most creative man when it comes to discipline. So let's see . . ."

Looking me up and down, the boy began to circle me. Okay, staring was one thing, but circling? Yeah, that was totally not cool. I moved around with him. "What are you doing?"

"You've definitely got that whole tough chick thing going on. Talking back, maybe? Shouting a four-letter word when you lost a relay race?"

"It's none of your business," I snapped, even as I glanced down and realized he was wearing pin-striped pants. I didn't even know those still existed. "Why aren't *you* in P.E.?"

He finally stopped circling and reached into the pocket of his coat. Pulling out an inhaler, he waggled it at me. "Asthma. But rather than just give me another elective, the fascists who run this school make me come to P.E. every day and sit out."

"So why don't you sit out in the gym?"

Grinning, the boy slid the inhaler back into his pocket. "I figured if all I was going to do was sit there, I could at least offer commentary on the athletic prowess of my classmates. Coach Lewis, sadly, did not agree. So now I'm banished to the wilds of the football field. Much like *you*."

He slid his sunglasses back on. "And now you know my deep dark secret, so it seems only fair that you share yours with me. Oh, I'm Dex, by the way," he added. "Just in case you feel weird sharing deep dark secrets with strangers."

Maybe it was his grin, which was a nice change from the glares/looks of horror I'd gotten in the gym, but I found myself giving a little smile in return. "Izzy. And there, uh, was a dodgeball incident."

"Perhaps the most intriguing phrase I've heard uttered in some time," Dex said, rocking back on his heels. "I'm obviously going to need you to elaborate."

"This jackass hit a girl too hard with one of the balls. So I . . . hit him back."

Dex ducked his head, regarding me over the top of his sunglasses. "Aaaand?"

"And maybe I threw it a little too hard and . . . dislocated his shoulder."

"Whoa, for real?" Dex asked, and for just a second, the act—or whatever it was—slipped, and he just seemed like a normal teenage boy.

A normal teenage boy wearing a cravat, but whatever.

"It was an accident," I said hurriedly, but Dex shook his head.

"Which girl and which jackass?"

"Romy Hayden and Ben . . . something. I don't remember."

"You knocked out Ben McCrary?" he asked, eyes wide.

"It was an accident," I said again. "I threw the ball harder than I meant to."

Dex burst into laughter. "Oh my God, that is the greatest thing I've heard all week. You are my new hero."

Squinting at me, he leaned in and said, "Seriously, I might actually be in love with you now. Would it be awkward if we made out?"

Head spinning, I stepped back. I thought of my cousin, Sophie, and her boyfriend, Archer. The way they were always zinging one-liners back and forth. I should have a one-liner. Instead, I said, "Yes, it would be."

I waited for his smile to falter, for a little bit of that light to fade from his eyes. But if anything, he looked *more* delighted. "Well, then we'll just have to hold off until we know each other better."

Wait, did that mean he actually *wanted to make out with me?*

"And not only did you assault Ben McCrary—"

"I didn't *assault* him," I muttered, but Dex ignored that.

"You did it in defense of Romy Hayden, who is one of the least useless people at this school. I'm not joking. You are my favorite person today."

From somewhere in the distance, I heard the electronic whine of the bell, and Dex frowned. "Sadly, our time together has come to an end. Unless you have Algebra Two next?"

I shook my head, thinking back to the schedule I'd shoved into my back pocket. "European history."

"Ah, you're a sophomore. I'm a junior, so ships in the night are we," Dex said, heaving a sigh. "In that case, I'll see you on the bus tomorrow."

I blinked. "You ride my bus?"

"You didn't notice me this morning? I'm wounded."

I'd been too busy worrying about how I was going to navigate Mary Evans High to notice anyone, even a six-foot-tall boy wearing pinstripes.

"Not much of a morning person," I finally said.

Bouncing on the balls of his feet, Dex smiled again.

"Fair enough. I'll save you a seat tomorrow. Until then, Isabella."

"Isolde," I corrected, and his smile widened.

"Even better." He reached out to shake my hand.

Our palms touched, and a jolt went through me. He didn't seem to feel it as he gave my hand two firm shakes before dropping it. "Try not to kill anyone else today!" he called as he began walking backward down the track.

I was still reeling, so it took everything I had to muster up a weak smile in reply. Once he'd turned around and started walking like a normal person, I glanced down at my hand.

My skin still tingled, like a low electric current was running through me. It was faint, and I'd certainly felt stronger, but it was unmistakable. Magic.

Dex was Prodigium.

CHAPTER 9

The rest of the day passed uneventfully. I guess after you've beaten someone up with a dodgeball and flirted with a monster, most anything else will seem pretty tame.

I wasn't quite ready for another run-in with Dex, so rather than take the bus home, I decided to walk. It was a few miles, and by the time I got home, my calves ached, but the walk gave me time to think. What kind of Prodigium was Dex? Warlock seemed like the most reasonable explanation—I hadn't spotted a bloodstone on him, and without one of those, vampires become barbecue in the sunlight—and there hadn't been that weird animal smell that seemed to cling to shape-shifters. Wings were pretty conspicuous, so unless he was hiding them underneath that peacoat, I didn't think he was Fae. But I'd been around lots of witches and warlocks, and I'd always been able to sense their power once I got within a few feet of them. I'd never had to *touch* one to feel their magic.

As I unlocked the front door, I tried to think of who I could ask about this. I knew I should tell Mom, but I'd never had trouble identifying a Prodigium before, and it wasn't something I was ready to own up to. Besides, this was meant to be my case. My chance to prove myself.

I wondered what Finley would say if she were here. Probably something like, "Stab him with silver and see if it kills him."

So that left me with only one option.

The house was quiet and dark when I stepped into the foyer, and Mom's car wasn't in the driveway. Still, I found myself walking softly as I made my way to the third bedroom. I hadn't been in there since we'd moved in, and when I opened the door, it was like being punched in the stomach.

Finley's things were in here. By which I meant her pillow and a photograph she'd had stuck to the mirror in our bedroom. It showed us when I was around six, Finn eight or nine. We were in the training yard, two little redheaded girls with our arms around each other's shoulders. It was a sweet picture (if you ignored the fact that I was holding a miniature crossbow and Finn's fingers were wrapped around the hilt of a sword), and

I wished I remembered the day it had been taken.

There was also her belt, the one I'd found that night, slung around one of the bedposts. I wanted to go over to it, to hold it in my hands. Instead, I walked past the bed and over to the mirror that hung on the wall. It was, as usual, covered with a heavy piece of canvas. When I pulled it back, Torin was there, hip propped against the bed behind me.

He was examining his fingernails, bored, but when he realized I was there, his face brightened. "Hullo, Isolde. Pleasant day at school?"

"Not really," I told him. "But I needed to ask you something."

Torin folded his arms. "I'm not in much of a prophecy-spouting mood today, to be honest."

"I don't need to know the future. I need to know . . . I don't know, the present, I guess. I met this boy today, and he's . . . I don't know, he's something."

"Something as in he is handsome and you fancy him, or something as in he's one of my kind?"

Scowling, I replied, "He's Prodigium. I think. I don't know He felt strange when I touched him."

The second the words were out of my mouth, I regretted them. Torin's sly grin only intensified that regret.

"This is why I told Aislinn she should have more

blokes around. A boy touches you, and you mistake hormones for magic."

I wanted to shake the frame, but I crossed my arms, mimicking his pose. "It wasn't hormones. It was magic. Or some kind of power. But not like any power I've felt before. It's . . . I don't know, really weak."

Finally, the grin slipped and Torin managed to look a little serious. "Weaker than mine?"

Even trapped in the mirror, Torin radiated power, and I nodded. "Yeah. I can usually pick up on a Prodigium within a few feet. But this guy, I didn't get it until he shook my hand. Could he just be . . . like, a really, really bad warlock?" But then I shook my head. "No, wait. He had asthma. If he were a warlock, he would've cured that." One of the benefits to being a magical being was that they almost never get sick.

Torin gave an elegant shrug. "Perhaps he's faking it. And something could be diluting his power. A counter-spell or a binding charm. Did he seem odd?"

I thought back to Dex, to his weird, formal way of talking, and strangely old-fashioned, if stylish, outfit. "Yeah, but I'm not sure that's magic."

"If you find out where he lives, I can always slip into his mirror, find out for certain," Torin offered. "It would be, as you like to say, a gigantic pain in my backside, but I could try."

71

Torin moved pretty easily through the mirrors in our house because his original mirror was housed here. Getting into mirrors in other locations was tough for him, but I'd seen him do it before. And I'm not going to lie: the idea of sending Torin to check up on Dex was tempting. What if Dex was something dangerous? Okay, so maybe an asthmatic guy rocking a cravat didn't seem all that threatening, but what did I know? And I was here to investigate supernatural shenanigans.

But I couldn't get over the feeling that sending my pet warlock into a dude's mirror to spy on him was . . . well, icky. Especially when he was one of the few people at school who'd been nice to me today. So I shook my head. "No, let's not go that far. I'll work it out on my own."

"As you like," Torin said, going back to studying his cuticles. "But the offer stands."

I leaned back on the bed, bracing my arms on the footboard. In the mirror, it looked like we were standing practically on top of each other. "You just want me to owe you a favor."

"There is but one favor you can do for me, Isolde, and that is to release me from this prison."

The words sent a shiver through me. "That's never going to happen."

He glanced up, raising an eyebrow. "Oh, so now it's

you with the gift of prophecy, is it? I know w
seen. You are my key and my salvation."

Without answering, I got up and went to cover the
mirror. His voice sounded muffled behind the canvas as
he called, "Remember, a favor for a favor, Isolde. I can
be very useful."

He could be. He *had* been. But his visions never
came when we most needed them, and from everything Mom had told me, Torin had a way of twisting
words and promises so that he got more than you were
willing to give, and always gave you less than you
wanted.

In other words, it wasn't worth it.

Sighing, I opened the door and walked into the
hallway.

"What are you doing?"

I jumped as Mom's voice rang out in the quiet house.
She was standing just inside the front door, frowning.
"Isolde?" she asked, her body stiff.

I froze, a million lies rushing to my lips. But Mom
always saw through those, and all lying did was piss her
off. "I was talking to Torin."

"About what?"

"Just my day at school." That wasn't *technically* a lie,
but Mom still frowned.

"Well, why don't you tell *me* about your day." Her

expression hardened. "Specifically the part where you hurt some boy in your P.E. class?"

Ugh. So that's why she was so pissed. "It was an accident," I said for what felt like the millionth time that day, but Mom gave a frustrated sigh as she tossed her bag onto the hall table. "Damn it, Izzy, I told you, keeping a low profile is an essential part of every job."

"I was trying!"

"And breaking someone's arm by second period? That was your attempt at *trying*?"

"It was only a dislocated shoulder," I muttered, sounding sullen even to my own ears. "And he was a jerk who purposely hurt this girl I think can help me with the ghost thing."

Mom gave a frustrated sigh, but then what I had said dawned. "What does that mean?"

Briefly, I told her about the Paranormal Management Society and Romy. As soon as I said the words "teenage ghost hunters," she sat down on the edge of the bed.

"Damn it. You know if there is a legitimate haunting happening here, they'll probably end up making things worse. Those types of kids always do."

"Yeah," I said, going to sit next to her. "But it's something. If nothing else, maybe they'll have information. Either about Mr. Snyder himself, or who could be haunting the school. Save me the hassle of going to the library."

Mom looked up, and something very close to a smile flickered on her face. "So you'd actually go to a library instead of plugging everything into the Google?"

Now I smiled. "Mom, it's just *Google*. And yeah, you always said books were the best for research. Even the Internet can't know everything."

"I know I said that; I'm just surprised you listened."

"I do that sometimes," I told her, and she reached out and patted my knee. Then, clearing her throat, she rose to her feet and headed for the door.

"Well, it's a start," she said, her voice slightly gruff. "Probably won't lead to much, but better than nothing. Now, come on. I don't like you spending too much time in here."

Swallowing my disappointment, I stood up, too. I had always been proud of my mom. So she'd never bake cookies, or sew a Halloween costume, but she could fight *monsters*. She was tough and smart, and maybe she didn't read bedtime stories, but she had taught me to defend myself against the things that lurked under beds.

But in that moment, I didn't want a smart, tough mother who kicked supernatural ass. I wanted to sit on the couch with her and tell her about my crappy day. And maybe about Dex, leaving out the possible magical powers part.

I wanted to tell her that I missed Finley, too.

Instead, I followed her out the door and said, "So, I . . . I guess I'll go do homework now."

"Right," Mom said with a brusque nod. "And I'll go, uh, clean up the kitchen. See you at six for dinner?"

"Sure," I said, turning to jog up the stairs.

When I was halfway up, Mom called, "Izzy?"

"Yeah?"

"I'm . . . you're doing good work," she said haltingly. "Other than the dislocated shoulder."

It wasn't exactly "Oh, Izzy, I am so proud of you, and I was wrong to ever give you such lame job."

But I'd take it.

CHAPTER 10

I sat up, confused. I was moving, and overhead, birds were chirping, and the scent of flowers was so heavy in the air, it made me feel a little light-headed. Sunlight sparkled on dark green water. When I threw up my hand to ward off the glare, I saw that once again, I was wearing a ton of rings that I had never owned.

Groaning, I sank back against silken pillows. "Why are we on a boat?"

At the other end of the little rowboat, Torin grinned at me, his long arms pulling the oars. "Thought a change of scenery might be nice."

"You know what would be nice? Not having you invade my dreams with these"—I waved my hand—"whatever this is."

"It's an outing, Isolde. And quite a nice one, too."

Much as I hated that, I couldn't argue. The sun felt good on my face, and there was something undeniably pleasant about drifting down a stream flanked with flower bushes and weeping willows. "Where is this?" I asked. "Someplace you knew?"

Torin abandoned the oars and leaned back, closing his eyes and lifting his face to the sun. "You know the answer."

"Set you free and I'll find out," I muttered.

He nodded, replying, "Even so."

"Since that's not going to happen, any other reason you decided we should row our boat merrily down the stream?"

"You were grinding your teeth as you slept. It was both annoying and concerning, so I thought an outing would do you some good."

"First off, don't watch me sleep, and secondly—"

"Oh, hush," Torin said with no real heat. "Can't you just lie back on your pillows and enjoy this lovely summer's day?"

"It's February, and I *am* lying back," I reminded him.

"In the outside world," Torin said. "But in here, it can be whatever we want."

That was a dangerous line of thought. Torin was good at this kind of thing: offering dreams and wishes and perfect days. But none of it was real, and none of it was free.

Still, it was nice to feel warm and drowsy in the sunshine, not worrying about Finley or Mom or ghosts or—*shudder*—high school.

Leaning over the side of the boat, I let my fingers trail in the cool water. It took me a second to realize I didn't have a reflection. Sitting up, I squinted at Torin. "I get the no-mirrors thing, but even water is unreflective?"

"My rules," he said easily.

There was a flash of movement on the far bank, and I lifted my head to see a woman moving along the shore. She was wearing a heavy dress of purple brocade, the sunlight picking up hints of blue in her black hair. "Who's that?"

"Hmm?" Torin turned his head, and seeing the woman, he scowled. "What is she doing here?"

A flick of his wrist, and the woman vanished; but Torin kept scowling. "That's odd. I didn't invite Rowena here." He squinted at me. "Did you?"

"Since I don't even know who Rowena is, no."

Torin turned his gaze back to the spot where she'd been. "Rowena was a member—" He broke off, brushing his hair out of his eyes. "No matter."

I sat there waiting for him to say more, but Torin simply closed his eyes, tilting his face to the sun. I didn't know much about the life he'd lived pre-mirror, and sometimes I wondered if that was for the best. It was too weird to think of Torin as just a normal guy—a normal *boy*, really—wandering around in the world.

We were quiet for a long time, and I might have dozed off. Was that even possible? Sleeping inside of a dream? With Torin, who knew? Still, I was startled when he suddenly said, "You should just be yourself."

"What?"

"You're afraid these children won't like you. That's what you were grinding your teeth over in your sleep. Worrying how to make them like you, how to infiltrate their little group."

He lifted his head, looking at me intently. "But the person you are is delightful, and they will like you if you'll just . . . be that."

I shifted, smoothing imaginary wrinkles in my heavy skirt. "So that's your big advice? Be myself?"

Torin grinned, his teeth slightly crooked, but very white. "That's it. Be yourself. Be Isolde Brannick, and they will have no choice but to adore you." He reached out and took my hand, pressing a kiss to the back of it.

I was too stunned to do anything but sit there, my hand limp in his.

When Torin lifted his head, his eyes were bright green, almost the same green as the water we floated on. "Now, wake up," he whispered.

I came awake almost instantly, my stomach in knots.

According to my clock, I had three minutes before my alarm went off, pale gray light shining around the edges of my curtains.

Immediately, my eyes shot to the mirror, but there was no trace of Torin there. Which, considering how weirded out I felt, was a good thing. What the heck had that been? The hand-holding in the last dream had been one thing, but hand-kissing was, to quote Maya, a whole 'nother ball of wax.

Still unsettled, I threw back my covers and headed downstairs.

Mom had already left. This time, there was no huge breakfast spread. Just a Post-it on the freezer reminding me that there were frozen waffles inside. I popped a couple into the toaster, then went back upstairs and took the hottest shower I could stand. As I stood under the spray of scalding water, I thought about my dream last night. Not the hand-kissing stuff—I definitely didn't want to think about that—but the stuff that came before.

Be yourself, Torin had said. I could do that. And hey, so maybe yesterday was less than ideal—ha! pun alert— but I had at least made friends with Romy. Kind of. So now all I had to do was talk to her about the ghost hunter club and see if she knew anything about the attack on that science teacher.

Easy.

I felt better when I got out of the shower, but I also discovered that my little inner pep talk had taken longer than I thought. My waffles were burned *and* I was in danger of missing the bus.

Throwing on some clothes—jeans, another black T-shirt, and, remembering the looks I got yesterday, the one pink hoodie I owned—I ran out the door. The stop was down the block, and the bus doors were starting to close as I rushed up. My hair was still damp on my shoulders as I hoisted myself up the steps, giving what I hoped was an apologetic smile.

The driver—Maggie, according to her name tag—gave a disdainful sniff. "I don't wait," she snapped at me. "You lucked out this time, girlie."

"Sorry," I mumbled, making my way to the back. I scanned the rows for an empty spot, and suddenly Dex stood up, waving his arms. "Isolde!" he called. "It's me, Dex, your new best friend! I saved you a seat!"

Several of the kids around him turned to glare, but Dex either didn't notice or didn't care. I lifted my hand, acknowledging him. He sat there beaming at me, looking as threatening as a golden retriever, but I couldn't forget what happened yesterday. If I knew Dex was Prodigium, did he know what I was? Is that why he was so buddy-buddy this morning?

The bus lurched forward just as I got to the back, and Dex reached out to steady me. I think he was trying to grab my waist, but his hand landed on my hip. Even through my jeans I felt that low hum of magic.

Dex jerked back, and for a second I thought maybe he'd felt it too. But then he winced and said, "Sorry. We probably haven't reached the inappropriate touching stage of our friendship yet."

Oh, right. I'd been so concerned with trying to figure out what Dex *was* that it didn't even occur to me that a boy had just touched my hip, which was definitely in the "bathing suit zone." That was as far as Mom had gotten in her Facts Of Life talk a few years back: "Don't let boys touch you in the bathing suit zone." Then the warlock she and Finn had been chasing chose that moment to leap onto the hood of our car, and the rest of her talk had gone unfinished.

I think Mom had been relieved.

Blushing, I sat down next to Dex, trying to keep our thighs from touching. (Thighs were not in the bathing suit zone, but I was pretty sure they were still kind of scandalous.)

As I reached behind me to start braiding my hair, Dex propped his ankle on the opposite knee. Today he was wearing gray corduroys and a deep navy V-neck that made his eyes look even bluer. The peacoat was balled up behind his head.

I nodded at it. "Were you napping?"

"Yeah. Bus gets to my neighborhood at six thirty, which is just inhumane, if you ask me. I usually sleep the whole way, but I'll endeavor to be an alert seatmate for you."

Securing a rubber band around the end of my braid, I looked at him. "Do you always talk like that?"

"Like what?"

I raised both eyebrows. "'Endeavor to be an alert seatmate'? Who says stuff like that?"

Chuckling, Dex elbowed me in the ribs. "Civilized people. People with names like Dexter and Isolde."

"Izzy," I told him. "Only my mom calls me Isolde, and even then, just when she's mad at me." I didn't mention that Mom had been calling me that a lot lately.

"So how did you end up in Ideal, Mississippi, Izzy?" Dex asked, sitting up. His hair was tangled in the back, and I had this completely bizarre urge to smooth it out. Just in case my fingers decided to do that, I clasped them together, laying my hands in my lap.

"We lived in Tennessee, but then my mom, um, lost her job. So she thought a change of scenery would be good for us." There it was, my first time using the cover story. Dex accepted it with an easy shrug.

"I'm new, too," he said. "Well, newish. I moved here back in the summer."

"From where?"

Dex linked his fingers and stretched his arms over his head. "New York."

"Did your parents want a change of scenery, too?"

"They're, uh . . . not around anymore."

Surprised, I twisted to face him. "Who do you live with?"

Dex widened his eyes in mock innocence. "Oh, I live by myself. Didn't I mention? I'm thirty-five."

When I just rolled my eyes, he relented. "I live with my Nana."

He said it lightly, but Mom had taught me and Finn to pay attention to body language. Dex was twisting the strap of his bag around his fingers so tightly that his knuckles were turning white.

Before I could ask anything else, a face suddenly popped up over the seat in front of me. "Hey," Romy said. "Izzy, right?"

"That's me," I said. "Have you, um, been there the whole time?"

"Romy's like me," Dex said, nudging the back of her seat with one pointy-toed boot. "Picked up entirely too early, sleeps the whole ride."

"Tries to sleep," she corrected. "This idiot usually keeps me awake." Despite the insult, there was affection in her voice, and Dex was grinning at her.

"Anyway, just wanted to say thanks for tearing Ben McCrary's arm off yesterday."

"I dislocated his shoulder," I said, but Dex waved me off.

"I like Romy's version better. And just wait, by spring break, the story will be that you tore off *both* his arms and shattered his spine."

Romy snorted. "Did you tell her about the meeting?" she asked Dex.

"No, I was boring her with my life history first," Dex replied. "Why don't you give her the hard sell?"

Eyes twinkling behind her glasses, Romy rested her chin on her hands. "Well, since you're such a rad chick and all, we thought you might want to join our club."

I hoped my face looked confused rather than relieved. All that worrying over how I was going to get into the club, and then, *bam*, I'm invited. Maybe today really *would* be better than yesterday.

Doing my best to furrow my brow, I looked back and forth between them. There was something unnerving about their identical expressions of glee. "Um, is this one of those clubs where the first rule is you don't talk about it?"

Dexter threw his head back and laughed, and Romy made that snorting noise again. "No," she said. "But if it were, I'd definitely want you in that one, too. This is actually a school-sanctioned thing, so it counts for extra-curricular stuff on college applications."

Oh, right. College. That was something I'd have to pretend to be thinking about, too.

But then Dex sat up and said, "Romy, I don't think Harvard is going to very impressed by your membership in something called PMS."

A startled giggle burst out of me. Paranormal Management Society. PMS. I hadn't even thought of it like that.

Romy looked a little chagrined. "I didn't come up with the name, and by the time we got it, Anderson had already made the T-shirts," she insisted, which only made Dex laugh harder.

"So what is PMS?" I asked, even though I already knew. "I mean, I know the traditional definition. . . ."

"Paranormal Management Society," Romy answered, swatting at Dex.

"Oh," I said weakly. "That's . . . um . . . that's awesome."

"Okay, see, I feel like when you're saying 'awesome,' what you mean is 'lame' and 'making me not want to be friends with you,'" Dex said.

"No." I shook my head. "That doesn't sound lame at all. It's just . . . I never heard of a school-sponsored monster-hunting club. What do you guys do?"

"Mostly we lurk around places at night with dorky

equipment purchased off the Internet," Dex offered, making Romy smack his arm again.

"We research local ghost legends, and then we . . . investigate them."

Dex leaned over and said in a stage whisper, "'Investigate' is code for lurking around places at night with dorky equipment purchased off the Internet."

"We're working on doing more," Romy said quickly. "Anderson—you'll meet him later—is our resident ghost-lore researcher, and he's looking into ways we can actually, like, banish ghosts and exorcise places."

She sounded so excited, and it was all I could do not to wince. Humans getting involved with the supernatural was bad enough, but exorcisms were way more than a bunch of teenagers could handle.

"Have you guys ever found anything?" I asked.

"We thought we got some ghostly voices on a tape recorder once," Romy offered. "At this creepy abandoned house in the next town over. And Anderson's closet door opened on its own one time."

"Because he had his window open," Dex muttered, and Romy shot him a look. "*Maybe* it was because of that. We don't know. It could've been . . . other stuff."

"Sure, why not? I just, uh, don't want to wear a T-shirt that says PMS, okay?" I added, and Romy stuck out her hand. "Deal."

CHAPTER 11

We shook on it just as the bus pulled up to the school. "Try to get kicked out of P.E. again today," Dex told me as he gathered up his stuff. "We can hang on the football field."

"Ha-ha," I muttered, slinging my bag over my shoulder.

Romy and I made our way to English while Dex sauntered off to his first class. We got to Mrs. Steele's room before the second bell, so Romy tossed her backpack onto the desk next to mine and said, "Gonna run to the bathroom. Watch my bag?"

"Sure," I replied as she dashed out the door.

As soon as she was gone, my eyes fell on her bag. Should I look through it really quickly? I wasn't sure if there was anything related to PMS or the case in there, but Mom said to check everything. If anyone asked what I was doing, I could just say I was looking for a pen.

My fingers were already reaching for the strap when something heavy landed on my desk. Startled, I looked up to see Adam sitting there.

"Hi," he said, smiling.

I drew back my hand. "Um. Hi."

"So I guess you decided to be a ghost hunter after all." He was still smiling, but there was something weird in his face. He looked kind of . . . bummed.

When I didn't say anything, he hurried on. "I mean, I just saw you talking to Romy and Dexter when you walked in, and you guys seemed really friendly. Especially you and Dex."

I was so confused that all I could do was stare at him while my brain raced for something to say. Why did Adam care who I was hanging out with? "They're nice," I finally said lamely, and Adam gave a little shrug.

"So, anyway, I was going to ask you this yesterday, but . . . you know."

Adam had gone kind of red and stammery, and I braced myself for whatever it was he wanted to ask me. "Anyway," he said again, "could I get your number?"

I blinked. What—oh, my cell phone number. Which he wanted. So he could call me.

"Sure," I said, hoping I sounded normal. Because

this was normal. Boys asking for your phone number. I scrawled it across a sheet of notebook paper and handed it to him. Adam grinned, looking relieved.

"Awesome," he said, nodding his head.

Romy returned, flopping into her desk with a huge sigh. When she noticed Adam, she gave a little wave. "Hey, Lipinski."

"Romy," Adam replied, but he didn't really look at her. To me, he said, "Okay, well, I'll, uh, see you around, Izzy." He waved the piece of paper. "And call you."

"Right," I said, still wondering what his deal was.

Once he was back at his own desk, Romy leaned over. "How do you have two dudes crushing on you in less than twenty-four hours at this school?"

I whirled around. "What?"

"Lipinski practically left a drool marks on your desk, and Dex is even goofier than normal in your presence."

The third bell rang then, saving me from answering. But as I pulled out a pen and paper for Mrs. Steele's vocabulary quiz, I snuck a glance at Adam a few rows over. He was sneaking a glance at *me*, so I quickly looked back to the front of the room. There had been something kind of . . . dreamy in his expression, but that wasn't because he liked me. How could he? We'd spent all of five minutes together yesterday.

As for Dex, well, he was Prodigium. And probably

only interested in me because of that. And Adam had asked for my number because . . . actually, I couldn't think of any other reason besides that he wanted to call me. And why do boys ever call girls if not to ask them out?

Scribbling out the definition of "moratorium," I tried very hard to ignore the sinking sensation in my stomach. All that TV I'd watched aside, I really didn't know anything about normal teenage interaction. I'd prepared myself for ghosts and keeping my cover story consistent, but the one variable I hadn't even considered was . . . humans. Regular people. With regular emotions and thoughts and wants that weren't all tied up in the supernatural.

I couldn't get suspicious over every single person who showed the slightest bit of interest in me. Clearly, I was going to have to brush up on my Normal People Skills.

Maybe a new season of *Ivy Springs* was already out on DVD. . . .

By the time English ended, I'd made myself a list of things I needed to get. More DVDs, obviously, but I also wanted some of those magazines I'd seen in drugstores and gas stations. The ones with glossy-haired girls on the cover and titles like *American Teen* and *Sassy Miss*. I wanted to be both of those things. Okay, so maybe I could do without being "sassy" for now, but there had to be good info on regular teenage stuff in there. Those magazines always had articles about "How to Tell if a

Boy Likes You!" and "Could Your Lipstick Kill You?"

I'd also added "makeup?" only to cross it out. Maybe I should read that article about killer lipstick first.

Making the list cleared my head a little bit, and I was actually in a good mood once we got to P.E., despite the fact that Coach Lewis handed me a uniform as soon as I walked in. Once I was changed into the ugliest T-shirt/ shorts combo on earth, I followed Romy out of the locker room and into the gym.

Ben was there, sitting on the bleachers, his arm in a sling. I waited for him to shoot me the Death Glare, but he was too busy talking to a blond girl next to him.

"Who's that?" I asked Romy, nodding toward the girl. I hadn't noticed her yesterday.

Romy heaved a sigh. "Beth Tanner, Ben's girlfriend since, like, the womb. They've been on and off for a while."

"Right now they seem . . . off," I said, which was kind of an understatement. Beth's face was the same bright red as the free-throw line, and I thought I could see tears shimmering in her eyes. Ben reached out with his uninjured arm to take her hand, but she threw it off. "Seriously, what is wrong with you?" she screamed, her voice echoing in the gym.

Now Ben was raising his voice, too. "It *wasn't me.*" He lifted his injured arm as far as it would go, thanks to the sling. "How could I have done it with *this*?" As he said it, his eyes fell on me, and I swear his face paled a little.

"Dude, Ben McCrary is so terrified of you," Romy whispered, and I frowned.

Beth was shaking her head, and I realized Ben wasn't the only one who was afraid; Beth's red face and shrill voice weren't just from anger. Her movements jerky, she turned to the bleachers and picked up her bag, rifling through it. "I know you were upset, but this?"

She whipped something out of her backpack, and I felt my muscles tense up, but Beth wasn't brandishing anything like a weapon at Ben. It was a doll. The Barbie's hair was the same bright gold as Beth's, and it was even wearing a little cheerleading uniform in green and white, which, from all the bunting and banners covering the gym, I knew were the school colors.

But even from this distance I could see that there was something wrong with the doll. Its plastic limbs looked twisted and mangled, and there was a bright splash of red over its stomach. "This is sick!" Beth shrieked, shaking the doll, and Ben seemed to go even paler.

"Beth, I swear to God, I didn't hang that thing up in your locker." Once again, Ben gestured to his arm. "There's no way—"

"Liar!" she screamed, the word bouncing around the gym. That was apparently enough for Coach Lewis. He turned around and blew his whistle. "Laps, all of you!"

"In here or out on the football field?" a girl asked. By this point, Beth was crying too hard to talk, and she was turning kind of purple. The coach was a similar shade, and seemed completely flustered. "I don't care!" he snapped at the girl. "Just . . . go run."

I turned to Romy, only to find her staring at Ben and Beth with a strange expression on her face. "Romy?" I asked. Half the class had already starting jogging lazily around the gym, while the other half was heading for the doors.

Grabbing my sleeve, Romy tugged me toward the second group. "We need to talk to Dex."

"About?"

But she didn't answer me.

Dex was on the bleachers again, huddled over a book. When he saw us, he waved and hopped down the steps.

"Did everyone get kicked out today? Was there a riot? Did you gang up to tear Ben McCrary limb from limb? Izzy led the charge, didn't she?"

"Shut up," Romy said, clearly thinking about something. In deference to Dex's asthma we walked around the track instead of running, while Romy filled Dex in on Beth's meltdown.

"Ah, high school romance. I never get tired of it," Dex said when she was finished.

"I think this is more than that," Romy said, chewing on a thumbnail. "What if the doll is like the frog?"

Dex stopped walking, shoving his hands into his coat pockets. "Okaaaay," he said slowly. "That's a . . . a point."

"What does any of that mean?" I asked. It was entirely too cold to be out there in a short-sleeve T-shirt and shorts, and I wished I'd brought my hoodie.

Seeing me shivering, Dex whipped off his coat and placed it around my shoulders. As he did, I caught a flash of silver on his wrist. At first I thought it was a watch, but it was actually some kind of bracelet. I was so busy trying to look for a bloodstone—I was pretty sure Dex wasn't a vamp, but it never hurt to check—that I nearly missed Romy answering me until I heard her say, "—like Mr. Snyder."

My head shot up. "What?"

"Mr. Snyder," Dex repeated. "Our current town scandal and PMS's ongoing case."

I took a deep breath, not sure how to proceed. I had to seem interested, but not *too* interested. "What happened?" I asked, figuring that was a safe question.

"He was nearly murdered by some sort of invisible being wielding a microscope," Romy answered.

"I'm going to need that explained to me," I said, and Dex mimed holding something over his head and bringing it down with force, making a sound like *Ka-DONK*.

I blew on my hands to warm them, smiling a little. "No, I understand how you can kill someone with lab equipment. It's the invisible part I'm not getting."

"Mr. Snyder was alone in that room," Romy said. "It was locked from the inside, and there aren't any windows in the lab."

That all lined up with what the newspaper article had said, although it had left out the microscope part.

"And what does the Beth doll have to do with any of that?" I asked. "And what frog?"

"About a week before Mr. Snyder nearly bit it, someone took one of the dead frogs he used in class for dissection," Dex answered, turning so that he was walking backward. "It was stuck to his door with its wee froggy head all bashed in."

I'd seen a lot of gross stuff in my day, but I still wrinkled my nose. "Ew."

"Indeed," Romy said with a shudder. "Poor frog."

"It was already dead," Dex reminded her, but Romy wasn't looking at him.

"And now the doll," she murmured under her breath.

Dex looked over the top of his sunglasses at Romy. "Sometimes I think you forget we can't all see directly into your brain, Romy. You're not exactly clarifying the situation for Izzy here."

Romy tucked her hair behind her ears. "Okay, so the police think that whoever attacked Mr. Snyder had some kind of personal grudge against him."

"Brilliant deduction on their part," Dex interjected, but Romy ignored him. "And the frog was meant as a kind of warning, some way of freaking him out. But, like we said, he was alone in the room. He swore up and down that there was no one in there and the microscope seemed to attack him on its own. Which obviously made us think *ghost*."

"It made *you* think ghost, Rome," Dex said, and Romy pushed her glasses up her nose.

"Can you think of a better explanation for a man being attacked in a locked room by something he couldn't see?"

When neither Dex nor I answered, Romy gave a brisk nod. "Exactly. And everyone knows that this place has a ghost: Mary Evans. She was the daughter of Ideal's mayor way back in the early 1900s. She actually went to this school."

"Was it called Mary Evans High then?" Dex asked. "Because that is an astonishing coincidence."

Romy was walking faster now, and both Dex and I sped up, too, Dex still walking backward. "No, back then it was named after some Confederate general. Anyway, Mary fell in love with one of her teachers."

"Gross," Dex and I said at the same time.

Ignoring us, Romy continued. "So they had this big secret romance going on for a while, and then she got knocked up."

"Double super gross," Dex said, turning on his heel so that he wasn't facing us anymore.

"So they were going to run away together," Romy said with a shrug. "Or at least that's what the teacher promised Mary. He was supposed to meet her in a cave right outside of town. It was where they'd been hooking up, apparently."

"But he lied, and then she froze to death waiting for him, and now her ghost haunts the school where she met him," I finished, almost without thinking.

It took me a second to realize that Romy and Dex had stopped walking. I stopped and glanced over my shoulder.

"How did you know that?" Romy asked. "You've lived here, what, a week?"

It had been less than that, but that wasn't how I knew this particular ghost story. There were versions of it all over the place. It didn't mean the story wasn't necessarily *true*; it was just . . . kind of boring.

I wasn't sure if I was disappointed or relieved. I'd told Mom this would be an easy case, but I hadn't expected it to be quite *this* easy. This had to be the ghost we were dealing with.

I realized Dex and Romy were staring at me, waiting for an answer. "Oh, right. The Mary Evans thing. It was, uh, in the brochure they gave my mom about the school."

Dex frowned. "We have a brochure? And it mentions the local ghost story?"

"Do you still have it?" Romy asked. "It would be a good thing to add to my file on Mary Evans."

"I think we threw it out," I said quickly, before trying to change the subject. "So you think that the ghost of Mary Evans is pissed at teachers or—"

Romy chewed her lower lip. "That's what we thought at first. But if the Barbie is a warning for Beth like the frog was a warning for Mr. Snyder, what does that—"

Suddenly, Dex stopped, pressing a hand against his chest. He made a kind of wheezing sound, and at first I thought he was joking. But then Romy grabbed his arm. "Dex?"

He fumbled in his pocket, getting out his inhaler. He took two deep pulls on it, and the wheeze slowly started to fade. One more pull and his breathing sounded normal, if kind of fast. "Sorry," he said. "Wasn't trying to be a drama queen."

"You shouldn't have been running," Romy chastised him, and he rolled his eyes.

"I was just walking quickly. And I'm fine now." He

raised his head, and while his face was a little pale, he didn't seem to be in danger of keeling over. "Anyway, why don't you go inform Anderson of this little *aha* moment? I think he has yearbook this period."

When Romy hesitated, Dex waved her on. "Don't worry. If Coach Lewis decides to grace us with his presence, I'll tell him you went to the ladies' room. That ought to scare him to death."

"You're sick, Dex," Romy told him.

"Which is why you like me. Now go."

Once Romy had dashed off, Dex turned to me. "Alone at last. So how's your second day stacking up against your first?"

"They've both been full of peril, but since today involved less maiming, I'm gonna give it the edge."

Dex laughed, but he still sounded out of breath. "I'm glad you decided to join our little ghost-busting gang."

Shrugging out of his jacket, I handed it back to him and tried to sound casual as I asked, "Yeah, what's with that? You don't strike me as the ghost-busting type."

Dex gave me a little half-smile, taking his coat. "I'm just full of mysteries, Miss Brannick," he said. "And now, if you'll excuse me, I think I'm going to head back to my bleachers and my book. But I'll see you on the bus."

I watched his retreating back, wondering just what Dex's mysteries might be.

CHAPTER 12

Id hoped to get right to my first meeting of the Paranormal Management Society, but on the way home that afternoon, Romy informed me that for "budgetary reasons," they could only meet every other week, which meant there wouldn't be another meeting until the next Thursday. That gave me nearly ten days to wait, which was a lot longer than I'd wanted—the sooner I got this case over with, the better—but in the end, I was kind of grateful for the time.

For one thing, school was tougher than I'd expected. English was good. We were reading *Macbeth*, and while I'd never read Shakespeare before, any story that involved witches, ghosts, and a bunch of violence seemed right up my alley. History was also okay, and I was holding my own in chemistry, but geometry was one of the more evil foes I'd ever faced. I hadn't really thought much about balancing ghost busting with math problems, so it was nice to let the case take a backseat for a little bit.

In addition to giving me time to figure out homework, those ten days let me get closer to Romy and Dex. I still hadn't met the mysterious Anderson. He drove to school himself, and since he was a junior, we didn't have any of the same classes. But I sat with Romy and Dex on the bus every day, and by the time the first PMS meeting had rolled around, I felt like I was already one of the group. I wondered if all kids made friends this quickly, or if this was just unique to Dex and Romy.

PMS was holding its meeting in one of the portable classrooms behind the school, and when the last bell rang on Thursday afternoon, Romy and I made our way out there. "The state outlawed these like a million years ago," Romy told me as we walked into what was basically a trailer, "but a few schools keep them around for art classrooms or yearbook offices." She snorted. "You know, classes that don't really matter, according to the fine state of Mississippi."

This particular trailer wasn't being used this year. It smelled like erasers and damp carpet, but it had a big whiteboard and a few desks that weren't covered in scratched obscenities, so it met all of Romy's requirements. "We used to meet in the lunchroom, but the janitors were always rushing us." Romy turned to the whiteboard, picked up a blue dry-erase marker, and scrawled *1st point: Izzy.*

"So how long have you been running this thing?" I asked her as she wrote, *2nd point: Gym Weirdness/Beth/Doll.*

"I tried to start a chapter back in junior high, but a couple of parents complained. Apparently, investigating the paranormal is the first step on the road to devil worship or something. But when we got to high school I was ready."

Once she'd written *3rd point: Tonight?* Romy turned to me with a broad smile. "I explained to Mr. Owens—he's our principal—that it wasn't, like, an occult thing." She raised her thumb, ticking off. "It's science. They study parapsychology at Duke, for heaven's sake. And"—she raised her index finger—"a few years back, Mary Evans High had a forensics club that studied old-timey murders. That is way more twisted than ghost hunting. And last but not least"—a third finger went up—"investigating popular ghost stories from this area increases our knowledge of local folklore and regionalism."

I sat on top of one of the desks, crossing my legs. "Wow. You really wanted to—I mean, to make this club." The door banged open, and a lanky boy, even taller than Dex, loped in. He had blond hair that fell nearly to his shoulders, and while he had a few acne scars and wasn't as handsome as Dex, he was still a pretty good-looking guy. Then his eyes landed on Romy, and his whole face seemed to light up.

"Hey, Rome," he said, his voice surprisingly deep. Then his eyes landed on me. "Oh. Hi."

I gave a little wave. "Hi."

"Anderson, this is Izzy," Romy said, and I noticed her face was kind of glowy, too. "She's gonna be in the club now, but we'll go over that when everyone gets here."

"Sounds good," he said affably, sitting on top of the desk closest to Romy.

"Everyone" turned out to be Dex. He arrived about five minutes later, sliding into the desk next to mine. "So, Izzy," he asked, turning those blue eyes on me, "suitably impressed by our headquarters?"

Romy tossed the dry-erase marker at him. "Okay, now that we're all here, I'm calling this meeting of the Paranormal Management Society to order. First point"—she gestured to the whiteboard—"is to welcome our newest member, Izzy Brannick. Izzy has only been at Mary Evans for about two weeks, but has already proven herself awesome by permanently crippling Ben McCrary."

"Whoa," Anderson said, looking at me with respect even as I said, "I just hit him with a dodgeball."

"I've had dreams about that," Anderson replied.

"Could you describe what happened in really precise detail?"

"Later," Romy answered for me. "We have a lot to cover today."

Reaching into her backpack, she pulled out a laptop. "Now, as you know, there have been several odd happenings around here lately. Today, Izzy and I observed something especially weird." Romy perched on the desk opposite from me, balancing the computer on her crossed legs. "Beth Tanner found a Barbie doll, dressed to look like her and seriously jacked up, hanging in her locker."

Anderson leaned forward in his desk. "Like Mr. Snyder and the frog," he said, eyes going wide.

"Possibly," Romy said, turning her computer so that we could all see it. There was a little folder on the desktop titled MARY EVANS, and Romy clicked on it. "Okay, so it's been common knowledge that Mary has haunted this place ever since she died."

"Forever condemned to high school," Dex said with a little shudder. "That would make me homicidal, too."

Romy didn't lift her eyes from the screen, but she frowned. "Why is she homicidal, though? I mean, over a hundred years, and up until a few months ago, the only ghostly activity was an occasional locker door opening, or things disappearing and showing up someplace weird." Clicking on an icon, Romy pulled up a document with

EVIDENCE typed in bold letters on the top. Several bullet points were listed below, including things like LOCKERS and CHALK.

When I asked what that meant, Romy closed the document, saying, "About ten years ago, an entire history class saw a piece of chalk float in midair for thirty seconds. But that's it."

Now I frowned. That did seem like quite a leap from floating chalk to dismembering frogs. It was really rare for a ghost to have that kind of control over its surroundings. If this was Mary Evans's doing, the sooner I got rid of her, the better.

Next to me, Anderson tapped a pencil against his braces. "If Mary left that doll for Beth, that kind of blows our whole teacher theory out of the water." He glanced over at me, cheeks reddening slightly. "We figured she went after Mr. Snyder because he was, you know, a teacher, and it was a teacher who, um . . . who, like—"

Sighing, Dex turned in his seat and propped his feet up on the desk next to him. "Got her in the family way."

As far as theories went, it wasn't a bad one, and I nodded. But Anderson was right: Why Beth now?

"Is there any connection between Beth and Mr. Snyder?" I asked, trying to look innocent. "Any reason the same thing that was after him would go after her?"

Romy pulled her knees up and stared into space.

"Nothing I can think of. Beth didn't even have biology this semester."

Silence fell over the trailer, the only sound Anderson's tapping at his teeth and the occasional car going by. Then Dex dropped his feet to the floor and proclaimed, "Look, I'm just going to say what everyone is thinking. Maybe history is repeating itself here. Maybe Beth and Mr. Snyder had a thing, like Mary and Mr. Gross Teacher."

Romy, Anderson, and I screwed up our faces at that, but I had to admit, it was a solid idea, and it did point even more to Mary Evans's being the actual culprit. And all I needed to know to make this place ghost-free was the "who."

Romy had clicked on something else now, a picture. It showed several people all dressed in clothes from the turn of the twentieth century. They were standing on a big lawn, and a few of the boys were holding tennis rackets. In the back, there was a girl with light hair and big eyes, a red circle drawn around her face. "That's Mary," Romy said, tapping the screen.

Dex leaned over my desk to get a better look, and I caught a whiff of some nice, woodsy scent. "She was pretty," he observed. "If I were her, I'd be chilling out in heaven, hitting on hot dead guys. Not hanging around here accosting chemistry teachers."

"She feels tied to this place," Anderson said, pointing his pencil at the laptop. "Until she gets some kind of justice, she's always going to hang around here."

It was very hard to bite my tongue on that, but I managed. Just like the rumors surrounding vampires, there's all kinds of wrong information about ghosts. If Mary Evans was stuck in this place, all the justice in the world wouldn't make her leave. She'd keep hanging around until someone put her to rest.

Romy shut down the computer. "So I'm thinking séance?"

My head shot up. "Wait, what?"

"We can contact Mary Evans through a séance," Anderson said. He nodded to the corner of the room, where a Ouija board, still in its box, sat on one of the desks. "See if we can talk to her, figure out if she's here. Maybe this weekend?"

Crap. I didn't know who invented Ouija boards, but whoever that guy was, he was a jerk. This place already had one dangerous spirit floating around; it didn't need something else called forth from a Ouija board.

"Are you guys sure that's the best idea? I mean, Ouija boards don't work, right?"

Anderson looked like I'd just insulted his grandmother. "Of course they *work*. I mean, we've never tried one before, but on TV—"

"On TV, EMP readers work," Dex threw in.

"And in reality, yours just has a lot of blinky lights."

"I've only had it for a few weeks, so we don't really know what the blinky lights do yet," Anderson replied, and Dex raised his hands in surrender.

"Boys." Romy sighed with a weariness that told me this wasn't the first time she'd stopped their squabbling. "Anderson's EMP reader is awesome and a very valuable tool for this club. And so is that Ouija board. So. As soon as I can find a free night when I don't have to babysit my brothers, we are going to get our séance on."

Dex snorted. "So we'll be doing the séance next summer, then?" To me, he added, "Romy is forever babysitting her little monsters."

He said it so easily, but most Prodigium I knew hate the term "monster." They find it offensive, and would never use it in casual conversation. Once again, I wondered just what the heck Dex was.

Sighing, he sat up and thumped his feet to the ground. "I for one cannot wait to hear the thrilling story behind why Mary Evans decided to upgrade from opening locker doors to attempted murder."

Romy ignored him and held up her hand for a high five. "So, Izzy Brannick, are you ready for your first experience with the paranormal?"

I slapped her palm, not sure whether I should laugh or cry. "As I'll ever be."

CHAPTER 13

"I don't think Everton really loves her."

"Of course he does," I told Torin around a mouthful of SpaghettiOs. "I mean, he gave up his dream of sailing across the world so that he could take her to prom. That has to mean something."

It was Friday night, and Torin and I were sitting in my room—well, I was. He was chilling in the mirror as usual, waiting for Mom to get home. When I'd come in from school, there'd been a note saying she'd be back later and I should fend for myself as far as dinner went. Hence the SpaghettiOs.

"No, I've known rogues like this Everton. He merely wants Leslie because he cannot have her. Once she succumbs to his charms, he'll tire of her."

I pointed my spoon at the screen, where Everton

and Leslie were currently locked in a pretty passionate embrace. "Think she's already succumbed."

"Bah," Torin said with a wave of his hand. "Mark my words, he'll discard her before this disk is completed."

I just shrugged, more interested in watching Everton and Leslie kiss than listening to Torin. I wondered if I'd ever have the chance to kiss someone. Didn't seem likely with all the monster hunting and family angst, but still. Kissing looked . . . nice.

"We could try that, next time I visit your dreams," Torin suddenly said, and my SpaghettiOs sloshed over the side of the bowl.

"What?"

Torin nodded toward the television. "Kissing. You've never done it, I'm quite good at it . . . seems like we should at least make an attempt."

Glaring at him, I scrubbed at the spot on my T-shirt. "I don't want to kiss you."

Raising his eyebrows, Torin leaned forward. "Do you not? Why?"

I sat my bowl on the desk, no longer interested in eating. "First of all, you're an evil warlock trapped in a mirror, and secondly, it would be . . . weird."

He shrugged. "Not unless you wanted it to be."

I had no idea what that even meant, so I just turned back to the TV. "I've known you my whole life," I told him, keeping my eyes on Everton and Leslie. "You basically used to babysit me when Mom and Finn were out on missions. So kissage is out of the question."

I expected him to tease me about that, but instead he waved it away. "Very well. Just thought I'd offer."

"Thanks but no thanks," I muttered, my face flaming. Now Everton and Leslie were arguing, but I'd missed what they were fighting about, and truth be told, I couldn't pay much attention anyway. I'd meant what I'd said about kissing Torin being weird. But then wouldn't it be weird with any boy I kissed?

I snuck a look at Torin out of the corner of my eye. Practice kissing in a dream wouldn't be like real kissing, after all. And—

No. No, no, no. That was a stupendously dumb idea. Torin was four hundred years older than me, and dangerous and trapped in a freaking mirror. My life had always been odd, but I wasn't about to let it get *that* odd.

I reached up and hit stop on the DVD player. "Okay, that's enough *Ivy Springs* for today."

Torin made a sound of protest. "But Leslie was just accusing him of fancying that other girl, Lila! And I was so sure Everton was moments away from throwing her over at last!"

"We'll watch more tomorrow," I promised him. "Now, you—"

I was interrupted by an insistent buzzing coming from somewhere in my backpack.

"What on earth is that?" Torin asked, and suddenly I remembered: my cell phone.

I scrambled to get it out of my bag. "Mom?"

There was a pause and then, "Um, no? Is this . . . is this Izzy?"

It was a boy. *What boy would be*—and then I remembered my second day of school, giving Adam this number. "Adam! Uh. Hi."

"Hi."

"Hi."

"Oh, this is scintillating," Torin muttered, and I threw him a look over my shoulder.

"So," Adam said, "I was calling because there's a basketball game tonight, and I thought you might want to, uh, come with me."

When I didn't say anything immediately, he rushed on. "I know it's really last minute, but it starts in like an hour, and we can just meet there if you want, or I can pick you up, or . . . whatever."

I glanced down at my SpaghettiO-stained T-shirt, my mind racing. A boy, coming to my house. To pick me up and take me somewhere. That was totally a date.

And I wasn't sure I was ready for that yet.

"I'll meet you there," I told him. Hopefully Mom

would be home soon, and if not, well, I could walk. After I changed into something not smeared with tomato sauce, obviously.

"Great!" he said, a little too loud.

"Yeah!" I exclaimed back, trying to match his enthusiasm. In the mirror, Torin didn't roll his eyes so much as his whole body.

"So an hour, at the school. I'll meet you there."

"Right," I agreed, hoping we could be done with this soon. My hands were starting to sweat. How come no one on *Ivy Springs* ever had these awkward phone moments? Leslie had probably never had sweaty palms in her life, not even when Everton called to tell her he was breaking up with her so that she could go to art school in Italy.

Finally Adam said, "See you then," and I breathed a silent sigh of relief. "Okay. Um . . . bye."

"Bye."

That done, I tossed my phone on the bed and turned my attention to my closet.

"Whatever shall you wear?" Torin observed, propping his chin in his hand. "Let's see, there's the black T-shirt with black jeans. Or perhaps, if you're going for elegance over function, you could wear the black T-shirt with black jeans. Ooh!" He sat up, widening his eyes. "Do you know what would be particularly fetching? The black—"

"T-shirt with black jeans," I finished for him. "Hilarious."

But looking at my closet, he did have a point. Other than that pink hoodie, my closet was a sea of sameness. A sea of black. And I didn't have the faintest idea what girls wore to basketball games.

Gripping the closet door with one hand, I leaned in and fished out a T-shirt. "You are being stupid," I muttered under my breath. "You have a ghost to hunt, and you are panicking over *clothes*."

Even though I hadn't been talking to Torin—and he knew it—he acted as though I had been. "But these things are all related, yes? The ghost and fitting in with these pathetic children. You are not fretting about clothing. You're merely trying to best maintain your cover."

Torin could be hugely annoying and a major pain in the butt, but every once and a while he said things I really needed to hear. So I threw him a very small smile before tossing a towel over my mirror.

"You know I wouldn't look," he said. "I am quite offended right now!"

Once I was in a clean shirt, I reached up to touch my hair. It was still back in the tight braid I wore every day, and for a second I thought about leaving it like that. But no, I needed to look a little different than I did at school, right?

So I unraveled the braid, combing it out with my fingers, until my hair fell in waves around my shoulders. That fixed, I grabbed a tube of lip balm out of my bag and coated my lips. I didn't own any makeup, and I knew Mom didn't have any either, so it was the best I could do.

Finally, I took the towel off the mirror to look at myself. Torin was still there, and I scowled, trying to see around him. "Lovely, Isolde," he told me, and I had to admit, I looked . . . Okay, maybe I was no Leslie, but my hair actually looked . . . pretty all down around my face like that.

Still, my hands itched to braid it again. Brannicks never wore their hair down, because it only got in the way of staking vamps or shooting shifters or taking out witches.

I heard the front door open. "Iz?" Mom called. I gave myself one last look before grabbing my jacket and heading downstairs.

Mom's hands were full of books, old ones that were flaking little bits of leather binding everywhere and filling the room with the smell of musty paper. "Everything I could get from the university library on— Oh."

She paused in the doorway. "That's a new look."

"There's this boy," I blurted out. "Adam. And he, uh, asked me to go meet him at the school for a basketball game, and I was thinking you could drive me there. If that's all right. It's part of my cover."

Mom blinked a couple of times before shifting her stack of books to her other hip. "Like a date?"

"Like a mission," I corrected, and I thought the corner of her mouth tilted up a little bit.

"Okay, then. Just let me . . . um, put this stuff away."

I walked over to help her, scooping up a few of the books. As I followed her to the guest room, I glanced at the spines. Two of them appeared to be about hauntings, but one had a title so faded I couldn't even read it. "What's the deal with all the books?" I still had no idea what Mom was up to while I was busy at school all day, although she'd mentioned driving to the university in the next town over to get some "materials."

Sighing, Mom shouldered the door open. "Research." From the tone of her voice, I knew that's all I was going to get.

Once again, a twist of guilt and anger coiled in my stomach. Did the research have something to do with Finn? If it did, I didn't understand why Mom was being so secretive about it.

"Izzy?" Mom said, and I realized she'd asked me a question.

"Sorry." I laid my books down on the bed next to Mom's half of the stack.

"I was just asking if you've found out anything at school yet."

"Yeah, actually," I told her, tucking my hair behind my ears. "For one thing, I'm pretty sure who the ghost is." I filled her in on Mary Evans and what I'd learned from PMS. When I was done, Mom raised her eyebrows. "Sounds pretty typical."

"That's what I was thinking." I perched on the edge of the bed. "Some stories become legends for a reason, I guess."

Mom nodded. "And how was the ghost hunter club? The usual?"

"Yeah. EMP detectors they ordered off of TV, files of local legends. That kind of thing. And they want to do a séance at some point, so I need to come up with a way of stopping that."

Sighing, Mom glanced down at one of her books, the one called *Ghosts and Hauntings*. "Make sure you do. Last time I dealt with one of those civilian ghost hunter groups, they did a séance. Ended up opening a portal to the Unseelie court instead, and brought through some seriously nasty faeries. I don't want to clean that up again."

I didn't know if she meant clean up in the "closing the portal, banishing the faeries" way, or if it was more a "and then I mopped the humans' blood off the wall" kind of thing.

I decided maybe it was better just to wonder.

"Anyway," I said, fiddling with the ends of my hair, "it seems pretty cut-and-dried. The frog and Barbie thing is odd, but—"

Mom held up a hand. "The what?"

Oh, right, I'd forgotten to tell Mom about Romy's theory that Mary was somehow warning her victims. As briefly as I could, I filled her in.

When I was done, Mom was frowning. "That is odd," she said. "But it doesn't really matter. If this Mary Evans is the ghost you're after, get rid of her."

"Planning on it," I told her. "But you have to do a banishing on the last day of the month, right? That's still a couple of weeks away."

Mom made a noncommittal sound in reply, and I thought of what Torin had said. Was coming here really about protecting the students of Mary Evans High? Or was it Mom's attempt at letting me have a taste of normal life?

"So this Adam," Mom said, sitting on the edge of the bed. "Is this part of the job, or is it—"

"Part of the job, for sure," I said quickly, and for some reason, Dex's face suddenly appeared in my mind. How would I feel if it were him I was meeting tonight? Just the thought sent my heart racing in a way that wasn't totally unpleasant.

Mom peered at me. "You're blushing."

I just stopped myself from covering my cheeks with my hands. "What? No, I'm not. I'm just . . . it's kind of hot in here."

But Mom was not so easily fooled. "Iz, I know we haven't talked much about boys."

"And we don't need to," I hurried on. "Dex is just a friend."

I didn't realize my mistake until Mom frowned at me. "I thought you said his name was Adam."

"It is," I said, turning away and heading for the door. "Dex is just this other boy. He's in that ghost hunter thing, and you had mentioned that, so it was on my mind. We should go if—"

Mom stood up. "Two boys?" she asked, and I wasn't sure if she was horrified or impressed.

"Friends," I said again. "Nothing else. And didn't you say it was important to blend in? Going on a . . . er, going to a basketball game is totally blending in."

I could tell Mom was struggling between the Brannick part of her that wanted to believe I was doing all of this for the mission—which I *so was*—and the Mom part that suddenly realized she had a teenage daughter. A teenage daughter who was hanging around teenage boys.

She reached out, and I think she was going to lay a hand on my shoulder or something, but in the end, she just let her arm drop to her side. "Izzy, I'm glad you're so dedicated to this, but . . . you have to remember that these kids you're spending time with are just part of a job. You can enjoy spending time with them, but in the end, there isn't any room for them in your life permanently."

I should have just nodded, but instead I said, "But you have friends. Or connections, or whatever. People like Maya. Like whoever found you this house."

Mom frowned slightly. "Those aren't my friends, Izzy, and they're not . . . civilians. They're people who are already wrapped up in this life. People who know about Prodigium and what we do. It's different."

"I understand that," I replied, but Mom just ducked her head to look into my eyes. "Do you? Do you *really*?"

I thought of Dex again, and the way it had been kind of . . . nice sitting with Romy in English class.

But I looked at Mom and said, "Absolutely. A job. Means to an end, all of that. On it."

Mom held my gaze for another beat before sighing. "Okay," she said at last. "Then let me grab my car keys and we'll get you to this game."

CHAPTER 14

The gym was brightly lit, and as I made my way down the hill from the parking lot, I could hear the banging of drums, the squeak of sneakers, and the occasional shout. Inside, it was even louder, and way more packed than I would have expected. Apparently sports are a really big thing around here.

Adam was waiting just inside the door, and I was relieved to see he was wearing more or less the same thing he'd had on at school today. That was one thing I'd gotten right at least. And from the look he gave my hair, I guess that had been right, too. "You look nice," he told me, waving his hand in my general direction.

"Thanks," I said, forcing myself not to shove my hair behind my ears again. "You, um, too."

On Everton and Leslie's first date, he'd taken her to

this fancy restaurant that had ended up burning down by the end of the episode. But before that, the date had looked like fun. I didn't remember them standing around awkwardly, struggling for things to say.

Because that's a TV show, dummy, and this is real life, I reminded myself.

Finally, Adam nodded toward the inside of the gym. "I, uh, usually play in the pep band, but I took the night off. Drums."

"Oh," I said, unsure what else to say. "Drums are . . . loud."

Adam tilted his head to one side, like he couldn't decide if I was being funny or not. Then he just shrugged and said, "Yeah, they are. So do you like basketball?"

I peeked around him, watching as boys in satiny-looking outfits raced up and down the court. "I don't know. I've actually never seen a basketball game before."

Adam's eyes widened. "Whoa, seriously?" From the tone of his voice, you'd think I'd said I'd never, I don't know, been outside before. Breathed air. "Like, you've never been to one, or you've never even seen one on TV?"

"Both," I told him. "We never had a TV before, so . . ."

Now Adam didn't just look surprised, he looked kind of horrified. Maybe that's what made me sound so defensive when I jerked my head toward the court and said, "I've seen stuff *like* this."

Then I remembered that that had been a "party" this coven of dark witches had been throwing, and it hadn't been a ball they'd tossed between them, but a human head.

That little story didn't seem like one I should share with Adam.

He shook his head. "Okay. Well, then I'm glad I could introduce you to your first real basketball game. I mean, our team sucks, but still, right?" He smiled at me, but it didn't reach his eyes, and I knew I wasn't the only one disappointed by the way this "date" was going.

"We should go in," he said, turning toward the gym. I did the same, and promptly collided with a boy.

"Sorry!" I said, reaching up to steady him without thinking.

But since it was Ben McCrary, and I'd just put my hand directly on the shoulder I'd dislocated, he gave a hiss of pain.

"Sorry, sorry, sorry!" I said again, holding my hands up. Ben just stared at me, pale and wide-eyed, and attempted to put as much space as possible between me and him.

"Just-just stay away from me," he sputtered before darting off.

Adam and I watched him go.

"I . . . um, I kind of dislocated his shoulder in P.E.," I said.

Adam was still staring after Ben. "Okay," he said slowly. "I heard that, but I thought it was just a rumor. I mean, no offense, but you're kind of tiny, and Ben McCrary is . . . not."

"I throw a mean dodgeball," was all I could think to say.

Turning back to me, Adam blinked a few times. "So you've never seen a basketball game, you didn't own a TV, and you can dislocate shoulders with dodgeballs?"

I didn't think any of that was meant to be a compliment, but I smiled anyway. "Yup."

Adam took that in. "I'm gonna grab us some Cokes," he finally said, nodding toward the concession booth. "If you want to go on in and grab a seat, I'll find you when I'm done."

"Great," I said, relieved for any suggestion that would put an end to us just standing there.

The game seemed to have just started, but the bleachers were already pretty full. I spotted a few empty spaces in the middle, and was just preparing to wade through the crowd when I glanced up and saw Romy, Anderson, and Dex sitting in the very top row.

They spotted me around the same time, and Romy

waved, gesturing for me to come join them. I picked my way up to the very top of the bleachers, trying not to step on anyone's hand.

Once I was there, Anderson scooted closer to Romy, leaving a space between him and Dex. I squeezed into it, and if my hip bumped Dex's, so what? Everybody was practically sitting in each other's laps as it was.

"Look at you," Dex enthused, leaning forward with his elbows on his knees. "Embracing school spirit, supporting school athletics."

"Yeah," I said, "I'm here—"

But before I could say anything about Adam, Romy leaned across Anderson and said, "It's actually awesome that you showed up. This is kind of an impromptu PMS meeting."

Dex rolled his eyes. "By which Romy means she tricked me and Anderson with the promise of manly things like sports only to foist her ghost-hunting agenda on us once we got here."

"I knew it was a PMS meeting," Anderson offered in his deep voice. "I hate sports."

Dex flung his hand out toward the court. "Well, I don't. I have a very vested interest in watching those dudes in blue beat the ever-loving crap out of the Mary Evans High Hedgehogs."

"Wait, our mascot is the hedgehog?" I asked.

"Up until a few years ago it was a Confederate soldier," Anderson told me. "But then everyone decided that was offensive, so they'd let the student body vote on a new one. That's how we'd ended up with the Mary Evans High Hedgehogs."

He nodded, and for the first time, I saw the mascot. He was standing near the cheerleaders. There'd been some attempt to make him look tough. The hedgehog's quills had been tipped with silver paint to make them look sharp, and his face was twisted into a snarl.

But all the quills and fierce expressions couldn't disguise the fact that, at the end of the day, the mascot was just a six-foot-tall hedgehog.

It was hard to tear my eyes away from that spectacle, but I finally turned to Romy and asked, "So what ghost business are you working on tonight?"

Romy huffed out a breath, ruffling her bangs. "Well, it was supposed to be the séance. My mom got off early tonight, so it was the perfect chance, but when we got here, the stupid trailer was locked."

Looking at me, she added, "I tried texting you like a billion times."

I'd left my phone at home. I still wasn't used to carrying it around, which I obviously needed to get better about. I really didn't want these three doing a séance.

"Romy asked us to break a window," Dex said, "but

I told her I was not prepared to commit a crime, even in the name of science."

"Any chance you'll have another free night soon?" Anderson asked.

Before Romy could answer, Dex said, "Why is Adam Lipinski coming toward us?"

"Oh!" I had kind of forgotten about Adam. But there he was, making his way up the bleachers with two cups in his hands. "He's, um . . . we're here together," I said, and almost as one, Romy, Dex, and Anderson turned to look at me.

"Like, you're on a date?" Romy asked, both eyebrows raised. "And you came to sit with us?"

"He said to find seats," I told her, lifting one shoulder in a shrug.

"He probably meant for the two of you," Dex said, pulling his leg as far away from mine as he could. "And preferably seats that didn't have you wedged between two other guys."

Romy was already at the very end of the row, and Anderson was as close to her as he could get. Dex had a little space on his side, and he scooted away from me, giving Adam just enough room to squeeze in between us.

He handed me my Coke, the cup icy and slick in my hand. "Thanks," I murmured, suddenly unsure and embarrassed again. Was I not supposed to sit with my friends? Was that why Adam's shoulders were all . . . weird?

Taking a sip of my drink, I wondered why it was there were a million books on ghosts and legends and monsters, and nothing useful like, *How to Go On a Normal Date Without Looking Like a Total Spaz.*

"You guys talking ghost stuff?" Adam asked, and next to me, I felt Anderson tense a little.

But Romy leaned over, pleasantly surprised. "We were, actually. Okay, so everyone knows that this place has a ghost, and—"

"And you guys are going to slap on your tinfoil hats and get rid of it?"

Adam said it with a little smile, but it still sounded . . . snide. Mean, even.

Romy's expression hardened and she turned her attention back to the court. "No, we only use our tinfoil hats when there are aliens involved."

On Adam's other side, Dex sighed dramatically and leaned back against the wall, pulling his sunglasses out and slapping them on his face. He then stretched out his long legs, crossing them at the ankle, and folded his hands over his stomach.

Frowning, I leaned forward a little, trying to see past Anderson. "So, since the séance didn't work out, what

PMS business are you dealing with tonight?" I asked Romy.

Her eyes flicked back to Adam for a second before she said, "I just thought with the mutilated doll and everything, we might need to keep an eye on Beth."

"She's cheering tonight," Anderson offered, nodding down at the gym floor. Sure enough, there was Beth standing in a line with a bunch of other girls in green and white, silver pom-poms in her hand. I remembered the doll wearing a rough copy of that same outfit, all mangled and covered in fake blood.

Then next to me, Adam snorted and said, "Oh, that psycho Barbie she found in her locker? Please, that was totally just Ben being a jerk."

"It's more than just that," Romy said, but Adam rattled the ice in his drink and rolled his eyes. "Of course it is. You know, Romy, this ghost hunter thing was cute when we were all in elementary school, but now it just makes you a weirdo. You get that, right?"

"Better a weirdo than a jackass," Dex muttered.

"You're one to talk, dude," Adam fired back, but Dex gave no indication he'd heard him.

"Whatever." Adam stood up and looked down at me. "I'm out of here. Izzy, you coming?"

As I stared up at him, I realized something. I wasn't irritated that Adam had interrupted Romy and screwed up my chances at getting more info. I was irritated because Dex was right. He *was* a jackass.

"No," I told him, curling my hands around the bleacher. "I think I'll stay here."

Adam hadn't been expecting that, I could tell. For a second he looked confused and then, I thought, hurt. But just as quickly, he gave me the same look he'd given Romy. "Okay, fine," he said, walking down a row. "The girl who's never seen TV before probably belongs with these freaks anyway."

With that, he turned and left. The four of us watched him go. Only when he was at the very bottom did Dex say, "Izzy, I don't think your new boyfriend is very nice."

I didn't bother to correct him about Adam being my "boyfriend." So my first date was a total bust, then. But why, watching him walk away, did I feel so . . . I don't know, relieved?

And then something else occurred to me. "Oh, crap. He was supposed to drive me home."

Dex slid his sunglasses down his nose, but before he could say anything, Romy leaned over. "My mom is coming to get me in like an hour. We can drive you home."

"Great," I told her, ignoring the tiny flicker of disappointment. I needed more of a chance to talk to Romy anyway.

There was a sudden shout from the crowd as—I guess—our team scored points. Everyone around us shot to their feet, clapping, but the four of us stayed in our seats.

"Well, Isolde," Dex said over the noise, "how does it feel to have declared for Team Outcast?"

I couldn't help but laugh. "Good," I told him, and I was surprised to discover I meant it.

CHAPTER 15

By the time the game was nearly over, I still didn't really understand basketball, but I did learn that Dex's Nana texted him about every ten minutes any time he was away from the house, that Romy twisted one strand of hair around her finger every time Anderson said something to her, and that Anderson had, up until junior high, actually been a pretty decent basketball player himself.

"Busted my knee waterskiing," he told me, tapping the kneecap in question. "But it was all good. Led to me looking for other ways to spend my time, and then I found Ro—uh, found the club. Ghost hunting seemed like a lot more fun than throwing a stupid ball into a basket, anyway."

"Anderson here is a reformed jock," Dex said. "Which he didn't bother to tell me until we'd already been friends for a month. By then it was too late to shun him, as I should have."

Grinning, Anderson reached over me and thwacked Dex's head, sending his sunglasses tumbling.

Dex gave an outraged cry. "I am affronted! That's it, friendship rescinded."

Anderson just leaned back against the wall and laughed. "Like you said, bro, too late." He turned his gaze down to me. "Of course, if you want to escape this madness while you still can, I wouldn't blame you."

"Hey!" Romy leaned over, laying a proprietary hand on my arm. "We finally have another girl in the group. Please don't run her off just yet."

It was weird watching their easiness with each other, and then seeing them treat *me* like that, too. I'd never really missed having friends—you can't miss something you've never had—but I hadn't realized how, well, awesome they could be, either.

I stood up. "I'm gonna run to the bathroom. Be right back."

Romy looked like she was about to get up, too. "Do you want me to come with you?"

I hesitated, one foot awkwardly lifted over the bleacher below me. "I know where it is," I told her, remembering that I'd seen a girls' room in the gym lobby.

But that must've been the wrong answer, because Romy seemed puzzled. "Oh, okay."

I made my way back down the bleachers, and when I got to the front of the gym, I suddenly saw why Romy had offered to come with me. There were . . . groups of girls huddled outside the bathroom, talking, laughing, some sharing lip gloss. Crap, was that a thing girls who were friends were supposed to do with one another?

Sighing, I turned to the gym doors, noticing that just up the hill there were lights on in the school. There were bathrooms up there, and maybe they wouldn't be so crowded.

It had gotten colder, and I shivered a little as I jogged up toward the school. Luckily, the main breezeway door was unlocked, and I knew the bathroom was just inside, past the lockers.

Flyers pinned to a bulletin board ruffled in the breeze as I yanked open the door. The hall was dark, although there were two rectangles of light from the bathroom doors. I was headed for them when a glow suddenly filled the hall.

For one second I thought someone had just flipped on another light, but no. This wasn't the harsh fluorescent of the hallway lighting, or the dull amber of the bathroom. This was slightly bluish and very, very familiar.

Taking a deep breath, I steeled my nerves and turned around.

Mary Evans floated in the hall just behind me, her long white dress barely brushing the ground. In the picture Romy had shown me, her hair had been styled into some sort of fancy updo, but now it straggled down her back. She didn't speak, but her eyes roamed over me, confusion on her translucent face.

"Hi, Mary," I said, my voice loud in the quiet hall. Okay. This was good. This was confirmation that the ghost stalking Mary Evans High was in fact Mary Evans. But it was hard to feel glad about that when I remembered that the same ghost had nearly killed a guy.

"You need to leave this place."

Her head jerked up, lips curling back in a snarl, and I stepped back. The cold metal of the lockers pressed against my shoulders, and I swallowed hard. "You can't stay—" I started, and then there was a rush of wind as she suddenly surged forward.

It was like I'd been dunked into a tub of ice water. I couldn't see anything but that blue light, and all around me there was this horrible sense of pressure, like hands were pushing on me as hard as they could. But that wasn't the worst part. The worst part was her voice in my mind, shrieking so loudly I could barely make it out. *Pay they have to pay have to pay,* over and over again. Images played behind my eyelids. I saw blood on a microscope, saw Mary's ghostly hand clutched around the base. Then there was a cave, and fire? Something bright, something that *burned*.

And then suddenly the cold and the pressure were gone, the shrieking was silent, and Mary was no longer up against me, all around me.

She hovered there in front of me, chest heaving in and out as though she were still breathing, and she had a frantic look in her eyes. Her mouth opened in a silent scream, head tilting back to cry at the ceiling.

And then she rose up, hovering high over my head before vanishing.

I stood there against the lockers, nearly panting. My knees felt watery, but I made myself stay on my feet. Brannicks don't slump to the floor just because a ghost gets up in their face.

Still, as I pushed myself off the lockers and scrubbed a shaking hand over my mouth, I had to admit that that had not been your run-of-the-mill ghost. I'd seen ghosts before. I'd seen them sad and confused, maybe a little irate. But I'd never seen one as furious as Mary Evans, and I'd certainly never had one try to . . . God, what *had* she been trying to do? It had almost felt like she was trying to climb inside my skin.

Shuddering at that thought, I pushed open the

bathroom door. Inside, I splashed cold water on my face and tried to get my heart rate back to something resembling normal. Reminding myself that coming face to face with Mary Evans was a good thing—hey, now I knew what I was up against—I stepped back into the hallway.

A shadowy figure suddenly appeared in front of me, and with a choked shriek, I reached out and grabbed the front of a shirt, slamming the person against the lockers.

Anderson blinked back at me.

"Oh!" Loosening my fingers, I let him go, smoothing his shirt out with the flat of my hand. "Sorry, you scared me. I startle kind of easily."

Tucking his hair behind his ears, he nodded. "I noticed that." I waited for him to give me the "You Violent Freak" Look Ben McCrary had given me, but to my surprise, Anderson just smiled and said, "I knew you dressed like a ninja, but I didn't think you actually were one."

I laughed. "I didn't hurt you, right?" I asked, but Anderson waved me off.

"No harm, no foul. Romy was looking for you. She took the gym while I headed up here."

"Where's Dex?" I asked before I could stop myself.

Anderson shrugged. "His Nana needed him, so he went home." He frowned, looking more closely at me. "Are you sure you're okay? You're kind of pale."

We opened the breezeway doors, stepping back outside. "Yeah, just . . ." I trailed off, and Anderson nodded.

"Overcome with the majesty of team sports. I understand."

Chuckling, I shrugged. "Something like that." The air didn't feel so cold now that I'd had a ghost trying to snuggle me, and I took a deep breath as we walked down the hill. We had just gotten to the gym when Anderson said, "Hey, Izzy."

I turned and he stood there, hands in his pockets, shoulders hunched. "Uh . . . thanks for being so cool with Romy. I know she likes hanging out with me and Dex, but with you . . . with you being, like, you know, a *girl* and stuff—"

I stopped Anderson before he could actually choke on his tongue. "It's easy to be cool with Romy. She's a cool girl."

Anderson wasn't as good-looking as Dex, but the goofy grin that spread across his face was seriously beautiful. "She's the *coolest* girl," he enthused, and even though I'd just been scared half to death not ten minutes before, I discovered I was grinning, too.

"Who is?" Romy asked, coming up behind him.

Anderson's ears reddened and he kicked at a nonexistent rock. "This girl," he babbled. "This girl who's cool."

Romy raised her eyebrows. "Huh. Informative, Anderson." Tugging at my hand, she started pulling me toward the parking lot. "Come on, Iz, my mom's here."

"Bye, Anderson," I called, waving to him with my free hand.

He gave a sheepish wave back and then turned away.

"So," Romy asked as we stepped into the parking lot, "other than getting ditched by Jerk-Face Adam, how was your first Official Mary Evans High Event?"

I looked back at the school, and even though I couldn't be certain, I thought I saw a flash of blue light.

"Eventful."

CHAPTER 16

Romy's mom drove a minivan, one of those fancy ones with the doors that open on their own and TV screens in the back of every seat. As we clambered into the back, I stepped on one doll, a handful of crackers, and a pile of Legos.

"My siblings are beasts, sorry," Romy said, flopping into her seat.

"They're also four," her mom informed me, catching my eyes in the rearview mirror. Her hair was a few shades darker than mine and pulled up in a haphazard ponytail. A large spot that looked like it might have been grape juice stained her T-shirt from the collar to the middle of her chest.

I noticed the booster seats and looked over at Romy. "You have three siblings?"

"Triplets," she said with a nod. "Three boys. Adorable and evil in equal measure."

"Romy," her mom admonished, and Romy leaned forward, holding on to the back of the seat in front of her. "Mom, I love them, you know I do. But even you have to admit they are five parts cute to five parts holy terror."

I could hear her mom sigh as she glanced down at the dark purple blob on her shirt. "All right, you may not be entirely wrong."

Settling back in her seat, Romy fished a sippy cup lid out from behind her back and tossed it to the floor. "At least I had nine years as an only child. My parents adopted me when I was two," she told me. "I was eleven when the triplets were born, and nothing in my life has ever been quiet again." But even as she said it, there was a kind of softness in her smile, and it twisted something in my chest.

A sensation that only got worse when Romy's mom asked, "What about you, Izzy? Do you have any brothers or sisters?"

"No," I told her around the sudden lump in my throat. "Just me and my mom." What else could I say? "My sister disappeared" was too bizarre and opened the door to too many questions. "My sister died" wasn't true. Or at least I hoped it wasn't. So this was the easiest answer I could give, no matter how much it sucked to say it.

"Your house must be super quiet, then," Romy said. "Now I know where I'm going the next time I need to escape." Her grin was bright.

"Sure," I said, even as I tried to imagine Romy in my house. I'd never had company before. Would Torin behave? Maybe if I talked to him beforehand . . .

"We may need to grab ice cream before taking Izzy home," Romy informed her mom. "She had a rough night."

I jerked my head in Romy's direction. I hadn't told her about seeing Mary's ghost, so what did she—

"Some jerk boy stood her up."

"I didn't get stood up," I said quickly, but Romy waved her hand.

"Okay, so technically you told him to get bent, but that in no way negates the need for ice cream."

"I think I'm good," I told her, but I was smiling.

"Are you sure?" Romy's mom asked. "Because I've taught my daughter well. When boys are jerks, only ice cream will suffice. Or shopping, maybe."

"Ooh!" Romy sat up in her seat. "Yes, shopping. That's what Izzy needs. I mean, not right now, obviously, but sometime in the very near future. No offense," she added, "but while I appreciate this whole goth thing you have going, you could seriously use some color."

Seeing as how tonight Romy was wearing a sweater

such a bright shade of yellow that it practically glowed in the dark, I was a little nervous about what her idea of "color" might mean. But hadn't I just been worrying that my normal Brannick wardrobe wasn't going to hack it at Mary Evans High?

"Okay," I said slowly. "I could . . . maybe get behind a shopping trip."

"Excellent!" Romy said. "Next week. Mom, can you take us? On Thursday?"

"I can," her mom agreed before catching my gaze in the rearview mirror. "Romy tells me you've joined her club. Are you into all things supernatural, too, Izzy?"

"You could say that," I told her. "Mostly I was just excited the school had something as cool as a Paranormal Management Society."

"Well, I'm glad you joined. Romy could use some girlfriends. Not that Anderson and Dex aren't nice boys; it's just that it's so hard for Romy to find girls who share her interests."

"Mom," Romy said, embarrassed.

I looked over at Romy, and felt guilt wash over me. I liked her, I did. But it wasn't like I was being her friend just because she was a cool person. I was . . . using her.

What was it Mom has said? *Remember, don't get too close. These people are a means to an end.*

That thought was still bothering me when Romy's

mom pulled up in our driveway, but I tried not to let it show. Instead, I put on my brightest voice, told Romy I'd see her tomorrow, thanked her mom for the ride, and went inside.

Mom was sitting at the kitchen table when I came in, one of those ancient books in front of her. She barely glanced up as I took the seat across from her. "How did it go?"

I shrugged. "Okay. I saw the ghost we're dealing with, and let me tell you, she is one seriously unhappy chick."

"Dangerous?" Mom asked, linking her fingers on top of her book.

"I can handle it," I said automatically, even as I remembered just how full of rage Mary had been. I thought about asking Mom if she knew much about ghosts possessing people—if that had been what the whole pushing thing had been about—but decided against it. Mom needed to think I could do this on my own.

Because I could.

So before she could ask me anything else, I said, "I think I cemented my friendship with the ghost hunter kids, but . . ."

"But?" Mom prompted.

Sighing, I propped my chin in my hand. "I think I'm really bad at dating."

Mom huffed out a laugh and turned her attention back to her book. "Is it awful that I'm kind of thrilled about that?"

I wanted to ask her more about it. Like, had it been wrong to sit with PMS? Was Adam being a jerk, or was that just teenage boys? I mean, sure, Dex didn't seem like that, but he *wasn't* a regular teenage boy, and . . .

"Did Finn ever date? When you guys had those longer jobs that took a few weeks. Was there ever, like, a guy or anything?"

Surprised, Mom looked up. "I . . . I honestly don't know. She never mentioned anyone."

If we found Finley—*when* we found her—I would ask her.

There were a couple of pens on the table, and I picked one up, poking at Mom's book. "So this research. What is it about?"

Curling her fingers around the edges of the volume, Mom scooted it away, just the tiniest bit. "Nothing you need to worry about. Just something I'm looking into for Maya."

She inhaled sharply through her nose, the same way Finn always did right after she told a lie. My chest tightened, and I fought the urge to yank the book back, to see for myself what Mom was so interested in. It had to be about Finley. But if it was, why wouldn't she tell me, let me help her?

Because she's afraid you're going to screw it up, a voice hissed in my head. *Because if you had just gone into the house with Finley that night, she might still be here.*

Blinking against a sudden stinging in my eyes, I just nodded. "Okay."

The silence that hung over the table was threatening to turn awkward, so I cleared my throat and said, "You know, the only part of the Mary Evans things that doesn't make sense to me is the frog and the Barbie."

Mom rested her elbows on the book in front of her. "You're right. There are plenty of stories about ghosts attacking people, but that level of physical manipulation . . . it would take a lot of energy. That's not just wielding a weapon; that's planning."

I nodded, drumming my fingers on the table. "It seems kind of advanced for a ghost."

"Advanced, yes, but not unheard of."

Mom and I both jumped as Torin's voice floated through the kitchen. I glanced around, wondering where he could be, and my eyes landed on the clock above the stove. It was framed in a beveled mirror, and even though all the little pieces of Torin were hard to make out, I could still see him in there.

"Torin, you know you're supposed to keep to your

mirror," Mom said, getting up and heading for the clock. She lifted it off the wall, and Torin made an aggrieved sound.

I stood up from the table, leaning one hand against it. "Have you seen something like this before?"

Mom stopped, the mirrored clock held out from her body. I couldn't see Torin's face, but I heard him clearly when he answered, "Only once. My coven raised a particularly nasty ghost. On their own, spirits are usually harmless, but if they've been summoned forth by any type of magic, well. Completely different kettle of fish."

Lowering the clock to the table, Mom considered that. "So you think a witch or a warlock could have somehow raised this spirit?"

"Possibly." Mom had put the clock facedown, so Torin's voice came out muffled. "Or, at the very least, powered it up. Isolde mentioned that there had been very basic haunting activity at this school for quite some time. So why now? What changed in the past few months to turn an ordinary specter into something that can perform such feats as securing a dead frog to a door, or mutilating a toy?"

I chewed my lip. How long had Dex been in Ideal? It couldn't be a coincidence that just when this guy, who was clearly *something*, showed up, Mary Evans had become Uber-Ghost.

But Mom just shrugged. "Well, it's not like it matters. Powerful or not, ghosts are easy to dispose of. And we just have a few more days until the full moon. Izzy will get rid of it, and that will be that."

Except that I wasn't sure that *would* be that. If someone was raising ghosts, what was to stop them from raising another one once Mary Evans was gone? For just a second, it was on the tip of my tongue to tell Mom about Dex. But what if I did, and she decided this case was too big for me after all, and just decided to take it over herself?

I glanced at the pile of books on the table—Mom's super-secret "research" that she still wouldn't tell me about.

If she was going to keep her secrets, I would keep mine.

CHAPTER 17

"Here." Romy added a sweater to the pile in my arms. "Redheads look good in green."

I cast a doubtful look at the sweater. "This . . . doesn't look like green."

The shade should've been called "Radioactive" or maybe "Noxious." That had been one of our vocabulary words this morning.

Frowning, Romy reached into the rack and pulled out a black skirt. "Here, Ninja Lady," she said, tossing it to the top of my stack. "You can wear it with black."

We'd been shopping for over an hour, and Romy had already talked me into a pink blouse, two pairs of jeans that were *not* black, three T-shirts in various shades of purple, and even a yellow sundress. "First day of spring, if I don't see you rocking this, I'm going to be very disappointed," Romy had said when she'd shoved it into my arms.

"Deal," I'd replied, even as a little voice inside my head reminded me that I wouldn't be in Ideal in the spring.

Now I gently put back both the green sweater and the black skirt. "I think we're set, Romy. My mom's credit card can only take so much."

Romy heaved a huge sigh and ran her fingers longingly over the green sweater. "What if I bought it, and then you could borrow it sometimes?"

I laughed. "Clearly, you and that sweater were meant to be."

Once we left the store, we still had nearly half an hour to kill before her mom was due to pick us up. Ideal had one mall, and while it wasn't exactly upscale, there were a few nice stores, and I had to admit, the smells wafting from the food court were pretty tempting. But rather than head that way, Romy steered us toward a particularly sad-looking toy store.

"You know, I'm actually all stocked up on My Little Ponies," I told her as she dragged me through the entrance. Romy rolled her eyes.

"First of all, no girl can ever have enough My Little Ponies. That's just science. But secondly, we're not here for those. I need to get a new Ouija board. The one we have is all scratched up and smells like school."

Oh, right. The séance was coming up. I'd promised Mom I'd stop it, and what had I been doing instead? Going to basketball games. Shopping for clothes.

"Are we really gonna do the séance thing?" I asked as Romy moved toward the board game section.

"Um, yeah. Whenever I get another free night, that is." Walking her fingers down stacks of boxes, she finally found the one she was looking for. "Aha!"

As she pulled the Ouija board from the shelf, I shifted my bags to my other arm and put a hand on the box. "Look, I love a good séance, but Ouija boards are so old-fashioned. Isn't there something more . . . technical we could use?"

Romy didn't take her hand away from the box, but she did frown thoughtfully. "Like what?"

"I don't know. Didn't Anderson just get a new EMP reader? Maybe let him use that. And, I mean, honestly, Romy, do you trust Dex with a Ouija board?"

It was the right thing to say. Romy visibly flinched. "Ugh. You're right. He'll just push it around to say inappropriate things and then swear it was Mary Evans, 'that saucy wench' or something."

I couldn't help but laugh. "Yes. Yes, he will do exactly that."

The box slid back onto the shelf. "Anderson *has* been

wanting to try out his EMP recorder. See if we can record any ghostly energy spikes. And even Dex can't screw that up." Then she wrinkled her nose. "Except he probably could."

I tried not to sigh with relief as Romy turned away from the board games. "Awesome," I said. "Besides, I've been wanting to see what kind of gear Anderson has." Mostly to make sure it didn't actually work, but I didn't tell Romy that.

We left the toy store, making our way down the mall toward the entrance. Some '80s soft rock ballad was playing, and a harried-looking mom walked past us, a little kid tugging on her hand. A few feet away, there was a big fountain splashing turquoise-colored water, a couple of girls sitting on the edge, giggling together.

"Are you an alien?"

"What?" I asked, turning to Romy. She was smiling, but there was genuine curiosity in her dark eyes.

"You're looking around the mall like you've never been in one before. And sometimes you look around the school that way, too."

"Oh," I said, heat rising to my face. So much for "blending in."

"Where did you live before this?" Romy asked, maneuvering around a couple of old ladies power walking.

"Tennessee." Immediately, I wondered if I should add more, so I hurried on. "I went to a really small all-girls school, so, yeah, this is all a little new to me."

That apparently satisfied Romy. "Okay. So why did your mom pull you out of that place and move you to freaking Ideal, Mississippi, a.k.a. The Most Boring Town on Earth?"

"Oh, I don't know," I said, swinging my bag. "My last school didn't have *ghosts*. Or ghost hunters for that matter." I thought about *Ivy Springs*, the way Leslie and her identical cousin, Lila, would sometimes laugh together and link arms and bump hips and stuff. I wondered if I should attempt a hip bump now.

But Romy was a lot taller than me, so my hip would just hit her thigh, and . . . yeah, we could skip that bit.

Suddenly her entire face brightened and she grabbed my arm. "Oh! Speaking of ghost hunters . . ."

She reached into her purse, fishing around for something. "Remember when you asked if there was some connection between Beth and Mr. Snyder? You know, something that wasn't gross and illegal?"

"Right," I said as I dodged a couple of kids with balloons tied around their wrists.

"Well, I did a little Internet sleuthing and found this." She pulled a folded-up piece of paper out and handed it to me. It was a mention on the Mary Evans High

Web site. The title read, MEHS CELEBRATES AN 'IDEAL' HISTORY.

"So last year, the school did this big thing about the history of the town and how many students and faculty had had family here when Ideal was founded. And check it." She pointed at the picture. "There's Beth, there's Snyder."

I recognized Beth easily enough, also noting that Adam and Anderson were in the picture. Mr. Snyder, a dark-haired guy who looked to be around thirty, was the only adult.

"I mean, it's not much, but it's something, right?" Romy was watching me with big dark eyes.

"Yeah," I agreed, studying the photo.

They have to pay, Mary had said. Thought. Felt. Whatever all of that shrieking in my head had been. But Mary had frozen to death, according to the legend. A crappy way to go, but not exactly something you could blame other people for. But what if Mary did hold some- one responsible and was seeking revenge through that person's descendants? Stranger things had happened.

"I still wonder why now, though. A hundred years she's been dead, and she just now decides to go crazy?" I glanced over at Romy.

She shrugged. "Who knows why ghosts do things?" Then she grinned. "Ooh, or maybe our town is, like, built over the underworld! And psychic evil energy is just now leaking into Ideal." She mulled that over like a little kid making a Christmas list. "Man, think of all the ghosts we'd have then," she said wistfully, and I nearly laughed.

I wasn't sure how anyone could be excited about their town potentially being a portal to Hell, but I clapped a hand on Romy's shoulder and said, "We can only hope."

CHAPTER 18

A few days later, I sat at the dinner table with Mom, twirling spaghetti around my fork. "So Mrs. Steele was telling us that Macbeth was a real person who really killed a king, but that the witches and the ghosts were all made up. Which, I mean, obviously they weren't."

I took a bite of pasta, chewing and swallowing before saying, "It's lame. I think everyone would be a lot more interested in the play if they knew how real it all was. Maybe I'll write something about that in my essay."

Mom gave me a weird look, so I quickly amended. "Not that I'd mentioned the witches and ghosts being real, but something about the way supernatural—"

"It's the last night of the month, Izzy," Mom said,

shaking her head. "You won't need to write that essay."

I lowered my fork. "Right."

Pushing her plate away, Mom rested her elbows on the table. "You hadn't forgotten, had you?"

Of course I hadn't. I just . . . maybe hadn't thought of leaving Ideal so soon after the banishing was done. Which was stupid. If Mary's ghost was put to bed, what reason did we have to stay?

Mom got up from the table, carrying her plate to the sink. "In any case, tonight's the night. I picked up a few canisters of salt at the grocery store. They're in the pantry."

Dishes clattered, and Mom turned on the faucet. "You did a good job," she said, her back to me. "You were able to figure out who the ghost was, and now you'll banish her, and no one's gotten hurt. No one except that boy in your P.E. class, at least. You want me to come with you tonight?"

"I think I can manage pouring some salt onto some dirt," I said, hating how petulant I sounded.

Mom must not have liked it either, because she sighed and turned to face me. "Not every case is glamorous, Isolde. Some of them are just . . . pouring salt. Saying a few words. Moving on."

"I guess," I replied. In the silence that followed, I could hear the steady *plink-plink* of water dripping from the sink.

Mom turned around. "Have you liked school?"

Surprised, I lifted my shoulders in a shrug. "Kind of," I told her. "I mean, I've only been there a month, and it hasn't exactly been a thrill a minute. Are all high schools so . . . dull?"

Mom's mouth quirked in what might have been a smile. "Mine was."

My fork skidded across the spaghetti. "You went to high school? Like, a regular one?" As far as I knew, no Brannick ever spent much time in the human world. We were too busy training and fighting and saving everyone from unholy evil.

"For a little while," Mom said. "Me and my sister. Our mom was working a job in California that ended up taking a lot of time. She thought it would be a good idea for us to at least try school while we were there."

"Did you like it?"

"That's like asking if I liked all my teeth pulled out through my nose," she said, and while I wanted to laugh, that sounded so much like something Finn would've said that my chest felt tight. "So that's a no, then," I finally managed to say, and Mom gave a dry chuckle.

"It wasn't all bad. I liked history, and there was

something . . . I don't know, novel about it, I guess. It wasn't for me, but I was grateful for the experience. Eventually." She hesitated again, like she couldn't decide if she should say anything else. Then she said, "It let me know what I didn't want."

Her eyes met mine across the kitchen. "And I'm sorry, Iz. For you and Finn. I should've let the two of you have a choice, too. Before now."

"You would let us . . . choose not to be Brannicks?" I asked. It seemed like the most impossible thing in the world. This was who we were, what we were born to do. You didn't just get to reject your entire bloodline and sacred calling.

But Mom nodded. "If it's what you wanted."

The words hung between us until finally Mom cleared her throat. "Anyway, yes, school is boring. And soul sucking. But everyone should go through it, even if it's only for a little while."

"So what now?" I asked then, pushing my plate away. "I pour some salt and we pack up and leave?" The idea should've filled me with jubilation. A month of regular high school was more than enough for anyone, and it would be nice to get back to our house. And sure, I'd miss Romy and Anderson. And Dex. But Mom was right: we didn't have room for friends in our lives.

Of course, there was one mystery that still needed

solving. One thing that might keep us in Ideal a little longer. "But if someone is raising ghosts, what's to stop him or her from just raising another one once we salt the grave?"

Mom pinched the bridge of her nose between her thumb and forefinger. "Good point."

I swallowed. Now or never. "Also, um, one of the kids in PMS . . . er, the ghost-hunting thing. He's Prodigium."

When Mom's brows shot up, I faltered a little. "Or at least I think he is."

"Think?" Mom repeated. "Iz, you always know when someone is Prodigium. You even know what type."

"Usually, yeah," I said, tucking my hair behind my ears. "But this guy . . . I can't tell. I didn't even know he was Prodigium until he touched me." Mom's brows went even higher, and I quickly added, "On the hand. In a handshake. No bathing suit areas involved."

She studied me for a long moment before saying, "Are you sure it was magic you felt, and not . . . other things?"

"Yes!" I exclaimed, throwing up my hands. "God, why does everyone keep saying that?"

Hand on one hip, Mom stared me down. "Who is everyone?"

I swallowed. "Just . . . just Torin."

"So you told Torin about this boy being Prodigium, but not me?"

It sounded kind of bad when she put it like that. "I just . . . I wasn't sure it was anything, and I didn't want to bug you while you were working."

"Isolde, I do not know how many times I have to tell you this, but Torin is useless more often than not. If you need advice or help with something, you come to me, and be honest and upfront."

"Like you're being with all your 'research'?" As soon as the words were out of my mouth, I regretted them.

Movements stiff, Mom walked to the pantry and pulled out two canisters of salt. "This should be enough," she said, handing them to me. "Go salt the grave, stop the haunting, and get back here. Then we can talk more about this Prodigium boy."

"Fine," I said, taking the salt more roughly than I'd intended. Mom didn't say anything, though, and I headed upstairs to get my backpack.

Torin was already chilling out in my mirror when I opened the door. He brightened when I came in. "Oh, good, you're here. Is it time to watch a new episode of *Ivy Springs*? If Everton asks Rebecca to the prom instead of Leslie—"

"I don't have time tonight," I told him, shoving the salt into my bag.

If I hadn't known better, I would've sworn that Torin seemed hurt. "You never have time anymore. I've barely seen you in the past few weeks, and what on earth could be more important than *Ivy Springs*?"

"Ghost busting," I answered.

"Ah," he said, nodding toward the backpack. "That explains it. And here I thought you perhaps had a sodium problem."

I picked up one of the ponytail holders by my bed and flicked it at him. It bounced harmlessly off the glass. "After you get back from destroying the ghost, then can we bemoan Everton and Leslie's tragic love?" he asked, picking at the lace on his cuffs.

"Sure," I said, but he frowned.

"Why do you seem so sad, Isolde?"

"I'm not," I answered immediately. "I'm just . . . Mom and I are having a thing right now."

Torin snorted. "You and Aislinn are always having 'a thing.' I think it's more than that." Leaning forward, he squinted at me. "Isolde, are you . . . are you saddened to be leaving this wretched place so soon?"

"No," I replied quickly. Too quickly. Torin settled back against my bed in the mirror, a smug smile on his face.

"You *are*," he said. "You don't want to leave. One mere sample of the cornucopia that is a regular American high school, and you have developed a taste for it."

Rolling my eyes, I shoved my arms through the sleeves of a black jacket. "You've completely cracked."

Scowling, Torin folded his arms over his chest. "You know I don't appreciate mirror jokes."

Doing my best to look contrite, I picked up my backpack. "I'm sorry, Torin. I'll try to *reflect* on my actions."

"All right, now you are just being mean."

He was still grumbling when I left, which should've made me smile. Annoying Torin was one of my favorite pastimes. But it was hard to grin when his words still sat in my stomach like a rock.

One of the great things about the tininess of Ideal was how easy it was to walk to everything. The graveyard where Mary Evans was buried was only a few blocks from my house. So even with all my deep thoughts weighing me down, I was there in no time.

Most people think graveyards are creepy, but I'd been in enough of them over the years that this one just felt kind of . . . homey. I made my way past the newer graves, into the older section of the cemetery. Mary Evans's grave wasn't hard to find. There was a huge marble statue marking her final resting place.

I paused, reading the inscription: MARY ANNE EVANS 1890–1908 FOREVER OUR ANGEL, FOREVER AT REST.

"I really hope so," I murmured as I pulled my

backpack off my shoulders. I grabbed one of the salt canisters and pried open its funnel. The entire grave would have to be covered with salt in order to bring her spirit back and lock her in.

"Sorry to ground you like this, Mary," I whispered. I had just started pouring when a voice said, "Fancy meeting you here."

I whirled around.

Dex.

CHAPTER 19

I froze, but the salt kept pouring out of the nozzle, making a little pyramid on top of the grave. For a long beat, Dex just watched it trickle out.

Once the container was empty, he looked at me. "Soooo . . . whatcha doin'?"

"What are you doing?" I fired back. The same night I go to banish a ghost that may have been raised by magic, Dex, who may be Prodigium, shows up. That was a little too coincidental for me.

"I followed you," he said, like that was every bit as normal as me and my salt. "I was on my way home from the store, and I saw you, so thought I'd see what the Illustrious Isolde Brannick was up to."

With as much dignity as I could muster, I spread the little pile of salt over the dirt with the tip of my shoe.

"You can't just go around following people," I told Dex as I tossed the empty salt carton into my backpack. "It's creepy. And inappropriate."

"Says the girl pouring salt onto graves."

I glared at him. "This is . . . part of my religion."

Smirking, Dex put his hands in his coat pockets. "Oh, so you belong to the Crazy Salt Freak Church?"

"It's an Irish-Celtic thing," I tried, but Dex just shook his head.

"I don't know whether to be more insulted that you're lying to me, or that you apparently think I'm some kind of idiot. Also, it hasn't escaped my knowledge that this"—he nodded at the tombstone—"is the final resting place of one Mary Evans. The very same Mary Evans who Anderson wants to EMP, and Romy wants to Ouija."

My mind raced, trying to come up with some plausible explanation. Unfortunately, all I could think was, *What would Leslie do if Everton caught her pouring salt on graves?* Since I was pretty sure the answer was *cry prettily*, I rejected that idea and decided to go for what Mom always said: *When you're caught in a lie, stick as close to the truth as you can.*

"Ouija boards don't work."

Dex rocked back on his heels, still grinning. "That a fact?"

"I'm just saying, I don't think that anything made by

Milton Bradley is much good for contacting the dark side, that's all."

"Meanwhile, the Morton Salt girl is totally connected to the forces of evil. That would explain her coat."

"Salt destroys evil spirits. I . . . I read it on the Internet this afternoon."

Nudging the salt pile with his foot, Dex shrugged and said, "Okay. I can buy that. But then why come out here by yourself? Why not meet with us and let PMS get their Salt Warrior on?"

Ugh, was he secretly a member of the FBI? I had never met anyone who asked so many questions.

"I thought you guys would think it was dumb."

At that, Dex threw his head back and gave a barking laugh. "For God's sake, Izzy, we call ourselves PMS. And trust me, your salt theory is no dumber than the time Romy investigated a Civil War graveyard with tinfoil on her head."

"That . . . actually happened?" I'd just assumed they were joking.

Dex nodded. "Or when Anderson spent every penny he made mowing lawns for two summers on a special tape recorder that was supposed to capture ghostly voices." His eyes met mine. They were very blue and . . . twinkly. "Besides, your weirdness is why I like you so much."

I didn't know what to say to that, but luckily, he

didn't seem to need a reply. "So. You've made this lovely little salt pile. What can I do?"

"You can go home," I told him, but he was already taking off his jacket—another peacoat, but this one was deep purple in the moonlight—and laying it gently over one of the angels' outspread wings. Then he knelt down and started spreading the salt with his hands. He had pretty hands, I decided. Thin and long-fingered and delicate. Like a pianist. I'd never really thought about boys' hands before, but looking at Dex's made me feel warm and shivery all at the same time.

Grudgingly, I knelt down next to him and pulled the other canister of salt out of my backpack. "Just . . . keep doing that. You have to cover the entire grave with salt to confine the spirit." Dex lifted his head, and I added, "I mean, that's what the Internet said."

Satisfied, Dex went back to the salt. After a while, he moved to the foot of the grave, pouring it there.

"This is fun," he said. "Weird and disturbing and possibly illegal, but still fun."

"Is it okay if we don't tell Romy and Anderson about this?"

He grinned at me. "Absolutely. Now we've formed our own splinter cell of PMS."

Leaning forward, he lowered his voice to a conspiratorial whisper. "We've gone rogue."

I made a sound almost like a giggle. Not that I did giggle. Brannicks aren't gigglers. Dex and I spent the next few minutes pressing the salt into the grass. We didn't say anything else, but there was something nice about the silence. It reminded me of when Finn and I used to hang out in the War Room, me reading, her sharpening weapons. Just being with her had been . . . comforting. Nice. That's how it felt now with Dex, even doing something as bizarre as sealing a ghost in its grave.

Then we reached for the same tiny mound of salt and our hands brushed. This time, Dex didn't apologize, but as soon as his skin touched mine, I felt that little hum. That reminder that Dex wasn't a normal boy. That I didn't know what he was. And the more time I spent with him, the less sure I was that even he knew what he was.

Sobered, I stood up, backing away from him a little bit. "Okay," I said, my voice unsteady. "That's . . . that."

"Excellent. So no more ghosts, no more science teachers getting brained, and lockers that open mysssterioooously," Dex said, wiggling his fingers at me. I almost made that giggle sound again, but I stopped myself. Confusion flashed across Dex's face, and he stuffed his hands into his pockets. "Well," he said, but he didn't add anything else.

Suddenly the silence between us wasn't comfortable

so much as awkward. I dusted my hands off on the back of my pants. "I better head home. Mom'll be pissed if I'm out late."

Dex twisted his wrist, glancing at his watch. "It's not even eight. Are your parents Amish?"

"My mom is just . . . strict."

"So is my Nana, but I get to stay out until at least nine. And I don't know about you, but all this salting the earth has me craving fries. You wanna go grab something to eat?"

Eating food together. At night. I didn't even need Everton and Leslie to tell me that was a date. Or had this been a date? We'd laughed and had fun and touched hands. That felt kind of . . . date-y even if it was on top of a grave.

But he was smiling at me again, and now that he mentioned it, I hadn't eaten much dinner. "Can you get me home by nine?"

His grin widened. "Isolde, my friend, I can get you back by quarter 'til." He held out his hand to help me to my feet. "Shall we?"

I only hesitated for a second before taking it, and this time, when a pulse shot through me, I wasn't a hundred percent sure it was only magic I was feeling.

CHAPTER 20

Several minutes later, Dex and I were seated in a bright red vinyl booth at a place that called itself the Dairee Kween.

"What's with the misspelling?" I'd asked when we'd pulled up.

"It used to be an actual Dairy Queen, but the corporate office made them close it down after a major rat outbreak in the kitchen. So the owners just reopened it, but changed the spelling to keep from getting sued."

"That . . . does not make me want to eat here."

Dex laughed. "The rat thing was like thirty years ago, according to my Nana. And it's probably just a rumor anyway."

He might have been right, but I made a note to skip the burgers. Besides, it's not like I was ever going to eat here again. Mary Evans's ghost was put to rest, and Mom and I would be moving on. Which was awesome and great and not at all sad-making.

"This is better than our regular PMS meetings," Dex said once we had our food. "Those are sadly lacking in fries, I've found." He reached past me for the ketchup. "And desecrating graves is a surprisingly fun bonding activity. I only defile the dead with my closest friends."

"So we're friends," I said hesitantly, swirling a french fry in ketchup. Dex snagged a fry from my plate and popped it into his mouth.

"Yes," he said, chewing. "And now that I've stolen food from you, it's official. You and me, friends for life."

"Good," I said. "I . . . I like being friends with you."

"Same." He made my favorite grin, the one that was surprisingly goofy for such a handsome guy.

Wait a second. I'd known him for a few weeks. How did I have a *favorite grin* of his?

Our eyes met and held, and it was like there was this . . . pulse between us. For a second I thought it was just Dex's magic or power or whatever it was that I was picking up on. But it didn't feel like that. It felt—

Dex's phone beeped, and as he looked down at it, the moment was lost. Which, to be honest, was kind of a relief. "My Nana," he sighed. "Why oh why did I ever teach that woman to text?" As his thumbs moved over the keypad, I pretended to be super-interested in my fries. Really, I was studying him.

He certainly didn't seem like a guy with anything to hide, but why had he been at Mary's grave? It couldn't just be a coincidence that he'd shown up when he did. Had he really followed me, or was there more to it than that? I needed to get closer to Dex.

The thought immediately sent a flutter through me, and I dropped my eyes back to my plate. Not close to him like *that*. Close in the general Finding Out Information way. "There," he said, sliding his phone into his bag. "Apparently my curfew has been lengthened by an hour since I'm with you." He waggled his eyebrows. "I told her I was with a lady who is quite the good influence on me."

"You *need* a good influence," I told him, smiling a little.

Dex sat back in his chair, impressed. "Isolde Brannick. Are you flirting with me?"

I tossed a fry at his head. It bounced off his shoulder, and he winced theatrically, pressing his hand to his clavicle. "Easy, slugger! In your hands, a french fry is a deadly weapon."

"No, I'm only deadly with dodgeballs," I said, and he laughed.

"Flirting and joking! Within a few minutes of each other! Is this the side of Isolde that only her friends get to see?"

He was teasing, but it gave me the opening I'd been hoping for. "Yup. And speaking of . . ." I ventured. "Friends . . . they can . . . they can tell each other stuff, right? I just mean . . . if you had some kind of secret, or something you hadn't ever told anyone, you could tell me. No matter . . . no matter what it was."

Oh, smooth, Izzy. Seriously. Why didn't I just grab him and yell, "TELL ME WHAT KIND OF MAGICAL POWERS YOU HAVE!" By the end of my little stuttering speech, I was blushing and Dex was frowning.

"A secret?" he asked, puzzled. Then his face suddenly cleared, and he shook his head. "Oh, right. Because of all the purple."

"Purple?"

"The clothes, I mean," he said, gesturing to his coat. "I know that I'm fashionable and well-groomed, and yes, I have been known to rock the occasional man-bracelet."

He lifted his wrist, jangling the bracelet I'd noticed earlier. I could see now that it was plain silver, just a series of links.

"But," Dex continued, dragging another one of my fries through ketchup, "I also like ladies. And not as shopping buddies, but in the carnal sense." His tone was light as always, but he wouldn't meet my eyes. Not to mention, that spiel was so smooth, he had to have done it before.

I'd only thought I was blushing before. Now my face was probably the same color as the tabletop. "Dex, I wasn't asking if you were . . . I didn't think you . . ."

"Oh." He took a drink of his soda. "Then you were just asking me to spill some . . . nonspecific secret?"

I shook my head. "Forget it." This was obviously getting us nowhere, so I decided to try a new subject. "Tell me more about your Nana."

Dex's face immediately brightened. "Basically, she is the bestest Nana in all the land. Bakes cookies, knits afghans, and lets me hang out past curfew with lovely ladies such as yourself. You should meet her someday. She'd love you."

Was meeting Nana a serious thing? It kind of felt like it. I *really* needed to get those magazines. Making a mental note to stop by the drugstore I'd noticed on my way to the graveyard, I nodded. "I'd like that. And your parents, are they also the bestest?"

If Dex's face had gone all shiny at the mention of his Nana, bringing up his parents had the opposite effect. His shoulders slumped a little, and something flickered in his eyes. "They died when I was little. Just me and my Nana for a while now." He took a long sip of his Coke, rattling ice in the cup. I had the sense that it was less about being thirsty and more about dropping the subject.

"My dad died when I was little, too," I heard myself say, and Dex lowered his cup.

This wasn't part of my cover; this was the real deal, but he had shared something with me, so it felt right to return the favor. "He, uh, was a soldier." That was literally all I knew about my dad. Men don't tend to stick around in the Brannick family.

Dex nodded slowly. "Sucks, doesn't it?"

I hadn't known my dad, so I didn't miss him the way I missed Finn, but still I replied, "It does."

A silence fell over the table, and I mentally kicked myself. I was supposed to be getting information out of him, not sharing personal feelings.

Ignoring the tiny voice that said maybe my interest in Dex was less than Brannick-y, I reached out and took his wrist. This time I was prepared for the little buzz that went through me. "You know, I actually like this man-bracelet," I said, turning his wrist for a better look. I hoped it came off as jokey and kind of flirty, but really I was inspecting it for . . . well, anything. Maybe there were runes or something carved into the links.

Preening a little, Dexter leaned closer to me. "That's because you're a woman of taste. My Nana gave this to me. I have very strict instructions never to take it off."

I looked up sharply at that. "Seriously? Never? Why?" For the first time since I'd met him, Dex seemed a little uncomfortable. Taking his hand back, he shrugged. "Superstitious thing, I think. Nana, like you, has a touch of the Irish in her." He turned his wrist, the silver gleaming in the fluorescent lights. "Supposed to be lucky, I guess." And then he flashed that grin again. "And clearly it has been lucky, because I was wearing it when I met you." He grabbed another fry from my plate. "My new best friend."

In spite of myself, I laughed. "Oh, so now we're best friends?"

He nodded very seriously. "Three fries I've stolen from you. That cements it."

By the time Dex drove me home, I was thinking less about his bracelet and his Nana and whatever it was I felt when I touched him and more about how nice it was talking and laughing with a boy. Leslie and Everton didn't seem to do much laughing. Mostly they were either crying or angsting or making overly dramatic declarations of love to one another. That had seemed kind of fun on the show, but I thought maybe this was better.

But those kinds of thoughts were pointless and stupid (and I clearly needed to stop watching *Ivy Springs*). *It's a job*, I reminded myself as Dex opened the passenger door for me. *He is a job. You don't get to think things like how soft his hair looks. Or how nice his eyes are.*

Dex walked me as far as the front door, and when he stopped there, my heart pounded in my throat. Oh, God, this was the part where kissing happened. I may never have been on a date, but I'd watched enough TV and read enough books to know that when you eat food with a boy and then he takes you to your door, kissing will occur.

And I was in no way ready for that. Kissing was another one of those things I'd meant to do more research on, just in case. Like, how did you know which way to turn your head? And what about teeth placement? What if there was a spit issue? Should I have taken Torin up on his offer to help me practice? Trying to keep the panic off my face, I turned toward Dex. "Right. So. Good night, then."

He gave a little bow. "Until tomorrow, Fair Isolde."

And then he leaned forward.

My heart was in my ears, and my hands were shaking. Okay, I could do this. It was just lips. Just lips pressing together, hopefully without spit. And tongues . . . tongues . . . Okay, actually, no. I could *not* do this.

I was just about to pull back when Dex reached out and . . . ruffled my hair. "Sleep tight!" he called cheerfully as he jogged down the front steps.

"Um. You too," I replied, but I was so dazed that I

didn't get that out until he was already in the car, pulling away.

Was he going to ruffle my hair all along? Had I just imagined the way he'd looked at my mouth? Or had he seen the naked panic on my face and changed his mind?

I walked into the house and turned to face the little mirror in the hallway. At least that confirmed that, yup, hair and face, totally the same shade. "Magazines," I whispered firmly at myself. "Tomorrow."

Torin's face suddenly appeared, frowning. "Are you talking to me? And why are you all beet colored?"

Luckily, Mom walked around the corner, and Torin immediately vanished. "That took longer than I'd expected," she said, drying her hands on a dish towel.

"I ran into that kid. The one I think is Prodigium. We, uh, grabbed some food."

"And?" Mom asked expectantly.

"And I still don't know what he is." Taking a deep breath, I pushed my shoulders back. "So I wanna stay. A little longer. Just until I find out." After all, there was a chance this whole thing wasn't really over, no matter all the salt thrown on Mary's grave. If Dex's Possible Prodigium Powers had had anything to do with raising her ghost, I needed to know.

Frowning, Mom tossed the towel into the kitchen. "Do you think he's anything dangerous?"

My knees felt watery and my heart was racing. Yeah, Dex was dangerous, all right, but not in the way Mom meant. I gave her my best Tough Chick Grimace. "No. But if he is, I'll take care of it."

She watched me for a long time, so long that I was afraid she was about to say no. Instead, she shrugged. "Okay, then. This one is all yours."

I told myself that the relief flooding through me had everything to do with Mom's trusting me, and nothing at all to do with getting to stay in Ideal.

"But you just get one more month," Mom said. "No more. Anything longer than that can be dangerous for us."

"Right," I said, nodding. Mom never liked to work long jobs. The way she saw it, the longer you were in a place, the more you were expected to make connections, friends even. And Brannicks could never afford that. Too many questions.

"Mom," I said, scuffing my toe against the linoleum. "About earlier—"

The light in the hallway was too dim to see clearly, but I could practically feel Mom frowning. "It's nothing. Just . . . just, good night, Mom."

The words seemed to hang there in the hallway. Then Mom turned away. "One month, Izzy," she called, heading into the kitchen. "And then we're going home."

CHAPTER 21

The next day, Dex wasn't on the bus, but Romy and Anderson were. As soon as Romy saw me, she grinned and waved me over.

"Hey," I said, finding my seat. "What are you doing here?" Anderson didn't usually ride our bus since he had his own car.

He slumped in his seat, a little sheepish. "My parents may have gotten their credit card bill this month, and they may have discovered that I used their American Express to buy some stuff for PMS."

"Check it," Romy said, nudging Anderson. He opened his backpack, and I could make out some black plastic device that I guessed was his EVP recorder. "I'm totally going to pay them back," Anderson said, zipping up his bag. "But it was on sale, so it made sense to go ahead and buy it, you know?"

"Absolutely," Romy agreed. "But it sucks that they took your car away."

Anderson shrugged. "Just for a few weeks. And hey, it means I get to hang out with you guys more."

I was apparently included in the "you guys," but you wouldn't have known that from the way Anderson's gaze lingered on Romy.

Covering a smile, I asked, "So where's Dex this morning?"

"He texted me that he was running late," Anderson offered, lifting his legs to prop his feet on my seat. As he did, his leg brushed Romy's, and I saw her give a little jump.

She cleared her throat, twisting her ponytail around one finger. "Did he say why?"

Anderson rolled his eyes. "You know Dex. He said it was because his Nana needed him to deliver a covert message to a Colombian drug runner, but he'd be in by lunch."

I snorted with laughter, but Romy frowned. "I bet it was another asthma attack. He's been getting them more often lately."

"Is it bad?" I asked. "His asthma?"

Romy and Anderson nodded in unison. "He laughs it off, but yeah," Anderson said. "It can be scary."

The image of Dex gasping for breath suddenly flashed in my brain, and I felt my chest tighten. *A job, a job, a job,* I repeated in my head.

"He hasn't lived here long, has he?"

Romy shook her head. "Just since August." And then suddenly she turned to Anderson and said, "Okay, you need to go away for a second."

His sneakers, which had been resting on the back of my seat, thudded to the floor. "Why?"

"Because Izzy and I need to talk girl stuff, and you can't be a part of that."

I don't know if Anderson was just used to following Romy's orders, or if he was terrified we'd start talking about Tampax, but in any case, he moved pretty quickly a few rows away. Reaching over the seat, Romy tugged my hand. "Come here."

Moving over to the now-vacant seat beside her, I raised my eyebrows. "What is it? Something about PMS? I mean, the ghost-hunting PMS, not the . . . regular kind. Unless you want to talk about that, because we can."

Romy waved her hand. "No, no business and not that kind of girl stuff. The more fun kind of girl stuff." She leaned closer, her dark eyes sparkling. "Do you like Dex?"

She'd whispered it, but I still looked around, hoping

no one had overheard. "First off, shhhh! And . . . yeah, of course I do. I like all of you."

"No, but I mean do you *like* him? You know, in the carnal sense."

I rolled my eyes. "You've clearly been spending too much time with Dex."

Romy smiled and poked me in the middle of my chest with one lime-green fingernail. "And so have you, if what my sources at the Dairee Kween tell me is correct. Were you two on a date there last night?"

"Please," I hissed. "The shushing. Could you at least try? And no, we weren't on a date. We were just . . . hanging out."

"In the sexy way."

There it was again. That giggle. That sound I supposedly didn't make. "No," I whispered, trying to look stern. "In the *friendly* way."

"Mmm-hmm," Romy said, narrowing her eyes.

"What about you?" I said, ducking my head closer. "I saw you jump when Anderson's leg brushed yours."

Now it was her turn to hiss, "Shhhhh!"

Smiling, I leaned back in my seat. "Ah, I see. It's different when the shoe is on the other foot."

"There are no shoes on any feet," Romy insisted, but the tips of her ears had gone pink. "Anderson and I are just friends."

"So we're just two awesome, ghost-hunting girls with two boys who may be cute, but are most definitely nothing more than friends," I said, and Romy grinned.

"We are. Which is why I'm going to share this with you, even though I was going to hog it all to myself for the ride."

With that, she reached into her backpack. I don't know what I expected her to pull out. A tinfoil hat, maybe. A pamphlet on twenty-first-century ghost-hunting techniques.

Instead, she whipped out a glossy issue of *Rockin' Grrls!* magazine, complete with articles like, "What His Dog Says About His Kissing Style!" and "Is It Wrong to Be in Love with Your Stepbrother?"

"Perfect," I said.

Romy and I spent the rest of the bus ride reading *Rockin' Grrls!*, and then I spent the walk to class telling her all about *Ivy Springs*.

"So this Leslie chick works at a circus?" Romy asked as we slid into English.

"Not, like, all the time. Only since her mom married a trapeze artist."

Romy stared at me. "Okay, I clearly need to see this show immediately. You said you own it?"

When I nodded, Romy pointed at me. "Then you are

going to bring it to my house next week, and we're going to watch all of it."

"There are over sixty episodes," I told her, raising my voice a little to be heard over the third bell.

"Make it next Friday, then. You can spend the night, and we'll do a whole marathon."

"Awesome," I said, and was surprised to find that I really meant it. And not so that I could ask her more about Dex, or try to find out what she knew about supernatural stuff. Just because hanging out with Romy and watching Leslie and Everton fight/make out/break up/ get engaged for a few days sounded like . . . fun. Lots of it, actually.

Mrs. Steele announced that we'd be doing group work this morning, so we all started moving our desks, forming little circles. Apparently we'd been paired up based on who sat closest to us, so in addition to Romy, our group included Adam.

Ugh.

I braced myself for the awkward, and Adam more than delivered. Barely looking at me, he opened his binder and leaned as far away as he could.

Another desk bumped mine, and I glanced up to see Beth, Ben McCrary's girlfriend. I expected her to give me the cold shoulder, what with my dislocating her *boyfriend's* shoulder, but she didn't even seem to know who

I was. In fact, as we got to work on the assignment—answering a series of discussion questions about *Macbeth*—Beth didn't pay attention to any of us. Her eyes were far off, distracted, and when Romy asked her to copy down question four, Beth blinked at her like she wasn't even speaking English.

"What?"

"Question four?" Romy repeated, lifting her eyebrows. " 'How does the supernatural influence Macbeth's actions?' "

Beth just shook her head. "I . . . I don't know." She gave a little shiver and crossed her arms tightly over her chest. "And can we please skip the questions about the supernatural?"

Romy glanced at me. "That's, like, half the questions."

"Lotta ghosts in *Macbeth*," I offered, tapping my pen against my paper. Beth looked me, huge dark circles under her eyes. She blinked twice before turning back to Romy.

"You do that ghost-hunting club, right?"

On my other side, Adam snorted but didn't say anything. Romy flashed him a quick glare.

"Yeah," she told Beth. "Why?"

Beth swallowed, her throat working convulsively. "Have you ever seen a ghost?"

Now Adam folded his arms, entire body radiating disdain, but neither Romy nor I paid him any attention.

"Not seen, exactly," Romy said, her eyes practically glowing as she moved closer to Beth. "But sensed, sure. I can show you all kind of notes on ghostly activity in—"

"I saw a ghost in my house," Beth blurted out. Then she swung her head from one side to the other, making sure no one could overhear. Her blond hair hung limply around her shoulders, and when she laid both hands on her desk, I saw that they were trembling. "I mean . . . I think I did. For the past few nights, I've heard these weird sounds outside my room, like someone was walking down the hall. But when I got up, th-there was no one. And I thought I was just hearing things, but then last night—" She broke off, chewing her lip. Romy had her fingers curled around the edge of her desk, and even Adam seemed interested now. There was no disguising the real terror in Beth's voice. "I woke up, and there was this . . . this shape standing by my bed. All glowing and hazy, and I tried to yell, but it was like my throat wasn't working, and then it just . . . it just vanished."

Romy was practically vibrating with excitement, but I frowned. Last night? I'd sealed Mary Evans in her grave last night. There was no way she could be floating around Beth Tanner's house.

Beth caught my expression. "You don't believe me," she said flatly.

"No," I said, shaking my head. "It's not that, it's just—"

"Maybe you were dreaming," Adam suggested, and Beth's lower lip wobbled.

"I wasn't . . . You know what? Just forget it. It was stupid anyway." With that, she slammed her notebook shut and got up, asking Mrs. Steele if she could go to the restroom.

As she left, Adam folded his arms on top of his desk, leaning toward me. "Do you think it's drugs? I bet it's drugs. I took an awareness course about drugs last year. At the *community college*."

I was still staring at the door, so it took me a moment to realize Adam was looking at me.

"Huh?"

"Beth Tanner. On drugs. Is she? Because I'm voting yes."

"Don't be a jerk, Adam," Romy snapped. "She was really freaked out." Twisting in her desk, Romy faced me. "We should talk to her. When she gets back. Maybe PMS could go over to her house, see if we can pick up any energy readings—"

"You have got to be kidding me," Adam groaned, and Romy turned back around.

"You should take this more seriously," she said. "Look at what happened to Mr. Snyder, and now Beth. You could be next."

I knew Romy was doing that thing she did a lot—assuming everyone knew exactly what she was thinking. But Adam didn't know about the picture of him with Beth and Mr. Snyder, or Romy's theory that Mary was seeking revenge on the founding families of Ideal, so he just stared at her, eyes wide.

"Um . . . what the hell does that mean?"

Romy's face was bright red, but the bell rang, saving her from having to answer. Adam shoved his desk back and began gathering his things, muttering something about "freaks" under his breath.

As Romy and I headed for the door, she turned to me. "It had to be Mary that Beth saw, right? Which means her spirit isn't just tied to the school."

I just nodded, lost in thought. It *couldn't* be Mary. I knew how to deal with ghosts, and the salt thing had never failed. Was there another ghost prowling the halls of the school?

I saw Beth one more time, during P.E., but she just sat on the bleachers, surrounded by her friends and still looking kind of gray. I tried to catch her eye, hoping to talk to her a little more about what she'd seen, but every time our eyes met, she looked away.

By the end of the day, I'd nearly convinced myself that Beth was wrong. The doll had unsettled her, and who could blame her? A mutilated Barbie that looks like you strung up in your locker? That would upset anyone. Still, worry slithered through me. This was supposed to be a simple, easy job. I couldn't have screwed *this* up, too.

Romy and Dex were both waiting for me by my locker when the last bell rang, and if a little thrill ran through me at seeing Dex standing there, seemingly okay, I tried my best to ignore it. He had his shoulder against the door, leaning down to listen to Romy. As I got closer, I could hear her saying, "Maybe Mary has some sort of grudge against those families."

"So the ghost of Mary Evans is pissed off at the descendants of *some* people who did some*thing*. For some *reason*," Dex summed up. When Romy nodded, he bent down, taking her shoulder. "Rome, can you hear yourself when you talk?"

Irritated, Romy rolled her shoulder, knocking Dex's hand off. "Why are you even in PMS if you don't believe in this kind of stuff?"

"Because this school is so boring, I thought I might actually die, and ghost hunting seemed like a fun way to spend some time," he replied. "And it is fun. I like creeping around abandoned buildings, and scouring cemeteries, and pouring salt on— Oof!" He grunted as my elbow slammed into his ribs.

Looking down at me, Dex made a face, but added, "Fries. I like pouring salt on fries after I've creeped around abandoned buildings and scoured cemeteries. It's just . . . this seems like a stretch, Romy."

Romy pressed her lips together, and I wasn't sure if she was hurt or angry. Finally, she spit out "Whatever" and stormed away from us. I stood there, torn. Dex and Romy were both my friends, but now they were mad at each other. Was I breaking some kind of girl code by *not* walking away with Romy?

"Rome!" Dex called after her. She didn't turn around but she did raise her hand and flip him off.

Dex just sighed. "Well, that'll be with us for a while. Romy can hold a grudge like no one's business."

"You shouldn't have picked on her," I told him as I put my things in my backpack.

"I didn't!" he cried. "I just pointed out that her theory is insane."

"Which she saw as picking on her," I said once we'd joined the flow of students heading toward the parking lot. The buses lined up under an awning.

"Okay, so maybe I could have phrased it a little nicer, but life at Mary Evans High is rough enough for Romy. The PMS thing has already made her a target. If she starts spouting off about a ghost wanting to kill the home-coming queen . . ." He shook his head. "There would be no end to the crap they'd give her."

"So you were trying to protect her by . . . being mean to her?"

By now we were outside. While the other, luckier kids who had their own cars walked through the parking lot, Dex and I took our places on the sidewalk. Romy was several feet away, very pointedly not looking at us.

"I just know how tough it can be when everyone thinks you're some kind of freak," Dex said, his voice suddenly tight. "When I was a kid—"

He broke off, staring somewhere beyond my shoulder. "What the hell?"

I turned, catching a sudden movement out of the corner of my eye. A car down at the far end of the parking lot was driving toward us. And it was going . . . fast. Way too fast considering the fact that kids were walking out to their cars. One of those kids passed me, and I realized it was Beth.

She froze, staring down the parking lot at the car. "Oh my God," I heard her mutter. And then the car was moving faster, and it seemed to dawn on me and Beth at the same time that it was headed for her.

And that no one was behind the wheel.

I didn't think. I launched myself toward Beth,

shoving someone out of my way. I heard a pained cry, but by then I was already to Beth. The two of us went stumbling into a parked car, my elbow smacking the side-view mirror so hard I bit my lip. Beth crumpled to the ground between two cars as I fell nearly on top of her.

Just behind us, I could hear the squeal of rubber, the sick crunch of metal on metal. And shrieking. There was a lot of shrieking.

"Are you okay?" I asked Beth, which was probably a stupid question seeing as how she was pale and sobbing. "What happened?" she kept asking. "What was that?"

It was a really good question.

I stood up and took in the chaos raging around me. The car had plowed right into one of the parked buses. Luckily, no one had been on it, and all the kids waiting to board seemed to have gotten out of the way.

A flash of movement caught my eye, and I turned back to Beth's car. There, sitting in driver's seat, was the spirit of Mary Evans. She was a lot fainter than she'd been the night of the basketball game, and no one else seemed to see the ghost, but there was no doubt in my mind that's who she was.

In a flash, she was gone, and I could almost convince myself that it had been a trick of the light.

I had laid salt all over that grave. It wasn't possible for her to be out and wreaking havoc.

Unless I'd screwed up somehow. But it was spreading salt. How hard was that?

But Dex had been there that night. Could he have done something that made the banishing not take? I scanned the crowd for Romy and Dex, finally finding them back on the sidewalk, near the school. I made my way toward them, stepping over Ben McCrary. He was lying on the grass, clutching his shoulder. Apparently he was who I'd shoved. Oops. "Um . . . sorry," I said, but he made a shrieky sound and scuttled farther away from me.

"Are you guys okay?" I asked once I'd reached Romy and Dex.

"Us?" Romy asked, pushing her hair out of her face. "You're the one who just leapt on Beth Tanner like a ninja."

"Yeah," Dex added. "That was . . . if I say hot, does that make me a perv?"

In spite of all the adrenaline coursing through me—or maybe because of it—I started laughing. And once I'd started, Dex joined in, and then Romy was laughing, too. The three of us stood there for a long time, cracking up while everyone around us looked horrified.

But when I turned back to the bus, my laughter died in my throat. Two teachers were helping Beth up from the ground. Coach Lewis was there, too, gesturing at the crowd. "Back up, back up!" By now, a siren was wailing in the distance, and a group was starting to form around the wrecked car.

"Wow," Dex said softly, as though the seriousness of what had happened was just starting to sink in. "She really could have been hurt."

I watched him carefully. None of this made sense. If Dex had screwed up the banishing on purpose, he was the best actor in the world. He looked genuinely freaked out right now.

"She could have *died*," Romy said, and then she closed a hand around my wrist. "But you saved her."

I tried to smile back and not think that if I'd done my job right, she wouldn't have needed saving at all.

CHAPTER 22

"I used enough salt," I told Torin later that evening. We'd just watched three episodes of *Ivy Springs*, but I hadn't concentrated on any of them. I'd been too busy going over everything that had happened that afternoon. "I know I did. But it didn't lock Mary in."

Torin scratched his chin. "That's exceedingly unusual."

I know Mom had said to stop going to Torin for advice, but, well, he was here and she wasn't. And this was definitely a day that required advice. Lots of it.

"It's more than just that; it's impossible," I replied, flipping onto my back to gaze at the ceiling. Whoever had lived here before us had put up a bunch of those plastic stars. "Ghosts can't fight the salt thing. It's part of why they're so un-fun to hunt."

Torin was quiet for a moment before saying, "You said both the teacher and the student received little . . . gifts. Warnings of their impending fate."

"Yup. A squashed frog and a jacked-up Barbie."

"That's smart," Torin said. "Fear makes spirits stronger. It's why older hauntings are so hard to dispose of. The longer a spirit can build up and live off of fear, the more powerful it is."

I turned over, facing Torin. "I've never heard that before."

Torin crossed his arms, smug. "Oh, how I love knowing things you don't. It's such a satisfying feeling."

"Well, now I *do* know it, so thanks for that."

"Hmm," Torin acknowledged with a nod. "That is the price for sharing my wisdom."

With a huge sigh, Torin flopped down onto my bed in the mirror. Looking at the reflection, it was like we were lying side by side. "So the ghost is strong because of fear," I said, dangling my legs off the bed. "But . . . ghosts are pretty much always scary. Why go the extra mile?"

"There's a difference between fear and terror," Torin said. "Terror is a much stronger emotion. It feeds all sorts of negative energy. Appearing in her ghostly form to these people would have, to use your vernacular, freaked them out. But leaving little gifts telling them how they'd be attacked? That builds a sort of anticipatory terror. Like fuel for a ghost. And when you have a ghost that's already terribly strong due to being summoned by magic, well. You end up with a problem like this on your hands."

I mulled that over. "But why summon a ghost?"

Torin was uncharacteristically silent, and when I tilted my head to look at him, he was fiddling with his cuff. "Torin?" I prompted.

"Spirits are not always summoned on purpose," he said at last. "There are times, if one is doing a particularly advanced spell, for instance, that the magic can have . . . unintended consequences. If, for example, one was attempting to raise the dead—"

"You can't do that. It's not possible to bring somebody back to life."

Sniffing prissily, Torin dropped his sleeve. "Of course. I'm sure your vast amounts of knowledge amassed over the past sixteen years greatly outweigh my own centuries-long existence and personal experiences."

Torin tended to get extra-flowery when his feelings were hurt, and I sat up, moving a little closer to his mirror. "I'm sorry," I said, meaning it. "It's just . . . Wait, have you raised the dead?"

"I'm not saying that," Torin replied, but he didn't quite meet my eyes. "I'm only saying that if you have a ghost who is resistant to salt, you probably have a witch as well, and one attempting seriously dark magic at that."

Chewing on my lower lip, I thought about Dex. He'd been there the night I'd tried to seal Mary into her grave, and it hadn't worked.

"You have that expression on your face that speaks of incipient moral dubiousness," Torin observed, making me glad I'd bought that thesaurus a few years back.

"Yeah, I'm about to get super morally dubious, Torin. Remember the other day, when you asked if I wanted you to go in Dex's mirror?"

"I do," he said, narrowing his eyes.

"And remember how I said I didn't want you to?"

"Indeed."

"I take it back." It was awful, I knew that. No matter what Dex was, he was my friend, and using my magic mirror to spy on him was most definitely Not Okay. But people were getting hurt, so I couldn't afford to be a good person right now. And somewhere deep inside, I must've know this was going to happen. Otherwise, why had I studied his mailbox number when he'd driven me past his house the other night?

I gave the address to Torin, telling myself that this was the only way. Being a Brannick meant making hard choices. Mom had once said it meant choosing what was right over what our hearts wanted. I thought she might have been talking about my dad, but I hadn't had the courage to ask.

Still, when Torin gave me a flourishing salute and vanished, I had to swallow the urge to call him back, tell him to forget it. But it was too *late*.

Sighing, I turned to my TV, hoping Everton and Leslie's problems could distract me from my own. I was only about five minutes in when there was a soft knock at my door. Even though I knew Torin was long gone, I shot a glance at the mirror before calling, "Come in!"

Mom opened the door and leaned against the jamb. "There was a car accident at your school today," she said without preamble. "Anything to do with you?"

"Kind of?"

Mom took that in. "Anything I need to know about?"

I glanced at my mirror. "No," I said at last. "I got this."

Mom took a deep breath through her nose, but in the end, she just nodded. "Okay. Anything more on that boy?"

I tried hard to keep my eyes off the mirror this time. "He invited me to his house to meet his grandmother. Figured I'd take him up on that, see if there are any clues."

"Good idea," Mom replied with a little nod. "Have you finished your homework?"

"Yes." We'd had lots of extra time to wait while they

towed the car and the dented bus, and I'd tackled the rest of my *Macbeth* questions as well as the first few paragraphs of my essay. Dex and Romy, thankfully, had made up. When a new bus had finally arrived, they were joking and teasing each other again.

"Okay," Mom said slowly. When I glanced up, she was still hovering in the doorway.

"I thought we might go out to dinner tonight."

"Does this town have restaurants?" I asked. "I mean, other than the Dairee Kween?"

Mom gave a snort that sounded close to laughter. "I passed that place today. I don't think I can trust anywhere that mangles the English language like that."

"I think I saw a Chinese place next to Walmart." I said. "I could go for some lo mein."

"Chinese it is," said Mom, pushing off of the jamb. "Meet me downstairs in ten."

The drive to the restaurant was quiet, but in a nice way. We didn't mention the case during dinner. Instead we talked about school, and I told her about Romy and PMS and one of the articles I'd read on the bus: "Twenty Uses for Your Hair Dryer You've Never Thought Of!" Mom didn't talk much, but she listened, and I decided that was good enough.

Once we were done and Mom had paid the bill, I figured we'd head home. I was kind of anxious to see if

Torin was back yet. But instead, Mom started the car and said, "Why don't we drive around for a bit?"

"Um . . . sure."

If the drive over to the restaurant had been pleasant, this one was just . . . weird. When I flipped on the radio, Mom immediately reached out and turned it off. And she kept leaning over the steering wheel and peering out into the darkness, cocking her head like she was listening for something.

But it wasn't until she pulled in front of a house and shut off the ignition that I finally got what was going on.

"A job?"

She shrugged. "Maybe. The other day I was having breakfast at the Waffle Hut, and these two guys there seemed shady, so—"

I rolled my eyes. "Mom, everyone at the Waffle Hut is shady. That's why they go to the Waffle Hut. To . . . be shady. And eat waffles. Shadily."

Mom sat back in her seat. "I just . . . I needed to do something."

"Something other than your research?" I asked, and Mom's sigh seemed to come up from the soles of her feet.

"Why won't you tell me what you're looking into?" I asked, and to my horror, my voice came out thin and high, like I was on the verge of tears. "If it's about . . .

about Finley, at least let me try to help. I know I messed up that night, but I wouldn't—"

She turned to me, and once again I was struck by how much she looked like Finn. All high cheekbones and pouty lips and strong jaw. "What happened to Finley was not your fault, Isolde," she said, using that commanding tone again. "I don't think that, and I never want you to think it, either."

I tugged at the drawstring of my hoodie. "I miss her a lot."

A car drove past us, and it must have been a trick of the light, because I could've sworn Mom's lower lip trembled a little. "I know you do."

It wasn't, "me, too," but at least it was something.

Leaning back, I thumped my head against my seat. "We're not going to find her, are we?"

Mom was quiet for so long that I wondered if she would even answer. And then she said, "I don't know."

Something about being in the dark in the car made all of it easier to say. "What are we going to do? If we *don't* find her. We're the last two Brannicks in the world. Do we just keep hunting monsters even though it's crazy dangerous? Until there are no Brannicks left?"

A muscle worked in Mom's jaw, but she didn't answer. For a long time, the only sound was the ticking of the cooling engine. Then, sounding as tired as I felt,

Mom said, "I don't know, Isolde. All I know to do is . . . this." She nodded toward the house, but I knew she didn't mean this specific job. "My mother died in the field. So did my cousins and aunts and nearly every Brannick I have ever known. But I don't know what to do with myself if I'm not doing this. And searching through ancient, useless books for some clue as to what happened to Finn . . . I just feel like I'm going crazy. Following those guys from the Waffle Hut, thinking they might be Prodigium, was the first time I've felt happy in weeks."

I turned to stare at her. "Mom. That is . . . deeply effed up."

She gave a harsh bark of laughter, but there was no humor in it. "That's being a Brannick, Izzy. Now come on. Let's get home."

We didn't say anything else the whole way home, both of us lost in our own thoughts.

Back in my room, I searched the mirror, but Torin was still gone. I didn't know if that was good or bad.

I shucked my clothes, got my pajamas on, and spent the next few hours on my computer searching for anything to do with Mary Evans and ghost summoning. Mom was right: this is what Brannicks do. We hunt monsters, we save people, we keep our eyes on the ball. I had let myself get too distracted with Dex and Romy and

Macbeth essays. . . . It was time to solve this case and get out of Ideal. Time to let Mom get back on a case, too, rather than just following some possibly creepy dudes at the Waffle Hut.

When Mom knocked on my door and called, "Lights out," I knew what my next step would be.

I closed the laptop and got into bed, thinking I was too keyed up to sleep. But I must have dozed off at some point, because the next think I knew, Torin was there, whispering, "Isolde."

I sat up, afraid that I was in another one of my Torin-created dreams. But no, there he was, standing in my mirror. "Torin?" My voice was thick with sleep.

"If your lad is up to mischief, he wasn't indulging tonight," Torin said, and I was shocked by the wave of relief that flooded through me. "Nothing supernatural about him except just how many hours he can play video games," Torin added, giving a massive yawn.

"Good," I told him. "And thanks."

In the glass, he seemed to be sitting in my desk chair, leaning back with his arms folded behind his head. "Is that it, then? Are we done?"

I rolled back over in bed, looking out my window. "No," I said softly. "We're just beginning."

CHAPTER 23

"Okay, so if everyone will just look at their handout, we can get started."

Romy, Dex, and Anderson watched me with varying degree of "WTF?" stamped on their faces as I stood at the front of the portable classroom, dry-erase marker clutched in my hand. I'd called an emergency meeting of PMS that morning before class, so we didn't have much time before the bell rang. The sooner I got them on board with this idea, the sooner we could stop Mary.

"When did you have time to make handouts?" Dex finally asked.

"That's not important. The important part is highlighted halfway down on page two."

There was a rustling of papers as they all flipped to that section. "This . . . this says 'On Witches, Ghosts, and

Summonings.'" Anderson stared at me with wide dark eyes. "Summonings? Are we dealing with, like, exorcist-level stuff here?"

"Not exactly." I turned back to the whiteboard and began writing. "Okay, so Mary Evans's ghost was summoned by a witch. I'm not sure why, but that doesn't matter so much right now. The main thing is to find out *who* raised her."

Behind me, I heard Dex say, "Um, Professor Brannick, I have questions. And they are legion."

"I'll take questions at the end."

"I was joking," Dex murmured, but I was on a roll. "So, ghost summoning is not that hard if you know where to do it. And there are two places where a witch could've summoned Mary Evans. One, the place where she's buried, and two, the place where she died."

I turned to face the other members of PMS. "Now, we know where Mary is buried, and according to the legend, she died in the cave where she used to meet her teacher. If you'll flip to page three, you'll see I've attached a map of where I think this cave probably is. Tomorrow night, we're going to split up and go to those places. Dex and Anderson, you take the grave; me and Romy will take the cave." I paused. "Hey, that rhymes. Anyway, once we figure out who raised Mary's ghost, we can figure out why, and we can stop it. And now I'll take questions."

Three hands went up.

I called on Dex first. "Um, yes. We have this friend, Izzy Brannick? She's about your height, has your color hair, and she is a normal, sane-type person. And you, Crazy Lady, seem to have replaced her. Can we have Izzy back now please?"

Rolling my eyes, I pointed at Romy. "Next."

"Actually, I kind of want you to answer Dex's question. Seriously, Izzy. What is going on with you?"

"Just trying to be a . . . a productive member of PMS. So are we all agreed? Friday night, the boys deal with the cemetery, the girls handle the cave."

"Um," Anderson said, flicking his hair out of his eyes, "I, uh, was wondering if I could be paired up with Romy instead. No offense, Dex, it's just . . ."

Dex held up a hand. "None taken." Then he gave an exaggerated leer. "I'd much rather spelunk with Izzy, anyway."

I knew that spelunking meant exploring caves, but I glared at Dex like he'd said something inappropriate.

"Now see, there's the Izzy I know," he teased, and I suddenly found myself smiling back. Ugh. I was clearly losing it.

Shaking my head, I rattled my own handouts. "Okay, so me and Dex take the cave; Romy and Anderson, you're on grave duty. We'll be looking for anything that suggests a ritual has taken place. Candles, burn marks, funky smells . . ."

"Salt all over the grass," Dex said under his breath, but neither Romy nor Anderson paid him any attention.

"So . . . witches," Romy said, frowning at the paper.

"Yes. Well, witch, singular at least."

She looked up at me, squinting behind her glasses. "Pointy-hat-wearing, broomstick-riding witches."

"They don't actually do any of that stuff. At least most of them don't. Some of them like to be retro every once and a while."

Anderson lifted an eyebrow. "And you know this because?"

I glanced over at Dex. "I read a lot. On the Internet. And also I went to this fancy all-girls' school, and we had a whole class on . . . witches."

When the three of them just continued to stare at me, I added, "It was a really progressive school. Anyway, tonight, PMS patrol, cool?"

"I don't have anything better to do tonight," Anderson said, draping his arm around the back of Romy's chair.

Her dimples deepened as she tried to hide a smile. "Me neither," she said.

"You know I'm always up for weirdness my Nana won't approve of," Dex said, clapping his hands together. "Speaking of, since you'll have to ride with me tonight,

Izzy, why don't we get off the bus together this afternoon? You can meet my Nana."

"Right," I said. I'd been meaning to do that, and while I wish I'd found time to see if any of those magazines had articles like, "Meeting His Nana: What Does It Mean?" there was no time like the present. "That . . . yeah, sure, that'll be fine."

Dex leaned forward, his blue eyes bright. "So let's do this. PMS's first witch hunt!"

The bell rang, and the four of us hurried to gather up our stuff and get back into the main building. The boys loped off ahead while Romy and I hung back a little.

"Anderson was in that picture," she said, worrying her thumbnail between her teeth. "If I'm right, and Mary's after the descendants of certain people—"

"There were lots of people in that picture, Romy," I said, looping my arm through hers. I still hadn't found the appropriate time to do a hip bump, but arm-looping felt right. "And Anderson is going to be fine because we're going to find out what's causing the haunting and put a stop to it. Besides, Mary's nice enough to leave us little warnings when she picks a victim. If anything freaky happens to Anderson, he'll tell us, and we'll know."

That didn't seem to make Romy feel better, so I tightened my arm in hers. "Or hey! Maybe she's done with the whole revenge thing. Maybe it was just Snyder's and Beth's relatives she was pissed at."

That theory lasted until second period. Just after P.E., Romy and I were standing by her locker when there was suddenly an explosive *bang* from farther down the hallway.

"The hell?" I heard someone squawk as a cloud of gray smoke began pouring out of a locker.

"Anderson?" Romy cried, but it wasn't Anderson standing in front of the Exploding Locker. It was Adam, his face a mask of fear and annoyance.

Rushing down the hall, I grabbed his arm. "Are you okay?"

Irritated, he threw off my hand. "Yeah, fine. Just some jackass put a firecracker or something in my locker." Waving the smoke away, he peered inside, and I leaned over his shoulder to do the same. All that was left of Adam's textbooks was a smoldering pile of ash.

"All right, people, make a hole," Mrs. Steele said, pushing students out of her way. Grimacing, she took in the mess. "First someone's car malfunctions, now lockers are exploding? What has gotten *into* this place?"

Behind her back, my eyes met Romy's. Apparently, Mary was far from done.

CHAPTER 24

"**O**kay, please do not be alarmed by our yard situation," Dex said as I followed him up the driveway. "Nana is a fearsome cook but a truly dreadful gardener. It is known."

Dex exaggerated about a lot of things, but the state of his yard was not one of them. Even though it was late February and nothing was exactly blooming, every bush and blade of grass in Dex's front yard was brown and crispy-looking. Even the pear tree looked in danger of keeling over.

But the house itself was pretty. Nicer than ours and a little bigger, there were cheerful yellow curtains in the windows, and when Dex opened the front door, I froze and took a deep breath.

I don't know what heaven smells like, but if it doesn't

smell like freshly baked cookies, I will be really disappointed.

Seeing my rapturous expression, Dex grinned. "This way," he said, tugging me into the kitchen.

A woman in a light blue sweater and a pair of what I'm pretty sure could be described as Mom Jeans—Nana Jeans?—was pulling a tray of cookies out of the oven as we walked in.

"Dex!" she cried happily. And then her eyes swung to me. They were the same bright blue as Dex's, and they nearly matched her sweater. "And who is this?"

"Izzy, my Nana, Nana, my Izzy."

I shot Dex a glare as his Nana put the tray of cookies on the counter. "Oh, my!" she exclaimed, flapping her hands. "Dexter, if you're going to have company, especially such lovely company, you need to warn your Nana! I look a *mess*."

She actually looked pretty nice, in my opinion. Her hair, like Dex's, was black and curly, with only a few touches of gray at her temples. Glasses perched on the edge of her nose, fastened to a sparkly chain draped around her neck. As she reached out and enfolded me in a hug, I caught a whiff of vanilla and baby powder.

Basically, Dex's Nana was the Perfect Grandmother. When she pulled away, she even patted my cheek. "Oh, aren't you a pretty thing. Dex said you were, but it's nice to see he didn't exaggerate for once."

My cheeks flamed at that, and next to me, Dex nudged my ribs. "If anything, I undersold her, didn't I, Nana?"

She swatted at his arm. "Now, Dexter, you're making her blush. Come on and grab a couple of cookies, and tell me all about yourself, Izzy. What a sweet name. Is that short for Isabelle?"

"Isolde," I told her, scooping up a cookie from the tray. Dex sat down on a gingham-covered stool and patted the one next to him. I sat, taking a bit of my cookie. It was everything I had hoped it would be and more. I wondered if Dex's Nana would consider adopting me.

"How pretty," she said. She moved to the giant stainless steel fridge and pulled out a carton of milk. "Wasn't there a famous story about an Isolde? Something beautiful and tragic?"

"Tristan and Isolde," Dex said before I could answer. "And quite frankly, I'm hoping the romance of Dexter and Isolde ends up with a lower body count."

Nana tittered, and I brushed stray crumbs of cookie from my mouth. "There is not a romance of Dexter and Isolde," I said, but I caught myself smiling anyway. Then I remembered. Dex was not just some boy, and I was not just some girl sitting in his Nana's kitchen, eating the most wonderful cookies ever created by woman. He was some kind of Prodigium, and I was here to find out what.

And even if there hadn't been that, romance between me and Dex was totally out of the question. I tried to imagine taking him home to Mom, introducing him as my boyfriend. Brannick women were always very careful about the men they chose. They had the bloodline to think about, after all, which was why they tended to pick warriors. Soldiers, Navy SEALS. My grandfather had even been a Green Beret.

Whenever Mom had talked about Finley's and my dad, the one word that always came up was "strong." Dex couldn't even jog around the football field without his asthma flaring up.

And it wasn't just that. How would Mom react to a boy who was so purely . . . decorative? Sure, Dex had salted a grave, but he'd taken his nice coat off first.

I shook those thoughts off. They were unproductive and pointless. Instead, I smiled at Nana and said, "So you and Dex moved here from New York?" I thought as far as questions went, it was fairly harmless. But I didn't miss the way Nana stiffened slightly. "We've lived a little bit of everywhere. And I've told Dex that the important thing is the future, not the past."

She stroked his hair. "He's here now, and that's all that matters."

Dex smiled at her, but there was something kind of puzzled about it. Maybe he thought her answer was as weird as I did, but it almost seemed like more than that. It was the same look Finn used to get when she couldn't remember where she'd put her crossbow. (That happened a lot more often than it should have, if you asked me. You should always know where you've left deadly weapons.)

"Nana's right," Dex finally said, slapping a hand on the counter. "As Shakespeare said, 'Don't look back, you should never look back.'"

"That was a Don Henley song, dear, but it's an excellent sentiment nonetheless," Nana said, patting his hand. Weirdness passed, she smiled at me again. "Izzy, will you be staying for dinner?"

If the rest of her food was as good as her cookies, I'd be an idiot not to.

Dex answered for me. "She will be. And then we're going to go out for a while, if that's okay with you."

Nana's face creased into a frown. "Are you sure that's a good idea, sweetie? Your asthma has been so bad lately—"

But Dex just waved that off. "I'm fine. It's the time of year or something. Asthma season. But I have my trusty inhaler"—he pulled it out of his coat pocket, shaking it—"and the Fair Isolde to protect me if need be."

When Nana didn't stop frowning, Dex dropped the act, leaning in closer to her. "I'll be fine, Nana," he said, his voice softer. He laid a hand over hers, and his bracelet caught the light. "You worry too much."

She touched the silver links around his wrist. "I'm your grandmother," she said. "It's allowed."

Watching them together made me smile, and started this kind of warm, blooming feeling in my chest. Not only was Dex cute and smart and funny, but he loved his Nana—

And that's when something occurred to me. Dex's Nana. She was related to him by blood. That meant if he was Prodigium, then so was she. That's how that worked; there was no skipping generations, no freak human kid born to Prodigium parents.

There were no vibes coming off of Nana, and she'd hugged me. Touched my cheek. I hadn't felt anything. Not even the slightest hint that she was Prodigium. Still, just to be sure, I leaned forward and said, "That's a pretty ring."

Just as I'd hoped, she pushed her hand toward me so that I could get a better look. As she did, I caught her fingers.

Nothing. Not even the slightest tingle.

"Thank you, sweetheart," she said. "I got it from one of those home-shopping shows. You know, the ones that come on late at night and make silly old ladies like me spend more than they should."

I laughed harder than necessary, trying to cover my confusion. Nana wasn't Prodigium, so Dex couldn't be one either. But if that was true, what the heck was I feeling? No matter what everyone kept saying, I knew that little hum of magic when I touched him wasn't just hormones.

I turned my head and looked at him grinning at his Nana, his silver bracelet winking in the sun, his coat just impossibly, stupidly purple.

Or did I just want Dex to be Prodigium because the idea of liking him was a lot scarier?

CHAPTER 25

Dex and I spent the rest of the afternoon playing video games. I'd never done that before, but it turned out all those years of training paid off in wicked hand-eye coordination. So while I couldn't beat Dex at Dragon Slayer IV, I didn't get totally embarrassed either. Once we'd slain dragons, we ate with Nana. Like her cookies, her spaghetti recipe clearly came from heaven, and by the time we left for the cave, I felt happier—and fuller—than I had in weeks.

Okay, so maybe Dex's Nana seemed a little overly protective. But Dex was her only grandkid and all the family she had. That was probably normal. And Dex was normal, I reminded myself as we drove to the outskirts of town. In the dim blue lights of the dash, I studied his profile. Normal. I'd never thought that word could sound so appealing.

The cave was easier to find than I'd thought it would be. There were signs and everything. Granted, they didn't mention Mary Evans or ghosts, but according to the legend, this had been where Mary and Jasper—the teacher—had met, and done . . . whatever. And, more important, where Mary had died.

Once we got there, Dex opened my door for me, holding out his hand. "Milady."

The night was cold enough that I wished I'd brought a heavier jacket. Dex was decked out in a new purple jacket, a thick green scarf knotted at his throat. He looked warm and cozy, and I wondered if his jacket was as soft as it seemed.

Dex must've picked up on my longing, because he went to unbutton his coat. "Cold? You can have it."

"No," I said quickly. "It's just . . . purple suits you. Which is good since you wear so much of it."

Preening, Dex raised his head and pushed his shoulders back. "It brings out the color of my eyes."

I didn't giggle this time, but I did give him a playful shove as I moved past him and into the cave. Once we were inside, we turned our flashlights on.

"Well, this is . . ."

"Creepy," I finished.

"I was actually going to go with 'pants-wettingly terrifying,' but, sure."

"You really think Mary and Jasper used this place to get all . . . romantic?" Running a hand over the damp walls of the cave, I shuddered a little. "Because seriously, I wouldn't even take my *hat* off in here."

"Their relationship was already pretty gross. Maybe they were going for some kind of grossness record."

"Lovely," I muttered, walking farther back into the cave. As I did, I had to crouch slightly. Dex had to practically fold in half. "Whoever used to hang out here, they must have been pretty tiny," I joked.

Dex turned his flashlight on me. "Um, Iz, pretty sure they weren't standing up," he said, and I blushed.

"Right," I said, trying to sound extra brusque so that he wouldn't notice my discomfort. "Okay, so. Proof of the supernatural. Let's find some."

Kneeling down, Dex yanked a melted candle off a little shelf carved in the rock. "You think this was supposed to be sexy or spooky?"

I was never going to stop blushing. I was actually going to die of blood loss because there wasn't any left to pump through my heart. It was all in my face.

"Nothing in this place is sexy," I told him, and he laughed.

"Oh, come on, Izzy. Even you, Miss Anti-Romance, can admit there's something just a little bit appealing about making out in a candlelit cave."

"Bats live in caves," I reminded him. "And where there are bats, there's bat poop. Lots of it. Did you know there's a cave in Mexico where they have a whole mountain made of guano?"

Dex leveled a fake-sultry gaze at me. "Are you coming on to me?"

I shined my flashlight at him, making him throw up a hand to guard his eyes. "Hey, watch it! You want me to actually see the ghost stuff, right?'

"Just . . . start looking, okay?"

"Fine," he grumbled, and we made our way deeper into the cave. The ceiling got lower and we both had to drop to our knees and crawl.

"Salting graves, crawling underground . . . you really are the most fun date ever," Dex mused. I bumped him with my shoulder and kept crawling. After a few feet, the cave opened up again, the ceiling soaring at least twelve feet overhead. Dex stood up and stretched with a happy groan, but all I could focus on was the magic bouncing off the rocks, filling the air, making my hair nearly stand on end. "This is it."

Frowning, Dex spun in a circle. "What, this? This is where the ghost stuff went down? How can you tell?"

"I just . . . can." It was maybe not the greatest answer ever, but I couldn't think of any other way to explain to Dex how I could sense magic.

Luckily, he didn't question it. "Whoa!" he cried.

"What?" Had he felt it? Was it just a delayed reaction? But Dex wasn't exclaiming over all the magic radiating inside the cave. He was walking forward to another little alcove carved in the rock.

"Aha," he said, poking around on the ground. "You're right, this is it."

I knelt next to him, turning my beam of light onto the cave floor. There was another melty candle and a few scraps of charred paper. Rooting around a little more, he uncovered a tiny golden charm. I leaned in closer as he laid it in his palm and shined the flashlight on it.

"A heart," he murmured.

I was suddenly aware that our heads were very close together, and took a deep breath. "Yeah."

His eyes dropped to my mouth. "That's both sexy and spooky, don't you think?"

"Depends on how you look at it, I guess," I said.

Now I was watching his mouth. Like his hands and eyes, Dex's lips were pretty. Beautiful, even. And suddenly I wanted them on mine more than I had ever wanted anything. Even as we moved closer together, some tiny part of my brain that was still a Brannick and not a silly girl losing her head over a cute boy registered what the magic in this cave must be. No ordinary spell had happened here. This was different. This was a love spell.

And now here Dex and I were, soaking in all this love spell energy. That was why he was staring at me like he wanted to devour me. Why I *wanted* him to devour me. It was residual energy from the spell, nothing else. I don't know how I did it, but I managed to get to my feet and back away from him.

Clearing my throat, I started shining my flashlight around the rest of the cave. "There might be more stuff. I mean, that's definitely magiclike, and—"

"I've never kissed anyone in a cave," Dex mused. When I turned around, he was still on his knees, watching me. "Or in any kind of underground structure, really. Cave, bomb shelter, secret government bunker . . ." His light was on me again. "What about you? You seem like the kind of girl whose romantic life is full of thrills and danger."

My "romantic life" consisted of watching cheesy teen soaps and sneaking the occasional drugstore romance novel, but wasn't the kind of thing I wanted to share.

And I definitely wasn't telling him that I'd never kissed anyone anywhere before. "Lots," I told him, going for breezy. "There was a secret tunnel connecting my school to the boys' school down the road. So it was all underground making out all the time."

"I knew it," he said, making me laugh. "So these boys you were sneaking off to meet in tunnels. Was there a . . . special one?"

Since there hadn't actually been *any* boy, much less a special one, I wasn't sure what to say. Finally I settled on, "I didn't have a boyfriend, if that's what you're asking."

"I was trying not to be that tacky about it, but yes, I was asking if you had . . . or if you *have* a boyfriend." My heart was pounding fast now. This time I couldn't tell myself he was being friendly, or that this was "just Dex." Boys don't ask if you have a boyfriend unless they are interested in you.

And then something else occurred to me. I could tell him I did. Invent some long-distance guy, someone I e-mailed and Skyped with. And that would be that. Dex and I could be friends, nothing more. He might feel a little disappointed, and maybe he'd pull back a little.

Just the thought of that hurt. I hadn't known Dex very long, but I liked him. Genuinely. Hanging out with Romy was fun, but it wasn't the same as the time I spent with Dex.

I'd been quiet too long. "So that's a yes, then?" he asked, his voice every bit as light as mine had been moments ago. But I heard the hurt creeping around the edges.

Tell him yes. Tell him yes.

Turning around, I let the beam of my flashlight fall on the floor. "No. I don't have a boyfriend."

I thought I'd seen every one of Dex's smiles. The goofy one, the ironic one, the delighted one. But the grin that broke across his face was a whole new specimen: the sexy one.

"Oh, thank God," he breathed, and then he was crossing the cave and pulling me to him.

CHAPTER 26

Dex was taller than me, and as he pressed me against him, he actually hauled me up on my tiptoes. His arm was around my waist, his other hand plunged into my hair, and he was kissing me. I mean, really, really kissing me.

I was kissing him back. And I was *good* at it.

I didn't know if it was the spell, or if I was some kind of kissing prodigy. Everything I'd worried about—weird head movements, awkward lip placement, the Spit Dilemma—none of it was an issue. Dex and I kissed like we'd been doing it forever. That buzz I felt every time I touched him was still there, but now it was wrapped up in all these other feelings, feelings that seemed a lot more potent than any magic.

My fingers curled against his shoulders, the material of his jacket as soft as it had looked, and I shivered.

When we finally broke apart, his eyes were bluer than normal. He seemed dazed—and I wasn't feeling particularly clearheaded either. "Izzy," he murmured.

I pulled back. "It's a spell."

Dex blinked twice, shaking his head. "What?"

I was still trying to catch my breath. Trying to keep myself from jumping back into his arms. "This place. It's got some kind of love spell thing happening. That's the only reason we . . . we, uh . . ."

I was moving back toward him, my hands already itching to grab his lapels. One of his fingers curled around my belt loop, pulling me in, but before our lips could meet again, I slammed both of my palms against his chest. "You don't really want to kiss me," I blurted out.

"I . . . I'm sorry, what?"

Stepping back, I crossed my arms. "This cave. Someone did a love spell here. That's what all this—" I went to point to his hand, but it was empty now. Somewhere in the middle of . . . everything, Dex had dropped the heart charm. Clearing my throat, I rushed on. "Anyway, love spells are, like, crazy powerful. They can . . . seep into places. Make other people feel the effects of the magic. That's what's happening to us."

I was babbling and I knew it, but I just wanted to find something I could say that would erase the dawning horror on Dex's face.

"So . . . we kissed because of *magic*?"

"Right," I said, relieved. "So it doesn't mean anything."

His expression twisted, and now he didn't seem horrified. He seemed . . . *angry*.

"Is this something else you learned on the Internet?" he asked, his voice cold. "The effects of love spells on people who don't like each other?"

Confused, I shook my head. "I do like you."

Dex laughed, but it was a laugh I'd never heard him use before. It was sarcastic and harsh. "Of course you do. As a friend, right?" And then suddenly, all the anger seemed to drain out of him. He ran a hand over the top of his head, ruffling his hair. "Look, it's fine. We kissed because magic made us do it. Whatever. Let's just . . . let's just go."

He moved toward the tunnel and made what I thought was another harsh laugh. But it wasn't. It was a cough. Then a wheeze. And suddenly he was sliding to the floor, his shoulders and chest working, but no air coming in or going out.

I rushed over to him, thrusting my hands into the pockets of his jacket, but he shoved me off.

"I know things are weird with us, but now is *not the time!*" I shouted. In the dim glow of the flashlight I could see the skin around his lips turning blue. Dex made

231

another wheeze, but this one sounded like it was trying to be a laugh. "Car," he mouthed.

I was bolting out of the cave the second the word was out of his mouth. Ducking to keep from whacking my head, I crawled faster than anyone has ever crawled before. By the time I got out to the car my hands were shaking. I yanked open the door and started pawing through the glove box. All that got me was a box of tissues and some hard peppermints.

Every bad word I knew was spilling from my lips as I thrust my hands between the seats. Finally, my fingers closed over metal, and I could've wept with relief when I pulled out Dex's inhaler.

When I got back to him, the wheezing had given way to a terrifying silence. Fumbling, I shoved the inhaler at him, sinking back on my heels when I heard him take several deep pulls on it.

It took much longer than it had that day on the football field, but after several agonizing seconds, Dex started breathing again. Color rushed back into his face, and he closed his eyes, shaking.

"Well, that was different," he whispered once he could finally talk. He opened one eye. "Never had an asthma attack from making out. You are one heck of a kisser, Izzy Brannick."

I would have hit him, but I was so glad he wasn't

dying that I just patted his shoulder instead. "I think it was the arguing rather than the kissing."

"Heh," he breathed. "Maybe." Both eyes opened. "I'm sorry, by the way. I shouldn't have gotten so pissed, but—"

"Forget about it," I said. "And . . . maybe it wasn't just the magic that made me kiss you. But, Dex. I can't . . . we can't . . ."

I didn't know what else to say. That seemed to sum it all up. I couldn't. *We* couldn't. My life was full of ridiculously dangerous stuff. And Dex, in his own way, was ridiculously brave. I thought about the clothes he wore, the unabashed affection he showed toward me, Romy, even his Nana. Every day of his life, Dex was uniquely himself, and he didn't care what people said about it. And I knew that if he really knew what my life was like, he'd want to be a part of it. That was the kind of guy he was—all in.

And being "all in" with me would get him killed.

"It's fine," Dex said, breathing more slowly. "As long as we can be friends, I'm . . . I'm good with that."

"Me, too," I said. And even though I knew that was true, I wondered why it made me so sad.

CHAPTER 27

"So . . . Everton likes Leslie?" Romy asked around a mouthful of popcorn.

"Yeah. Loves her, actually. But that was before the amnesia."

We were sitting in Romy's room on Saturday night, a big bowl of popcorn on the floor, two different kinds of sodas on her desk, and all three seasons of *Ivy Springs* sitting beside her TV.

I'd filled in her on what had happened at the cave. Well, the love spell part. Not the me and Dex kissing bit. Romy had told me about her and Anderson finding salt on the grave—and I tried to act very surprised about that—but in the end, both of us agreed that Friday night's field trips had been pretty successful, all things considered.

Then we'd put in *Ivy Springs* and let the trials of Leslie

and Everton distract us from our failure. Romy had already changed into her pajamas—naturally, they had cute little ghosts on them—and I was painting my toenails. Well, trying to. Since I'd never done it before, my feet looked like I'd accidentally stepped into a meat grinder. As I dabbed at the bright scarlet mess, Romy glanced up.

"Whoa," she said, eyes going wide. "What have you done?"

Sighing, I yanked a tissue out of the box on Romy's nightstand and began trying to wipe off the worst of it. "I think I used too much."

Romy laughed as she sat up. "Think? Iz, it looks like you poured half the bottle on your foot. Here, give me that." She snatched tissues away from me and rummaged in her nightstand drawer until she emerged with a bottle of nail polish remover. I reached for it, but she held her arm over her head. "Uh-uh. You cannot be trusted with dangerous chemicals, clearly. Give me your foot."

Hesitantly, I stretched out my leg, and Romy doused a few tissues with the polish remover. As she went to work scrubbing the worst of the mess off my right foot, she glanced at me over the top of her glasses. "You've never painted your toenails before, have you?"

I thought about lying, but seeing as how I'd somehow managed to get It's a Bit Chili in Here *between* my toes, I didn't think Romy would buy it.

"No. My mom is really strict about makeup."

Giving a low whistle, Romy shook her head. "Never played dodgeball, never been kissed, never used makeup . . ."

My face was nearly as scarlet as my toes. Well, my whole foot, actually.

When I didn't say anything, Romy raised her eyes. "Izzy?" she prompted.

I cleared my throat and tucked a strand of hair behind my ear. I hadn't planned on telling Romy about the kissing, but my stupid fair skin had given me away yet again. "I, um . . . me and Dex, we—"

Romy sat up so quickly she nearly turned over the bottle of polish remover. I caught it, but she didn't seem to notice since she was too busy clapping and squealing something that sounded like, "Ohmygodohmygodohmygodohmygod!"

Leaping off the bed, she paused the *Ivy Springs* DVD just as Everton was about to kiss Lila, Leslie's identical cousin. "I cannot believe we've been sitting here for an entire hour, painting nails and watching TV, when you could have been telling me every last detail about yours and Dexter O'Neil's mega-hot makeout session."

"It wasn't like that," I protested. "It was . . . Okay, it was exactly like that, but—"

Romy cut me off with another squeal, and I couldn't

help but laugh. "This is so very excellent," she said, flopping back down on the bed. "So when? Where? How?"

I drew back my now-polish-free foot, wrapping my arms around my knees. "Last night, at the cave, and, um, with our mouths?"

Romy rolled her eyes and hit me with one of the bright green throw pillows covering her bed. "I figured that last part. I just meant did he kiss you first, or beneath that shy exterior, are you secretly a seductive vixen?" She waggled her eyebrows, and now it was my turn to toss a pillow at her.

"He kissed me. Well, he asked me if I had a boyfriend, and I said no, and then we . . . kissed."

Telling it like that, it sounded so flat, so uneventful. But I didn't know how girls talked about this kind of thing. And besides, I kind of wanted to keep it private. It was almost like I was afraid if I shared all the details—how warm his lips had been, the softness of his jacket under my hands—it wouldn't feel as special anymore. And since it was probably the only time it was ever going to happen, I wanted it to stay special for a long time.

Something must have shown on my face, because Romy's giddy grin slipped into a puzzled frown. "Why did you make Sad Face?"

Before I could say anything, Romy rushed on. "Was it bad? I mean, I always thought Dex would be pretty good at kissing despite his general spazziness, but I could be wrong, and if I am, just tell me. I know he's my Boy Best Friend, but you're my *Girl* Best Friend, and that trumps him—"

I help up my hand like that could stop the rush of words. "No, it was not bad. And . . . I'm your best friend?" I'd never had a best friend unless you counted Finley. But even though she'd been my sister, and I'd loved her, it wasn't like we'd ever painted each other's toenails, and I shuddered to think of what she would've said about *Ivy Springs*.

Romy smiled, almost shyly. "Um, duh, of course you're my best friend. What do you think all this means"—she waved her hand, taking in the popcorn, the polish, the TV—"if not your initiation into Best Friendom?"

In my head, I could hear Mom's voice: *These people are not your friends, Izzy. They are a means to an end, and as soon as this job is over, you'll never see them again.*

But Romy was my friend. When she'd asked me to spend the night, I hadn't agreed so that I could pump her for more information about the hauntings. I'd said yes because I'd wanted to hang out with her. To paint nails and talk about boys and watch Everton and Leslie make idiots of themselves.

"Okay, see, there you go with Sad Face again," Romy said, and I sighed. "It's just . . . the kiss with Dex was good. And I like him. Lots. But I can't exactly do the boyfriend thing."

Now it was Romy's turn for Sad Face. "Why not?"

Because I'm a monster hunter and this whole thing was just a job and I have to tell my mom that Dex isn't really Prodigium soon and then she'll make us leave.

The words were right there, desperate to tumble out of my mouth in one big avalanche of overshare.

Instead I shrugged and said, "I need to concentrate on school. You know. For, um, SATs. And college. And . . . stuff like that."

I expected Romy to argue, but she just sighed and picked up the nail polish remover. "I get that," she said. "But it sucks. You guys seem like a weird fit at first glance, but I don't know. I think you'd be good together."

"Yeah," I replied.

And then I got off the bed and restarted *Ivy Springs* before Sad Face became Crying Face.

"Isolde. Isolde. ISOLDE."

Blinking, I sat up. Ugh, another Torin dream. Something I was definitely not in the mood for. "Go'way," I mumbled at him. "Don't wanna play dress-up."

But when I flopped over onto my stomach, I realized I wasn't in a ball gown. I also wasn't in a ballroom or on a boat. I was lying on the trundle bed in Romy's room,

239

and Torin wasn't in my dreams, he was in her mirror.

Fully awake, I shot out of the bed and made my way as quietly as possible to Torin. My face nearly against the glass, I hissed, "What are you *doing*?"

"Dropping in," he said, raising his hands innocently. "Isn't that what blokes are supposed to do? Raid slumber parties?"

"No," I shot back, my voice barely audible. "At least I don't think so. But it doesn't matter. *You* should not be here."

Behind me, Romy made a snuffling noise in her sleep and turned over. I didn't think it was possible to be any quieter, but I tried anyway. "Go. Away."

"I miss you," he said suddenly. Our faces were very close to each other, and even though I knew it was impossible, I could've sworn I felt a puff of breath on my cheek. "You never talk to me anymore. And that?" He pointed to the stack of *Ivy Springs*, eyes narrowing. "Traitor."

"This is my job," I told him, ignoring the pang of guilt in my chest. What was wrong with me? I didn't have anything to feel guilty for. So I chose to watch the show with a real girl my own age instead of a four-hundred-year-old warlock trapped in a mirror. Surely, that wasn't anything to feel guilty about. Or at least I thought it wasn't. *Sassy Miss* hadn't exactly covered that.

"These people aren't a job to you anymore, Isolde," Torin said, voice low. "They're your friends. And while it causes me actual physical pain to admit this, your mum is right. In the end, getting close to humans can only hurt you."

I backed away from the glass, but he kept going. "I've watched generations of Brannick women get close to regular people. Fall in love, make friends. It ended in tragedy every single time, Isolde. I know you don't believe a large percentage of what I say, but believe that I have no desire to ever see you hurt. And these people will hurt you."

Romy rolled over again, and I looked back at her. "Romy is . . . she couldn't hurt me."

"Could she not?" In the glass, Torin walked over to Romy's desk and opened the top drawer, pulling out something thin and golden.

My heart sank, but I made myself cross the room and open that same drawer. There, hidden under a stack of purple Post-its, was a charm bracelet. There was a ballet slipper and a tiny golden unicorn and horseshoe and what I think was supposed to be a pot of gold. And in between the slipper and the unicorn was a space where, I had an awful feeling, a heart was supposed to go.

I put the bracelet back where I found it, silently slid the drawer closed, and walked back to the mirror. "It makes sense," Torin said as soon as I was in front of him.

"She finds a harmless little love spell somewhere, decides to try it out. And then she tries another spell, and another. And what do you know, she runs a ghost-hunting club, but there are no ghosts. So she works a little hedge magic, does a summoning or two. Just to make things interesting. And then it very quickly gets out of hand."

I wanted to deny it. To say there had to be some mistake. But Torin was right. It made total sense.

"What do I do?" I asked, but I wasn't sure if I was talking to Torin or myself.

"Tell your mum. Or tell that bloody Prodigium Council and let them deal with it. Let this girl know there are consequences for messing about with the unknown."

Both of those were technically good ideas, but they made my stomach twist in really awful ways. What if it turned out the only way to break this particular spell was to kill her? Mom would do that. If it was the only way, I had no doubt she could. And as for the Council . . . my cousin Sophie may have been in charge, but she wasn't there right now. Who knew what those people would do to Romy?

"I can't," I said, and Torin watched me with an unreadable expression.

Finally he said, "This is being a Brannick, Izzy. No one said it would be easy."

And with that, he was gone.

CHAPTER 28

First thing Sunday morning I faked an upset stomach and left Romy's. She seemed a little down, but I let her keep the last season of *Ivy Springs*, which cheered her up. Instead of home, I headed for the library. Unfortunately, Ideal's library wasn't exactly the best resource, and I quickly saw why Mom had needed to drive three towns over to get her books. Looking for anything on "hedge magic" only got me a bunch of volumes on how to grow hedges. Thinking of Dex's horrible lawn, I wondered if I should check one out for Nana. Then I remembered that everything between me and Dex was kind of awful right now. Besides, I had the case to focus on.

That night, Mom and I went back to that Chinese place, and I told her I was ready to leave. She raised her eyebrows. "Case closed?"

"Almost," I said. I still hadn't figured out how to stop Romy. Part of me wondered if I could just talk to her like . . . like a friend. Or maybe sneak a fake article into *American Teen* that said something like, "Why Hedge Magic and Raising Ghosts Is So Last Year!"

By Monday, I still hadn't found anything. Dex had saved me a seat on the bus like usual, but he was very careful not to sit too close to me. I think both of us were relieved when Romy turned around and started telling Dex about her and Anderson's night.

"And there was salt, like, everywhere," she said, pushing her glasses up. "I mean, that was all we saw, but that has to mean something, right?"

Dex made a sort of choked laugh that he quickly turned into a cough. Romy's brow furrowed. "You okay?"

"Yeah, just . . . Anyway, Izzy, why don't you fill Romy in on our night?"

"She already did," Romy said, barely suppressing a smile. She winked at me, and I wanted to be able to wink back so badly. Instead, I reached into my pocket. "I left out a part. We also found this." Before leaving the cave Friday night, I'd searched the floor for that heart charm. I pulled it out of my pocket now.

Romy plucked the charm from my hand, a weird expression on her face. As she studied it, I studied *her*. "Have you seen it before?"

Startled, she raised her head. "I have a charm kind of like this, but it doesn't look all blackened and stuff." She handed it back to me. "Maybe it belonged to Mary."

I don't know what I'd expected. Not for her to be like, "Oh, right, this is mine! I did some kind of freaky spell at that cave, and whoops! Now we're plagued by ghosts." But I'd thought she'd show a little more reaction than that. If anything, she just seemed kind of confused.

We had a test in English and a freaking relay race in P.E., so I didn't get a chance to talk to her any more that morning. Then she didn't show up at lunch, so I made up my mind to talk to her during history, only to find out class wasn't meeting because there was a pep rally for the basketball team. There had been, like, eight in the first season of *Ivy Springs*, but I'd never actually been to one. And I have to admit, my curiosity to see what an actual pep rally looked like almost outweighed my need to know what was up with Romy.

The gym was already full by the time we got there, but Romy and Anderson had saved a couple of places at the very top of the bleachers, just like the night of the basketball game. Dodging other kids, Dex and I carefully made our way up there. At one point, I nearly stumbled and he reached out, catching my hand. It was the first time we'd touched since the cave, and the feel of his hand on mine made me remember his lips on mine, his hands on my back. But the instant I had righted myself, Dex dropped my hand.

It was for the best. Really. Dex and I couldn't be together, not like that. And I wouldn't be at the school for much longer. The less I had to miss, the better.

Once we reached the top of the bleachers, I sat by Romy, and Dex went over beside Anderson. Even with two people between us, I was so aware of him my skin felt charged.

Trying to take my mind off of that, I nodded down at the gym floor. "So what exactly is going to happen?" I asked Romy.

She turned to me, surprised. "You've seriously never been to a pep rally?"

"They, uh, didn't do them at my old school. We didn't have sports." I was too distracted to sound sincere, but Romy didn't seem to notice.

"Okay, well, basically, it's a stupid and pointless ritual wherein we all cheer for our stupid, pointless basketball team. We'll shout some stuff, the cheerleaders will do a dance, and then the mascot will come out and we'll shout some more."

"That sounds . . . dumb."

Romy nodded. "It is. Intensely. But it's better than history, I guess."

At that, the basketball team, all wearing their

warm-up suits, jogged out into the gym and everyone started hooting and clapping like these weren't the same guys we saw every single day. About half the kids in the bleachers even leapt to their feet, but since Romy, Anderson, and Dex all stayed seated, so did I.

The band started up, and I saw Adam on the very edge, playing his drum. I'd kept a close eye on him since the locker thing, but so far there had been no sign of Mary. I wasn't even sure what she was planning for him. Snyder had gotten the frog with the bashed-in head, signaling that he was about to get his head bashed in. Beth had gotten the mangled Barbie a few days before she was nearly hit by a car. Adam had gotten an explosion. A month ago, I would have said a ghost making someone blow up was pretty much impossible, but if Mary could wield a killer microscope and manipulate a car, what was to stop her from sending Adam sky high? Still, I wondered how she was going to manage that, exactly.

Dex leaned closer to Anderson. I heard him murmur something, and all thoughts of Adam were forgotten.

Maybe I could try to talk to Dex on the bus. Tell him . . . I don't know, I'd lied about not having a boyfriend. And then I'd felt guilty about the kiss, and that's why I'd spazzed out. He was probably too smart to buy that, but it was worth a try. God, why were boys so complicated? I suddenly wished I had a ghost to fight right that second. Or a vampire. A werewolf. Heck, I'd even take a gollum, no matter how messy killing one was. Anything to make me feel like me again.

I sat there brooding through the rest of the pep rally. It worked pretty much exactly like Romy had said, and I had nearly tuned it out by the time the giant hedgehog rushed onto the court.

On the other side of Romy and Anderson, Dex snorted, and in that moment I wanted nothing more than to be sitting beside him, hearing whatever snarky comments he undoubtedly made about the mascot.

I hadn't realized I was staring at him until he turned his head and looked at me. Romy and Anderson were talking, their heads close together, but for a second it was like there wasn't anyone but me and Dex. A little smile drifted across his face, and just when I was thinking about returning it, there was a shout from the gym floor.

The hedgehog was wheeling out a big "cannon." As one of the cheerleaders handed him a sparkler, I leaned over and asked Romy, "What's the deal with that?"

She rolled her eyes. "Ugh, this is the *big finale* every time. He pretends to light the fuse, and then it shoots out glitter and confetti while we all ooh and ahh and pretend he hasn't done it a million times. On the upside, it means this stupid pep rally is almost over."

"So it's not a real cannon?" I asked.

Romy shook her head. "Nope. Just an air cannon."

"But . . ." I leaned forward. "It *looks* like a real one. Like that one that's outside the front of the school."

The hedgehog took the sparkler as the student body stomped their feet, chanting, "M! E! H! S!" He lit the fuse, and it kindled, smoking.

I sat up straighter. "Did he just really light that?"

Squinting, Romy peered down. "Huh. Yeah. Maybe this is a new part of the routine."

But the cheerleader who'd handed the mascot the sparkler was staring at the fuse in confusion. Then she started backing up, saying something over her shoulder to one of the other cheerleaders. And the hedgehog, suddenly looking a lot more malevolent than I'd ever thought a hedgehog could, pushed on the barrel of the cannon until it was pointing straight at the band. Or, more specifically, straight at Adam. I saw him drop his drumsticks, face wrinkling in confusion. A group of kids cheered, obviously expecting glitter and confetti, like Romy had said.

Shooting to my feet, I tried to make my way down the bleachers, but I was too high up and there were too many people. Distantly, I heard Dex call my name, but I was too busy trying to get to the floor.

One of the cheerleaders was shouting and pointing at the cannon, and I heard a chorus of shrieks go up from the gym floor. I wasn't going to make it.

But then, a basketball player darted from the first row of the bleachers, throwing all his weight onto the cannon. The sound its wheels made on the hardwood was awful, but the deafening boom that followed was much, much worse.

Thanks to the basketball player, the explosion pounded into the far wall of the gym instead of Adam—and all the kids within fifty feet of him. But it didn't matter. Everything descended into complete pandemonium as kids screamed at and shoved each other, trying to get off the bleachers and out of the gym. I hung on to the railing, inching down the side of the bleachers. Down on the floor, one of the basketball players was holding the hedgehog's arms behind its back as another boy reached up and tugged the mascot's head off.

The suit was empty.

As the boy holding the head staggered back, the suit slid through the other player's arms, pooling onto the floor.

I only *thought* there had been panic before. The screaming got louder, people started shoving harder, and the entire building seemed to quake.

Fear—thick, choking waves of it—rushed through the gym. More than fear, really. Terror. Horror. Dread. All of it pulsing in the air, and somewhere, I knew, Mary Evans was getting stronger.

Much stronger.

CHAPTER 29

Since the school had been evacuated, we held the emergency meeting of PMS at Romy's house. Romy's mom had gone overboard with the snack options, laying out three different kinds of chips on the counter, as well as two kinds of soft drinks.

Once we'd gotten our food we followed Romy up to her room.

Romy immediately clambered onto her bed, sitting cross-legged in the middle. Anderson sat next to her, while I took the desk chair and Dex folded his long body onto a bright green beanbag chair.

"Okay," Romy said, dusting crumbs off her hands, "I think we can all agree there's some seriously crazy stuff going on at Mary Evans High."

"I don't know, Rome," Dex said, crossing his ankles.

ledgehog violence is a lot more common than you'd think."

"What I still don't get," Anderson said, grabbing a handful of chips, "is why she went from floating some chalk to this whole reign of terror thing."

"There never was a haunting before," I said, finally getting it. "Floating chalk, locker doors opening, all of that was BS, just stories people told." I was too freaked out and thinking too fast to even pretend I didn't know much about the paranormal. "This is the only haunting Mary Evans High has ever had, and it's because someone used magic and freaking summoned a ghost."

All three of them stared at me, but I didn't care anymore. This had gone too far, and after what had happened in the gym today, Mary would be stronger than ever. We didn't have any more time.

I took a deep breath. It had come to this. "And I think I know who."

I walked over to Romy's desk and pulled out her bracelet, dangling it on one finger as my other hand fished in my pocket for the charm I'd found in the cave. "This belongs to you, doesn't it?" I asked her.

Very carefully, Romy put her can of soda down. "Yeah. What are you saying?"

I could feel Anderson's and Dex's eyes on me as I said, "You run a ghost-hunting club, but you didn't have

any ghosts to hunt. So maybe you stumbled across a spell somewhere. Hedge magic," I said. "You just thought you'd call up a couple of local spirits. Nothing too dangerous, nothing that could hurt anyone. But hedge magic can be tricky, and something went wrong. And people *are* getting hurt, Romy."

Her face was a mask as she took all of that in. Finally, she got off the bed and snatched the bracelet out of my hand. "That is my bracelet, and yes, that *is* my charm. But I lost it weeks ago. I certainly wasn't hanging out in a cave, conjuring up 'hedge magic.' And what does that even *mean*?"

"It's something—"

"Don't say you read it on the Internet."

"You *do* say that a lot," Dex said, and for once he didn't sound like he was joking. In fact, I could swear that was actual suspicion on his face as he watched me. "First the salt thing, now witches summoning ghosts . . .'"

Romy was looking at me weird, too. "What salt thing?"

Glaring at Dex, I said, "It was nothing. And besides, it didn't work."

"All this stuff did start happening when you showed up," Anderson said, his voice very quiet. I threw up my hands.

"What the heck? You said you'd been investigating

the Mary Evans thing since Mr. Snyder. And that was months ago."

"There weren't any hedgehogs trying to blow up the gym months ago," Anderson offered.

"It has nothing to do with me," I insisted, but even as I said it, a shiver ran down my spine. That was true. They'd had one incident before I came here. Now all hell had broken loose. Had I somehow unleashed all of this?

"You seem to know an awful lot about ghosts for someone who claims to not care about the paranormal," Romy spit out.

Anderson was nodding slowly, and even Dex seemed troubled. "The thing with the salt," he repeated. "The day after that, Beth ended up nearly becoming roadkill."

"I was trying to trap Mary's ghost," I fired back. "Not help her kill Beth."

It was the wrong thing to say. Anderson's face went hard. "You saw her at the graveyard the night before Beth nearly got mowed down?" he asked Dex.

Dex nodded. "She did say she was trying to keep the ghost in the grave."

"Which clearly didn't work."

"If I were trying to get Beth killed, why would I have saved her life?"

"Like you said, you didn't want anyone to get hurt," Romy said. "You felt guilty."

"No, I didn't!" I said. Or rather, yelled. Romy actually flinched. Trying to soften my tone, I added, "I didn't feel guilty because I have nothing to feel guilty about. I didn't call forth any ghosts. You did."

"No," Romy said through clenched teeth, "I. Didn't."

"Okay, fine," I said, so frustrated I wanted to shake her. "You didn't. Some other person came in here and stole your bracelet and started doing spells all over the place. The point is, we need to stop it. This ghost is dangerous, Romy. And you can't stop her with a blinking box and a tinfoil hat."

Romy swung an accusatory glare at Dex. "Stop talking about the hat."

"*That's* what you're choosing to be upset about?"

"If our blinking boxes and tinfoil hats are so stupid to you, Izzy, maybe you shouldn't be in PMS anymore," Anderson said.

I was surprised at how much that stung. And even more surprised that Dex stayed quiet. When I looked over at him in the beanbag chair, he was staring at the carpet, chewing his thumbnail.

"Fine," I said, wishing my voice hadn't wavered. "Go ahead. Deal with the crazy, murderous ghost on your own. I was just trying to help."

"We don't need your help," Romy said, and to my horror, my eyes started watering. Before the group could see that, I grabbed my backpack and, with as much dignity as I could muster, walked out of Romy's room, closing the door behind me.

The walk to my house didn't take long, but with every step, I got angrier and angrier. This is what happened when you get involved with regular kids. Stupid kids, who summoned a ghost and probably were going to get killed by it. And that was fine. That's what happened when people messed with stuff that was way over their heads. So sue me for trying to step in and use, oh, I don't know, *a thousand years of bloodline and experience and training* to keep them safe. Let them wear their tinfoil hats. And let Dex—

The tears nearly spilled over then, but I stopped just outside my front door and took a deep breath. No. I wasn't going to cry over him.

Them. Whatever.

Mom's car was parked in the driveway, so I called out for her when I went inside.

"In here," she answered from the kitchen.

I walked down the hall, and was surprised to find Maya standing next to the sink with Mom.

"What are you—" I started to say, but before I could get out any more, Mom turned to me. She wasn't smiling, but her eyes were practically shining. "It's Finn," she said. "We got a lead on Finn."

CHAPTER 30

"What?" was all I could say.

Moving quickly, Mom grabbed her jacket from a kitchen chair. "A girl just a few counties over disappeared last week. Same as Finley. Got involved with a coven of dark witches and vanished."

"Oh," I said, trying to keep the disappointment out of my voice. The news was great, better than anything we'd gotten so far. But it didn't seem like much. For some reason, when Mom said she had a lead, I thought it would mean . . . more. That we could have Finley back tonight.

I suddenly wanted that more than anything in the world. Finn and I had fought, and maybe we'd never painted our nails together, but she hadn't lied to me. She hadn't summoned ghosts and then called *me* a freak.

"Anyway, Maya is going to stay here with you until I

get back. Should be later tonight, maybe early tomorrow morning."

"I don't need a babysitter," I said, but Mom waved that off.

"Not now, Izzy. With everything that's been going on, I'd rather you didn't stay here alone."

"Besides," Maya said, moving to the stove, where she was boiling something that smelled like rosemary and death, "we'll have a big time. I can braid your hair, teach you a few incantations . . ."

I gave the least enthusiastic "Yay" of all time.

"As soon as I get back, we'll deal with your hedge witch friend, and then we can get home," Mom said, startling me.

I whirled around to face Mom. "You know? How?"

Flipping her hair over the collar of her coat, Mom glanced out toward the hall. "Torin is not always completely useless."

No, but he *was* completely slimy and untrustworthy. "He shouldn't have told you," I insisted. "This is my case, and I'm handling it."

"It was your case when it was a run-of-the-mill haunting. Or figuring out what kind of Prodigium that boy was. Which you never did, apparently."

"I was working on it," I told her, but Mom frowned.

"It's time to put an end to this entire case, Iz, and

you're too involved. As soon as I get back, we're finishing it. Besides, it's getting dangerous."

"It hasn't been *that* dangerous," I said, conveniently ignoring the whole pyromaniac hedgehog thing.

But Mom shook her head. "You're done. If we can't put a stop to this haunting now, it's only going to get worse. The more afraid people get, the stronger that ghost will become, and the stronger she becomes, the more people she can hurt. If we're not careful, this will become a cycle that pretty much can't be stopped."

"How will you stop Mary?" I asked Mom, and her eyes slide from mine.

"Stay here with Maya, and when I get back, we'll fix this."

"*You'll* fix this, you mean," I muttered.

Normally, that would've gotten me a sharp "Isolde!" and a remark about talking back. But to my surprise, this time, Mom just crossed the kitchen and laid her palm against my cheek. "You've done great here. You've proven yourself, and I am proud of you. But it's time to walk away now."

The last time Mom had touched my face I'd been ten years old and she'd thought I had a fever. That must've been why I just nodded and said, "Okay."

Mom dropped her hand with a little smile. "Good."

Turning to Maya, she lifted a canvas bag off the table. "I'll call from the road."

"Bring her home, Ash," Maya said, stirring her concoction.

"I'm going to try," Mom replied, and with one last look at me, she was gone.

As soon as the front door closed, Maya opened a cabinet and began pulling out a couple of bowls. "You want some?" she asked, gesturing to the stove.

"Um . . . no. I've got something to do."

Before she could offer me anything else—eye of newt tea, bird's feet stew—I took off to the guest room.

Once the door was shut behind me I marched over to Torin's mirror, smacking the frame as hard as I could. He stumbled, falling against the bed. "What in the world are you doing?"

"Don't." I pointed at him. "I wanted to figure out what to do about Romy on my own. I trusted you."

"And I was only trying to help," he insisted. "You could've been hurt, and for what? A trio of ungrateful children? They turned on you, didn't they." It wasn't a question.

His words stung, but I tried not to let it show. "They didn't turn on me. They had every reason to suspect I was a freak because hey, news flash, I *am* a freak. It doesn't make them ungrateful. It makes them . . . smart."

Torin frowned. "Isolde—"

I reached out and covered his mirror, suddenly tired and sadder than I'd thought possible.

After trudging up the stairs I spent the rest of the afternoon putting my few belongings back in the duffel bag, and watching the last few episodes of *Ivy Springs*, season three. But somehow, even Everton and Leslie finally getting together (and riding off in a hot air balloon, which may have been even weirder than the episode where Leslie dreamed she and Everton were on the *Titanic*) still couldn't cheer me up. Once it was dark, I decided to go down to the kitchen and talk to Maya. Hopefully, she was done cooking.

She was humming when I walked in and puttering with the sad little basil plant Mom had bought at Walmart. It had been sitting, pathetic and abandoned, on our windowsill for a while.

"No bird's feet, I'm guessing?" Maya asked as I walked in.

"Fresh out," I told her. Now that the kitchen no longer smelled like Evil Magic, I thought I might try to cook some dinner. Maybe carbs would cheer me up where *Ivy Springs* had failed. As I pulled out a box of macaroni and cheese, Maya gave a cheerful smile.

"No matter," she said, heading for the fruit bowl in the middle of the table. I'd just done the grocery shopping a few days ago, so there were several apples and a couple of bananas in there. My pasta forgotten, I watched as Maya picked up two apples and one banana and laid them on either side of the basil plant. Muttering something under her breath, she held on to the little pot of basil, and the leaves began to turn green and bright. But as they did, the apples and banana shriveled, going brown.

Once the basil was as perky as it could possibly be, Maya reached up and took off one of the several silver hoops in her ears. "That's . . . bizarre," I said at last.

"Hedge magic!" she trilled with a little shrug.

I scowled. Real magic, hedge magic, all of it apparently led to the same place: with everything crappy and awful. But it wasn't just that. Something was bothering me. It made sense that Romy was the one summoning ghosts, whether she'd meant to or not, but there was still this little niggling doubt in the back of my mind. Romy was a terrible liar, but she'd looked genuinely confused and hurt in her bedroom today. And there hadn't been any guilt in her face when I'd shown her the heart charm, just puzzlement.

"Maya," I said as she continued to cluck over the plant, "let's say you have a hedge witch summoning ghosts, and the one she's summoned is all big and scary and dangerous."

Maya turned back to me, her eyes sad. "Honey, most of the time, you can just get a witch to send the ghost back herself."

Breathing a sigh of relief, I sat the box of pasta on the counter. "That's what I'd been thinking—"

"But," Maya interrupted. "This is not a normal case. The ghost is too powerful. By this point, the only way to stop that ghost is to sever the connection with the witch who did the summoning. Hedge witch, 'real' witch, it doesn't matter. Stop the witch, you stop the ghost."

I tore open the box of macaroni even though I was far from hungry anymore. "And by stop, you mean . . ."

"Kill, yes." She touched one of the charms around her neck. "It's unfortunate, but that's the way of it."

My feet were bare, and when I looked down I saw my bright red toenails. A lump rose in my throat. "She made a mistake. She did a dumb thing, but she shouldn't have to pay for it with her life. There has to be some other way."

When I glanced up, Maya was wringing her hands. "What?"

"It's just . . ." She broke off, huffing out a breath. "Oh, your mama would kill me if she knew I was even whispering about this, but . . . there's maybe one way. To sever the connection without severing your friend's jugular."

I pushed the box of macaroni away. "Yeah, I'm going to need to hear about that."

"But it's dangerous and potentially unstable, and is really one of those tricks best left to those Pro-whatchamacallit witches."

Leaning forward, I pressed my hands on the counter. "Maya, whatever it is, I'll try it."

She filled me in on what exactly the ritual would require—and do—and while by the end of it, my heart was pounding and my eyes were huge, I agreed that it sounded a lot better than letting my mom run Romy through with a dagger.

"Okay," I said, pointing at Maya. "You go get the supplies you need, I'll call Romy and get her over here."

But when I dialed Romy's cell there was no answer. She was probably avoiding me, and I couldn't blame her. Luckily, I had her house number too, and I dialed that.

Romy's mom answered, and when I said who I was, she sounded surprised. "Oh! Izzy. I thought for sure you'd be out with the rest of them."

My heart lodged somewhere in my throat. "The rest of who?"

"The club. Romy said you'd called a special meeting tonight."

"Oh, right," I said, even as my grip threatened to shatter the phone. "I totally spaced. Could you remind me where it is?"

There was a pause, and then Romy's mom sighed and said, "God, Izzy, you are going to think I am the worst mother, but I honestly don't remember." She gave a little laugh. "Such is life with triplets, I guess."

I did my best to laugh back, but I couldn't get off the phone fast enough. Hanging up with her, I hesitated only the briefest second before dialing another number.

It picked up on the first ring. "Izzy?"

"Dex," I said, but before I could get anything else out, he rushed in.

"Izzy, I'm so sorry about what happened this afternoon. You know I—"

"DEX!" I said again, and mercifully, he stopped babbling. "Are you with Romy and Anderson?"

I could hear him sigh. "No. After you left, I may have quit the club. Very dramatically, I should add, complete with—"

I liked Dex. A lot. Heck, maybe I even more than liked him. But in a crisis, he was not exactly user-friendly. "Do you know where they were going tonight?"

"Yeah," he answered immediately, and I nearly sagged with relief. "They were going to the cave. You know, the one where we—"

"Right, right," I hurried on. "Okay, I think I've worked out a way we can stop Mary Evans without hurting Romy."

"I was unaware Romy getting hurt was ever on the table."

"It's not," I said, looking over my shoulder to where Maya was throwing every canister of salt we had into a duffel bag. *At least I hope it's not.*

"Do you want me to meet you there?"

There was no time to think, but I still hesitated, just for a little bit. I did want him to come with me. Because no matter how things went tonight, once everything was over, I'd leave Ideal. This was probably my last chance to see him.

"No." It came out like kind of a croak, and I cleared my throat. "No, there's no need for you to come. I just need to make things right with Romy."

"Okay," he said, his voice lower than usual. "Izzy—"

I hung up. Whatever he was going to say next would probably just make all of this harder than it was. Besides, Maya was ready and I needed to go.

"Thanks," I said, taking the bag and holding out my free hand. "If you'll just give me your keys—"

But Maya blocked the front door, hands on her wide hips. "No way," she said. "I promised your Mom I'd watch you, and letting you run off to fight a hedge witch and a homicidal ghost is probably one of those things she'd frown on. Besides, you'll need my help with the ritual."

Reminding myself that decking old ladies is wrong, I took a deep breath. "Maya, I appreciate that, but my friends are in danger, and I have to help them. On my own."

But instead of being impressed with what I thought was a pretty stoic delivery, Maya laughed. "You Brannicks are always saying that." She dropped her voice an octave or so. "'I have to do this alone. This is my sole duty. I cannot accept help.'" Shaking her head, she said, "But you don't do it alone. You *never* have. There's always people like me, or that weirdo you keep in a mirror, or these kids at your school."

Leaning forward, she took me by the shoulders. "You aren't alone, Izzy. You or your mom or, when we find her, Finley. And whether you like it or not, you need help. And you're getting it. So get your skinny little butt in my car, and let's go kick some ghost ass."

CHAPTER 31

Anderson's car was parked outside of the cave when we pulled up. Leaning over the steering wheel, Maya whistled low. "Well, if this isn't the perfect setting for a ghost face-off, I don't know what is."

I looked into the mouth of the cave, but everything was dark. Still, they were in there, I was sure of it.

Getting out of the car, I walked to the trunk. Maya and I were just hefting out our bag of supplies when a splash of headlights lit up the gloom. "Who on earth—" Maya started, but I recognized the burgundy town car immediately.

Even though I should have been horrified, I couldn't stop the giddy leap of my heart or the sudden smile that wanted to break out over my face. The car stopped, and Dex loped out of the passenger side.

"I told you not to come," I said, walking over to him.

He threw up his hands. "And yet. Now, what are we doing here?"

He squinted past me at Maya, who was already toting the bag into the cave.

"Dex," I said, pushing my hands into my back pockets so I wouldn't do something stupid like hug him. "This could get— Wait, you didn't drive."

Running a hand up and down the back of his neck, Dex sighed. "Yes, my Nana had to drive me. You see, apparently, nearly being blown up at school was somehow my fault, so now I'm grounded. But when I explained that my Fair Isolde had need of me . . ."

I looked up into his blue eyes, taking in tonight's scarf, which was a riot of turquoise and purple. His curly black hair was sticking up, and oh man, he was right. I did need him. Kind of a lot.

Which was just so, so unfortunate.

"Dexter!" Nana called, rolling down her window.

"Ah, yes." He jogged back to the car, resting his hand on her windowsill and ducking his head inside. "Nana, Izzy needs me to go into this cave to get our friends. I'm going to help her with that, while you wait right here."

Nana smiled at me. "Hello, Izzy. Dexter, you know I always appreciate your being helpful, but this seems . . ."

She looked past us toward the cave, and Dex craned

his head over his shoulder, following her gaze. "I know it looks vaguely unsanitary and potentially scandalous, Nana, but I promise that Izzy and I are only pursuing noble . . . pursuits. We've even got a chaperone! Izzy, who was that woman who went into the cave?"

I blanked, not sure how to describe Maya. I settled on, "My . . . also my Nana."

"See?" Dex said brightly, ducking his head in to kiss his Nana's cheek. "Izzy's Nana! We are totally safe and appropriate."

I wasn't sure Nana was convinced, but she pursed her lips and said, "No longer than ten minutes, Dexter."

He gave her a jaunty salute, and we turned and walked into the mouth of the cave.

Maya was in the first chamber, spreading salt. It was to Dex's credit that he just took her in with a "Huh," and followed me deeper into the cave.

"Okay, so—" I started, but then his hand grasped my shoulders, turning me so that my back was against the cavern wall.

"I like you."

Bewildered, I blinked at him. "What?"

"I. Like. You," Dex repeated, and for once there was no glimmer in his eyes, no smile lurking on his lips. "I have since that morning on the track, and I should've made that clearer by now."

Somewhere in this cave, Romy and Anderson were very possibly in danger. "Dex, seriously, now is not the—"

"No," he said, giving me a little shake. "There is never going to be the right time, Izzy. I've figured that out by now. Every time I try to tell you this, you brush it off or don't let me finish, or someone tries to blow up the gym. So I'm telling you now. I like you. And it has nothing to do with spells or near-death excitement or any of the other BS excuses you like to come up with."

"Dex," I said again, helplessly.

"And you like me, too," he went on, and there, at last, was the smile. "That's not just me being arrogant, by the way. Although I understand that that's sometimes a problem. But"—he hurried on when I opened my mouth to reply—"I can work on that. If you want. Even though I think you secretly like that, too."

Maybe it was knowing that we were about to walk into something really scary. Maybe I was afraid that, even if I didn't get killed tonight, Dex might. Or maybe I just really wanted to kiss him. In any case, I fisted my hands in the front of his shirt and jerked him to me. Our lips met, and if this kiss wasn't as . . . thorough as the first one, it felt bigger somehow. More important.

"You're right," I panted, once I'd wrenched my mouth from his. "I like you. A lot. And I just wanted you to know that, too. But—"

Dex just kissed me again, a quick peck on the lips, really. "No," he whispered. "No buts. Now. Let's go get Romy and Anderson."

Almost as though his words had summoned it, there was a sudden flare of blue light from farther back in the cave system. "Crap," I muttered, tugging Dex's hand.

We followed a twisting, narrow path that finally opened up onto a bigger chamber. Keeping Dex behind me, I walked in, not sure what I was going to see.

But it was just Anderson, his back to us. Dex blew out a relieved breath. "Oh, there you are, man. We were—"

But then Anderson began backing up slowly, his hands held out at his sides. As he turned, we could see Romy standing in front of him. Blue light pulsed all around her, and Mary Evans suddenly appeared, standing just in front of Romy, almost like she was superimposed over her. She wore a long white dress, and her blond hair was plastered to her face.

Then Mary vanished, and Romy was there again, holding a long silver knife to Anderson's chest.

Dex hissed a four-letter word under his breath, and I held my arm out, keeping him behind me.

Romy glanced over at me, her face briefly becoming Mary's again. The effect was unsettling and awful. "I wanted you," she said, two voices coming out of Romy's mouth. "You felt strong and . . . different. I thought if I could get inside of you, I could burn the world."

I stepped back slightly, pushing Dex. "I'm actually not much of a fan of world burning, so . . ."

Romy laughed, and it echoed eerily in the cavern. "It doesn't matter. I can make this one pay." She jabbed at Anderson with the knife, and he gave a startled sound of pain.

"Anderson didn't do anything to you," I said, but she laughed again, shaking her head, her features flipping between Romy's and Mary's so quickly they blurred.

"No, but the men who did are dead."

"No one hurt you," Anderson said, his voice wavering. "Y-you died of exposure."

Grinning, Mary/Romy flicked the knife. One of the buttons on Anderson's shirt went flying off into the darkness.

"That's what they say, isn't it? That I froze, all alone, waiting for my child's father. A tragic fate, but not a cruel one. Freezing to death is supposed to be peaceful. Like slipping into a warm bath and then a long sleep." She stepped closer, and I saw the very tip of the knife pierce Anderson's chest. "But burning to death? That is very. Far. From. PEACEFUL."

She screamed the last word, and all of us cringed as it bounced off the rock walls. "That's what they did, you know," Mary said. She was completely Mary now, even though it was Romy's face and Romy's body. Romy's eyes had never radiated that much hate. "My father and his friends. When they found me playing at spells. Nothing dangerous, nothing harmful. Just a love charm to make the man I wanted mine."

Smiling, Mary kept advancing on Anderson even as he backed up. A thin trickle of blood ran down his shirt. "And do you know what these good, righteous men of Ideal, Mississippi, did? They dragged me to this cave, saying 'thou shalt not suffer a witch to live,' and they set me on fire."

"I'm so sorry," I said, and I was. I thought of that sweet, shy, smiling girl in the picture. She hadn't deserved to die like that. No one did. But that didn't mean I could let her hurt innocent people.

"And now," Mary continued, "I will make everyone suffer."

She lunged forward, but I was ready. Grabbing Anderson's arm, I spun him away from Mary, shoving him toward Dex and the passageway. Mary's blade sunk into my arm, the pain somehow icy cold and burning at the same time, but I gritted my teeth and struck out with my other hand. The blow sent her reeling backward. "That's the thing with possessing people," I said, pushing the boys out of the cavern. "People have *bodies*, which makes them a lot easier to beat up than a ghost."

Mary screamed in rage, but I kept pushing Dex and Anderson, praying I'd given Maya the time she needed to set everything up.

We came tearing into the main cavern, our feet skidding on the salt covering the floor. Maya stood at the ready, and when Mary ran in, Maya shouted a word.

The effect was instant and painful. The whole cavern seemed to ring like a bell, and Mary shrieked, falling to her knees.

Once again, she started to flicker, part Mary, part Romy. Maya watched her, eyes wide.

"Where's the witch?"

"That's her," I said, breathing hard and pointing at Romy where she knelt on the ground. "The ghost is in her, it . . . it possessed her."

Maya was holding some kind of herbs in one hand and an ancient-looking book in the other. She let both drop to the ground. "Oh, hon," she said, so sad. "Then there's nothing I can do. The witch and the ghost, they have to be separate for this ritual to work."

Romy was writhing on the floor as though the salt was burning her. There was nothing of the girl I knew in her face, but I couldn't bear the thought of having to kill her. Not when she'd painted my toenails and made me laugh and been the first person I'd ever called friend.

Maya came to my side, holding out the small silver dagger she'd brought, *Just in case.*

Automatically, I tried to shove the dagger back toward her, but Maya gently pressed the hilt into my palm. "Sweetheart, she's in pain. A lot of it. If this doesn't work, you need to set her free."

Bile rose in my throat.

"Do you want me to do it?" Maya asked, and next to me, both Dex and Anderson stared.

"Do what?" Anderson asked just as Dex said, "I know you're not suggesting what—"

But I ignored them both. This was my fault. If I'd done something the instant I'd found out Romy had summoned Mary, maybe there would have been enough time. Maybe we could've fixed it before Mary got so strong. And if this didn't stop now, every person in Ideal would be in danger. Mary's rage would get stronger and stronger, her desire to hurt even more intense. This had to end.

And I had to be the one to end it.

My hand closed around the hilt of the dagger, but before I could take it from Maya, a voice rang out in the cave. "Dexter?"

The four of us turned slowly to see Dexter's Nana. She was wearing a sweatshirt embroidered with kittens, and the firelight turned her glasses into glowing orbs.

"Nana, I can explain," Dex said, as his gaze swung from me and the dagger back to Romy, crumpled on the floor, and back again.

"Oh, dear," Nana said, stepping forward. "I believe this may be all my fault."

CHAPTER 32

"Nana, how on earth could this be your fault?"

She nodded at Romy. "There's . . . there's a ghost in that young girl, isn't there?"

Dumbly, all four of us nodded.

Nana sniffed. "Yes, that's what I thought. Mary Evans. You know, she was the local legend when I was a girl growing up here. There were rumors she was a witch and . . ." She broke off with a chuckle. "Well, maybe I sympathized with her. I had always done the odd little charm myself."

She stopped suddenly, moving closer to Dex, who was watching her with a mixture of horror and confusion. "I didn't mean to do it." Her hand, as it cupped his cheek, was trembling. "But you were lying there on the floor, and you couldn't breathe."

Dex reared back slightly. "What?"

Nana shook her head, tears sliding down her face. "Your chest, it—it kept moving, but no air was getting in, and your eyes . . ." She gave a shuddering sigh. "Those beautiful eyes were so scared. I'd been doing hedge magic all my life. Bringing back plants, doing the odd luck spell. It's why my cooking is so good. So in that moment, I just . . . acted. Said the words to a spell I'd done a hundred times to make my petunias bloom."

Clearing her throat, she reached into her handbag and pulled out a tissue. As she dabbed at her eyes, Nana said, "And then you were back. Just like that. Killed every plant within a ten-block radius, but you were back. So I put my silver bracelet on you, and I . . . I hoped." She nodded at the bracelet. "That's what anchors the spell, what anchors your soul in your body."

"But it wasn't enough," I said softly, remembering Maya just that evening, bringing our basil plant back to life.

Nana gave a little laugh. "No, it wasn't. A human soul is a powerful thing, Izzy. It takes so much power to hold it. And no matter how many plants or birds or stray dogs I drained, it was like I could feel Dex's soul flickering. So I looked to other spell books, tried other rituals."

"And ended up summoning a really pissed-off ghost."

"An unfortunate side effect," she sniffed. "But really,

I've just been delaying the inevitable. Until an entire human life force is drained off, given to Dex, his existence is just . . . temporary."

Finally I understood what I'd sensed when I had touched Dex. No wonder he'd felt both magic and non-magic. Magic was keeping him alive. In his own way, he was a ghost. Or a zombie. Which meant I'd kissed . . .

No, definitely a ghost.

Dex was shaking his head and blinking, backing away from his Nana. "No," he said, hands trembling. "No, no, no, that is not possible. I can't be dead, and this"—he hooked one finger under his bracelet— "can't be the only thing keeping me alive."

Nana calmly regarded him through her glasses. "Take it off, then."

"No!" I cried, as Dex started to tug at the silver around his wrist. But he froze, finger coiled around the metal. "I can't."

"Compulsion spell," Nana said. "I didn't want to risk anything."

Knees giving out, Dex sunk to the floor, head in one hand. "No," he said, but I could see a tear splash down into the salt. When he lifted his face, his eyes were red. "Nana, how could you do something like . . ." Trailing off, he looked at Romy, crumpled and sobbing, clearly in pain. "That's because of me. Mr. Snyder, a-and Beth

Tanner, and the gym. And now Romy, the first friend I made at that stupid school, is possessed by a freaking vengeful ghost that you summoned because you were so busy trying to keep me alive."

Dex was crying, but he got up off the floor, dusting the salt from his pin-striped pants. "I'm not letting that happen. If I die, will this stop? Will the-the energy or whatever is powering the ghost shut down?"

Behind him, Maya shook her head no, but Dex was already tugging at his bracelet again. "Because I'll take this off. If me dying means that Romy can be okay, then I'm fine with that. Apparently I've been living on borrowed time anyway."

His whole body was shaking, but he held his chin high and his gaze was steady. He would do it, I had no doubt.

Nana stepped forward, trying to cup his face, but he flinched from her touch. "No, sweet boy," she said gently. "This isn't all your fault. It's mine. I just . . ." Her voice wavered, and this time, when she tried to touch him, Dex let her, albeit reluctantly. "I just loved you so much. And I'm so sorry I've hurt people, but I'm so glad I got this extra year with you."

Confused, Dex shook his head, but Nana was already moving toward Romy. Kneeling down, she patted Romy's hair and then reached into her handbag and pulled out a tiny blade. I stepped forward, but Maya caught my arm.

In a series of quick moves, Nana sliced an X into her palm and laid her bloody hand on Romy's back. Then she smiled at Dex. "I love you," she told him.

Dex, still shaking, only stared at her.

Nana looked to Romy, who had flickered back to Mary. "I'm sorry," she told her. "I should have let you rest. I had no idea what had really been done to you, or how angry you were."

"Nana—" Dex said, but she just ducked her head and whispered something. The light that filled the cave was blinding and sudden, and came with a concussive boom that made us all stagger backward.

When I could finally see again, Romy was sitting up, blearily shaking her head while Anderson knelt down next to her. "Um, ow," she murmured, and it was so clearly Romy—only Romy—that a sudden sob of relief welled up in my throat.

But then there was another sob. Dex was on his knees by his Nana. Her eyes were closed and she was smiling slightly, but there was no doubt she was gone.

He lifted his tearstained face to me and Maya. "What happened?"

Maya shook her head. "I'm not sure. I've never heard that spell she used before." Crouching down, she gently

lifted Dex's hand from Nana's back. His shoulders were heaving, and I wanted to say something, do something, but I had no idea where to start.

Without warning, Maya flicked the clasp on Dex's bracelet and I darted forward, hand out. "Maya!"

The bracelet fell harmlessly to the ground, but Dex stayed right where he was. Still breathing—well, wheezing actually. He fished his inhaler out of his pocket and jammed it into his mouth, eyes on the bracelet.

Once his breathing sounded normal again, Maya laid a hand on his shoulder. "That's what I thought. She knew that the only way to stop Mary was for her to die. But whatever that spell was, it didn't just kill her, it . . . transferred her. Put her life energy into you."

Dex lowered the inhaler. "So, I'm . . . not going to die?"

Shrugging, Maya picked up the bracelet and pressed it into Dex's palm. "Well, eventually you will, just like we all will. But not today." With that, she pulled Dex into a hug.

In shock, Dex raised his arms almost numbly and draped them around her neck.

"Nana did the right thing in the end," Maya said. "And she did it for you."

If Dex replied, I couldn't hear it.

CHAPTER 33

"So, you were . . . dead."

"Romy," I warned, but she just shrugged and pulled the blanket tighter around her.

"Look, I get that he's traumatized, but hey, I am, too."

"We all are," Anderson muttered.

The four of us were sitting in my living room, Romy and Anderson huddled on the couch, me in the one recliner we had, and Dex at my feet, his arms wrapped around his knees, a blanket over his shoulders. He hadn't said anything since we'd left the cave.

But now he looked at Romy, and a ghost of his old grin crossed his face. "Yeah, I was. And *still* better looking than any of the other guys at Mary Evans High." His voice wavered a little at the end, and he went back

to chewing his thumbnail. I wanted to lay my hand on top of his head or pat his back. Something. Instead, I crossed my arms over my chest.

"So he was dead," Romy reiterated, nodding at Dex. "And you"—she looked at me—"you're some kind of awesome monster slayer."

"I don't feel so awesome right now," I muttered. Maybe because no monsters had been slain. Sure, we'd stopped the hedge witch and brought an end to the hauntings, but this didn't feel even a little bit like winning. Not when I looked at Dex's shattered expression. His Nana hadn't been evil. Just wrong. And to be honest, I wondered if she'd even been that. What would I have done to bring Finley back if I could've? Or my mom if something happened to her? When you don't have much family left, you'll do anything to protect what you have.

The front door opened and we all jumped, but it was just Maya.

Dex stood up as she came in. "You took care of her?" he asked. "You didn't just . . . leave her there?"

Maya had stayed behind at the cave to, in her words, "put things to rights." Now she patted Dexter's arm, sympathy written all over her broad face. "I did. With respect. She was a sister, and we have ways of handling these things."

Confused, Dex stared at her. "A sis— Oh, right,

because you were both witches. Because that's real. That's a thing that really happens, and my Nana was one."

He went back to sitting and chewing.

Letting him have a moment, I turned to Romy and Anderson. "So if it was Dex's Nana accidentally raising ghosts, why was your charm in that cave?" I asked Romy.

Grimacing, she took another sip of the tea Maya had made. "I told you, I have no idea. I lost the stupid thing."

From the other end of the couch, Anderson cleared his throat. "Um . . . I might actually know why. I took the charm."

Romy's blanket slipped off her shoulders as she sat up. "You what? Why?"

Anderson's face was bright red, matching the plaid throw draped around him. "I saw this thing on the Internet about doing a . . . a love spell." He mumbled the last words so much that it sounded like he said, "abub-smell."

"You did a love spell on me?" Romy said, her "me" becoming a shriek.

"Yes!" Anderson said, tossing the blanket off and getting up to pace the living room. "And I know that's awful, and I shouldn't have, but . . . I liked you, and I thought it couldn't hurt." He hung his head a little. "So that's why we kissed at the graveyard that night. I'm sorry."

Huh. So Dex and I hadn't been the only ones using our PMS field trip romantically.

Romy slugged Anderson on the shoulder. "You idiot," she cried. "Did you do the love spell in eighth grade?"

"What? No. I did it, like, last month."

"Well, eighth grade is when I started liking you," Romy said, hitting him again. "So no, it wasn't the love spell that made me kiss you in the graveyard. And it's not the love spell making me kiss you now."

With that, she grabbed the front of his shirt and yanked his mouth down to hers.

It had been an awful night. A night so full of bad, even Everton and Leslie would've shuddered, and they had once spent a night getting chased by a serial killer on a train. But seeing Romy and Anderson kiss, I smiled. They were safe and happy, and that had to be worth something.

Looking over at Dex, I saw that he was smiling, too. Our eyes met, and I wondered if he was thinking the same thing.

The four of us, plus Maya, sat there for another hour or so before Romy and Anderson decided they should head home. As they walked to the door, I stopped Romy. "Look, I'm sorry about—"

She pulled me into a hug before I had time to finish. "I'm sorry, too."

I wrapped my arms tight around her, hugging her back, and when she pulled away, I hoped she wouldn't see the tears in my eyes. "I'm probably going to take tomorrow off from school," she said. "And you should, too. Maybe you could come over? See if Leslie survives that polar bear attack?"

My throat tightened, but I made myself nod. "Sure. I'd like that."

Once they were gone, Maya went into the kitchen, ostensibly to make some more tea, but really to give me and Dex some alone time, I think.

I counted sixteen of my own heartbeats before he said, "She won't see you tomorrow, will she?"

There was no sense in lying. "No. As soon as my mom gets back, we'll leave."

"And do what?" he asked, looking up at me. "Go to some other town? Fight some other evil?"

"Your Nana wasn't evil, Dex," I said, but he shook his head.

"You know what I mean."

I sighed. "Yeah. We will."

Standing up, clutching the blanket in front of him, Dex met my eyes. "Great. Because I'm coming with you."

"Dex," I said, but he cut me off.

"Look, I know you have to do the big hero thing

of, 'no, I must work alone, my love for you can only be a hindrance,' but . . . Izzy, what else am I supposed to do?" His voice quavered. "My parents are dead. My Nana is . . . is dead. And magic and monsters are apparently *real*. I can't just forget that. And I get that if you more or less adopt me, that will make things weird for us, but we don't have to be . . . We could just be friends."

I looked into Dex's blue eyes, remembering how brave he'd been. He'd been willing to die to save Romy's life, willing to do it in an instant. He might not be able to run or fight, but Dex had the biggest heart of anyone I knew. And I needed that. I needed him.

"I think there may be a friend-shaped spot for you, yeah," I said softly, and he smiled.

"But first—" I hesitated, chewing my lower lip. "I . . . I need to show you something."

Turning, I led Dex down the hall to the guest room.

I paused with my hand on the doorknob. "What I'm about to show you, it . . . it's pretty weird," I warned him.

"Oh, right, because everything else that happened tonight was totally typical." He was going for quippy, but there were tears streaking his cheeks and his voice sounded shaky.

Normally, I would've smiled at his attempt at humor, but what I was about to do was too big for smiling, and

Dex must've sensed that. "Sorry," he said, laying a hand on my arm. "I just mean . . . whatever weirdness there is, I'm prepared for it."

I didn't think there was any way he could be, but I nodded. "Okay, then."

Torin's mirror was covered up when I opened the door, but I could hear him as he said, "Ah, you're back! All hail the conquering hero."

Dex paused in the doorway. "Who was that?"

"You're braced for weird, right?" I asked, moving toward the mirror.

He visibly swallowed, but after a second, Dex nodded. "Braced. Weird. Bring it."

I pulled the canvas down from the mirror, and there stood Torin, leaning against the bed as always. Dex glanced back and forth between the bed in the mirror and the bed in the room before letting out a slow breath. "Okay. Yeah, that is . . . that is weird, all right."

"Who the sodding hell is this?" Torin narrowed his eyes. "Oh, right. That boy who plays all the video games. The one Isolde fancies."

"Torin," I said warningly, but Dex smiled a little even as his eyes roamed over Torin's mirror.

"Oi," Torin snapped. "Fancy-dress boy, my eyes are up here."

Dex met those eyes, one corner of his mouth still

290

lifted in a half-grin. "'Fancy-dress boy?' This from a dude who dresses like Prince?"

I snorted with laughter and Torin scowled. "Prince who?"

Then Dex laughed, too, and after a while, the sound actually sounded normal and not choked with tears.

"I do not like him," Torin declared, pointing at Dex. "I disapprove of your choice of paramour *immensely*."

"He's not my paramour," I said, rolling my eyes. "He's my friend."

"Right," Dex said, finally letting the blanket slip from his shoulders. Rolling them as though he were free of a great weight, he looked down at me and stuck his hand out. "Friends."

We shook on it, and there was no tingle of magic this time. But that didn't mean I didn't feel anything. Dex's eyes held mine and I knew I should pull my hand back, but suddenly that was the last thing I wanted to do.

"I am going to be sick," Torin muttered, turning away. "Completely, riotously sick right here in the mirror; and let me tell you, that is *quite* a mess."

"So is this." Dex and I both turned to see Mom in the doorway, but before I could say anything, she strode in, a hammer raised high in one fist. With a shriek, we jumped apart as Mom brought the hammer down as hard as she could on Torin's mirror.

CHAPTER 34

"Mom!" I cried as a few shards flew up, making tiny scratches along Mom's arms. But she didn't seem to feel them. Torin staggered backward, and in the mirror, the table teetered, nearly falling.

For four hundred years, Torin had aggravated and frustrated Brannicks, but he'd always been a part of our lives. I'd always assumed there was some kind of rule that we couldn't hurt him. After all, if he could be destroyed, wouldn't someone have done it by now, to heck with prophecies?

The frame shook, and Torin grimaced. Or at least I thought he did. It was hard to tell what was going on in all those fractured pieces.

Mom stood there, breathing hard, the hammer raised. Blood dripped down her arms, but she didn't seem to notice it. I waited for the glass to fall out of the frame, for Torin to become nothing more than a handful of shards.

There was no flash of light or smell of smoke. None of the stuff you expect when magic is happening around you. Just a soft *pop!* and suddenly Torin was complete again. The glass wasn't even scratched, much less cracked.

"That was uncalled for," he said, straightening his jerkin.

"You lied to me," Mom growled. "You told me you had seen Finley, and then sent me on a wild-goose chase while Izzy nearly got killed."

Her gaze moved to me, her face full of anger and worry and something else I couldn't name.

"*He* was your source?" I asked, pointing at Torin. "You're always telling me not to trust him, and—"

"With good reason," Mom said, and now I understood what was in her voice. She was angry not just with Torin, but with herself.

"Izzy needed a chance to spread her wings, Aislinn," Torin said, giving a bored shrug. "And you needed to get out of her way. She handled herself masterfully tonight. Proved to be a true Brannick."

Mom watched him for a long time. "She's always been a true Brannick," she said at last. Then she strode forward and grabbed the canvas, covering Torin. "We're done," she said, more to herself than anyone else. "We should've been done with him a long time ago."

She turned back, and for the first time seemed to notice Dex. "Who is this?"

"I'm Dexter O'Neil, Mrs. Brannick," Dex said, offering his hand to shake. "And I'm hoping you'll adopt me."

Mom looked back and forth between the two of us before muttering, "I need a drink," and walking out of the room.

In the silence that followed, I raised an eyebrow at Dex. "So . . . this is my family. Sure you want in?"

Dex looked back and forth between the door and Torin's mirror. "My Nana was a witch who kept me alive by raising evil ghosts. The bar for family dysfunction has already been set pretty high."

Half an hour later, we all sat at the kitchen table—me, Dex, Mom, and Maya. I told Mom everything that had happened at the cave. When I got to the part about Maya handing me the knife, she looked up. "Would you have killed her?" she asked. "If it meant destroying the ghost?"

I thought about it, turning my cup of tea around in my hands. "I don't know," I finally said. I knew it probably wasn't the answer Mom wanted, but it was the honest one. "I don't think so. I think I would've tried to find some other way, no matter what."

To my surprise, Mom smiled and reached out. She didn't quite tousle my hair—her hand moved too roughly for that—but it was an affectionate gesture nonetheless. "You're a good kid, Izzy," she said. "Sometimes that's what being a Brannick means. It's not always about storming in and saving the day yourself. It's about the willingness to do whatever it takes to keep people safe. I still don't like that Torin lied to me—especially about Finn—but—"

"I don't like him either," Dex said, speaking up for the first time since we'd sat down. "Both for lying to you, and just sort of on general principle. For the record."

The corner of Mom's mouth lifted in a half smile. "Good to know. So what are we supposed to do with you, Dexter O'Neil?"

Dex leaned back in his chair, trying to affect that super-casual thing he usually did so well. But his hands were shaking and his face looked ravaged. "Well, I may not have superpowers, and it's true my asthma may get in the way of much monster chasing, but I did used to be dead, and I faced down a terrifying ghost tonight. So, I'd like to . . . join your gang. Or whatever. There aren't any initiation rituals involving blood, are there?" He shuddered, and Mom cut her eyes at me.

I gave a little shrug.

"You understand why I might be hesitant to let my daughter's boyfriend move in with us, right?"

"I'm not her boyfriend," Dex said, his voice

completely serious. "I'm just her friend. I swear." He lifted his hand in what I think was supposed to be a Boy Scout salute but just ended up looking like a vaguely obscene gesture.

Mom turned back to me. "That true, Iz? This guy is nothing more than a friend?"

I looked at Dex and ignored the twisting in my heart. He was right. So we had liked each other. We could get over that. Especially if it meant Dex could stay with us.

"It is," I told her.

Sighing, Mom stood up and braced her hands on her lower back. "Well, we've solved Ideal's ghost problem. So where to next?"

Maya leaned back in her seat. "I have at least three file folders for you to look through. Couple of interesting cases just came in over the last few weeks."

Mom nodded. "Good. And there's another thing." She laid both hands on the table, leaning in so that she could meet my eyes. "Yes, the research I've been doing is about Finley. I've been trying to track the history of the coven Finn was with the night she disappeared, reading up on other vanishings, seeing if there's anything, any scrap that can help us find her. And I didn't tell you because I . . ." She looked down, flexing her fingers. "I didn't want to get your hopes up if it all came to nothing."

I reached out and covered her hand with my own. "Mom, knowing is better than not knowing every time, okay?"

After a moment, she squeezed back. "Okay." Then, slapping her palms on the table, she straightened up. "So we have more monsters to fight, places to go, and your sister to find. We have our work cut out for us."

Clearing his throat, Dex leaned forward and raised his eyebrows. "And does that 'we' include me?"

Mom looked down at me, and I could read the question in her eyes. If I said yes, she'd let Dex come with us. Which would mean traveling with Dex. *Living* with Dex.

But that would be fine. So we'd kissed a few times. It wasn't like we'd had some long-lasting relationship or anything. Surely downgrading to "just friends" and, basically, "work partners" would be easy enough. No matter how blue his eyes were.

I gave Mom the tiniest nod, and she returned it.

Putting one hand on Dex's shoulder, Mom gave him a little shake, making him wince. "Welcome to the Brannick family, Dexter."

Acknowledgments

Massive thanks to my editor, Catherine Onder, for all the hard work she put into making Izzy, Dex, Torin, and Company be the best and shiniest they could be! Also thanks to Lisa Yoskowitz for taking such good care of me and the book; and to Hayley Wagreich for being such a freaking Wonder Girl.

As always, thanks to my Agent of Amazingness, Holly Root, without whom none of my books would ever have been written, much less published.

Hugs and tea for Victoria Schwab, who claimed Dex as her own roughly five minutes after she read his first scene, so sorry, ladies (and Izzy).

Thanks to everyone at Disney-Hyperion for giving me and my books such a lovely home over the years.

Big, big thanks to all of my family and friends, who put up with me when I lock myself in a room for days, muttering things like, "But how would you kill a ghost?" Y'all are the bestest and I love you.

And to all of my readers: thank you, thank you, thank you. You're all lovely and amazing, and I'm so lucky to have each and every one of you.

STORM TRACK

Margaret Maron

Thorndike Press • Thorndike, Maine

Published in 2000 by arrangement with Warner Books, Inc.

Thorndike Press Large Print Mystery Series.

The tree indicium is a trademark of Thorndike Press.

The text of this Large Print edition is unabridged.
Other aspects of the book may vary from the original edition.

Set in 16 pt. Plantin.

Printed in the United States on permanent paper.

Library of Congress Cataloging-in-Publication Data

Maron, Margaret.
    Storm track / Margaret Maron.
       p. cm.
     ISBN 0-7862-2465-7 (lg. print : hc : alk. paper)
     1. Knott, Deborah (Fictitious character) — Fiction.
  2. North Carolina — Fiction. 3. Women judges — Fiction.
  4. Hurricanes — Fiction. 5. Large type books. I. Title.
  PS3563.A679 S76   2000b
   813'.54—dc21   00-026167

For Sarah Nell Johnson Weaver:
First cousin, friend first

Acknowledgments

As always, I am indebted to many for their help and technical advice, in particular: District Court Judges Shelly S. Holt, John W. Smith, and Rebecca W. Blackmore of the 5th Judicial District Court (New Hanover and Pender Counties, NC).

Belated thanks to Gail Harrell, Regional Library Supervisor of the Southeast Regional Library, who let me plug my laptop into her office socket when Hurricane Fran took away my electricity for a week.

Thanks also to Irv Coats, the generous and knowledgeable proprietor of The Reader's Corner, who always hands me the perfect source book.

Man is tinder, woman is fire,
and the devil is a mighty wind.

Attributed to St. Jerome

DEBORAH KNOTT'S FAMILY TREE

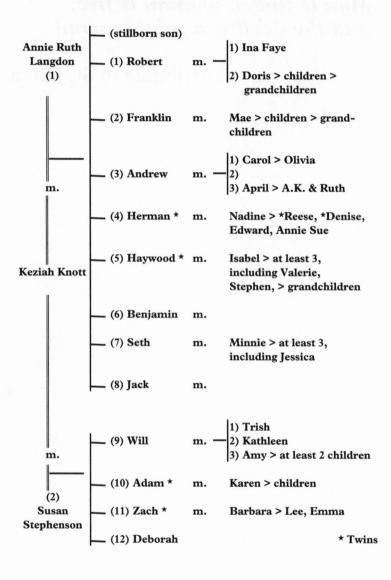

Late August

Afternoon shadows shaded the dip in the deserted dirt road where a battered Chevy pickup sat with the motor idling. On the driver's side, a puff of pale blue smoke drifted through the open window as the old man inside lit a cigarette and waited. The two dogs in back tasted the sultry air and one of them stuck its head through the sliding rear window. The man reached up and rubbed the silky ears.

A few minutes later, a green Ford pickup approached from the opposite direction and pulled even with the Chevy. The old man acknowledged them with a nod, then stubbed out his cigarette and dropped it on the sandy roadbed.

"Evening, Mr. Kezzie," said the stocky, heavyset driver who appeared to be in his early fifties. His hair was thinning across the crown and his face was lined from squinting through a windshield at too many sunrises.

The other, younger man was probably early thirties. He wore a neat blue shirt that had wet sweat circles under the arms.

Kezzie Knott peered past the driver. "This your cousin's boy?"

The older man nodded. "Norwood Love, Ben Joe's youngest."

"I knowed your daddy when he was a boy," Kezzie said, tapping another cigarette from the crumpled pack in his shirt pocket. "Good man till they shipped him off to Vietnam."

"That's what I hear." Norwood Love's jaw tightened. "I only knowed him after he come back."

And won't asking for no pity, thought Kezzie as he took a deep drag on his cigarette. Well, that part won't none of his business. Exhaling smoke, he said, "He the one taught you how to make whiskey?"

"Him and Sherrill here."

"I done told him, Mr. Kezzie, how you won't have no truck with a man that makes bad whiskey," his cousin said earnestly. "Told him ain't nobody never gone blind drinking stuff you had aught to do with."

"And that's the way I aim to keep it," Kezzie said mildly as he examined the cigarette in his gnarled fingers. There was no threat in his voice, but the young man nodded as if taking an oath.

"All I use is hog feed, grain, sugar and good clean water. No lye or wood alcohol and I ain't never run none through no radiator neither."

Kezzie Knott heard the sturdy pride in his voice. "Ever been caught?"

"No, sir."

"Sherrill says you got a safe place to set up."

"Yessir. It's —"

Kezzie held up his hand. "Don't tell me. Sherrill's word's good enough. And your'n." His clear blue eyes met the younger man's. "Sherrill says you was thinking eight thousand?"

"I know that's a lot, but —"

"No, it ain't. Not if you're going to do a clean operation, stainless steel vats and cookers."

He leaned over and took a thick envelope from the glove compartment and passed it across to Norwood Love. "Count it."

When the younger man had finished counting, he looked up at the other two. "Don't you want me to sign a paper or something?"

"What for?" asked Kezzie Knott, with the first hint of a smile on his lips. "Sherrill's told you my terms and you aim

11

to deal square, don't you?"

"Yessir."

"Well, then? Ain't no piece of paper gonna let me take you to court if you don't."

"I reckon not."

"Besides" — a sardonic tone slipped into his voice — "there don't need to be nothing connecting me to you if your place ain't as safe as you think it is."

As Norwood Love started to thank him, Kezzie Knott touched the brim of his straw hat to them, then put the truck in gear and pulled away through August heat and August humidity that had laid a haze across the countryside.

Ought to've paid more mind to the noon weather report, the old man told himself as he headed the truck toward home. Thick and heavy as this air was, he reckoned they might get another thunderstorm before bedtime.

Automatically he took a mental inventory of the farm — not just the homeplace but all the land touching his that his sons now owned and farmed.

Cotton was holding up all right, and soybeans and corn could take a little more rain without hurting bad, but all this water was leaching nutrients from the sandy soil.

Bolls was starting to crack though so it was too late to spray the cotton with urea to get the nitrogen up enough to finish it off. Tobacco had so much water lately, it was all greened up again. Curing schedule shot to hell. Just as well, he supposed, since the ground was so soggy along the bottoms you couldn't get tractors in without bogging down.

Playing hell with the garden, too. Maidie was fussing about watery tomatoes and how mold on the field peas was turning 'em to mush. That second sowing of butter beans won't faring so good neither — them fuzzy yellow beetle larvy making lace outen the leaves. Every time him or Cletus dusted 'em, along come the rain to wash off all the Sevin before it had a chance to kill 'em.

The boys was worried, but that's what it was to be a farmer. First you lay awake praying for rain, then you lay awake praying for it to quit. You done it 'most your whole life, he thought. All them years Sue tried to make you put farming over whiskey. Got to be a habit after a while. Certainly was for the boys.

And now another round of hurricanes setting up to blow in more rain?

Deb'rah won't going to be any happier

'bout more rain than the boys. She said she was about to get eat up out there by the pond. Fish couldn't keep up with the eggs them mosquitoes was laying in this weather.

Through the open back window, Ladybelle's nose nudged the back of his neck. Kezzie took a final drag on his cigarette and stubbed the butt in his overflowing ashtray.

"Still don't see why she had to go and build out there when the homeplace is setting almost empty," he grumbled to the dogs.

Chapter 1

The situation . . . is portrayed day by day exactly as it existed, and is not the product of imaginings of writers who put down what the conditions should have been; the storm has been followed from its inception.

August 31 — Hurricane Edouard is now 31° North by 70.5° West. Wind speed approx. 90 knots. (Note: 1 kt. = 1 nautical mile per hour.) (Note: a nautical mile is about 800 ft. longer than a land mile or .15 of a land mi.)

Math was not Stan Freeman's strongest subject. In the margin of his notebook, the boy laboriously scribbled the computations so he'd have the formula handy:

90 kts. =

90 + (90 x .15) =

He rummaged in his bookbag for his calculator.

The fan in his open window stirred the

air but did little to cool the small bedroom. Perspiration gleamed on his dark skin. His red Chicago Bulls tank top clung damply to his chest. It'd been an oversized Christmas present from his little sister Lashanda, yet was already too tight. His distinctly non-stylish sneakers lay under the nightstand so his feet could breathe free. Three sizes in six months. After he outgrew a new pair in one month, Kmart look-alikes were all his mother would buy "till your body settles down."

At eleven and a half, it was as if his limbs had suddenly erupted. The pudginess that had lingered since babyhood was gone now, completely melted away into bony arms and legs that stretched him almost as tall as his tall father. He was glad to be taller. Short kids got no respect. Now if he could just do something about his head. It felt out of proportion, too big for his gangling body, and he kept his bushy hair clipped as short as his mother would allow so as not to draw attention to the disparity.

At the moment, though, he wasn't thinking of his appearance. Using his light-powered calculator, he multiplied ninety by point fifteen, then finished writing out his conversion:

$90 + (13.5) = 103.5 \ mph.$

For a moment, Stan lay back on his bed and imagined himself standing in a hundred-and-four miles per hour wind.

Freaking cool!

And never going to happen this far inland, he reminded himself. He sat up again and picked up where he'd left off in his main notes: *Hurricane warnings posted from Cape Lookout to Delaware, but forecasters predict that Edouard will probably miss the North Carolina coast.*

Gloomily, he added, *Hurricane Fran downgraded to a tropical storm last night.*

With a sigh as heavy as the humid August air the fan was pulling through his open window, Stan took out a fresh sheet of notebook paper and made a new heading.

NOTES — Meterolg

He paused, consulted the dictionary on the shelf beside his bed, tore out the sheet of paper and began again.

NOTES — Meteorologists say we're getting more tropical storms this year because of a rainy summer in the deserts of W. Africa. (Reminder — look up name of desert) (Reminder — look up name of country) This makes tropical waves that can turn into storms. At least they think that's what caused Arthur and Bertha so early this year.

He couldn't help wishing for the umpteenth time that he'd known about this new school's sixth-grade science project earlier in the summer. If he had, he might have thought about documenting the life and death of a killer hurricane in time for it to do some good. Unfortunately, nobody'd mentioned the project till this past week, a full month after Bertha did her number on Wrightsville Beach. Cesar and Dolly had been right on her heels, but both of them wimped out without making landfall.

Like Hurricane Edouard was about to do.

Just his luck if the rest of hurricane season stayed peaceful. When he came up with the idea of doing a day-by-day diary of a killer storm, Edouard was still kicking butt in the Caribbean and had people down at the coast talking about having to evacuate by Labor Day. Now, though . . .

He wasn't wishing Wilmington any more bad luck, but a category 3 or 4 hurricane would sure make a bitchin' project.

Sorry, God, he thought, automatically casting his eyes heavenwards.

"Son, I know you think you have to say things like that to be cool with the other kids," Dad chided him recently. "But you let it become a habit and one of these days, you're going to slip and say it to your mother and how cool will you feel then?"

Not for the first time, Stan considered the parental paradox. His father might be the preacher, but it was his mother who had all the Thou Shalt Nots engraved on her heart.

As if she'd heard him think of her, Clara Freeman tapped on the door and opened it without waiting for his response.

"Stanley? Didn't you hear me calling you?"

"Sorry, Mama, I was working on my science project."

Clara Freeman's face softened a bit at that. Guiltily, Stan knew that schoolwork could always justify a certain amount of leeway.

Yet schoolwork seldom took precedence over church work.

"Leave that for later, son. Right now, what with all the rain we've been having, Sister Jordan's grass needs cutting real bad and I told her you'd be glad to go over this morning and do it for her."

Without argument, Stan closed the notebook and placed it neatly on his bookshelf, then began cramming his feet into those gawdawful sneakers. His face was expressionless but every cussword he'd ever heard surged through his head. Bad enough that this wet and steamy August kept him cutting their own grass every week without Mama looking over the fences to their neighbors' yards. Sister Jordan had two teenage grandsons who lived right outside Cotton Grove, less than a mile away, but Mama could be as implacable as the Borg — which he'd only seen on friends' TV since Mama didn't believe in it for them. If ever she saw an opportunity to build his character through Christian sacrifice, resistance was futile.

Any argument and she'd be on her knees, begging God's forgiveness for raising such a lazy, self-centered son, begging in a soft sorrowful voice that always cut him deeper than any switch she might have used.

On the other hand, if he spent the next hour cutting Sister Jordan's grass, Mama wouldn't fuss about him going over to Dobbs with Dad this evening.

This was the second time they'd made love. The first had been in guilty haste, an act as irrational as gulping too much sweet cool water after days of wandering in a dry and barren land.

And just as involuntary.

Today they lay together on the smooth cotton sheets of her bed, away from any eyes that might see or tongues that might tell. Despite the utter privacy, and even though her mouth and body had responded just as passionately, just as hungrily as his, her lovemaking was again curiously silent. No noisy panting, no long ecstatic sobs, no outcries.

Cyl moaned only once as her body arched beneath his, a low sound that was almost a sigh, then she relaxed against the cool white sheets and murmured, "Holy, holy, holy."

"Don't," Ralph Freeman groaned. "Please don't."

She turned her face to his, her brown eyes bewildered. "Don't what?"

"Don't mock."

"*Mock?* Oh, my love, I would never mock you."

"Not me," he said miserably. "God."

She traced the line of his cheek with her fingertips. "I wasn't mocking," she whispered. "I was thanking Him."

Over in Dobbs, Dr. Jeremy Potts decided he'd put it off as long as he could. Having slept in this morning, he'd had to wait till late afternoon to go running. This hot and humid August had kept his resentments simmering. If not for the three biggest bitches of Colleton County, he told himself, he could be working out in the lavish air-conditioned exercise room at the country club instead of running laps on a school track under a broiling sun. He could follow that workout with a refreshing shower instead of driving back to his condo dripping in sweat. Thanks to his ex-wife who'd been wound up by her lawyer's wife, not to mention that judge who gave Felicia everything but the gold filling in his back molar, it would be at least another two years before he could afford the country club's initiation fees and monthly dues.

Thank you very much, Lynn Bullock, he thought angrily as he laced up his running shoes.

Jason Bullock hefted his athletic bag over his shoulder and paused in the doorway to watch his wife brush her long blonde hair. She had a trick of bending over and brushing it upside down so that it almost touched the floor, then she'd sit up and flip her head back so that her hair fell around her pretty heart-shaped face with a natural fluffiness.

"See you later, then, hon. I'll grab a hot dog at the field and be home around eight, eight-thirty."

"For the love of God, Jase! Don't I mean *any*thing to you?" Lynn asked impatiently, speaking to his reflection in her mirror. She pushed her hair into the artfully tangled shape she wanted and set it in place with a cloud of perfumed hair spray. "I won't be here later, remember? Antiquing with my sister? Her and me spending the night in a motel up around Danville? I can't believe you —"

"Only kidding," he said. "You don't think I'd really forget that I'm a bachelor on the prowl tonight, do you?" With his free hand, he stroked a mock mustache and gave her a wicked leer.

"And don't try to call me because we're going to ramble till we get tired and then stop at the first motel we come to."

It pleased her when his leer was replaced by a proper expression of husbandly concern.

"You'll be careful, won't you, honey? Don't let Lurleen talk you into staying somewhere that's not safe just because it's cheap, okay?"

"Don't worry. It'll be safe. And I'll call

you soon as I'm checked in."

In the mirror, Lynn watched her husband leave. Not for the first time she wondered why she bothered to try and keep this marriage going. Except that Jason was going to *be* somebody in this state someday and she was going to be right there by his side. No way was she planning to wind up like her mother (after three husbands and five affairs, she was living on social security in a trailer park in Wake County) or Lurleen (only one husband but God alone knew how many lovers, one of which had left her with herpes and she was just lucky it wasn't AIDS). Besides, she'd busted her buns working double shifts at the hospital while Jase got his law degree so they wouldn't have a bunch of debt hanging over them when he started practicing. Now that the long grind was finally over, now that they could start thinking about a fancier house, a winter cruise, maybe even a trip to Hawaii, she wasn't about to blow it.

But that doesn't mean I've got to keep putting my needs on hold, Lynn thought, absently caressing her smooth cheek. Jase used to be such a tiger in bed. This summer, between long hours at the firm and weekends at the ball field or volunteer fire department — "building contacts" was

24

how he justified so much time away — all he wanted to do in bed most nights was sleep.

Not her.

She took a dainty black lace garter belt from her lingerie drawer and put it in her overnight case. Black hose and a push-up bra followed. She dug out a pair of strappy heels from the back of her closet and put those in, too. Panties? Why bother? You won't have them on long enough to matter, she told herself with a little shiver of anticipation.

She thought about calling Lurleen, but her sister was going to Norfolk this weekend and wouldn't be home to answer the phone anyhow if Jase should call. Not that he would. He wasn't imaginative enough to play the suspicious husband. And no point giving Lurleen another hold over her. She already knew too much.

Chapter 2

The origin of a hurricane is not fully settled. Its accompanying phenomena, however, are significant to even the casual observer.

"C'mon, Deb'rah, we're one man short and what else you got to do this evening?" Dwight wheedled. "What's-his-face didn't change his mind and decide to come, did he?"

Sometimes Dwight can be even more exasperating than one of my eleven brothers. At least *they* like Kidd and Kidd seems to like all of them. Dwight's been the same as a brother my whole life — one of my bossier brothers, I might add — and he knows Kidd's name as well as he knows mine, but he'll never come right out and use it if he can help it. Don't ask me why.

Kidd Chapin's a game warden down east, Dwight Bryant is Sheriff Bo Poole's right-hand man and heads up Colleton County's detective squad here in central North Carolina, so they're both law enforcement agents and they both like to hunt and fish and tromp around in the woods. There's no reason for them not to be friends. Nevertheless, even though they both deny any animosity, the two of them walk around each other as warily as two strange tomcats.

"No, he hasn't changed his mind," I said, with just the right amount of resigned regret.

Dwight would worry me like a dog at a rat hole if I gave him the least little suspicion of how sorry I'd been feeling for myself ever since Kidd called yesterday morning to say he couldn't come spend this Labor Day weekend with me as we'd planned. Kidd lives in New Bern, a hundred miles away, and we've been lovers for over a year now. But let his teenage daughter Amber crook her little finger and he drops everything — including me — to run see what she wants.

I know all about non-custodial angst. Not only do I see a lot of it when I sit domestic court, I've watched my own brothers struggle with their guilt. Hell, I even watch Dwight. Let Jonna call and say he can have Cal a day early, and what happens? Ten minutes after she hangs up, he's rearranged the whole department's schedule so he can head up I-85 to Virginia.

All the same, knowing about something in theory and liking it in practice are two entirely different things, and I was getting awfully tired of watching Amber jerk the chain of the man who says he loves me, who says he wants to be with me.

I brushed a strand of sandy blonde hair back from my face. It had bleached out this summer and felt like straw here under the torrid afternoon sun. When Dwight drove up in his truck, I'd been standing in the yard of my new house with a twenty-foot length of old zinc pipe in my hands.

"Here," I said, handing him the pipe. "Hold this and move back a couple of feet, would you?"

"Why?" he asked, as he held it erect and moved to where I'd pointed. "What are you doing?"

"Planning my landscape and I think I want a maple right about — stop!" I cast a critical eye on how the pipe's shadow fell across my porch. "Right where you're standing would be good. It'll shade the whole porch in August."

Dwight snorted. "It'll be twenty years before any tree's tall as this pipe. Unless you buy one with some size on it 'stead of digging a sprout out of the woods?"

Until the spring, my yard had been an open pasture with only a couple of widely scattered oaks and sycamores to shade a few of my daddy's cows. None of those trees shaded the two-bedroom house I'd had built on a slight rise overlooking the long pond. (A house, I might add, that was supposed to give Kidd and me some privacy. A supposition, I might add, we've had too frigging few weekends to test out, thank you very much, Amber.)

"I've already root-pruned six or eight waist-high dogwoods, three oaks and two ten-foot maples," I told him as I marked the spot where he stood with a cement block left over from laying the foundation. "Robert's going to take his front-end loader this fall and move them here for me. Want to come help me dig some five-dollar holes?"

He smiled at that mention of my daddy's favorite piece of planting advice: "Better to put a fifty-cent tree in a five-dollar hole than a five-dollar tree in a fifty-cent hole."

"Tell you what," Dwight bargained. "You play second base for me this evening

29

and I'll come help you dig."

"Deal!" I said, before he could figure out that he'd just swapped half a Saturday of my time for at least two full Saturdays of his. "Give me ten minutes to wash my face and change into clean shorts. Make any difference what color shirt I wear?"

Back when I was playing regularly, the closest we came to uniforms was trying to wear the same color tops.

He turned around so that I could see JAILHOUSE GANG stencilled on the back of the red T-shirt that stretched tightly across his broad shoulders. (And yeah, long as I was checking out his back, I took a good look at the way his white shorts fit his backside.) Dwight's six three and built tall and solid like most of my brothers. Not bad-looking either. I can't understand why some pretty woman hasn't clicked on him and moved him on over to her home page before now. My sisters-in-law and I keep offering suggestions and he keeps sidestepping us.

"I brought you a shirt," he said, reaching into his truck for one like his.

I had to laugh as I took it from him. "Pretty sure I'd come, weren't you?"

He shrugged. "Been a couple of years since you played. Thought you might enjoy it for a change."

"So who're we playing?" I asked as I headed up the steps, already unbuttoning my sweat-drenched shirt as I went inside.

"Your old team." Dwight followed me as far as the kitchen, where he helped himself to a glass of iced tea from my refrigerator.

"The Civil Suits?" I asked through my open bedroom door as I stepped out of my dirty shorts and pulled a pair of clean white ones from my dresser drawer. There were enough law firms clustered around the courthouse in Dobbs to field a fairly decent team and I'd been right out there with them till I was appointed to the district court bench and decided I probably ought to step back from too much fraternization with attorneys I'd have to be ruling on. "They as good as they used to be?"

"Tied with us for third place," he drawled. "Today's the playoff. You still got your glove or do we need to borrow one?"

"I not only have it, I can even tell you where it is," I bragged. My sports gear was in one of the last boxes I'd hauled over to my new garage from Aunt Zell's house, where I'd lived from the time I graduated law school till this summer.

I found myself a red ribbon, and while I tied my hair in a ponytail to get it up off my neck, Dwight spent a few minutes rubbing neat's-foot oil into my glove. The leather wasn't very stiff. Half the time when they come over to swim in the pond, my teenage nieces and nephews wind up dragging out balls and bats. Just like their daddies — any excuse to play whatever ball's in season — so my glove stays soft and supple.

I poured myself a plastic cup of iced tea and sipped on it as we drove over to Dobbs in Dwight's pickup. He was going to spend the night at his mother's house out from Cotton Grove and since neither of us had plans for later that night, there was no point taking two vehicles.

Our county softball league's a pretty loosey-goosey operation: slow pitch, a tenth player at short field, flexible substitutions. It's played more for laughs and bragging rights than diehard competition because the season sort of peters out at the end of summer when so many people take off for one last weekend at the mountains or the coast. Instead of a regulation field, we play on the new middle school's little league field where baselines are shorter.

For once, Colleton County's planners had tipped a hat to environmental concerns and hadn't bulldozed off all the trees and bushes when they built the new school. They'd left a thick buffer between the school grounds and a commercial zone on the bypass that lies north of the running track. Mature oaks flourished amid the parking spaces and a bushy stand of cedars separated the parking lot from the playing field.

Dwight's team, the Jailhouse Gang, are members of the Sheriff's Department, a couple of town police officers, a magistrate and some of the clerks from the Register of Deeds's office.

The Civil Suits are all attorneys with a couple of athletic paralegals thrown in, and sure enough, Portland Brewer called to me as I was getting out of Dwight's truck.

"Hey, Deborah! Whatcha doing in that ugly red shirt?"

Portland's my height, a little thinner, and her wiry black hair is so curly she has to wear it in a poodle cut that makes her look remarkably like Julia Lee's CoCo. We've been good friends ever since we got kicked out of the Sweetwater Junior Girls Sunday School Class one Sunday a million years ago when we were eight. Her Uncle Ash is married to my Aunt Zell, which also makes us first cousins by marriage.

Back when I was on the verge of messing

up my life for good, I noticed that Portland was the only one of the old gang who seemed to be loving her work. It wasn't that I had this huge burning desire to practice law. No, it was more like deciding that if she could ace law school, so could I. She snorts at the idea of being my role model, but I laugh and tell her I'm just grateful she wasn't happily dealing dope back then or no telling where we'd've both wound up.

"Cool shirts," I said when Dwight and I caught up with her and her husband Avery, who's also her partner in their own law firm.

Their T-shirts didn't have the team's name on the back, but they *were* printed to look like black-tie dinner jackets, if you can picture dinner jackets with short sleeves. Black shorts completed an appearance of wacky formality that was a little disconcerting when they joined us down the sidelines for throwing and catching practice while a team from the fire department and faculty members from the county schools battled it out on the field.

I was rusty with my first few throws, but it's like riding a bicycle. Before long, I was zinging them into Dwight's glove just like old times when I was a tagalong tomboy and he'd drop by to play ball with my brothers.

I was soon just as hot and sweaty as back then, too, and more than ready to take a break when someone showed up with the team's drink cooler.

Quite a few people had come to play and were either waiting to start or still hanging around after their own games. There were also forty or fifty legitimate spectators in the stands, and among the kids who stood with their noses to the wire behind home plate, I recognized Ralph Freeman's son Stan.

Ralph was called to preach at one of the black churches this past spring, but Balm of Gilead is in the midst of a major building program and membership drive and they can't afford to pay him a full-time minister's salary yet. In addition to his pastoral duties, he was going to be teaching here at the Dobbs middle school, and I wasn't surprised to see him out on the field with other Colleton County teachers.

"Who's ahead?" I asked Stan. "And what inning is it anyhow?"

"Dad's team's up by six," he said with a smile as wide as Ralph's. "Bottom of the fifth."

So it'd be another two innings before our

game started, and the way both pitchers were getting hammered, it could be six or six-thirty.

By now, the westering sun sat on a line of thin gray heat clouds like a fat red tomato on a shelf, a swollen overripe tomato going soft around the edges. All this heat and humidity made it look three times larger than usual against a gunmetal gray sky. The air was saturated with a warm dampness. Any more and it'd be raining. A typical summer evening in North Carolina.

Portland's team and ours clustered loosely on the bleachers near third base and we sounded like a PBS fund-raiser the way all the pagers and cell phones kept going off. I hadn't brought either with me since I had no underlings and was no longer subject to the calls of clients, but Dwight had to borrow Portland's phone twice to respond to his beeper. Both were minor procedural matters.

Jason Bullock was on the row behind me and his phone went off almost in my ear. Nice-looking guy in an average sort of way. Mid-twenties. Brown hair with an unruly cowlick on the crown. He's so new to the bar that the ink on his license is barely dry. He's only argued in front of me four or five times. Seems pretty sharp. Certainly sharp enough that Portland and Avery had taken him on as a junior associate. I didn't know his marital status, but I figured he was talking to either his wife or live-in.

I heard him say, "Hey, honey. Yancey-ville? Already? You must've made good time. Didn't pick up another speeding ticket, did you? . . . No, looks like our game's going to run late. We haven't even started yet, so I'll be here at least another two hours. . . . Okay, honey. Any idea what time you'll be home tomorrow? . . . Yeah, okay. Love you, too. . . . Lynn? *Lynn?*"

Beside me, Portland turned around to ask, "Something wrong?"

"Not really. She hung up before I thought to ask her what motel she's at. She and her sister have gone antiquing up near the Virginia border."

"I didn't realize Lynn was interested in antiques," said Portland, who'd rather poke through junk stores and flea markets than eat.

"Yeah, she'd go every weekend if she could. She loves pretty things and God knows she's earned the right to have them. Not that she buys much yet. But she says she's educating her eye for when we can afford the real things."

37

"Take more than a few antique stores to educate *that* eye," Portland murmured in my ear when Bullock got up to stretch his legs.

I raised my eyebrows inquiringly, but for once Portland looked immediately sorry she'd been catty.

"Jason's smart and works hard," she said. "Lynn, too, for that matter. He'll probably be a full partner someday."

In other words, it's not nice to be snide about a potential partner's wife.

"Why are all the cute ones already married?" sighed one of the Deeds clerks on the row in front of us as she watched Bullock walk toward the concession stand.

"Because they get snagged early by the trashy girls who put out," said her friend.

"Trashy?" I silently mouthed to Portland, but she just shook her head and said, "So where's Kidd? I thought he was coming this weekend."

"Me, too."

She immediately picked up on my tone. "Y'all didn't have a fight, did you?"

I shook my head.

"Come on, sugar. Tell momma."

So we moved up and back a few bleacher rows away from the others where we wouldn't be overheard and I spent the next half-hour unloading about Amber and how she seemed to be trying to sabotage my relationship with Kidd.

"Well, of course she is," Portland said. "You're a threat to the status quo. She's what — sixteen? Seventeen?"

"Sixteen in October."

"Give her till Christmas. Once she gets her driver's license and a taste of freedom, she'll be more interested in boys than her father."

"Don't count on it," I said bitterly. "It just hurts that Kidd can't see how she's manipulating him."

"You haven't said that to him, have you?"

I shook my head. "I'm not that stupid."

"Good. He may be subconsciously putting the father role above the lover, but you don't want him making it a conscious choice."

"I *said* I wasn't that stupid," I huffed. "I do know that if it's a choice between Amber and me, I'll lose. I just wish he could understand that he doesn't have to choose. I'm willing to take my turn, but she wants her turn and mine, too, and he has to start thinking more about *my* needs once in a while."

"Oh, sugar," Portland said, squeezing my

hand. "Just keep thinking license, license, license."

I gave her a rueful smile and promised I would. Portland likes Kidd fine, but what she really likes is the idea that he might be for me what Avery is for her, somebody to love and laugh with and keep warm with on cold winter nights.

Despite the still evening air, the smell of popcorn and chopped onions floated up to us as the sun went down. People were coming and going with hot dogs so we succumbed to the temptation of one "all the way." Here in Colleton County, that's still a dog on a bun with chili, mustard, coleslaw and onions. Enough Yankees have moved in that some of us've heard about sauerkraut on hot dogs, but Tater Ennis, who runs the concession stand, doesn't really believe it's true and he certainly doesn't sell it.

As we waited in line, I was surprised to suddenly spot Cyl DeGraffenried, an assistant DA in Doug Woodall's office, among the spectators. Cyl is most things black and beautiful, but I've never heard of any interest in sports. In fact, in the three years she'd been on Doug's staff, this was the first time I'd seen her at a purely social community gathering with no political

40

overtones. She's the cat who walks alone and her name is linked to no one's.

While I watched, Stan Freeman stopped in front of her, and from their body language I could tell that they were having the same conversation he and I'd had earlier. He pointed to his father out on the field and I saw her nod. After the boy moved on, I tried to see who she was there for — volunteer fireman or school member — but she didn't cheer or clap so it was impossible to know even which team, much less which man.

"Is Cyl seeing someone?" I asked Portland.

She shrugged, as ignorant as me.

("As *I*," came the subliminal voice of my most pedantic high school English teacher. "As is not a preposition here, Deborah, and it *never* takes an objective pronoun.")

More friends and relatives, teenage couples looking for a cheap way to spend the evening, town kids and idlers began to trickle into the bleachers through an opening in the shrubbery that surrounded the parking lot. School had opened last Monday and this was day one of the Labor Day weekend, the last weekend of long lazy summer nights. Our weather would probably stay hot on into early October, but

41

psychologically, summer always feels over once school starts and Labor Day is past.

A few families had spread blankets on the grass out beyond the centerfield fence where they could picnic and let their children run around while watching the game, and several hardy souls were even jogging along the oval track that circles next to the trees bounding the school's perimeter. As I munched on my hot dog, it made me hot just to watch them.

Coming down the homestretch was a man dressed in one of those Civil Suit T-shirts, but at that distance, I couldn't make out his face under his black ball cap.

"Millard King," said Portland when I asked.

"That's Millard King? Last time I saw him, he was carrying at least fifty more pounds."

This man was trim and fit.

Portland nodded. "Love'll do that."

"Who's the lucky woman?"

She shrugged. "Some Hillsborough debutante's what I heard. Old money. Very proper. I think her father's on the court of appeals. Or was it the state Supreme Court?"

The parking lot was gravel over clay but with all the rain we'd had in the last couple of weeks, we didn't have to put up with the clouds of dust that usually drifted up over the tall shrubbery as cars pulled in and out with some people leaving and more arriving.

The game in progress wound down to the last two outs, and Avery and Dwight, the two team captains, started counting heads and writing down the batting order.

"Where the hell's Reid?" Avery asked Portland. "He swore he'd be here by five-thirty."

"Reid?" I asked. "Reid Stephenson's playing softball?"

Reid is a cousin and my former law partner when the firm was Lee, Stephenson and Knott, before I took the bench. He's the third generation of Stephensons in the firm and I was fourth generation because his grandfather was also my great-grandfather. (The Lee is John Claude Lee, also my cousin, but no kin to Reid.) Generationally, Reid's on the same level as my mother and Aunt Zell. In reality, he's a couple of years younger than I am, although John Claude, who's been happily married to the same woman for thirty-five years, has made it clear more times than one that he considers us both on the same emotional level.

That's not particularly accurate.

Or fair.

I think of myself as serially monogamous and I don't mess around with married men, but ever since Reid's marriage broke up, he seems to be on a sybaritic mission to bed half the women in Colleton County, married or single.

"Reid's always been a sexual athlete," I said. "That's why Dotty left him. But when did he take up outdoor sports?"

Portland laughed. "Back in July. Right after he pigged out at your pig-picking. One of the young statisticians in Ellis Glover's office said something about his cute little tummy and Reid signed up for our team the next day."

"Unfortunately, he still has his own idea of warm-up practice," Avery said dryly. "And he never gets here on time."

Ralph Freeman's team held on to their comfortable lead in the bottom of the sev enth and our game could finally get underway.

First though, each team had to line up at home plate and let the *Ledger* photographer take a group picture. The picture itself only took a minute, but we had to stand in place another five minutes while the photographer laboriously wrote down every name, double-checking the spelling as he went. He must've been reamed good by Linsey Thomas, the editor and publisher, who believes that the *Ledger* thrives because Colleton County readers like to see their names in print. *And* spelled correctly.

Dwight won the coin toss, elected to be the home team, and we took the field a little before six-thirty.

Colleton County is mostly sandy soil, but the ball diamond has a thick layer of red clay that was dumped here when the Department of Transportation widened the four-lane bypass less than a quarter-mile away as the crow flies.

With so much humidity, my feet soon felt as if I had about five pounds of clay clogged to the bottom of each sneaker, but that didn't stop me from making a neat double play when Jason Bullock hit a grounder through the box in the first inning.

Reid had arrived, cool and debonair, just in time to have his picture taken, but I didn't get to speak to him till the bottom of the second when I hit a double, then moved to third — Reid's position — on a pitching error.

He just smiled when I needled him

about getting there late.

"Is she in the stands?" I asked. "Or doesn't she care for ball games?"

"Not *soft*ball games," he said with a perfectly straight face as one of the dispatchers popped up, leaving me stranded.

Top of the seventh, tied three all, and Millard King doubled to score Portland before we could get them out. Heat lightning flashed across the sky and there were distant rumbles of thunder. As shadows lengthened across the field, the floodlights came on. We were down to our last out when Avery walked me. Then Dwight stepped up to the plate and smacked the first pitch clear over the right field fence for the only home run of the game. I was waiting for him at home plate and gave him an exuberant hug.

A gang of us went out afterwards for beer and pizza — Portland and Avery's treat. Jason Bullock and one of their paralegals joined the two Deeds clerks who'd scored in the fifth inning, the dispatcher, Dwight and me. Everybody else, including my randy cousin Reid, pled previous commitments. Our waiter pushed two tables together and we sat down just as the rain started.

"They say Edouard'll probably miss the

coast," Avery said as fat drops splattered against the window behind him. "Fran's still out there though."

Lavon, the small trim dispatcher, said, "And Gustave's tooling along right in behind her."

"I'm real mad at Edouard," said the paralegal (Jean? Debbie?), giving him a pretty little frown. "I bought me a brand new bikini to wear to the beach this weekend but I was afraid to go with a hurricane maybe coming in. And then it blew right on past us so I stayed home for nothing."

I instantly hated her. It's taken constant vigilance to keep my weight the same as it's been since I was twenty, but even on my skinniest days, there's no way I'd ever have the nerve to wear a bikini in public.

Beneath her mop of tight black curls, Portland was looking indecisive, but not about bikinis. She and Avery have a condo at Wrightsville Beach and a small boat with an outboard motor for waterskiing and puttering around the shoals. "Bertha didn't hurt us, but if we're going to keep getting bad storms — ?"

Avery nodded. "Maybe we'd better run down tomorrow, close the shutters and bring the boat back up here."

Our pizzas arrived amid trash talk and laughter as we rehashed the game. Jason jazzed me that he'd given me such an easy double play that I owed him a good decision on his next DWI defense. We didn't get into courthouse gossip till there was nothing left of our pizzas except a logpile of crusts. As I suspected, the paralegal had her eye on Lavon and cut him out of the pack as soon as we'd finished eating.

That broke up the party.

Rain was falling heavier as Dwight and I drove back toward Cotton Grove, with the taillights of Jason Bullock's car ahead of us all the way till we turned off onto Old 48 and he kept going on into town.

By the time we drove into my yard, the rain was coming down so hard that we sat in the truck a few minutes to see if it'd slack off.

"You were right," I told Dwight as rain thundered on the truck roof. "Tonight was fun. I'm glad you asked me to fill in, but I have a feeling I'm going to be sore tomorrow."

"You probably ought to soak in a hot bath and take a couple of aspirin before you go to bed."

"Come in for a nightcap?"

"Naw, I'd better get on. Mother'll be expecting me."

He reached out and gave my ponytail a teasing tug. "Out there on the field tonight, with your hair tied up in that red ribbon, you looked about fourteen again."

I grabbed my glove, leaned over to give him a goodnight kiss on the cheek, and opened the door.

"Deb'rah — ?"

I looked at him inquiringly.

He hesitated, then turned the key in the ignition. "Let me see if I'n get a little closer to the door so you don't get wet."

"Don't bother." I opened the truck door wide and stepped out into the downpour. "Feels good."

I held my face up to the sky and let the warm rain pelt my face. I was instantly soaked to the skin with my clothes plastered to my body, but since I was going straight in the bathtub anyhow, what difference did it make?

"You're crazy, you know that?" said Dwight. "*And* you're getting my seat wet."

I laughed and slammed the door. He waited with the lights on till I dug the keys out of my pocket and let myself in the house, then gave a goodnight toot of his horn and drove off through the rain.

I'd forgotten to leave my answering machine on, so there was no way to know if Kidd had tried to call.

Chapter 3

Husbands lost their wives and wives their husbands, and the elements were only merciful when they destroyed an entire family at once.

September 1 — Edouard missed us completely. Down from a category 4 hurricane to a category 3, and heading out to sea. (Note: Make a chart that shows all 5 categories on the Saffir-Simpson scale.) Winds still up to 100 knots but dropping.

Tropical Storm Fran reclassified yesterday as a hurricane. 22°N by 63°W, winds at 70 knots and gathering strength. Tracking west-northwest at about 7 mph. Tropical depression #7 has moved off the African coast out into the Atlantic and is now called Tropical Storm Gustav.

Stan paused and compared his maps to those in the newspaper. His were slightly more up-to-date because the newspaper went to press with Fran's position as of eleven p.m. last night, while he had the radio's report from only a few minutes ago.

The radio was old and the original aerial had long since been replaced by a straightened wire hanger, but it had shortwave capabilities and when atmospheric conditions were right, it really did pick up stations far beyond the range of his regular AM/FM radio and tape player. In bed at night, he kept it tuned too low for his mother to hear and he often fell asleep with voices whispering foreign languages past the static, into his ear. Spanish and French, and occasional bursts of Slavic or German, twined through his sleeping brain and dreamed him into worlds beyond Cotton Grove.

The radio had come into its own with this science project. Its weather band made keeping up with all these hurricane movements almost as easy as watching the weather channel on his friend Willie's television.

Too bad Mama was so against television, Stan thought wistfully. (And good thing she didn't know that this radio could pick up the audio of some local TV stations.) Still, it was sort of fun to pinpoint the storm's positions just by listening and to try and guess where they'd be at the next reading. Right now, if Fran kept going straight, it'd hit between Cape Canaveral and Jacksonville, yet forecasters were beginning to predict that it'd turn north before that and could make landfall between Charleston and Wilmington by the end of the week if it didn't get pushed out to sea sooner.

He read over the sheets he had photocopied from a reference book at the county library over in Dobbs before the ball game yesterday, then began to write again, conscientiously casting the information he had gleaned into his own words. Intellectual honesty was one of the few things Dad preached about at home and Stan frowned in concentration as he wrote, skirting that fine line between plagiarism and honest summation.

NOTES: Here's how tropical storms strengthen into hurricanes: Warm air rises, cold air sinks. Warm humid air rises from the tropical waters of the Caribbean. As it rises, the water vapor condenses and forms clouds. That releases heat, which warms the upper air around it and that makes the upper air rise even higher. More air [cooler] flows down to the water surface to replace the rising air [warmer] and that starts a spiral of wind around a center of rotation. These storm winds speed up as they near the eye and form spiraling bands. Each band is like a separate thunderstorm and the heaviest are the ones that surround the eye.

He had already begun to consider the problem of constructing a 3-D model of a hurricane. Bands of cotton arranged in spirals on top of a map of the ocean? Build up the Caribbean Islands with a salt and flour dough that he could paint green?

He scissored the weather map from the paper and dated it for his growing file of clippings, then neatly refolded that section and carried it back to the living room.

The house was wreathed in Sunday silence as he stepped into the hall. Dad would be thinking out tonight's sermon, Mama would be talking in low tones with her prayer partner at the dinner table or on the back porch, her Bible open between them. No sound from Lashanda's room. She'd probably fallen asleep on the floor in the middle of her dolls.

The carpet let Stan move so noiselessly that his father did not stir when he entered the room and laid the paper on the coffee table with the rest of the Sunday pile.

The big man's breaths continued deep and regular, never quite breaking into a snore, but heavier than if he were awake. The soft leather Bible lay open on the arm of his lounge chair. Several index cards had fluttered to the floor. Ralph Freeman seldom wrote out his sermons, but he did make notes of the points he wished to cover. Stan tiptoed closer to the lounge chair, torn between wanting to look on his father's face without being seen, yet feeling vaguely guilty at doing so.

Was this what the Bible meant when it condemned Noah's son for looking upon Noah's nakedness? Because even though Dad was certainly dressed in suit pants, white shirt and tie, there was something naked about his face with the lines smoothed out, his eyes closed, his mouth relaxed.

For one confused moment, Stan wished he were a little kid again so he could crawl onto that lap, lay his head against that crisp white shirt and hear his father's heart beating strong and sure.

Seeing him like this with all the tension gone out of his body made Stan realize how much things had changed since they moved to Colleton County this spring.

Especially in the last month.

And it wasn't just because Balm of Gilead had been burned to the ground six weeks after they arrived. The person who set the fire had nothing against them personally or the church either and was now locked up in a Georgia penitentiary. Dad knew before they came that he was called to help Balm of Gilead's congregation raise a bigger, finer church and he'd been excited about it. Made them excited, too.

Not Mama though.

She hated to leave Warrenton but she hadn't tried to talk Dad out of it when he brought it to family council. "I'm called to be your wife," she'd said. "If you're called to go down there, then it's my duty to go with you."

"I would hope it's more than duty," Dad had teased, but Mama hadn't smiled back.

"If we're moving, then I'd better get some boxes tomorrow," she'd said. "Start packing."

"If you don't want to do this, Clara, tell me."

"No, it's fine," she'd said.

Looking at his father's sleeping face, the worry lines smoothed out for the moment, Stan realized that it wasn't fine, hadn't been fine even before they left Warrenton. More and more, it was as if he and Dad and Lashanda were in a circle together and

Mama was on the outside with her back to them.

A scrap of a verse he'd learned in Sunday school when he was younger than Lashanda came to him. Something about a person standing apart.

> *But Love and I had the wit to win:*
> *We drew a circle that took him in.*

That image suddenly troubled him so much that he slipped out of the room as silently as he'd come. What did circles of love have to do with this anyhow? They loved Mama and Mama surely loved them.

Look at the way she took care of them, the way she cooked good food and kept the house so neat and clean. Not like Willie's mom, who half the time sent him out for pizza or KFC and didn't seem to care if dishes piled up in the kitchen or if people dropped clothes and toys and schoolbooks wherever they finished with them so that she couldn't have vacuumed or dusted even if she'd wanted to.

Unbidden though came memories of the way Mrs. Parrish could throw back her head and roar with laughter over something Willie said, how Sister Jordan would reach out and suddenly crush her grandsons with big warm hugs for no reason at all, how old Brother Frank and Sister Hathy Smith still held hands when they walked across the churchyard despite their canes.

When did Mama quit laughing and hugging them? he wondered. Or holding Dad's hand? Because she did use to.

Didn't she?

He shook his head angrily, hating himself for these disloyal thoughts. Mama loves us, he told himself firmly, and we love her. She's just busy doing good things for people. She sees that Sister Jordan's grass is cut, sees that nobody at Balm of Gilead goes hungry, and even though she doesn't like dealing with white people, she doesn't let that stop her from driving over to Dobbs whenever some of the congregation need help signing up for benefits.

She makes sure all the shut-ins get their Meals on Wheels and that they have a ride to the clinic for their checkups.

And look how she loaned her car to Miss Rosa yesterday so Miss Rosa wouldn't lose her job when her car broke down Friday.

Mama's prayer partner was a cheerful person. Rough as she had it, she could always find things to laugh about when she came to visit, outrageous things white people did where she worked, things that made Mama shake her head and cluck her tongue.

Dad thought Miss Rosa was using her, but Mama just shrugged at that. "We're here to *be* used, Ralph," she reproached him. "How can I see your church members struggling and *not* try to help?"

As Stan entered the kitchen, he could see his mother and Rosa Edwards through the open door that led out to a screened porch. The two women sat facing each other across a small wicker table. The Bible was open between them, but their hands were clasped, their heads were close together and Miss Rosa was speaking with low urgency.

Both of Clara Freeman's children knew better than to interrupt a parent's conversation, so Stan went to the doorway and waited quietly until one of the women should notice him.

Miss Rosa saw him first and sat back abruptly, as if startled.

"What is it, Stanley?" his mother asked sharply.

"May I have a glass of lemonade, Mama?"

"Yes, but be sure and wipe up the counter if you spill any. I don't want ants in my kitchen again. Lemonade for you, Rosa?"

"I shouldn't. In fact, I probably ought to go." The other woman shifted in her chair, but didn't get up. "I've hindered you too long already."

"You never hinder me," said his mother with a smile for her friend. She closed her Bible and put it aside. "Stanley?"

Without spilling a drop, he brought a brimming glass out to the porch and set it down in front of Miss Rosa.

"Thank you, honey," she said.

"You're welcome."

As he returned to the kitchen, he heard Miss Rosa say, "You're raising you a fine young man, Sister Clara."

"We're real proud of him," his mother said.

As she always said.

Sunday dinner long over, the kitchen restored to order, the chattering nieces and nephews and their noisy children now departed, Cyl DeGraffenried's grandmother rested drowsily in her old oak rocking chair. The chair had a split willow seat that her own mother had woven half a century earlier and Mrs. Mitchiner kept it protected with a dark blue cushion. No one else ever sat there and the child who dared put his skinny little bottom on that cushion without being invited risked getting that bottom smacked.

Mrs. Mitchiner gave a dainty yawn and settled herself more comfortably in the chair.

Cyl nudged a small footstool closer and said, "Wouldn't you rest better if you went and lay down for a while?"

"I'm not ready to take to my bed in the daytime yet," Mrs. Mitchiner said tartly.

As Cyl had known she would. Unless she were sick, her grandmother never lay down until bedtime. If the sun was up, so was she. Her only concession to sloth was to lean back and let her spine actually rest against the cushion.

"See you next Sunday, then," said Cyl as she bent to kiss that cool pale cheek. "Call me if you need anything."

The older woman caught her hand. "Everything all right with you, child?"

"Sure," Cyl said cautiously. "Why?"

"I don't know. This last month, there's something different. I look at you in church. One minute you be sad, next minute you be lit up all happy."

Green eyes looked deep into Cyl's brown.

"Oh, baby, you finally loving some-body?"

"You, Grandma," she parried lightly. "Just you."

"I may be old, but I'm not feeble-minded," said Mrs. Mitchiner. "Just tell me this. Is he a good Christian man?"

"He tries to be," Cyl whispered.

Satisfied, Mrs. Mitchiner leaned back in her chair. "That's all God asks, baby. That's all He asks."

At the Orchid Motel, Marie O'Day was showing her newest employee the ropes. Mrs. O'Day didn't speak much Spanish and if Consuela Flores understood much English, it wasn't obvious. Nevertheless, they managed to communicate well enough that when they came to the last room at the back of the motel and found a Do Not Disturb sign on the door, Consuela pointed to the work sheet and made an inquisitive sound.

"Good!" said Mrs. O'Day with an encouraging nod and exaggerated panto-mime. "*Este* guest no check out at noon, and it's past three o'clock." She tapped her watch and held up three fingers. "*Qué más?* What you do now?"

Confidently, the apprentice maid

stepped up to the door and rapped smartly. "Housekeeping!" she called in a lilting accent.

Sunlight played on the low bushes that separated walkway from parking lot and a welcome breeze ruffled the younger woman's long black hair as she listened for an answer. When no one responded, she used the master key to open the door, again announcing herself.

Inside, the drapes were tightly drawn, but enough sunlight spilled through the doorway to show that the king-sized bed had not been slept in. The near side pillow had been pulled up against the headboard and the coverlet was rumpled where someone had sat. Otherwise the bed was still made. An overnight case sat open on the luggage bench under the window and a cosmetic bag lay on the dresser next to a bottle of wine and two plastic goblets, familiar signs that this guest was still in residence even though the room had been booked for only one night.

Consuela Flores looked to the motel owner for instructions.

"Start with the bathroom," Marie O'Day said briskly, pulling the curtains to let more light into the room, "then we'll —"

"¡Cojones de Jesús!" Consuela shrieked.

Crossing herself furiously, she recoiled from her path to the bathroom and slammed into Mrs. O'Day.

A torrent of Spanish poured from the terrified maid and she clung to her employer, who looked over her shoulder to the figure that sprawled on the floor between the bed and the far wall.

It was a slender blonde white woman.

She was naked except for black bra, a black lace garter belt and stockings. One sheer black stocking was on her leg. The other was knotted tightly around her neck.

Chapter 4

A faint rise in the barometer may be noticed before the sharp fall follows. Wisps of thin, cirrus cloud float for 200 miles around the storm center.

Election day was still two months away and I had no Republican opposition. Nevertheless, I continued to hit as many churches as I could every Sunday I was free. Today was homecoming at Bethel Baptist, the church that my mother and Aunt Zell had grown up in, not to mention my sister-in-law Minnie and Dwight Bryant as well. I hadn't planned to go, but then I hadn't planned to be free either.

Instead, I dragged my aching bones out of bed early and with my own two hands and a recipe off the Internet, I made a perfect pan of lemon bars for the picnic dinner that followed the preaching services. I also contributed a deep-dish chicken pie prepared from ingredients I'd bought Friday evening when I still thought Kidd was coming.

"Didn't know you could cook anything besides popcorn," said Dwight, helping himself to a spoonful.

"And you still won't know till you actually taste it," teased Seth, who was right in behind him.

Seth's five brothers up from me and likes to pretend I can't tie my own shoelaces yet.

"Y'all leave Deborah alone," said Dwight's mother. "I know for a fact that Sue started teaching her how to cook before she was five."

I love Miss Emily. Whenever she's putting Dwight in his place, she always looks like a militant Chihuahua up against a Saint Bernard. I'm told that Dwight and his sister Nancy Faye take after their dad, a big slow-moving deliberate man who was killed in a farming accident when his four children were quite young. The other two look like Miss Emily, who is small and wiry and has bright orange hair.

She's the enormously popular principal of Zachary Taylor High School and drives an elderly TR that she turns over to the vocational kids for a new paint job every spring. They think she's pretty cool because no matter how outrageous the color or detailing, as long as it isn't pornographic, she drives the results for a year. Currently, the car's a midnight blue with a ferocious cougar splayed across the hood. Last year it was turquoise with flamingoes and palm trees and the year before that, a neon purple with red and yellow racing stripes.

I took a serving of her pear salad. With so many newcomers from all over the whole country, Colleton County church picnics are no longer just home-fried chicken and ham biscuits. These days the chicken's likely to come out of a fast-food bucket that'll be plonked down alongside a bowl of guacamole or eggplant parmigiana. But Miss Emily's pear salad is unpretentious comfort food from my childhood: canned pear halves on buttercrunch lettuce with a blob of mayonnaise in the center and a healthy sprinkle of shredded American cheese. Even though I wind up scraping off most of the cheese and mayonnaise, I still put it on my plate every time it's offered.

Miss Emily was pleased and took me around and introduced me to all the new people who've moved in since I last visited.

In between, we paused to hug and reminisce with old-timers who remembered my mother and still knew Aunt Zell. If everybody was speaking gospel truth that Sunday, I could count on a hundred votes right here.

I was surprised Aunt Zell and Uncle Ash hadn't come, but Minnie said they were spending the weekend with cousins down on Harkers Island. "I think she was hoping they might could have a hurricane party."

People were talking about beach erosion from the storm surges Edouard had kicked up as it passed by our coast, but a hundred and fifty miles inland, the weather here was downright pleasant — low 80s, low humidity, nice breeze. In fact, the day was much too beautiful to stay inside and after all the preaching and handshaking (*and* a helping of fresh banana pudding from the dessert table), I wanted some physical activity. My whole body was still a little sore and achy from last night and I knew just what it needed.

"Anybody for a swim off my new pier?" I asked when I'd worked my way back around to Seth and Minnie.

"You know, that sounds like fun," said Minnie with a pleased smile. "I haven't been in the water this whole summer."

Miss Emily begged off, but Dwight thought he'd swing by for a while if he could find an old bathing suit at her house.

"Come on anyhow," said Seth. "I got an extra, don't I, hon?"

"If you don't, Robert or Andrew will," said Minnie.

I packed up the remains of my chicken pie and lemon bars and stopped at a store on the way home for a bag of ice, some soft drinks, salsa and several bags of tortilla chips in case this turned into another picnic.

The long pond that my house overlooks is actually more like a small lake that covers about five acres. Years ago, Daddy scooped out a marshy bottom when the little twins thought they wanted to raise catfish as a 4-H project. When they got over that enthusiasm, the original pond was drained, bulldozers and backhoes enlarged it to its present size and it was restocked with bass, bream and crappies.

The land Daddy deeded me takes in only the eastern third of the pond. The rest is part Haywood's and part Seth's, but of course, the whole family use it as freely as if all the land still had Daddy's name on the deed.

When I drove into the yard, I saw two

fishermen in our old rowboat at the far end of the water. One was definitely Daddy — I could see his truck parked under a willow tree down there. I assumed the other was one of my brothers or nephews. At a distance, they tend to look a lot alike. I waved before taking my bags into the kitchen and putting the ice in a cooler.

By the time I got the food stowed and then called around to the rest of my brothers who still live out this way, cars and trucks were pulling into my yard — Minnie and Seth, Andrew and April, Andrew's A.K. and Herman's Reese. Haywood and Isabel were in Atlantic City this weekend, Robert and Doris weren't home, and Zach's wife and daughter Emma were visiting Barbara's sick grandmother in Wilson, but Zach said he'd come as soon as he could find out what she'd done with his swimsuit. (Half of my brothers still act like they're guests in their own homes and don't have a clue as to where anything's kept even though their wives have been putting stuff back in the exact same places since the day they were carried across the thresholds.)

Long as I had the phone in my hand, I called Will and Amy over in Dobbs and they said they'd try to make it before dark.

That's when I finally noticed the message light blinking on my answering machine. Two messages actually. The first was from Kidd and came about five minutes after I left for church this morning: "I know I said I couldn't come, but this is dumb when we both have Labor Day off tomorrow. Call me back and say if it's okay if I scoot on up there this afternoon. I really miss you, Ms. Judge."

All *right!* His words zinged a warm flush through my body. "Take *that,* Amber, baby!" I thought gleefully.

A moment later, my emotions took a plunge into ice water as I listened to Kidd's second message.

"I guess you must be at church or something. Oh, God, Deb'rah, I sure do hate to have to say this. Some asshole hunter took a potshot at Griggs this morning. Got him in the shoulder. He's going to be okay and the shooter's in jail, but they just called me out to cover for him. Damn, damn, *damn!*"

My sentiments exactly as I angrily reset the message tape.

"Hey, it's not Kidd's fault that his colleague got shot," reasoned the preacher who lives in the back of my head.

The pragmatist who shares head space agreed. "The situation's exactly what it was

71

before you heard his message. Nothing's changed."

"Except that he lifted me up and then let me drop again," I sulked out loud.

"So? Since when do you take all your emotional cues from somebody else?" they both asked.

Point taken, I decided, and I made myself breathe deeply till I calmed back down. Just in time, too, since my yard seemed to be filling up with large animals. Through the window, I saw Zach's teenage son Lee, Andrew's Ruth and Seth's Jessica arrive on horseback, escorted by Blue and Ladybelle, the farm's boss dogs, and a couple of Robert's redbones.

How Herman's Annie Sue over in Dobbs had heard so quickly, I didn't know, unless she was already on the farm, but here she was, getting out of her car with her friend Cindy McGee, and both wore bathing suits under their T-shirts.

Since it was just family and nobody I needed to impress, I changed into a faded old black bathing suit and topped it with a "big-and-tall" white cotton dress shirt that Haywood outgrew this spring. It's loose and airy on me, perfect for keeping the sun off my bare arms.

Until I had this house of my own, I

hadn't quite realized how much I loved giving parties and having people come.

Seth, who was helping me carry lawn chairs from the garage, smiled when I said that. "Must be the Mama Sue in you."

"That woman sure did know how to throw a party," agreed Dwight, putting a couple of chairs under each arm. He'd arrived in a bathing suit and T-shirt as faded as mine, his Sunday-go-to-meeting clothes on a hanger in his truck.

Mother's parties and her hospitality were legendary. I had neither the space nor the help that she'd had, but I liked the thought that I might be carrying on her tradition.

The kids were jumping in and out and Minnie was bobbing around on a big fat inner tube when I got down to the pier. We'd had so much rain this month that the pond's surface was almost even with the pier and I jumped right in. The water's deep enough there to take a running dive off the end, but I've resisted all entreaties for a real diving board.

"Only if you all agree to wear helmets," I tell my nieces and nephews, having seen too many head injuries for one lifetime.

(They tell *me* I'm starting to sound like their parents.)

"Here comes Granddaddy!" called A.K. "Race y'all to him."

The water boiled with furiously stroking arms and kicking legs as they churned off toward the approaching rowboat. I let them go. After yesterday's ball game, the muscles in my arms were too sore for competition.

Daddy and whoever was with him had either fished all they wanted or else the bass weren't biting because my swimming area was too far away to seriously disturb the fish at that end.

Dwight pulled himself onto the pier and he slicked his wet hair back with both hands, then shaded his eyes against the sun. A pleased smile lit his face as the boat came closer. "Well, looky who's here."

It was Terry Wilson, a special agent with the State Bureau of Investigation and one of my favorite ex-boyfriends. Terry came between a law professor at Carolina and the current assistant secretary of a state department in Raleigh that shall remain nameless. I came between wives number two and three. Daddy's crazy about Terry and had sort of hoped I might be number three, the good woman that would settle Terry down and give him a stable home life.

As if.

Kidd included, Terry's more fun than any man I've ever known, but I wasn't reared to take a backseat to any body or any thing and he'd made it clear up front that his boy Stanton came first and the job came second. Since he was working undercover narcotics back then, I soon saw the futility of trying to take our relationship beyond the fun and games. Wife number three didn't last long enough to wreck our friendship and Terry still makes me laugh with the best war stories of any of my law enforcement friends.

I had a matching grin on my face as he rowed the old boat toward my pier.

Terry and Dwight and some of my brothers played baseball in the same high school division. They still go hunting together and he has standing fishing privileges in all the ponds on the farm.

Just as Terry threw the rope to Annie Sue to tie up, Dwight's pager went off.

He muttered a mild oath and looked around as if to see a phone magically appear.

Actually, one did. Annie Sue's friend Cindy had her cell phone tucked into the pocket of her T-shirt that was hanging on one of the pier posts. "Help yourself," she told him.

I pulled myself out of the water and listened unabashedly.

Dwight still had his watch on and I saw him check the time. "Around three-thirty, you say? And you got there ten minutes ago? Good. Secure the scene and call for the van and backups. I'll be there" — again he checked his watch — "in, say, twenty-five minutes, thirty at the most."

He replaced Cindy's phone and said, "Okay if I change clothes up at the house, Deb'rah?"

"Of course," I said.

Terry shipped the oars and stepped up onto the pier. "You got to leave the minute I get here?"

"Yeah," said Dwight. "Somebody went and got herself killed at the Orchid Motel over in Dobbs."

Chapter 5

What caused the mighty elemental disturbance, the possibilities of its recurrence and the danger which constantly hangs over other cities are given in detail.

A murder out on the bypass? Naturally enough, we assumed that whoever got killed at the Orchid Motel was a tourist who probably brought her own problems as well as her killer from somewhere outside the county. Nothing to concern us beyond the usual curiosity. Our momentary gloom was perfunctory and more because it was dragging Dwight away than because of an anonymous death.

"Too bad," we said. We clicked our tongues and shook our heads, then went back to the pleasures of a lazy warm Sunday. As the sun began to set in a blaze of gold and purple, the menfolks dressed the bucket of fish Daddy and Terry had caught while Minnie and I made cornbread and salad.

My back porch is fully screened and plenty big for a large round table and lots of chairs. The table was one I'd found in Robert's barn and works just fine when I hide the water stains and scratches with a red-checkered tablecloth. The chairs at the moment are cheap white plastic deck chairs and I only have four. Even with the four from my dining area inside, we were going to have to fill in with those folding aluminum lawn chairs that are always just a little too low for any eating table.

Some of the kids don't like fish, so I fetched a couple of twenties and was going to send Reese and A.K. out for pizzas, but they'd already conferred with the rest of their cousins and decided that the seven of them would stop somewhere on their way into Garner for a movie they all wanted to see at the new multiplex.

"But we sure do 'preciate your generosity," said Reese, plucking the bills from my hand with a big grin.

Zach had to leave, too. "Barbara'll be home soon and we're supposed to go over and take supper with her sister." He cast a regretful eye at Minnie's cornbread.

With the dogs milling around his feet, Daddy sat on the porch steps downwind from Terry and lit a cigarette while they watched Andrew and Seth fuss with getting the charcoal hot enough. The grill was one that Haywood and Isabel gave me when they bought a new gas model last month and this was the first time I'd had it out.

April murmured sounds of dismay as she rummaged in my sparsely filled kitchen drawers and cabinets for plates, glasses and flatware. All she could find were three or four mismatched plates and mugs, four glasses and some odds and ends of tableware — discards Aunt Zell had given me till I could get around to buying new.

"Over there," I said, gesturing toward the cupboards Will had built into the wall behind my dining table.

Mother was townbred and of the generation of young women that picked out table patterns by the time they were sixteen and registered them at Belk's or Ivey's. Her family was solidly middle-class, with a wide circle of equally well-to-do friends who gave her at least a dozen bridal showers, which means that she brought a ton of china, silver, and crystal to the farm when she married Daddy, a dirt farmer who'd never before even held a silver spoon, much less eaten from one.

She had willed it all to me, her only daughter, and when I moved into my new house, Daddy boxed it up and brought it over on the back of his old Chevy pickup. Full-service china for sixteen with meat platters, lidded bowls, and tureens. Silver for twenty. Enough crystal wine goblets to drink France under the table. It took up every inch of Will's cabinets.

"You can't serve cornbread and pond fish on Royal Doulton," April protested. "Do you know how much it would cost to replace one of those plates?"

"Why?" I asked with a perfectly straight face. "Did you plan on breaking some?"

"Deborah!" It was the same voice she would have used on one of her sixth-grade students.

"Look," I said. "This stuff hasn't been used since Mother died and Christmas was about the only time she ever used it herself. It's either that or paper plates and plastic forks and I hate plastic forks."

We compromised. Paper plates, plastic cups, sterling silver.

"We should have given you a proper housewarming," Minnie said and April nodded.

I laughed. "Come on, you two! Cotton Grove may *think* it's ready for the twenty-first century, but house-warmings for single people?"

"We could have started a trend," Minnie said regretfully.

"Never mind," April told her. "It'll make Christmas easy on all of us for the next few years. You've always been hard to shop for, Deborah. Now we can give you house stuff. Stainless flatware and water glasses." An impish grin spread over her freckled face. "And cute little napkin rings and salt-and-pepper shakers shaped like kittycats."

"Don't forget Tupperware," said Minnie.

"Teflon!"

"Aprons!"

"Oven mitts that look like vegetables!"

Laughing, they stepped onto the porch to set the table and Seth called through the screen. "I guess we're skipping church tonight?"

Minnie gave him an inquiring look. "Unless *you* want to go?"

"Well, I believe I'd rather sit right here and give thanks for this fish and this company," Seth said happily.

In the end, nine of us sat down to supper because Amy and Will arrived just as the first, smaller fish were coming off the grill.

"Sorry we couldn't get here in time to help," Amy said.

"That's okay," Terry said magnanimously, as if catching half the fish cleared him of further obligations. "You and Will can wash dishes."

Will took one look at the disposable plates and cups and said, "Done!"

Amy took one look at the silver and said, "You don't put *this* in your dishwasher, do you?"

"Why not?" I asked.

April had just taken a bite of crusty cornbread, but she rolled her eyes at Minnie, who laughed and passed me the salad.

Pond fish, bass excluded, are too small to split or scale if you're going to grill them, and they're full of bones. They're also wonderfully succulent and these were cooked to perfection.

"Fresher'n this and they'd still be swimming," said Daddy, as he expertly laid open a little sunperch and deboned it.

The first few minutes were devoted to food talk, then Seth mentioned Dwight and how he had to leave for a homicide at the Orchid Motel.

Amy looked up in interest. "Any of y'all

know Lynn Bullock? We heard that's who it was. One of the EMS drivers told somebody in ER that she was choked to death. They say Tom and Marie O'Day found her stark naked with just a black stocking tied around her neck. Stiff as a board, too."

Amy works on the administrative side at the hospital and hears every rumor that floats through the medical complex.

"Lynn Bullock?" I asked, removing a small bone from my mouth. "Not married to Jason Bullock?"

Amy nodded. "She's one of our LPNs."

I put down my fork. "That can't be right. I was sitting next to him at the ball game last night when she called him from a motel in Yanceyville."

"How'd he know?" asked Will.

"I assume he knows his own wife's voice."

"No, I mean how did he know she was calling from Yanceyville?"

"Because she and her sister had gone antiquing up there."

There was a slightly cynical smile on Will's lips, a smile just like the one on Terry's. Though butter wouldn't melt in either mouth these days, both men know a thing or two about creative cheating.

There's a reason they've both been married three times.

Seth and Andrew merely looked interested. Seth because he's never looked at another woman since Minnie, Andrew because, even though he messed up two marriages before April came into his life, infidelity was never the problem.

"Bullock," said Daddy. "Didn't one of Vara Seymour's girls marry a Bullock?"

"I believe her mother's name *is* Vara," said Amy. "But I was thinking Lynn's maiden name was Benton."

"Likely was," Daddy said, helping himself to another fish. "Vara, she sort of got around a bit."

"Who's Vara Seymour?" Minnie asked.

"Charlie Seymour's girl. Little Creek Township. He used to do some work for me. She were a pretty little thing, Vara were, but her mammy died when she was just starting to ramble and Charlie didn't know nothing about raising a girl."

From his tone of voice, I could guess what work Lynn Bullock's grandfather had done for him. He's out of the business now, of course, but Daddy was once one of the biggest bootleggers on the East Coast and he'd financed a string of illegal moonshine stills all over this part of the country before Mother reformed him.

"I don't know what kind of a woman her mother was," said Amy, "but Lynn herself was bright as sunshine."

"Won't never nothing wrong with Charlie Seymour's brains," Daddy said mildly.

"Excellent LPN," Amy said. "She was really good with scared pre-op patients. One of those people who never saw a stranger. She'd start in talking to them like she'd known them all her life. Didn't mind getting her hands dirty either. A lot of doctors are going to miss her."

"But not all?" I asked, picking up on something in her tone.

"Well-l-l."

"What?"

Amy shrugged. "I don't think we have to worry about Dr. Potts crying at her funeral. Lynn got her husband to represent Felicia Potts for their divorce."

"What's so bad about that?" asked Terry as he took another piece of cornbread.

"Ask Deborah."

The Potts divorce took place in May so it was still quite clear in my mind. It was the first case Jason Bullock had argued before me. Might have been his first case in association with Avery and Avery, for all

I knew. Equitable division of marital property in a bitterly contentious divorce.

Felicia and Jeremy Potts had met and married at Carolina. Felicia soon dropped out and went to work full-time in order to help Jeremy get his undergraduate degree, then to send him to med school. Nine years later, having completed medical school and his residency at Dobbs Memorial, and having passed all his boards, he was poised to join a lucrative private practice there in Dobbs. At that point, Dr. Jeremy Potts suddenly decided Felicia hadn't "grown" as a doctor's wife and he had filed for divorce.

They had been formally separated for over a year when the case came to me for final disposition. There wasn't much marital property beyond the furniture in their rental apartment and two five-year-old cars, and Dr. Potts generously offered her all the furniture and a ten-thousand-dollar settlement. He also offered to pay college tuition if Felicia now wished to go back for a degree.

Jason Bullock, who had only recently taken on Mrs. Potts's case, asked me to consider Dr. Potts's own degrees as marital property.

"You think you can split up a medical

license like a set of dining room chairs?" sneered the good doctor.

His attorney asked to speak to his client in private. When they came back to the bargaining table, the attorney announced that Dr. Potts was also willing to pay reasonable room and board while Felicia was in college, a term not to exceed three years.

Jason Bullock smiled, then produced pay stubs and cancelled checks to prove that Felicia had indeed financed most of Jeremy Potts's medical education.

Although our State Supreme Court has ruled that professional licenses aren't marital property, it has ruled that "any direct or indirect contribution made by one spouse to help educate or develop the career potential of the other spouse" could be taken into consideration when granting alimony. Bullock's argument and those cancelled checks convinced me that Potts would still be slogging through medical school without his wife's help and I granted Mrs. Potts so much alimony that my clerk's jaw dropped. I even provided for an annual accounting of his income with an accountant of her choice if she decided later to come back for a bigger bite sometime in the future.

Potts's attorney gave immediate notice of appeal.

"You're free to take it to Raleigh," I had told him, feeling pretty sure that my ruling was solidly grounded in the law. "In the meantime, her alimony payments start now."

Most of this occurred in open court and the results were public record so it wasn't a betrayal of anyone's confidence to tell about the case over fish and cornbread.

"But why would Potts be angry at Lynn Bullock," I asked, "when it was Jason Bullock that handled the wife's divorce?"

Again, Amy knew the details. "Felicia Potts studied accounting before she quit school and when they came to Dobbs, she got a job in Ralph McGee's office till he died."

(The late Ralph McGee, father of Annie Sue's friend Cindy, had been a CPA over in Dobbs.)

"That's how she met Lynn. Ralph did the Bullocks' taxes."

"And that affected the Potts divorce?" asked Minnie.

"Absolutely! Felicia was going to accept the good doctor's first offer," said Amy, "and Lynn heard him bragging about it at the hospital. I told y'all Lynn Bullock was one smart cookie? When Jason was in law school, she used to read some of his case-books and one of those cases covered a similar situation. Felicia didn't have any money to hire a good lawyer and it'd never dawned on her that a degree could be like marital property, but once Lynn talked Jason into taking the case on a contingency basis, Felicia went back and pulled every tax record and every receipt from their whole marriage."

Daddy nodded. "Sounds like something a granddaughter of Charlie Seymour's would think of."

"Lynn Bullock?" Will cocked his head at his wife. "Long blonde hair? Built like a brick outhouse? Wasn't she the gal we saw Reid with at the North Raleigh Hilton last Christmas?"

"Well, I wasn't going to speak ill of the dead," Amy said, "but yes, she *did* play around on the side a little."

Again Daddy nodded. "Just like her mama."

Chapter 6

Such a night of horror as the unfortunate inhabitants were compelled to pass has fallen to the lot of few since the records of history were first opened.

September 1 — cont'd.
— Edouard 37.5 N by 70 W. Winds 85 knots & dropping fast as it heads to N. Atlantic. No longer a threat to anybody.
— Hurr. Dolly pounded Mexico. At least 2 people dead.
— Fran 23.9 N by ?? W. Winds steady at 75 kts.
— Gustave —

Stan threw down his pencil, unable to concentrate.

Upon returning from evening worship, he had come straight to his room and turned on his radio to the weather station, but he'd been too distracted to copy off all the numbers accurately, much less put them in coherent order. There were floods in Sudan, monsoons in Pakistan, earthquakes in Ecuador and maybe he'd use them in his report and maybe he wouldn't, but right now, all he could think about was the storm raging behind the closed door of his parents' bedroom.

A quiet storm. No flying shoes or hair irons crashing into lamps. No shrieked accusations or thundering counterblasts. Even with his own door cracked, he could barely hear his mother's low voice, quick and tight and cold with a towering anger usually reserved for racist whites who threatened the dignity of her world.

Normally when she raged, his father's voice would be heard rumbling beneath hers, soothing, reassuring, reasoning. Tonight, he seemed to speak only when she paused after a torrent of questions, and even then, his words were short and fell away to a silence quickly filled with more of her anger.

Bewildered, Stan remembered how the evening had started normally enough. After a heavy Sunday dinner, supper was always sandwiches and milk. Then Mama and Lashanda would neaten up the kitchen while he and Dad went on ahead in the van to get things set up.

Ever since Balm of Gilead burned to the ground back in July, services had been held in an old-fashioned canvas gospel tent with folding chairs. In just the few short months Dad'd been here, the congregation had grown to over a hundred and it looked as if they could begin breaking ground for a new sanctuary next month. Meantime, everybody was sort of enjoying the outdoor preaching. There were inconveniences, of course. No Sunday school rooms, no choir stalls, no screens, no air-conditioning, not even overhead fans, only the hand-held, cardboard-and-stick fans with a picture of Jesus knocking at the door on one side and an ad for a funeral home on the other.

But tent revivals were a tradition that had almost fallen out of use and the older folks beamed when they sang,

Gimme that ol' time religion, that ol' time religion,

Gimme that ol' time religion — It's good enough for me.

That evening, he'd helped Dad set up the simple sound system, then he'd taken rubber gloves and a bucket of soapy water out to the two portable toilets that stood modestly on opposite sides of a large holly tree at the back of the lot and wiped down the seats and floors so everything would be neat and fresh.

When he came back to the tent, Sister Helen Garrett and her daughter Crystal were there, arranging a large bouquet of deep blue hydrangeas in front of the pulpit, the only piece of church furniture to survive the fire. At least Crystal was at work on the flowers, trying to keep the heavy flower heads from tipping over. Her mother was at the pulpit in deep talk with his father.

"Hey, Stan," Crystal said shyly. They were in the same class, but different homerooms at school, and he'd only started to know her a little when Sister Garrett joined their church last month. "Could I borrow your bucket to get some water for these?"

"I'll get that for you," he said, glad for a chance to be alone with her a few minutes before his friends arrived and started clowning around, teasing them. He'd always had friends who were girls, but never a real girlfriend. Not that Crystal *was*, he thought confusedly as he fetched the water and poured it into the vase. But if he did have a girlfriend, Crystal Garrett sure would be *fine*. That smile. Those eyes. Smart, too. Her science project was on the life cycle of the black-and-yellow argiope.

Only thing wrong was her mother, who embarrassed both of them the way she put herself forward at calls for rededication, clinging to Dad as she sobbed out her sins in his ear. Now that his own body was so aware of girls — and not just Crystal — it had only recently dawned on him precisely why Sister Garrett and one or two other of the church women took any opportunity to convert Dad's "right hand of fellowship" into a warm hug. He hated the way those women pulled at him and touched him and brushed up against him like they wanted more from him than what a pastor was supposed to give.

Crystal wasn't responsible for her mother any more than he was for Dad, who couldn't help reaching out and touching whoever he was speaking to at the moment. Like now, when one of the deacons approached and he drew Brother Lorton into the conversation with a hand-clasp and an arm around the older man's shoulder.

Predictably, once the conversation quit being one-on-one, Sister Garrett turned her attention back to the flowers and, to his dismay, to him. "You're looking more like your daddy every day, Stanley. No wonder my little Crystal's so sweet on you."

Crystal looked as if she wanted to go crawl under the pulpit and Stan escaped by suddenly remembering that he was supposed to distribute hymn books and fans along the chairs. More church folks arrived and he answered politely as they greeted him. He hadn't noticed Mama and Lashanda's arrival until his little sister edged up to him while he was plugging in the lights and whispered, "Mama's real mad."

Guilt had instantly seized him. A dozen possible transgressions immediately tumbled through his mind.

"What's she mad about?" he asked cautiously.

The seven-year-old shook her head, her brown eyes wide with unhappiness. "I don't know. I think she found something in Daddy's desk."

Four things were off-limits without permission: the refrigerator except for milk or carrots, the cookie jar, their parents' bedroom unless Mama or Dad was there, and Dad's desk in the living room.

Doors and drawers were left unlocked. It was enough for Mama to say "Thou shalt not" to ensure that neither he nor Lashanda would open any of them unbidden. They knew that Dad kept his pastoral records in the desk and often sat there to counsel troubled church members.

Maybe that's what Mama's found, he thought. Maybe there were some notes about a member of the congregation who'd done something so steeped in sin that the church needed to cast them out.

There was that time in Warrenton when she'd urged Dad to take such a step, but Dad had brought the sinner back to Christ. "And if Jesus can forgive him, Clara, who are we to cast stones and cast him out?"

But he couldn't say all this to his sister. She was still too little to understand.

"Don't worry. Dad'll take care of it," he reassured her, and she'd skipped away to join her friends.

Crystal had saved a place for him among their friends near the back but he kept a wary eye on his mother's profile. She sat in her accustomed seat, the very last chair on the front row.

As the pastor's wife, Mama knew all eyes were always upon her and her children and she preached to them constantly.

"It's up to us to set good examples," she said. "Think before you act. Weigh your words before you speak. The Bible tells us that the ungodly are like the chaff which the wind driveth away. The Devil is a mighty wind, children, and he'll blow your bad words and bad deeds to where they'll do the most hurt to your father if you're not mindful of who you are."

So Mama had sat in her usual seat and kept her face turned to Dad's with her usual expression of solemn attention. But when preaching was over and everything was stowed in the back of the van, Mama gave her keys to Miss Rosa, who was still without her own transportation to work, and she and Lashanda rode home with them. That's when he realized that Dad was the focus of her anger.

As his parents approached the van, he heard Dad say, "What were you doing in my desk, Clara?"

"I was looking for a rubber band for my prayer cards." Her words lashed out like a switch off a peach tree. "Instead, I found —"

She hushed when she realized that the van windows were open and that Stan and Lashanda were sitting wide-eyed.

There was utter silence as they drove home and he and Lashanda had immediately gone to their rooms without being told. It was like seeing bolts of lightning flash across a dark sky and scurrying for cover before the storm broke.

He couldn't imagine what Mama had found to set her off like that.

"Rubbers!" Clara Freeman's face contorted with distaste as she voiced a word that raised images of filth and abomination in her mind. "An open pack. I had my tubes tied after Lashanda, so why do you have rubbers in your desk, Ralph? What whore you lying down on? I'm your true wife, the mother of your children. I yoked my life to yours, walked beside you in righteousness, sacrificed myself to your calling."

"Clara, don't," Ralph said. It was worse than he'd imagined when he let himself imagine.

"Haven't I done what I promised the day you asked me to marry you?" she raged in quiet fury. "Haven't I been an upright and faithful helpmeet? Taught our children to walk in the ways of our Lord Jesus Christ and respect your position?"

Battered by her anger, knowing he was responsible for her scalding humiliation, he mumured, "You have."

"What more could a man of God require of a wife?"

He shook his head, suddenly deeply

tired. "Sometimes, even a man of God just wants to be treated like a man, Clara."

She drew herself up icily at this allusion to sex. "I've done my duty to you in this bed."

"Your duty," he repeated, feeling numb.

"So now it's my fault? Because I won't be your whore in bed, you've gone to a whore's bed?"

"I never meant to hurt you," he said quietly.

"Hurt *me*? It's not just me that's hurt, it's you, it's the children, but most of all, it's God. When people see a preacher turn to adultery and fornication, they laugh with the Devil and it's God who's hurt."

"Clara —"

"Did you think you could keep her a secret? When all the eyes of the church are on its shepherd? I'm your true wife, Ralph, and I call you back to the paths of righteousness. Like Sarah to Abraham. In the name of God, I tell you to cast out your concubine like Abraham cast out Hagar."

"Oh, Clara —"

The sound of her name upon his lips fed her scornful rage like kerosene on an open flame. Suddenly, she whipped her dress over her head and flung it to the floor. Her slip followed, then her bra and panties. For the first time in years, she stood naked before him.

Naked with all the lamps on.

"Is this what you want from me, Ralph?" She cocked her hip at him and did an awkward parody of a bump and grind. "Is this what it takes to redeem your soul?"

A sheen of perspiration covered her face and light gleamed on her full breasts and smooth belly. She was thirty-six years old and had borne two children, yet her body seemed as slim and firm as on their wedding night, the night he realized he had made a huge error that could never be rectified, when he understood that he'd mistaken her passion for God as a passion for him.

She had given him her virginity as a burnt sacrifice to God, not as a celebration of God's greatest gift between man and woman.

Now she slowly turned around, displaying herself openly, front and back. "Am I not comely in your sight?"

As she came back full circle, she saw the pity in his eyes and abruptly tried to cover herself with her arms and hands.

"Oh, God!" she moaned and dropped to her knees at the foot of their bed, clasped her hands and began to pray, wordlessly, silently, with tears streaming from her closed eyes.

Ralph opened their closet, took her white cotton robe from the door hook, and gently draped it around her shoulders. Without opening her eyes, she pulled the fabric across her naked breasts and continued to pray.

As Ralph stepped out into the hall and closed the door behind him, he saw that Stan's door was slightly ajar and he pushed it open.

The boy looked at him. "Is something wrong, Dad?"

He had never lied to his children. "Yes, but it's between your mother and me and we'll work it out. Try not to let it trouble you any more than you can help, okay?"

Wanting to be convinced, his son nodded.

"Don't stay up too late," said Ralph.

"I won't. 'Night, Dad."

" 'Night, Daddy," echoed Lashanda's little voice from next door.

His daughter was already in bed with the lights out, but enough spilled in from the hall when Ralph opened her door to see that she was still wide awake. He adjusted the fan in her window and asked if she was cool enough.

"Is Mama still mad?" the little girl whispered.

"She'll be fine in the morning," Ralph said, knowing that Clara would be in firm control of her emotions by breakfast time. Even if she were still angry with him, she would try not to let the children see it.

He kissed Lashanda goodnight and went down the hall to the living room. The telephone sat on the desk that had betrayed him and for a moment he was tempted to call.

But what he had to say to Cyl couldn't be said on a telephone, he decided. He pulled his keys from his pocket and walked out into the night.

The Bullocks lived in a small rental house at the edge of Cotton Grove.

There was only a single streetlight at the far end of the quiet block, but a light was on by the front door, and as soon as Dwight pulled up to the curb in his Colleton County cruiser, he saw a man come to the front window and peer out at him.

The door was opened before Dwight could cross the yard.

"What's happened?" he called from the porch. "Is it my wife? Is she all right?"

"Evening, Mr. Bullock," Dwight said.

Even though both had played softball together the night before and eaten pizza at the same table afterwards, Dwight was now in full official mode and Jason Bullock stopped dead on the porch steps as he registered the deputy sheriff's formality.

"Was she in a wreck? She always drives too fast. Oh Jesus, I'll *kill* her if she's gone and hurt herself!"

The contradiction of words would have been funny if Dwight didn't know what was going on in the man's head, that he was bracing himself to hear what a rumpled officer of the law had come to tell him at ten o'clock at night.

"I'm sorry," Dwight said. "There's no easy way to say this —"

"She's *dead?*"

All the air seemed to go out of Jason Bullock and Dwight put out his hand to steady him.

"Oh, Jesus," he moaned. "I told her and told her, but she wouldn't slow down. I swore I was going to buy a clunker that wouldn't go over forty miles an hour and she just laughed. Oh, Jesus. What happened?"

"Where was your wife this weekend, Mr. Bullock?"

"She drove up toward Virginia — there

were some antique stores near Danville. Look, are you absolutely sure? I mean, her sister was with her. Maybe they made a mistake?"

Dwight shook his head. "No mistake."

"She called me just before our game. She said she'd bought me a surprise. She said she loved —"

His face crumpled and he sank down on the wooden steps that led onto the porch.

Awkwardly, Dwight patted his shoulder.

"Sorry," Bullock said. He fumbled at his pockets, stood up and went into the house.

Dwight followed through the open door and into the kitchen where Bullock pulled a handful of paper towels from the dispenser by the sink and blew his nose.

The kitchen table was set for two with a bowl of slightly wilted salad in the center. A couple of steaks had thawed on the drainboard and runnels of blood had dried on the white porcelain.

"What about Lurleen?" asked Bullock when he had his emotions in check. "Her sister. Is she okay?"

There was no way to mask the truth. Quietly but succinctly, Dwight explained that his wife had never left Colleton County. That she hadn't died in a car crash, that she'd been murdered in the

Orchid Motel out on the Dobbs bypass.

"What?" Bullock was looking like someone had sucker-punched him. *"Why?"*

As neutrally as possible, Dwight described how his wife had been found — the wine glasses, the black lingerie, her partial nudity, how the door showed no sign of being forced.

Bullock listened numbly, his jaws clenching tighter and tighter with each new humiliating detail, till faint patches of white appeared along his chinline.

"I'm sorry," Dwight said again.

"Where is she?" he asked abruptly. "What do I need to do?"

"We sent her body to Chapel Hill for the autopsy," said Dwight, "but they're fast. If you have a funeral director call, they'll probably be finished within twenty-four hours."

He pulled a plastic bag from his pocket. Inside was a slim ballpoint pen. Sterling silver and expensive. Not an advertising gimme, although it looked elusively familiar to him for some reason. They had found it under Lynn Bullock's body though he didn't tell her husband this.

"Is it hers?" Dwight asked.

Jason Bullock took the bag and looked

closely at the sleek design. "If it is, I never saw it before."

He looked at Dwight bleakly. "But I guess there's a lot I didn't see, huh?"

Chapter 7

These storms, which are common to the southern and southeastern coasts of the United States, invariably originate in "the doldrums," or that region in the ocean where calms abound.

Monday morning — Labor Day — and I was surfing channels, trying to find more details about Lynn Bullock's death while waiting for the coffee to perk. All I was getting were the bare facts voiced over uninformative shots of the Orchid Motel draped in yellow police tape from yesterday afternoon, although a helicopter view from above showed me that the motel was closer to the ball field than I'd realized. All the time Jason was talking to his wife, thinking she was a hundred miles away, she was right there less than half a mile from us.

The TV reporters didn't seem to know

as much as Amy had. I felt sorry for Tom and Marie O'Day, who bought the motel six years ago and have worked hard to make it succeed. This wasn't the kind of publicity they needed. Tom appeared on camera long enough to say they had nothing to say, and viewers got to see a draped gurney being wheeled from a ground-floor room at the back of the building.

The radio was even less informative.

What I really needed was a newspaper.

When I lived with Aunt Zell and Uncle Ash, the *News and Observer* was lying on the breakfast table every morning when I came down. The *Dobbs Ledger*, too, if it were Monday, Wednesday or Friday. (With all the new people and new businesses coming into the county, the *Ledger* has also grown. Back in June, Linsey Thomas started publishing it three times a week instead of twice.)

Now that I have my own house, I also have my own subscriptions and both papers are delivered right on schedule.

The difference is that Aunt Zell has merely to open her front door and pick up the papers from her welcome mat. My mail and paper boxes are just over half a mile away from my front door, down a long and

108

winding driveway, and this presents me with something of a moral problem.

Only a total sloth would use a car for a one-mile round trip, but I'm a pitiful jogger and walking takes too long. So I half-walk, half-run and when I get back, all hot and sweaty, with *Ledger* newsprint smearing my hands because Linsey won't change the presses over to smudgeless ink, I might as well jump in the pond and swim till I'm out of breath before I shower and shampoo my hair.

Keep in mind that I am *not* a morning person. Before eight o'clock, all I really want is a reviving cup of coffee and a quiet moment to read the paper. Being forced to work out first thing is not my idea of how to start the day, although I have to admit that the new regime's done wonders for my muscle tone.

Some days, if I'm pressed for time, I do drive down, but I always feel so guilty that it takes the edge off the morning. You think it's silly to equate walking with righteousness and driving with sin?

Me, too.

But my Southern Baptist upbringing is such that nine mornings out of ten will find me puffing down the long drive. Which is why I was standing in a clump of yellow coreopsis at the edge of the road reading about Lynn Bullock's death when Dwight drove by around nine that morning and stopped to ask if I wanted a lift back to the house.

"Sure," I said, opening the passenger door of his cruiser. (Riding in someone else's car doesn't seem to bother my conscience.)

I was wearing sneakers, a sports bra and denim shorts with no underpants because I planned to swim as soon as I got back and half the time I don't bother with a suit.

"So who killed the Bullock woman?" I asked. By then I'd scanned both papers and seen little new since both went to press before the victim's identity had been announced.

"Now you know I can't talk to you about this."

"Sure you can," I wheedled. "I don't gossip —"

He snorted at that.

"I've never repeated anything you ever asked me to keep to myself," I said indignantly, "and you know it."

"True."

"And homicide cases are never heard in district court, so it's not as if you're tainting a trial judge."

"Also true." He gently braked and I felt the underside of the car scrape dirt as we eased over a patch where the tire ruts were deeper than the middle.

"Well, then?"

"You need to get Robert or Haywood to take a tractor blade to this drive again," he said.

"Dwight!"

"Okay, okay. Not that there's much to tell yet. Bullock gave me his sister-in-law's number up in Roxboro, but she never answered her phone till this morning. Said she hadn't talked to Mrs. Bullock since Tuesday night. Didn't know anything about a trip to Danville this weekend. She herself spent the weekend with a sailor in Norfolk."

Dwight pulled into my yard and cut the engine when I invited him in for coffee. I'd turned on the coffeemaker just as I left for the papers and it was fresh and hot. I poured us each a mugful, toasted a couple of English muffins, added figs from Daddy's bush and the last of the blueberries from Minnie and Seth's and then carried the full tray out to the porch table. Dwight had switched on the paddle fan overhead and it stirred the air enough to make the difference between pleasant and uncomfortable.

Hurricane Edouard was still dumping water on New England, but here in Colleton County the skies were bright blue with a few puffy clouds scattered overhead.

We buttered our muffins and topped each bite with the fresh fruits.

"Anybody see anything at the motel?"

"We don't have statements from all the help yet, but so far, nothing. That unit was the end one on the back side of the building and the trees and bushes back there are so thick that Sherman's army could've camped for a week without anybody seeing 'em. The people in the nearby units checked out yesterday before the body was found and we're trying to contact all of them. The O'Days run a clean business, but if someone wants to pay by cash, they don't ask to see ID and that's what happened with the guy in the next unit. Connecticut license plate. We're just hoping he didn't lie about his plate number."

"How's Jason really taking it?" I asked, popping a plump and juicy blueberry against the roof of my mouth.

" 'Bout like you'd expect. Doesn't know whether to be mad or sad. She was his wife, but she was screwing around on him."

"Any chance he could've done it?"

We're both cynical enough to put spouses at the top of any list of suspects.

Dwight shrugged. "Always a chance. He seemed pretty shook when I told him last night. He was at the ball field when you and I got there and his car was in front of us all the way back to Cotton Grove. Of course, he could have got home, found something that told him where she really was, and roared back to Dobbs by ten-thirty. We'll have to wait for the ME's report. One good thing though — they ought to be able to pinpoint the time of death pretty close."

"Oh?"

"Yeah. The motel's shorthanded right now since school started, so Tom and Marie were both working the weekend. He had a bowl of peanuts on the registration counter and she ate a few when she checked in. Tom thinks that was around four-thirty, quarter to five."

He didn't have to draw me a picture. Depending on how far along digestion was, the ME should be able to bracket the time of death rather narrowly.

"Tom had never met her, didn't know who she was and he didn't think twice when she paid cash in advance and gave him a phony name. Benton."

"Her maiden name," I said.

"Now how you know that?"

"She was an LPN at the hospital. Amy and Will got here after you left yesterday."

That was enough. He knows Amy, knows where she works, knows how she picks up information and stores it like a squirrel laying up pecans for winter.

"Amy says she played around."

"Any names?"

"Not recent ones," I hedged as I nibbled more blueberries.

"Her sister swears she'd hung up her spurs and was walking the straight and narrow these days," said Dwight, "but you wouldn't know it from the way that room looked."

He took another swallow of coffee. "Anyhow, Tom O'Day says she knew exactly where she wanted to be. Asked for a ground-floor room in back, said she liked it quiet and didn't want stairs. It was the last non-smoking room left on that side. According to the switchboard records, she made only one outgoing call on her room phone after she checked in. Around five."

"To her husband. I was sitting in front of Jason when he talked to her."

"And the switchboard says she received

an incoming call about ten minutes after that, someone who asked if Lynn Benton had checked in yet."

"Male?"

"The operator thinks so, but can't swear to it. She also says somebody called around three o'clock asking the same thing and that it could've been the same person."

"Impatient lover just waiting to find out what room she was in before rushing over?"

"Sounds like it, since he knew what name she was using."

"Nobody saw her at the drink machine? Filling her ice bucket? Letting strange men into her room?"

"If they did, they're not saying."

"I guess you're pretty sure it *was* a man?"

"Dressed like that? Or rather, undressed like that? And she was pretty well-built. Taller than you. Probably stronger, too. Nurses do a lot of lifting and pulling. It would've taken somebody just as strong."

"He could've caught her off-guard," I said, picturing the scene. "He could've been undressing her, took off one of her stockings. Maybe trailed it along her neck."

115

My mind flinched from the rest of the scenario. Lynn Bullock had thought he was making love to her. Instead —

Across the table from me, Dwight pulled a fig apart to reveal the soft fleshy interior and I wondered what he was thinking as he ate it. Ever look closely at a fig? It's male on the outside, explicitly female on the inside. Erotic as hell, but I doubt if Dwight notices.

"We bagged her hands," he said, "but if the killer came up from behind with that stocking and threw her down face-first, she may not've had time to do more than claw at the thing that was choking her. If that's the case, we'll only find her own DNA under her nails."

"Poor Jason Bullock." I sighed and got up to fetch the coffeepot for refills.

When I came back from the kitchen, Dwight was holding a couple of plastic evidence bags in such a way that his big hands concealed the contents.

"What's that?" I asked.

"These really do stay confidential," he warned me. "Ever see this before?"

Inside the first plastic bag was the top part of a gold-toned tie tack. Less than half an inch wide, it was shaped like a tiny American flag.

"Ambrose Daughtridge wears tie tacks," I said. "And so does Millard King, but I never paid much attention to them."

"What about this, then? We found it under the victim's body. For some reason, it makes me think of you. Why?"

It was a silver ballpoint pen.

"Because I had one just like it on my desk at the law firm," I said promptly. "You must have seen it there. John Claude gave them as Christmas presents three or four years ago."

Mine was in a pencil cup by the telephone in my bedroom and I brought it out to show Dwight. "I don't carry it in my purse because I'm afraid I'll put it down somewhere and walk off without it."

Dwight smiled as he compared the two. He knows my theory that there are probably only about fourteen ballpoint pens in Colleton County and everybody keeps picking them up at one business counter and putting them down at another counter somewhere down the road.

These pens were sterling silver — John Claude doesn't give cheap presents — and were distinctively chased with tendrils of ivy that twined along the length of the barrel.

"Any fingerprints?"

"Just smudges. Who else got one besides you?"

"I'm not sure. You'll have to ask John Claude." I didn't like where this was going. "Reid got one and Sherry Cobb."

Sherry is the firm's small, bossy office manager and Reid, of course, is the current generation's Stephenson.

Lees and Stephensons have been law partners since John Claude's father (a cousin from my Lee side) began the firm with Reid's grandfather (my great-grand-father) back in the early twenties. South-erners sometimes exaggerate the ties of kinship, yet family loyalties do exist and most of us will always give a cousin the benefit of doubt, even a first cousin once removed, as Reid was. His sexual develop-ment may have stopped when he was in junior high, but that doesn't make him a killer.

I didn't care if Will and Amy *had* once seen them together, there was no way Reid could be involved in Lynn Bullock's death, and I wasn't going to offer him up as a candidate to Dwight.

"I think John Claude bought them at a jewelry store at Crabtree Valley," I said. "Dozens of them are probably floating around the Triangle."

"We'll check," Dwight said mildly. "Long as Reid has his, no problem, right?"

I keep forgetting how well he knows me.

Chapter 8

Ordinarily, men and women have enough to do in attending to their own affairs, expecting others, of course, to do the same, and consequently they pay small attention to what is going on around them.

After Dwight left, I finished reading the paper. Polls showed Jesse Helms with his usual slim lead over Harvey Gantt in the senate race — what else was new? — and NASCAR champion Richard Petty was several points ahead of Elaine Marshall for Secretary of State, though that gap had closed a little since the last poll. Nothing to get our hopes up about though.

The *Ledger*'s front-page story carried a studio portrait of Lynn Bullock. Even in black and white, her makeup looked overdone and her long blonde hair was definitely overteased. More Hollywood than

Colleton County.

("Meow," scolded my internal preacher.)

Sheriff Bo Poole reported that his department was following up several important leads and he appealed to the public to come forward if anyone had seen Mrs. Bullock or anything suspicious at the Orchid Motel between five p.m. and midnight on Saturday.

In true *Ledger* fashion, the story ended by listing Lynn Bullock's survivors: her husband, Jason Bullock "of the home"; her sister, Lurleen Adams of Roxboro; her mother, Vara Fernandez of Fuquay-Varina; and her father, Cody Benton of Jacksonville, Florida.

I was mildly bemused to see Dr. Jeremy Potts pictured at the bottom of the same page, along with another white-jacketed doctor. They flanked a piece of diagnostic equipment that was evidently state-of-the-art. The story was about the machine, not the doctors, so I turned to the sports pages to check out the softball pictures.

Linsey's new photographer might have been slow with names, but he was expert with the camera. White or black, all our faces were crisp and clear. I never push, but I do make sure I'm always on the front row. Every bit of public notice, no matter how tiny, has to help subliminally at the polling booth.

Putting the plates and mugs Dwight and I had used in the dishwasher, I wiped down the countertops, then swept the kitchen and porch floor clean of crumbs and sand from last night. It'll be next spring before my centipede grass is thick enough to make a difference with tracked-in sand. In the meantime, no matter how many doormats I scatter around, I live with the sound of grit underfoot. It's almost as bad as a beach house.

At Aunt Zell's, I kept my two rooms picked up and I chipped in on her twice-a-month cleaning woman, but that was about the extent of my domestic labors. Now I'm doing it all myself and part of me is amused to watch the surfacing of a heretofore latent pleasure in housework, while the other part is horrified to see myself slipping into such a stereotypical gender role.

"Long as you don't start crocheting potholders or make people take off their shoes before they come in," soothes my mental pragmatist.

By noon I had changed the linens on my bed and had just thrown sheets and towels in the washer when my friend Dixie called from High Point. She said she'd get me a visitor's badge if I wanted to come over at the end of next month's wholesale furniture market to pick up a few floor samples at dirt-cheap prices.

"Should I keep my eye out for anything in particular?" she offered.

Standing in the middle of my house and looking around at all the bare spots that surrounded a handful of shabby family castoffs, I hardly knew where to start. "A couch?" I said. "And maybe a really great coffee table? That's all I can afford right now."

We talked about styles and colors and whether her love life was as stalled as mine seemed to be at the moment.

Yet, as if to give lie to all my grumbling, the phone rang the instant I hung up and it was Kidd, who did a lot of grumbling on his own about having to work time and a half to compensate for his wounded colleague when he'd rather be upstate with me.

"Tell me what you're wearing," he said.

"Right this minute?"

"Right this minute."

I slipped off my sneakers and curled up on the old overstuffed couch handed down from April's aunt. "My purple knit bra and a pair of cutoffs."

"That's all?"

"Hey, I'm decent."

"Not for long."

I smiled. "Why not?"

"Because I'm sliding the straps down off your shoulders and over your arms."

"You are?"

"I am."

"And I'm letting you?"

"You have no choice," he teased. "The straps are keeping your arms pinned to your side while I pull the bra down around your waist and kiss you all over."

"Um-m-m," I murmured, settling deeper into the cushions. "Feels wonderful." It seemed so long since we'd touched that I closed my eyes and drifted as his voice added detail upon erotic detail.

"I'm not as helpless as you think, though," I warned him softly. "You've pinned my arms, but my hands are free and I'm unbuttoning your shirt . . . running my hands across your chest." My voice slowed and deepened. "I'm touching your nipples very lightly, barely brushing them with my fingertips."

My own breasts began to tingle as he told me where his lips were and described what his hands were doing. I could almost

124

feel the roughness of his stubbled cheek, his face pressed hotly against me.

"Now I've unbuttoned the top of your shorts," he said huskily. "My fingers are on the zipper . . . Slowly, very slowly I —"

The screen door slammed and a male voice said, "Hey, Deb'rah? You home or not?"

I was so into the spell Kidd was weaving that for one confused moment, I felt as if I ought to clutch a cushion to my chest to hide my nakedness. Between telephone and washer, I hadn't heard Reid Stephenson's car drive up.

"Oops!" he said as he poked his head through the door and saw me. "Sorry. Didn't realize you were on the phone. I'll wait. Go ahead and finish."

As if.

Mood shattered, I told Kidd I'd call him later.

" 'Fraid I won't be here," he said with a long regretful sigh. "Roy and me, we're patrolling the water tonight. Lot of drunk boat drivers'll be out. But, Deb'rah?"

"Yes?"

"Remind me to punch your cousin in the nose the next time I come up, hear?"

"Hey, you didn't have to get off the

phone on my account," said Reid.

"Yes, I did," I said grumpily. "What're you doing out this way anyhow?"

Dressed in dark red shirt, white sneakers, no socks, Reid just stood there happily jingling his keys in the pocket of his khaki shorts. Not only is he cute as a cocker spaniel puppy with his big hazel eyes and his curly brown hair, he has a puppy's sunny good nature and isn't easily insulted, which is probably why he's so successful with women. Takes more than a whack with a newspaper to discourage him when there's a tasty treat in sight.

"I brought you a housewarming present."

He beckoned me out to the porch. There on the table was a long flat box wrapped in brown paper, tied with a gingham ribbon and topped with a spray of what looked like dried grasses.

"What's that stuff?" I asked.

He grinned. "Hayseeds, of course."

It's been a running joke with some of my town friends that my move to the country was the first step toward turning into a country bumpkin, that I'd soon be coming to court with a stem of broomstraw dangling from the corner of my mouth.

Inside the box were two smaller packages. The first was a yellow-backed booklet covered with dense black type-script that advertised things like blackstrap molasses, copper arthritis bracelets and diuretics — an old-fashioned farmer's almanac.

"You need to know what signs to plant your crops under," Reid said.

I had to smile because Daddy and Maidie still consult this same almanac before they plant — a waxing moon for leafy vegetables, dark of the moon for roots, zodiac signs for everything else.

The other package contained a rather handsome walnut board, inset with three brassbound dials. The top one was a ther-mometer (86°), the middle was a barom-eter (29.6"), and the bottom recorded the humidity (58%) — actually a pleasant day for the first week in September.

"How about beside your bathroom door?" Reid suggested as I looked around for a place to hang it. "You can see what the weather's like as soon as you get up every morning."

As if I couldn't just look out the window. But he was so pleased with himself and his gift that I held my tongue.

We carried it into my bedroom and he was right, as he usually is about spatial concepts. It was a perfect fit. One of the reasons Reid's such a good trial lawyer is that he notices details. So far as I knew, he'd only been in this room once since I moved in, when he brought out a small bookcase from my old office a few weeks back, yet he remembered the narrow wall between my closet and bathroom doors.

"Get me a screwdriver and I'll go ahead and put it up for you," Reid said.

I fetched one from the garage and we hung it in less than five minutes.

"Dwight see you this morning?" I asked as we walked back through the kitchen and I transferred my wet laundry to the dryer.

"About that pen he found under Lynn Bullock?"

"He told you that?"

"Come on, Deborah. I'm an attorney, remember? I don't answer any questions from a deputy sheriff without a good reason. Soon as you told him they were Christmas presents from John Claude, you knew he'd come asking to see mine."

"And you showed it to him?" I asked casually.

"Not yet. It's back at the office. He's going to come by tomorrow when I'm there. But I got to tell you, it pisses the hell out of me that he won't take my word for it. Has anybody *ever* seen me raise a hand to a woman? Ask Dotty. Bad as we used to fight, the only thing I ever slammed was the door."

"But you did have an affair with Lynn Bullock," I said.

He shook his head. "Nope. We went out twice last winter, I slept with her once and that was it."

Genuinely curious, I asked, "What's your definition of an affair?"

"More than a quickie and two suppers, that's for sure," he said virtuously. "Not to speak ill of the dead, but she turned out not to be my type."

"Oh?" I hadn't realized there *were* such creatures.

"Lynn Bullock was a sexy woman and she really liked to —" He hesitated. John Claude's lectured him so many times about using the F-word in front of women that it's starting to sink in. "— to do it. The thing is, she was just a little too trashy for me."

He spoke with such a straight face that I couldn't control my laughter.

"After Mabel, the motorcycle mama?" I hooted. "Or little Cass with the big —"

"You don't have to call the roll," Reid said, offended. "Look, you know Dolly

Parton's famous remark?"

" 'It takes a lot of money to look this trashy'?"

"Right. But Dolly goes for that look deliberately. It's her stage persona. Earthy. Playful. Lynn Bullock wore the same big hair, flashy clothes, and gaudy costume jewelry, only she was dead serious. She thought it made her look upper-class — I swear to God, she must've spent her formative years studying *Dynasty* as if it were a documentary on tasteful dressing."

"I never knew you were such a snob," I said.

"I'm not! Lynn was though. The first and only time I f— I mean, laid her, she spent the rest of the evening classifying half the people in Dobbs — this person was, quote, 'society.' That one was 'low-class.' I thought at first she was being funny but, no, ma'am! She was dead serious and she had the pecking order in this county down pat. I told her that if she wanted to see a real pecking order, she ought to come with me to the Rittner-Kazlov Foundation reception at the North Raleigh Hilton and watch artists and musicians put each other in their places. Mother wanted me to go represent her and I'd had just enough bourbon to think it might be amusing to watch Lynn watch them."

(Between them, Brix Jr. and Jane Ashley Stephenson have sat on half the non-profit boards in the Triangle.)

"I'm guessing all the women showed up in earnest black gowns and ceramic necklaces?"

"I believe there were two maroon velvets and an authentic batik with strings of cowrie shells."

"And Lynn Bullock wore — ?"

"A bright green satin cocktail suit with the skirt up to here, hair out to there, gold shoes, gold purse, chunky gold earrings and gold glitter in her hair. She said she hoped the glitter wasn't too much, but after all it was Christmas."

"Oh, Lord." I've always disapproved of extramarital sex, but I could almost find it in my heart to feel sorry for someone that tone-deaf about clothes. "How on earth did she get out of the house dressed like that without her husband noticing?"

"He was in Charlotte that weekend."

"So how did the artsy crowd react?"

" 'Bout like you'd expect. Polite for the most part, but there was a lot of eye-rolling and the older women became very, very kind to me, almost motherly. They did

131

everything except cut up my carrot sticks for me."

"Poor you."

"The worst was running into Amy and Will as we were leaving. Amy took one look at Lynn and then sort of glazed over. But what really iced the cake was the way Lynn thought those women were jealous of her style. She didn't have a clue." Reid shook his head.

"The weird thing was that even though she was out with *me*, cheating on *him*, she kept talking about how great it was going to be when her husband joined Portland and Avery's firm — how much money Jason was going to make and how they were looking forward to the day when they could afford to sponsor civic events because money's the way you get your nose under society's tent."

"She got that right, didn't she?" I said cynically.

More than forty years ago, my daddy's own acquisition of respectability was based on the illegal production and distribution of moonshine. Mother's people were higher up the social scale and after they fell in love and married, she made him quit bootlegging. Without that early seed money though — the whiskey money that bought good bottom land, decent equipment, and a fair amount of respect — he probably would have stayed too dirt poor to court her in the first place.

"Who would kill her, Reid?"

"Hell, I don't know. Usually you'd say the husband, but Bullock was on the ball field, right? Millard King, too."

"She slept with Millard King? When?"

He shrugged. "Before me, after me, during me — I don't keep tabs. I just remember hearing their names linked." He paused a moment. "Come to think of it though, not recently. I heard he's hoping to marry the daughter of one of our Justices."

He shook his head again. "I really don't know who was sleeping with her. Not me, though."

"Any problem walking away?" I asked, trying to get a feel for the murdered woman.

"Not for me," he said, with that male arrogance that always annoys the hell out of me. Then he gave a sheepish grin. "Cost me a bundle to get the smell of dog dirt out of my car, though. She dumped a whole pile of it all over the front seat."

Chapter 9

Dejection and despondency succeeded fright.

September 3 — Edouard — no longer anything but an extratropical storm at 6 a.m. — just south of Nova Scotia — winds only 55 kts. Large swells, minor beach erosion, some coastal flooding from NC–Maine. Some damage to small boats at Martha's Vineyard & Nantucket. At least one drowning.
— Fran 24.4°N by 70.1°W — still a Category 1 hurr. & getting stronger. Will prob. be upgraded to Category 2 by tonight.
— Gustave's collapsed.
— Hortense

"Stan? Mama says come to breakfast *now* or we're gonna be late for school."

Reluctantly, the boy turned off the radio, shelved the notebook and followed his sister down the hall to the kitchen. Yesterday's breakfast had been so strained that he'd volunteered to help Dad cut the grass around the church tent without being asked, just to get away from the house. Not that Dad hadn't been quiet and withdrawn himself. But his silences were always more comfortable than Mama's.

To Stan's relief, his mother seemed to be in her normal school morning mode. Wearing a pink-and-green-checked cotton dress, she gave him a good-morning smile as she sliced bananas and peaches over their bowls of cold cereal. His father asked the blessing, then she poured Lashanda's milk and handed the carton on for him to pour his own. Her voice sounded just like always as she passed out lunch money, looked critically at his shirt to see if it was a clean one, and reminded Lashanda that she had piano today, "so don't forget to take your music. I don't want to have to come rushing over to the school this morning, you hear?"

"Yes, Mama." The little girl smiled, too young to worry whether everything really was back to normal. As long as no visible storm clouds hovered over their heads, the semblance was sufficient and she chattered so freely that even Stan felt the tension level go down.

Ralph Freeman finished eating first and went to brush his teeth. When he came back to the kitchen with his backpack hanging from one shoulder, he said, "I have to leave now, Clara, if I want to get to Dobbs on time. You sure you don't want me to drop the children off on my way?"

"You go on ahead," she said, from the kitchen sink. "Rosa gets off at seven and she'll be here in plenty of time. You'll probably pass her on the way."

That's when Stan realized that his mother's car wasn't in the drive. Miss Rosa must've worked the night shift again. As his father bent to kiss them goodbye, he also realized that Mama still had her back to them. Spoons and dishes rattled against each other beneath the running water and she acted too busy to turn around and lift her face for his usual kiss on her cheek. Dad must not have noticed either, because he didn't hesitate, just went on out to the van and drove off.

Rosa Edwards gave a mighty yawn as she drove through morning traffic. Not that she was all that sleepy, merely ready for her own bed after two nights away from it. Sunday night was payback for when Kaneesha covered for her a couple of weeks back, and last night was her own regular night. For people on the house-

136

keeping staff, night duty at the Orchid Motel was mostly a matter of just being there in case a bed suddenly needed changing or fresh towels were required in the middle of the night. Otherwise, there were a couple of lounge chairs in a little room off the main desk where you could put your feet up and doze after you'd tended to all your chores.

The O'Days were good bosses. For white people. They paid better than minimum wage and were real easy to get along with. Of course now, they had their own ideas about how to run a motel and it might not be the way Motel 6 or the Marriott did things, but long as you did your job and did it right, you didn't have to act extra busy when they were around. And they were fair about dividing up the night work. You didn't get hired unless you were willing to take your turn. But you could trade off if you needed to, long as you knew it was your responsibility to see that your hours were covered. That was the one thing they were bad about: show up late or don't show up at all without being covered and, child, the doo-doo don't get no deeper. They didn't want to hear about flat tires, dead batteries or how the babysitter bailed at the last minute. You got one second chance and that was it.

Long line of women be happy to have your job 'stead of picking up sweet potatoes, she told herself. Mexicans, Asians, A-rabs, you name it these days.

Must've been like the United Nations when the police tried to talk to Numi and Tina, who worked the noon to eight shift Saturday and Sunday. Here it was Tuesday morning and that was still all anybody could talk about — that naked body, the black stockings, the fancy wine, the man who'd called twice to see if she was there yet. Not that they were saying much more than that, 'cause nobody'd really noticed the murdered woman when she checked in except for Mr. O'Day.

Sister Clara's car radio was always tuned to a gospel station and Rosa sang along with one of their favorite hymns, but her mind wasn't with the words.

Even though she was on duty Sunday night when yellow tape was being strung all over that end of the place and police cars and ambulances were coming and going, nobody'd interviewed her 'cause they must've been told that she got off work at four on Saturday, before the murdered woman arrived.

None of the others seemed to remember

that she came back around five-thirty after doing her weekly shopping because she'd gone and left her Bible in her locker. She hadn't thought anything about it herself till she got there Sunday night and they told her what'd happened in Room 130.

That's when she remembered driving around the back corner of the Orchid Motel in Sister Clara's quiet little car and there was this white man coming out of that very same room. He closed the door and hung the Do Not Disturb sign on the knob and soon as he saw her, he turned away quick-like.

"Jesus, lift me up and lead me on," she sang along with the radio. *"Till I reach your heavenly throne."*

If any policeman had've asked her Sunday night, she might've told about that man right then and there, but all the guests down at that side of the motel, them that didn't just up and check out, had to be moved over to the front side and Mrs. O'Day had kept her hopping till after the police left.

And if anybody'd been with her in the bathroom at two o'clock this morning when she was sitting on the stool reading the *Ledger*, she might've bust out with it then, but they weren't and she didn't. By the time she returned to the lounge, she'd had second and third thoughts about what this secret knowledge could do for her.

"For my sins you did atone," sang the choir.

Yesterday's *Ledger* lay on the car seat beside her, neatly folded so that the man's picture was staring right back at her.

Probably had plenty of money. White men like him usually did. And here she was, needing a new car real bad, what with winter coming on. That old rustbucket of hers stayed in the shop more than it stayed on the road. Wouldn't have to be a fancy car, just something nice and dependable like Sister Clara's.

Sister Clara was always warning her to stay out of white people's business.

Easy enough for her to say, thought Rosa, and her a preacher's wife with a husband to give her everything — nice house, nice car, nice clothes she don't have to go out and work among white folks for. Still, it won't none of her business to bear witness against that man. "Thou shalt not suffer a whore to live." Isn't that what the Bible said? Not up to her to avenge the killing of a white harlot.

Anyhow, she didn't have to decide right now, she told herself. Like Mary, she was going to sit back and ponder all these things in her heart.

"Jesus, lift me up and lead me on."

He couldn't believe his luck. Ever since it happened, he'd checked his rearview mirror for every white Civic that he met, noted every white Civic parked on the streets — who knew Honda had such a big slice of the car market? And didn't they make Civics in any damn color *except* white?

Then suddenly, there it was!

He was waiting at a stop sign when the car sailed by, the gold cross affixed to the license plate, the Jesus bumper stickers with their blood red letters on a white background. The one on the left read, "Jesus loves *YOU!*" The one on the right, "Jesus died for your sins."

Without thinking twice, he immediately switched his blinker from a left-turn arrow to a right-turn. As soon as the westbound lane cleared, he pulled out and headed after the white Civic, his heart pounding. He didn't have a plan. All he'd hoped — a blind illogical hope, he'd begun to think — was that he could somehow find her before she heard about Lynn's death, connected it with him, and went to the sheriff.

Finding her was first. He hadn't really thought about what he'd do after that.

She drove as if she were late, weaving in and out of morning traffic. Fortunately, the heaviest traffic was leaving Cotton Grove, not entering it, and he was able to close the gap between them. Nevertheless, she was four cars ahead of him and he almost lost sight of her when she suddenly whipped into the central turn lane and zipped across in front of an oncoming car with only inches to spare.

He was forced to wait for six cars before he could follow and by then, the white Civic was nowhere to be seen.

Damn, damn, *damn!*

To be this close and then lose her.

He kept to the posted thirty-five miles per hour even though every instinct told him to go even slower so he could look carefully. Unfortunately, this was a residential street in a black neighborhood with black kids collecting on the corner to wait for their school buses. He couldn't afford to drive too slowly or they'd notice him.

Notice and remember.

He told himself that Cotton Grove was a little town and this black neighborhood was proportionately small, too. How long could it take to quarter the whole area?

As it turned out, he didn't have to. Two blocks down, he spotted the white Civic parked in the driveway of a neat brick house. He carefully noted the house number as he drove by but didn't have time to make out the name on the mailbox, too.

At the next corner, he made a left, then three right turns to bring him back down this street. As he passed the house a second time, he saw two women and two children getting into the car and he immediately pulled in ahead of a green van parked at the curb. He waited there with the motor running till the Civic backed out of the drive. Only the little girl's head turned in his direction when they passed him, and even she didn't seem to notice as he trailed them through town.

First stop was the middle school where she let off the boy, then the elementary school for the little girl. Finally, she stopped in front of a small house at the end of a shabby, unpaved, semi-rural street and the second woman got out. He was too intent on the driver to pay much attention to her passengers. A quick stop at a convenience store, then she drove straight back to the first house.

He was right behind her all the way, and

by the time she got out of the car and went into the house with her purchases, he'd begun to formulate his next move. She had to know about the murder by now, yet he hadn't been arrested. Either she hadn't looked at him closely enough to give the police a good description or she hadn't connected him with the murder room. But how could that be unless she was dumber than dirt? She'd driven around the corner of the motel just as he pulled the door closed behind him. He'd certainly registered a black female face and the car's religious symbols as she passed within fifteen feet. It seemed impossible that she wouldn't recognize him the minute she saw him face-to-face again.

He slowed down enough to read the name on the mailbox.

Freeman.

It was a sign.

Take care of that woman and he'd stay a free man.

The blue LCD numbers on her bedside clock marched inexorably toward eight o'clock. Lying there, watching the numbers reconfigure themselves to show every passing moment, Cyl DeGraffenried wondered dully who it was that first realized it would take only seven straight little segments of liquid crystal to display every digit.

She was supposed to be in court at nine, but she couldn't seem to pull herself out of bed. All she wanted to do was lie here and watch those little segments light up or then go dark as the numbers changed.

As an assistant district attorney, she'd seen her share of people with clinical depression and she knew that staying in bed was a classic symptom of withdrawal, but knowing it and being able to resist were two entirely separate things.

Like falling in love with Ralph Freeman. She had known it was stupid and wrong, and she hadn't been able to resist that either.

She considered herself religious, yet she'd never daydreamed of loving a preacher. And certainly not a married preacher.

Two months of unimagined happiness, followed by these last two nights of misery. Just thinking about Sunday night made her eyes fill up again with tears. Such delight when she'd opened her door to find him standing there.

Such grief when he told her why he'd come.

"You don't love her," she'd said and he didn't deny it.

Instead he took her in his arms as if reaching out for salvation and held her against his heart. "If it were just you and me, I'd walk through the fiery furnace to stay here with you forever. I love you more than I ever dreamed I could love anyone. The smell of you, the softness —" His voice broke with sorrow. "She's the mother of my children, Cyl, and she's done nothing to be humbled like this."

"But she doesn't love you!"

"No," he said bleakly, as his arms fell away from her. "No. But we both love God."

Coming from anyone else, it would have sounded sanctimonious. To Cyl, it sounded hopeless.

"What kind of God would keep the two of you in a loveless marriage?" she had wept. "God *is* love."

"If I left Clara, I'd be turning my back on His love," he said dully. "Breaking all the vows I ever took. I'd be saying that all the things I've preached, all the things I've believed in my whole life, were hypocrisy. I can't do that, Cyl. I can't live without God in my life."

"But God forgives the sinner," Cyl

argued, calling upon all the forensic skills that made her such a skilled prosecutor. "He'll forgive us. If you believe in Him, you know that's true."

"Could we forgive ourselves? Could we build a life on the wreckage of Clara's? Break my children's trust?" He touched her cheek, wet his fingers in her tears and brought his finger to his lips, almost as if it were a communion cup.

"These are my tears which are shed for you," she sobbed, seeing the sacrifice in his eyes. "Take. Drink."

He had crushed her in his arms then with all the intensity of his bitter grief, then, very gently, he had kissed her forehead and walked away.

Leaving her to lie here alone in an empty bed, numbly watching the blue segments come together and fall apart, endlessly marking a time that no longer had meaning.

The partnership of Lee and Stephenson, Attorneys at Law, had begun in an 1867 white clapboard house half a block down from the courthouse back in the 1920s. More than seventy years later, they were still there. When Dwight Bryant stopped in a little after nine, however, he found that this generation's Stephenson hadn't yet arrived.

"Only thing I'm getting's his voice mail," Sherry Cobb apologized. "I'm sure he'll be here directly. Let me fix you some coffee."

Dwight accepted readily. Of all the law firms in town, Lee and Stephenson had the best coffee.

Hearing their voices, John Claude Lee came to the door of his office.

"Got a minute?" asked Dwight.

As soon as he explained what he wanted, John Claude brought out a folder from the file drawer in his desk. As precise and well-ordered as John Claude himself, it was labeled "Christmas Gifts, Office" and after a quick perusal, he was able to give Dwight the brand name and model number of the silver pens, as well as the name of the jewelry store at the Cary Towne Center Mall.

"I bought three," said the white-haired attorney. "One for Reid, one for Deborah, who was still in partnership here that year, and the third for Sherry. Those were my personal gifts to my colleagues. As a gift from the firm the rest of the staff received silver pins shaped like snowflakes with their bonuses."

He returned the folder to its proper

place and closed the drawer. "May I assume your interest in my choice of Christmas gifts somehow relates to the death of that unfortunate Bullock's wife?"

"It might, but don't let it get out, okay?"

"My lips are sealed," said John Claude. "Sherry's on the other hand — Would you like for me to ascertain if she still has hers?"

"That would be a big help," Dwight admitted. In addition to having the best coffee, Lee and Stephenson also had the most gossipy office manager. While she was fairly reticent about the firm's business affairs, everything else seemed to be fair game.

"And of course, you'll want to see Reid's." The older man shook his head in weary resignation. His partner's randy nature was a constant trial.

Through the window behind John Claude's head, Dwight spotted Millard King heading down the sidewalk toward the law office next door.

"I'll check back by in a few minutes," he said and hurried out.

Talk about banker's hours, thought Dwight as he cut across the grass on an intercept path. Attorneys don't do too shabby either. Here it was almost nine-thirty, yet Reid wasn't in and King was just arriving.

"Overslept," said Millard King, although he looked alert enough to have been up for hours as Dwight followed him into the two-story white brick building that housed the firm of Daughtridge and Associates. "And I have a ten-fifteen appointment, so I can't give you but just a minute."

"Actually, it may take ten," said Dwight, settling into the comfortable leather chair in front of Millard King's shiny dark desk. "I understand that you were seeing Mrs. Bullock?"

King had worked hard to lose weight this last year, but he was still robustly built and inclined to perspire a little when nervous. He mopped his brow with a snowy white handkerchief, then took off his beautifully tailored gray jacket and hung it on the antique cherry coatstand behind the door before taking a seat behind his executive-sized desk. His shirt was pale blue with white cuffs and collar, his dark blue tie was held in place, not by a tie tack, but by a narrow gold clip. Late twenties, he had the slightly beefy, very blond, all-American good looks of an ex–college half-back who wasn't quite good enough for the pros. Rumors were that he was a fair-to-middling attorney with political ambitions beyond this junior partnership in Ambrose Daughtridge's firm.

King leaned back in his leather armchair, elbows on the armrests, and tented his fingers in front of his chest. "Am I a suspect in her death, Bryant?"

"Should you be?" Dwight asked mildly.

"I'd appreciate it if you wouldn't play games."

The judicious tones would have been more effective without that light sheen of perspiration on his forehead.

"This belong to you, by any chance?" Dwight asked, handing him the bagged flag-shaped tie tack they'd found near Lynn Bullock's body. "I'm told you had one like it."

"Sorry," said King. "I don't recognize it."

"You've heard how she was found?" Dwight asked. "The way she was dressed?"

"And you think *I* was the one going to meet her that night? I was on the ball field," he said indignantly. "You saw me. I hit a double off you, for God's sake!"

"We don't know yet when she was killed," said Dwight. "No one saw her after five or spoke to her after five-ten. Our game didn't start till well after six."

"Well anyhow, I'm covered from around five till our game ended," said King. "I try to run at least five miles a day and on Saturday, I used the school track to run laps from about five-fifteen till shortly before six when I joined the team."

"There's a footpath from the far end of the track, through the trees, out to the bypass. The Orchid Motel is exactly three-tenths of a mile from the track," said Dwight. "We measured."

"But I never left the track," he said tightly. "Dozens of people would have seen me leave or come back. Ask Portland or Avery Brewer."

"Were they out there running with you?"

"Of course not!" King snapped. "I was running alone. I mean, there were other people on the track, but not *with* me."

"Can you give me their names?"

Millard King frowned in concentration, then shook his head. "I didn't know any of them. One man looked a little familiar. He might be a doctor at the hospital, but I couldn't swear to it. Wait a minute! One of the women. She had on red shorts and a white shirt and I think she works in the library. Peggy Somebody."

"Peggy Lasater?"

"Yeah, that sounds right. She'll tell you."

Dwight wrote the name in the little ringbound notebook he carried in his jacket pocket. "What about after the game?"

"Straight home," King said virtuously.

"Which brings me back to my first question. Were you seeing her?"

It was clearly not a question King wanted to answer, but he leaned forward with the earnest air of a man about to put his cards face up on the table.

"Look," he said. "I'm twenty-eight, single, and if a woman comes on to me, looking for a roll in the hay with no commitments, why not?"

"And that's what happened with Lynn Bullock?"

King hesitated. "Is this off the record?"

"I'm not looking to jam you up," said Dwight. "If it's not relevant to our investigation, it stays in the department."

"Okay then. Because, see, I'm about to ask someone to marry me. Someone whose father's in the public eye and who wouldn't take kindly to having his daughter's name linked with a murder investigation. I've been absolutely faithful to her since we first started getting serious this past June and I intend to be faithful from here on out if we marry. I'm not going to have some little passing affair jump up and bite me in the ass ten or fifteen years down the road, if you get my drift."

Dwight nodded, suppressing a grin. Say what you will about Clinton, he thought to himself, but for young men with their eyes on future elective office, he sure had provided a real good object lesson for keeping their peckers in their pants.

"It was at the Bar Association dinner back in April. She was there with Jason in this tight red dress." He shook his head reflectively. "If it'd been New York — hell, if it'd even been Raleigh! But this was Dobbs and you should've seen all those other women looking at her sideways and reining their husbands in. Well, I didn't have any wife and neither did one or two others. You talked to Reid Stephenson yet? Or Brandon Frazier?"

"Frazier's a new one on me," said Dwight, noting down the name. "Didn't her husband mind?"

Millard King shrugged. "Some men like it when their wives make other men hot. Sorta like 'Yeah, you'd like to get in her panties, but I'm the one she goes home with.' Jason doesn't miss a trick in the courtroom but he didn't have a clue about his wife. Lynn and I got it on a couple of times, but right around then's when I got serious about the gal I'm hoping to marry and decided I didn't need that complication."

Something in his virtuous tone made Dwight ask, "Your idea or Mrs. Bullock's?"

"I guess you could call it a mutual decision," King admitted.

"In other words, she wanted to break it off more than you did."

"I told you —"

"So if she called you and invited you to join her at the Orchid Motel, you wouldn't have gone?"

"Absolutely not," Millard King said firmly.

At Memorial Hospital in Dobbs, Amy Knott stuck her head in the staff lounge and flourished a manila envelope. "I just wanted to tell everybody that we're collecting to make a donation to pre-op in Lynn Bullock's name."

"I'm sure going to miss her there," said one of the women doctors, handing Amy a ten-dollar bill. "She always went the extra mile. When's the funeral?"

"She's being cremated." Amy held the envelope open as other doctors dug in their pockets. "I understand there'll be a memorial service next month."

The door opened and a white-jacketed doctor came in. He had poured himself a cup of coffee before the unnatural silence finally registered. Spotting Amy's envelope, he said, "Taking up a collection?"

"For Lynn Bullock's memorial," Amy said with a rueful smile. "I don't guess you want to contribute."

"On the contrary." Dr. Jeremy Potts set his coffee down, opened his wallet, and made an elaborate show of pulling out a twenty-dollar bill. "I can't think of anything that would give me more pleasure."

Back at Lee and Stephenson, Dwight was amused to see that Sherry Cobb was using her silver ballpoint pen as she and one of the clerks proofed a long legal document. John Claude smiled benignly from his doorway.

"Reid's in his office," he said, pointing down the wide hallway to what used to be the dining room when this was a private house.

The door was ajar and Dwight rapped on it, then pushed it all the way open. Reid was on the phone and he motioned the big deputy sheriff to come on in as he pushed back his chair so he could open the long center desk drawer. He held the phone in one hand while he rummaged with the other.

"Okay then, Mrs. Cunningham. I'll draft that new codicil and . . . ma'am? . . . No, no, that's quite all right. It'll be ready for your signature tomorrow at ten."

He hung up and continued his search. "That old lady changes her will every time the moon changes. Ah, here it is. *Voila!*"

The morning was so overcast that Reid had his lights turned on and the silver pen gleamed in the lamplight as he fished it out from the back of the drawer and handed it over to Dwight.

Same make, same twining ivy leaves engraved along the length of the barrel.

Reid watched him compare the two pens. "Would you really have thought I killed her if I couldn't put my hands on it?"

Dwight shrugged. "Let's just say it moves you down the list a couple of notches."

"Come on, Dwight. I'm a lover, not a killer. You know that. I've told you — I saw her twice and that was one time too many."

Dwight just nodded and took out his little notebook. "Now as I recall, you got

157

out of somebody's bed and over to the ball field around six. But you left as soon as the game was over. Where'd you go after that?"

"I came back here, showered and changed, then drove over to Raleigh. You remember Wilma Cater?"

"Jack Cater's sister?"

"We went to see that new Tom Hanks movie, then stopped by the City Market for a couple of drinks."

"Who's *she* married to?" Dwight asked sardonically.

Reid laughed. "Don't let it get around, but I do go out with *un*married women every once in a while."

At noon, Deputy Mayleen Richards appeared in Dwight's doorway with some papers in hand. "I called the jewelry store and spoke to the manager. The *current* manager."

"Oh?"

"Yes, sir." A tall and solidly built ex-farmgirl, Richards had only recently been pulled off patrol duty. Dwight had decided that her diffidence with him and Sheriff Bo Poole was because she was still ultraconscious of protocol. "There's been a complete change of personnel from when

Mr. Lee bought those pens four years ago."

"But?"

"But they do keep pretty good records."

Dwight waved her over to the chair in front of his desk. "So what do these pretty good records show?"

Richards sat down stiffly. "Well, for one thing, the store makes a point of offering exclusive merchandise. They won't carry items you can find at every mall in North Carolina. The pens were made in England and distributed only through an importer in New Jersey. So I went ahead and called them and they confirmed it. The store in Cary Towne Mall was the only outlet between New York and Atlanta that carried the line. There's one in Boston, another in New Orleans." She looked down at her notes. "The rest are Chicago, Scottsdale, Vail, Seattle and L.A. for a total of six hundred pens — a hundred and fifty of them were this design."

"Good work," Dwight said approvingly. "So who owns ours?"

"The jewelry store's old invoices show that they stocked twenty silver pens from that company in four different designs. Five were the 'Windsor Ivy.' They have no documentation as to who bought three of the pens — those have to be Mr. Lee's three — but they do know that two pens were sold at employee discount to the then-manager, who now works in their flagship store in New Orleans."

"Did you call him?" asked Dwight.

"Her," said Richards, allowing herself the smallest of smiles for the first time. "She's not there today, so I left a message that I'd call tomorrow."

"Excellent," said Dwight. "Keep me informed."

"Yes, sir." She handed him some papers. "These are Jamison's interviews with the rest of the motel staff. Nothing useful. And the ME faxed over his preliminary report."

Dwight skimmed through the technical terms that basically said yes, Lynn Bullock had indeed died of strangulation. And based on testimony that she had been seen eating peanuts at approximately 4:45 p.m., it was safe to say that death occurred between the hours of 4:45 and 7:45 p.m.

"Cremated?" gasped Vara Seymour Benton Travers Fernandez. "We ain't never had nobody cremated in our whole family. My daughter ought to've been buried proper and decent, *in* her body, not burnt to ashes."

Jason Bullock looked at his mother-in-law and took a deep breath. "I'm sorry, Vara, but it's what Lynn wanted. We discussed it when I drew up our wills and that's what we both decided to do."

"She never!" Vara said stubbornly. "She ever tell you that, Lurleen?"

"Wills?" said Lynn's half-sister. "She always said she was going to will me her pink ice necklace and earring set. Did she?"

The older woman was skinny as a tobacco stick inside a pair of tight black slacks and a sleeveless top patterned in tiger stripes. Her orangy-blonde hair had been colored and bleached so many times it had thinned until you could see the scalp between the hair follicles. "You mean they's not going to be a church service or nothing?"

"We don't — Lynn didn't — neither of us belong to a church, Vara. It was something we meant to do, but . . ."

Jason Bullock's voice trailed away in regret. A church would have given structure to this hopeless morass he seemed to be floundering through. There would have been churchwomen bringing food and offering comfort, a minister who could have guided him into a traditional ceremony. Instead, he was suddenly thrust into unfamiliar territory and Lynn's only two relatives (if you didn't count her father and a bunch of half-siblings in Florida, and Lynn certainly never had) weren't making it any easier.

He hadn't been able to reach either of them by phone till early Monday morning. Lurleen immediately drove down from Roxboro, swinging through Fuquay to pick up Vara and bring her over. Now they were back again this afternoon and while there was grief in their eyes, there was also greed in Lurleen's.

He himself was so numb and conflicted at this point that he thought, Well, why not? What else was he going to do with Lynn's things?

"You and Vara can take what you want," he told Lurleen, "but first you've got to tell me. Who was Lynn sleeping with?"

"Just you, honey," she answered guilelessly.

"Ah, cut the crap, Lurleen," he said, suddenly angry. "You know where she died. And how."

She gave a petulant shrug. "She didn't tell me and that's the gawdawful truth. We used to be like this." She held up two crossed fingers. "But ever since y'all got so high and mighty with your fancy jobs and fancy money, she didn't tell me shit. And every time I asked, she'd just smile and say nobody, so she could've been blowing the governor, for all I know."

Tears and mascara cut dusky tracks through Vara's makeup. "Poor little Lynnie. She wanted to be somebody and now she's just ashes. And I didn't even get a chance to kiss her goodbye."

At the stoplight in Mount Olive, as a patrol car pulled even with him in the next lane over, Norwood Love kept his face expressionless, but his eyes went nervously to the pickup's rearview mirror. Everything back there was still secure. There was no way that trooper could see what was beneath the blue plastic tarp covering the truck bed. Besides, even if he *could* see them, there was no law against hauling a load of empty fifty-gallon plastic pickle barrels. For all anybody could say, he was maybe planning to store hog feed in 'em. Or turn 'em on their sides and use 'em for dog kennels. Till they were full of fermenting mash, couldn't nobody prove different.

The light changed to green and the young man pointed his truck back toward

Colleton County.

Reid Stephenson's first court appearance of the day was scheduled for two o'clock. As he left the office, he tucked the silver pen securely in the inner breast pocket of his jacket and wondered if Deborah by any chance left her doors unlocked out there on the farm.

Otherwise, he was going to have to figure out another excuse to drop by and get her pen back on her bedside table before she missed it.

Chapter 10

The air is calm and sultry until a gentle breeze springs from the southeast. This breeze becomes a wind, a gale, and, finally, a tempest.

Despite the long Labor Day weekend in which to get it out of their systems, courthouse regulars were still titillating each other with gossip of Lynn Bullock's death on Tuesday. Who was she having an affair with? Reid? Brandon Frazier? Millard King? Or was it someone yet unnamed? The more malicious tongues favored Millard King, simply because he'd become more priggish now that he was romancing the very proper Justice's debutante daughter. Malice is always entertained when prigs try to squeeze their clay feet into glass slippers.

There were those who thought it was tacky of Lynn Bullock to sleep with so many of her husband's peer group. "Why didn't she keep it at the hospital?" they asked. "All those beds going to waste. Why didn't she crawl into one with a doctor?"

"How you know she didn't?" came the cynical reply. "And come to think of it, wouldn't a doctor know exactly how much pressure it takes to strangle somebody?"

I'd never met the dead woman and I'd had very little to do with her husband so I shouldn't have been drawn into the discussions, yet, given Reid's peripheral involvement, I couldn't help being interested.

Unfortunately, I wasn't hearing much new.

I sat juvenile court that morning — emancipation, termination of parental rights, even a post-termination review, where I learned that two badly neglected twin brothers had been adopted into a loving family. In fact, the new parents were there with the babies, who were clearly thriving. Seeing your decisions vindicated like that is one of the happier aspects of being a judge.

In the afternoon, it was domestic court. There were the usual no-shows and requests for delays, along with a couple of unexpected meetings of minds that only required my signature rather than a formal hearing. By three o'clock, I was down to the final item on the day's docket.

Jason Bullock was scheduled to argue a domestic case in front of me that afteroon — contested divorces seemed to be turning into his specialty, and, under the circumstances, I would have granted a delay. But the plaintiff, one Angela Guthrie, wanted to be done with it and was willing to let Portland Brewer, one of Bullock's senior associates, represent her since she clearly felt any judge in the land would side with her.

Daniel Guthrie was represented by Brandon Frazier, a lean and intense dark-haired man who was also one of the men linked to Lynn Bullock's name. Frazier was about my age, divorced, no children. A lot of women around the courthouse, single *and* married, thought he was sexy-looking with those smoldering, deep-set eyes, but I've never much cared for hairy men. Not that I've ever seen his chest. Looking at the wiry black hair that covers the backs of his hands and wrists gives me a pretty good idea though.

It was the first time I'd seen Frazier since the murder, and if he was walking around with a load of guilt, it wasn't immediately visible. But then it wouldn't be, would it? Every good attorney — and Frazier's pretty good — is an actor and a con man. He has to be able to sell snake oil to a licensed doctor and he does. Why? Because he can make the doctor believe that he himself believes in it — one honorable man to another.

The Guthries were both in their mid-thirties. They had a nine-year-old son and an eleven-year-old daughter. Mr. Guthrie looked somewhat familiar. I seemed to recall him sitting in the witness stand to testify, but for what? Something criminal? My memory was that he'd sat up resolutely and spoken confidently. Today, he had a half-sheepish, half-defiant look about him.

His wife was suing for a divorce from bed and board (which in North Carolina is basically a court-approved legal separation) on the grounds of mental and physical cruelty. She asked for retention of the marital home, custody of the two minor children, child support and post-separation support — what used to be called temporary alimony. Whatever Danny Guthrie had done to her, it was still a burr under her saddle. According to the papers before me, she'd filed her complaint almost a full month earlier, yet, as she took the stand, I could see that she was madder than hell and it was scorched-earth/ sow-the-land-with-salt time.

My friend Portland led her through a recap of marital frictions, all the ordinary, but nonetheless irritating, things that finally drive a spouse to say "Enough!" — his disregard for her plans, his lack of involvement in their children's school activities, his excessive drinking, his erratic work hours.

That was when I realized why Danny Guthrie looked familiar. He was a former K-9 officer with the Fayetteville Police Department, now working dogs for the Drug Enforcement Agency.

"And when did you realize that your differences were completely irreconcilable, Mrs. Guthrie?" asked Portland Avery.

"It was sometime after midnight, the seventh of August. Or more accurately, between the hours of one a.m. and five thirty-eight on the morning of August eighth," Angela Guthrie answered crisply.

"That's remarkably precise," Portland said. "Would you elucidate?"

Green eyes flashing, Mrs. Guthrie described how her husband hadn't come home from work that evening, despite their earlier agreement that they would get up at dawn the next morning and drive to the mountains for a family vacation.

"A vacation that was supposed to give us a chance to relax together and learn to be a family again," said Mrs. Guthrie.

Instead, ol' Danny and Duke didn't come rolling in until well after midnight.

"Duke?" I asked.

"His dog. A Belgian Malinois."

As a judge, I've attended impressive demonstrations of what Malinois can do for law enforcement agencies. They're built like a sturdy, slightly smaller German shepherd and they're intelligent enough to understand several different orders. According to their handlers though, they have to be carefully trained to control a natural tendency toward aggressiveness.

Upset and angry, Mrs. Guthrie had smelled the whiskey on her husband before he got halfway across the kitchen.

"What did you say or do at that point?" asked Portland.

"I was really frosted that he didn't come home in time to help me get ready for the trip and now he was so drunk he wouldn't want to get up till late. *Plus* he'd been too drunk to drive, so we'd have to go get his car before we could get started. I just let him have it with both barrels. I told him exactly what I thought of him and his adolescent behavior," said Mrs. Guthrie, beginning to steam up all over again.

"And what did Mr. Guthrie say or do?"

"He never said a word. Just stood there swaying back and forth till I quit talking. That's when he looked at Duke, pointed at me and said, 'Guard!' and then staggered off to bed."

"What did you do next?"

"*Nothing!*" she howled, rigid with indignation. "Every time I tried to stand up, the damn dog started growling down deep in his chest. I sat there for four hours and thirty-eight minutes till my son came downstairs and I could send him back up to get Danny."

The bailiff and a couple of attorneys on the side bench were shaking their heads and chuckling.

Okay, I'm not proud of myself. I snickered, too. As a feminist, I was appalled. But as someone who grew up with a houseful of raucous brothers and dogs (dogs that half the time showed more sense than the boys), the thought of that dog and this woman eyeing each other half the night? I'm sorry.

Danny Guthrie misjudged my laugh and when he took the stand to tell his side of the story, he'd regained most of the easy confidence I remembered. He seemed to think I was going to be one of the guys, in full sympathy with what he clearly considered a harmless little prank.

"I'm no alcoholic," he said earnestly. "See, what happened was, our unit had just gotten a commendation for rounding up eight drug runners and we went out to celebrate. Yeah, I probably should've called her, but I didn't realize how late it was. Then I got home and I was really stewed. All of a sudden, that vodka hit me like a ton of bricks and she wouldn't shut up. All I wanted was to get away from her nagging tongue and go to bed. I honestly don't remember telling Duke to guard her. And it's not like he bit her or anything."

"But would he have if she'd tried to leave the room?" I asked.

"Maybe not bite exactly, but he'd of done whatever it took to hold her there."

"You're an officer of the law," I reminded him. "Didn't it occur to you that your wife could have had you arrested for false imprisonment? That you could be sitting in jail for a hundred and twenty days?"

"It was just a *joke!*" he repeated. "She doesn't have a sense of humor."

"Well, in this case, I'm afraid I don't either. What's the difference between what you did and hiring a man with a gun to keep her sitting there? And what happens when it's your weekend to have the children and you've been out celebrating? Would you have Duke guard *them?*"

Apprehensive of where I was going, Guthrie swore he never drank a drop when he was in charge of the children, that he would never put them in jeopardy.

When I asked Mrs. Guthrie the same question, she grudgingly admitted that he was, on the whole, a decent father. Not terribly attentive, but certainly never mean to them or physically abusive in any way.

In the end, despite an eloquent argument from Brandon Frazier, I granted the divorce from bed and board and gave Mrs. Guthrie most of what she was asking for.

The Colleton County Sheriff's Department is located in the courthouse basement and as soon as I'd adjourned court and stashed my robe, I went downstairs to give Dwight the swim trunks he'd left at my house on Sunday and which I'd forgotten to give him when he was out yesterday.

The shifts had just changed and he sat at his desk in short sleeves, his tie loosened and his seersucker jacket hanging on the coatrack. Labor Day might be the official end of white shoes for women, but Dwight never puts away his summer clothes till the weather starts getting serious about colder temperatures.

"Any luck with that man in the room next to Lynn Bullock's?" I asked idly. "The New Jersey license plate?"

We've known each other for so long and he's so used to me asking nosy questions about things that are technically none of my business that half the time he'll just go ahead and answer.

"Connecticut," he said now, distracted by a report he was reading. "No help at all. Turns out the guy's a sales rep for a drug company, on his way home from a sales conference in Florida. Got in around ten, left the next morning before nine. Says he didn't see or hear anything and probably didn't."

Dwight signed the paper he was reading, closed the folder, tossed it into his out-basket, then leaned back in his chair and propped his big feet on the edge of his desk.

"We got the ME's report. He says Lynn Bullock bought the farm sometime between five and eight, although we know she called her husband at five and someone called her at five-ten. That means she was dead before Connecticut ever checked in."

"What about John Claude's pens? Reid and Sherry show you theirs?"

"Yeah. But the store had five to start with. I've got Mayleen Richards working on it."

"There must be hundreds of them like that around," I speculated.

"Not as many as you'd think." He gestured toward the yellow legal pad that lay just beyond his reach. It was covered with doodles and notes that he'd taken when Deputy Richards gave her report. "The national distributor swears that he imported a hundred and fifty and only five of those were sent to this area. 'Course, the way people are moving in from all over, who knows? The whole hundred and fifty could've worked their way back east by now."

I smiled. "Good thing we still had ours."

"Good for Reid, anyhow."

Even though I hadn't *really* been worried about my cousin, I did feel a little relieved that the pen wasn't his.

"You're just going through the motions," I said. "You know you don't think Reid could do a thing like that."

"I quit saying what a person could or couldn't do a long time ago."

Dwight's only a few years older, but sometimes he acts as if those years confer a superior insight into human motivations. He gave a big yawn, stretched full length, then sat upright and opened another folder. "If we don't get a viable suspect in the next twenty-four hours though, I'm going to start looking at all her old boy-friends a little closer. Millard King says he was jogging. Brandon Frazier says he went fishing. Alone. And Reid didn't get to the ball field till after six. Remember?"

I wondered whose reputation would go in the toilet if Reid had to tell what bed he'd been in that afternoon.

Speak of the devil and up he jumps.

Thunder rumbled overhead and rain sprinkled the sidewalks as I hurried toward the parking lot before the heavens opened all the way and drenched my dark red rayon blouse. It isn't that I mind the wet so much, but that particular blouse starts to shrink the minute water touches it — rather like the wicked witch when Dorothy empties the water bucket on her — and I was supposed to attend an official function that evening.

I slid into my car just as the rain started

in earnest and there was Reid's car parked by mine, nose to tail, so that we were facing each other. Reid powered down his window. With the rain slanting into his window instead of mine, I did the same.

"Feel like going to Steve's for supper?" he said.

"Not particularly."

My cousin Steve runs a barbecue house down Highway 48, a little ways past the farm, and it's the best barbecue in Colleton County, but I was pigged out at the moment. During election season, that's all they seem to serve at fund-raisers. "Why?"

"No reason. Just thought it might be fun to go by for the singing. Y'all still do that every week?"

"Yes, but that's on Wednesdays."

I almost had to smile. My brothers and cousins and anybody else that's interested get together informally at Steve's after Wednesday night choir practice or prayer meeting to sing and play bluegrass and gospel. It's so country and Reid's so town. He doesn't play an instrument, he doesn't know the words and he's never dropped in when we were jamming except by accident.

"Well, maybe tomorrow night then?"

Rain pelted his face. His tan shirt and

brown-striped tie were getting wet, yet he didn't raise his window as he waited for my answer.

It was after five o'clock and I had plans for the evening, so I quit trying to figure out what he really wanted and said, "Sure."

Maybe he'd hit me with it before I had to watch him make a fool of himself at Steve's.

A month earlier, Cyl DeGraffenried and I had been asked to participate in a "Women in Law" forum at Kirkland Prep, an all-female school on the southwest edge of Raleigh. Since Cyl's apartment is on the way, we'd agreed that I'd pick her up early and we'd stop for supper somewhere first.

Cyl and I aren't best friends but we're working on it. Chronologically, she's five years younger. Psychologically, she acts five years older. She thinks my moral standards are too flexible, I think hers are overly rigid. When we argue politics and religion, she accuses me of being a flaming liberal. I *know* she's a social conservative. She's better read and more intellectual than I am, but she also has a dry, self-deprecating wit that keeps me off balance. Most true conservatives can't laugh at

178

themselves — they're too busy pointing a sour finger at the rest of us — so Cyl's mordant sense of humor gives me hope that I'll convert her yet.

I hadn't seen her around the courthouse during the day, but that wasn't unusual. She prosecutes cases all over the district, wherever Doug Woodall sends her, and I'd left a message on her voice mail that I'd be by her place around six.

Her apartment's in one of the new suburban developments that have popped up like dandelions between Garner and Raleigh. A swimming pool and fitness center surrounded by interlocking two-story duplexes that look more like yuppie townhouses than boxy apartments. Attractive low-maintenance landscaping. Tall spindly sticks that will eventually grow into towering shade trees if the whole place isn't first leveled for another mall.

It was still raining when I drove into the parking area in front of Cyl's ground-floor unit. The wind had died, and rain fell straight down from the sodden gray skies with a steady, almost sullen persistence, as if prepared to go on all night long. We'd had so much in the last few weeks that the ground was saturated, the creeks and rivers were swollen and it didn't seem possible that there was any more water left in the clouds.

I did the umbrella maneuver — the one where you crack the car door, cautiously stick the umbrella up into the air and try to get it completely open so you won't get drenched when you step out of the car? I managed to save my blouse, but when I reached back inside the car for my purse, I tipped the umbrella and dumped a gallon of water on my skirt.

One thing about platform shoes though: they do help you walk through shallow puddles without getting your feet wet.

I splashed over to Cyl's door and stood beneath its mini-portico to ring the bell.

No answer.

I rang again, then scanned the parking area as I waited. Yes, there was her car, two spaces over from mine. She was probably on the phone or in the shower.

This time I leaned on the button a full thirty seconds.

Nada.

The curtains were half open but I couldn't see any movement or much else inside the dark interior. On such a dreary late afternoon, her lights should have been on. Was the power out? Maybe the doorbell didn't work? I pounded on the wooden panel, then put my ear close to the door and mashed the doorbell again till I heard endless chimes echo around the rooms inside.

This wasn't like Cyl at all. She's not only punctual, she's usually punctilious.

I darted back to my car and used my flip phone to dial her number. The answering machine kicked in after the first ring and I said, "Cyl? Are you there? Pick up!"

I finally decided that maybe I'd gotten our signals crossed and that she'd probably gone on ahead with someone else.

Instead of a leisurely gossipy supper, I hit the drive-through at Hardee's and ate a chicken sandwich in my car while the rain drummed on the roof and the windows fogged over.

At Kirkland Prep, I joined Judge Frances Tripp, the appeals court judge who administered my oath of office when I was first appointed to the bench, and Lou Ferncliff, one of the highest-paid personal injury attorneys in Raleigh. But no Cyl. The facilitator was head of the social studies department and very p.c. In addition to enlightening the student body with our female insights into the field of law, we were also supposed to be a visual civics lesson: two white women and two African-Americans, colleagues in law and equals under the law.

Cyl DeGraffenried's absence skewed the balance and made the facilitator very unhappy. I wasn't happy either. This was so totally unlike Cyl that I was starting to worry.

Fortunately, Frances and Lou are troupers and had participated in panels like this so many times they could probably do it in their sleep. And I've never been shy about speaking up, so it was a lively discussion.

The students were bright enough to ask intelligent questions and we probably turned a half-dozen of them on to the law. ("Just what this country needs," Lou laughed as the forum broke up around nine-thirty. "More lawyers.")

I probably should have gone on home, but Cyl's apartment was only a couple of miles out of my way and I knew I wouldn't rest easy if I didn't satisfy myself that she was okay.

Her car hadn't been moved and this time I rang that damn bell for almost three solid minutes. Just when I was ready to give up and go call her grandmother, a light came on in the living room and a moment later, the door opened.

"Cyl?"

She looked like hell. Barefooted, wearing nothing but a long pink cotton T-shirt, her eyes were puffy and bloodshot, her face looked bloated, and she had a bad case of bed hair. She blinked at me as if disoriented.

"What's wrong?" I asked, startled by her groggy appearance. "Are you sick?"

She shook her head dazedly. "Deborah? What time is it? Why are you here?"

"The forum," I said. "Supper. Kirkland Prep. Did you forget?"

"Oh, Lordy, was that tonight? What day is it?"

I reached out and touched her forehead, but it was cool to my fingers, so she wasn't running a fever.

"It's Tuesday. When did you last eat?"

"Sunday? Sunday night?" Her shoulders slumped. "Sunday," she moaned.

I propped my dripping umbrella against the wall beneath the skimpy portico and moved past her. "You need food."

She made a gesture of protest but was too dispirited to do more than follow me into her kitchen and watch as I opened cabinets until I found a can of tomato soup.

I dumped it into a saucepan and while that heated, put some cheese on a slice of whole wheat bread and popped it into her toaster oven. "Are you on anything?"

Cyl shook her head, then paused in uncertainty. "Valium? I couldn't sleep. I think I took a couple sometime last night? This morning?"

I poured hot soup into a mug and put it in her hands. "Drink!"

Obediently, she did as I ordered.

Which only confirmed that something was definitely wrong here. No way does a functioning Cyl DeGraffenried take directions from me.

I made a pot of coffee and when it was ready, she drank that, too, and even nibbled at the toasted cheese.

While she ate, I chattered about the forum and how we'd covered for her and how brilliant Frances and Lou and I had been. Eventually, she almost gave a half-smile as the food and caffeine started to kick in a little and I said, "What's going on, Cyl? Something happen at work?"

She shook her head listlessly.

"Something wrong in your family?" So far as I knew, her grandmother was the only family member she truly cared about. "Your grandmother's not sick, is she?"

"No."

In my book, that left only one thing to make a woman like Cyl fall apart. "Who's the man, Cyl, and what's he done?"

A further thought struck me. "Oh jeeze! You're not pregnant, are you?"

"I wish I were!" she burst out passionately. And then her face crumpled.

If those red eyes were any indication, she'd already cried a river of salty tears. I put my arms around her and made comforting noises as she wept again, long hopeless sobs that echoed the rain streaming down her windows.

There was a box of tissues by the kitchen phone and as her emotional storm dwindled, I pulled out a handful and smoothed her hair while she wiped her eyes and blew her nose.

"Sorry," she said at last, making a visible effort to pull herself together. "This is so stupid. I'm sorry I forgot about the forum and thanks for fixing me the soup, Deborah. I'll be all right now."

Not the most tactful brush-off I've ever had. Not going to work either. If I thought she had a girlfriend to call or a sister she'd turn to, I'd have been out of there as soon

185

as she hinted. But Cyl's such a loner, I didn't think it'd be healthy to leave her to keep going round and around in her head as she'd evidently been doing these last two days.

"So when did he dump you?" I poured myself a cup of coffee and topped hers off again. "Sunday? Saturday?"

"How do you know I didn't dump him?" she asked, with a shadow of her old spirit.

"I've dumped and I've been dumped and I know which one makes me want to stay in bed with the covers pulled over my head. It's pretty bad, huh?"

"We were only together twice." Her voice was weary. "The first man I've been with since law school."

Why was I not surprised?

"I didn't want it to happen. Neither of us did. Not with him — not with him married."

Now that *did* surprise me. As many backhanded jabs as she's made at *my* love life, I knew that Cyl's personal code of morality was straight out of the Old Testament. She might be able to rationalize fornication but no way could she do adultery without a heavy load of guilt.

"We didn't realize what was happening until it was too late," she said. "It was just friendship. Talking. A cup of coffee. He helped me through that rough time, the day I found out what happened to Isaac. He was so easy to talk to. Almost like talking to Isaac when I was a little girl. I felt as if there was nothing I couldn't tell him, that he would just listen. Without judging or condemning."

Isaac was Cyl's uncle, a boy who'd been more like an older brother than an uncle, a brother she'd idolized. He disappeared when she was only eight or nine years old and everyone thought he'd fled to Boston without a backward look, which was probably why Cyl had grown up feeling betrayed and abandoned and wary of trusting again. I was there the day she learned how he died, a day of high emotions, another rainy day like this one, with Cyl so full of grief that —

"Ralph Freeman?" I exclaimed.

Cyl looked almost as shocked as I felt. "How did you guess?"

"Hell, I was standing right beside you when you asked him for a ride back into town. He shared his umbrella with you out to the parking lot. I remember asking about his wife and children and he said they were visiting her family back in Warrenton. Is that when it happened?"

"Nothing happened," Cyl protested. "Not that day, anyhow. We just talked. Then, two weeks ago, he came by the office to ask about a man in his church that he was trying to help. A misdemeanor. It was a Friday afternoon. Everyone else was gone. I pulled the shuck to check the charges. He was reading it over my shoulder. I looked up to say something. Our lips were so close. And then they were touching, and then —"

She broke off but I couldn't help wondering. Right there on Doug Woodall's couch?

"We knew it was wrong. But it felt so right." She sighed and shook her head sadly. "We knew we'd sinned, and we said we'd never do it again. But it was like not knowing how hungry you are till you see the food spread out before you and God help us, Deborah, we were both starving. Touching him. Being touched. It was a banquet. Afterwards, I guess we tried to pretend it was a one-time thing. An aberration. We stayed away from each other for a week and then, Saturday morning . . ."

She fell silent for a long moment and tears pooled again in her large brown eyes. "It was even more wonderful," she whispered.

I didn't know Ralph Freeman's wife except by reputation: a God-fearing, commandment-keeping woman who didn't trust white people. I did know his children though, an eleven-year-old son and a seven-year-old daughter who was an engaging little gigglebox. Kids like Stan and Lashanda are one more reason I don't mess with married men.

As if reading my mind, Cyl said, "He has children, a wife, a commitment to Jesus. And he's right. It could jeopardize my job, too. He can't — *we* can't — That's what he came to tell me Sunday night. We can't ever see each other alone again. And he's right. I *know* he's right. But, oh Deborah, how can I stand it?"

And she began to cry again.

Chapter 11

Never did a storm work more cruelly.

September 4 (Weds.)
— As of 6 a.m. Hurricane Fran 26° N by 73.9° W.
— Winds at 100 kts. (115 mph) — now a Category 3 hurricane.
— Predicted to hit land sometime tomorrow night.
— Hurricane watch posted last night from Sebastian Inlet, FL to Little River Inlet, SC.
— Evacuating coastal areas of NC, SC & GA.
— Trop. strm. winds 250+ mi. from eye & hurr. winds out 145 mi. — gale-force wind & rain if it hits NC.

Stan Freeman finished jotting his morning notes with a sense of growing excitement. Maybe they'd get a little action this far inland after all.

Certainly his parents seemed concerned when he joined them for breakfast. The kitchen radio was tuned to WPTF's morning weather report. Rain today and more predicted for tomorrow with gusty winds. Unless Hurricane Fran took a sudden sharp turn soon, North Carolina was definitely in for it.

"It's a biggie," Stan told them happily. "Almost three hundred miles across. A lot bigger than Bertha and you saw what *she* did. They're talking winds a hundred and thirty miles an hour! Storm surges twenty feet high! And if it comes in at Wilmington, we might even get tornadoes."

"Stanley!" his mother protested.

"Tornadoes?" Lashanda's eyes widened. "Like Dorothy? Our house will get blown away? Mama?"

"Your brother's talking about 'way down at the coast," Clara said with soothing tones for her daughter and a warning glare for her son. "That's a long way away. And it seems to me, Stanley, that you should be praying the storm passes by instead of hoping it hits and causes so many people grief."

"I'm not wishing them grief, Mama," he protested as the phone rang and his father got up to answer. "I'm just telling you what the weather reports say. I have to keep up with it for my science project. You want me to get a good grade, don't you?"

As he knew it would, citing school as a justification for his excitement somewhat mitigated her displeasure.

"Don't worry, Shandy," he told his little sister. "We'll be safe this far inland."

A drop of milk splashed on Lashanda's skirt and she jumped up immediately for a wet cloth to sponge it off. She was wearing her Brownie uniform since they were meeting immediately after school.

His father hung up the phone and came back to the table. "That was Brother Todd. He and the other deacons think we ought to cancel prayer meeting tonight, and spend the evening taking down the tent. The canvas is so rain-soaked that it's dripping through. One strong gust could send it halfway to Raleigh."

"When will you start?" asked Stan. "After school? I can help, can't I?"

"Me, too," said Lashanda.

"You're too little," Clara told her. "Besides, that's men's work."

"It's not fair!" Lashanda's big brown eyes started to puddle up. "Boys get to have all the fun."

"I thought we agreed not to stereotype gender roles," Ralph said mildly.

Clara's tone was three shades colder. "Wrestling with a tent in the wind and rain is not appropriate for a little girl."

"Or a little boy either," he said with a smile for his daughter. "But I bet we can find something that *is* appropriate. Maybe you can gather up the tent pegs, honey. Would you like that?"

The child nodded vigorously.

"We'll see," said Clara as the phone rang again.

"For you," Ralph told her, handing over the receiver.

"Sister Clara?" came a woman's strong voice. "This is Grace Thomas and I sure do hate to bother you this early in the morning, but I wanted to catch you 'fore you got off."

Grace Thomas was a fiercely independent old woman who lived a few miles out from Cotton Grove. She and her late husband were childless, her only niece lived in Washington, and there were no near black neighbors. Even the nearest white neighbor was a quarter-mile away. None of this had been a problem until she broke her leg last week.

"You're not bothering me a bit," said Clara. "How's that leg of yours?"

"Well, it's not hurting so bad, but I still

193

can't drive yet and with the hurricane coming and all, I was wondering if maybe you or one of the other sisters could fetch me some things from the store?"

"I'll be happy to." Clara signalled to Stan to hand her the notepad and pencil that lay on the counter.

She was in the habit of listing her plans for the day and the list already had four or five items on it.

Now she added Mrs. Thomas's needs: bread, milk, eggs, cat food, lettuce, lamp oil and a half-dozen C batteries.

"Batteries might not be a bad idea for us," said Ralph as he finished eating and carried his dishes to the sink. "I doubt we'll lose power, but you never know. Best be prepared. Isn't that the Scout motto, Shandy?"

The child wasn't listening. Instead, she wiggled her finger around in her mouth and pulled out something small and white.

"My tooth fell out! Look, Daddy! I wasn't biting down hard or anything and it just fell out. Am I bleeding?"

She bared her teeth and there was a gap in her lower incisors. Three of the upper ones had been shed so long that they were half-grown back in, but this was the first of the lower ones.

"Better hurry up and put it in a glass of water," Stan teased. "You let it dry out and the Tooth Fairy won't give you more than a nickel for it."

The Tooth Fairy had been yet another of the many forbiddens in Clara's childhood and she was eternally conscious of her father's strictures concerning anything supernatural. Ralph, though, likened it to believing in Santa Claus, just another harmless metaphor for an aspect of God's love. She suspected there was something faulty in his logic — Santa Claus might be an elf, yet he was modeled on a real saint, whereas the Tooth Fairy — ? But Ralph had more book-learning and he was her husband, the head of their household, she told herself, and it was her wifely duty to submit to his judgment in these matters. Besides, they'd allowed Stanley to believe and it didn't seem to have interfered with his faith in Jesus.

So her smile was just as indulgent as Ralph's when Lashanda carefully deposited her tooth in a small glass of water and carried it back to her bedroom.

Their shared complicity made it the first time since Sunday that things had felt normal to Stan. His mother's smile transformed her face. Forever after, whenever he remembered that moment, he was always glad that he'd reached out and touched her hand and said, "You look awful pretty today, Mama."

She was usually too self-conscious to accept compliments easily, but today she gently patted his cheek. "Better go brush your teeth, son, or we're going to be late."

When they were alone in the kitchen, Clara lifted her eyes to Ralph in a look that was almost a challenge.

He picked up his umbrella and briefcase. "I'll be home by four-thirty," he said as he went out to the carport.

In the days to come, it would be his burden that there had been no love in his heart for her this morning.

That he hadn't said, "Your mama *does* look pretty today."

That he hadn't even said goodbye.

"Hello? . . . Hello?" The man's voice became impatient. "Is anybody there? Hello!"

The rain was coming down hard, drumming on her red umbrella like the racing of her heart. Rosa Edwards swallowed hard and tried to speak, but she was so nervous, she knew she'd botch it.

Instead, she abruptly hung up and

moved away from the exposed public telephone outside the convenience store. She had thought out everything she meant to say, but the minute she heard his voice, knowing he was a murderer, she couldn't speak.

Telephones were so fancy these days. Buttons you could push and it'd call the person you last called. Another button and it'd tell you what number last called you. Not that it'd get him anywhere if he did find out she was calling from this phone. Wasn't in her neighborhood.

Her feet were soaking wet as she splashed back to her raggedy old car that just came out of the shop for $113.75. While rain beat against the piece of plastic she'd taped over the broken window on the passenger side, she rehearsed it in her mind all again, the way she'd just say it right out, no messing around. Then, when she was perfectly calm, she walked back to the phone, inserted her coins and dialed his number again.

As soon as he answered, she spoke his name and said, "This is the gal that saw you coming out of Room 130 at the Orchid Motel Saturday evening."

First he tried to bluster, then he tried to intimidate her, but she plowed on with what she had to say.

"Now you just hush up and listen. What you done to her ain't nothing to do with me. You give me ten thousand dollars cash money and I won't never say nothing to nobody. You don't and I'm going straight to the police. You get the money together and I'll call you back this number at six o'clock and tell you where to leave it."

She hung up without giving him a chance to answer, and even though the concrete was wet and her tires were almost bald, she laid down rubber getting out of the parking lot just in case there were fancier, quicker ways to find out where she was calling from.

The rain was starting to get on Norwood Love's nerves. The young man had worked his muscles raw these last few days, trying to get this underground chamber fitted out properly with running water, drainage pipes, air-conditioning, propane tanks, and ventilation ducts. His cousin Sherrill had helped some. Sherrill was the only one he trusted to help and keep his mouth closed. Most of it, he'd done alone though, keeping it secret even from his wife. Not many women want their husbands to mess with whiskey and JoAnn was no different.

Fortunately, she worked regular hours in town, so it wasn't all that hard to do things without her noticing.

With the money from Kezzie Knott, he'd bought some stainless steel vats second-hand at a soup factory over in Harnett County. He'd fashioned the cooker to his own design, did the welding himself. The copper condensing coil was one his dad had made before he flipped out the last time — *Only thing he ever give me that he didn't take back soon as he sobered up,* thought Norwood. The fifty-gallon plastic barrels from that pickle factory out near Goldsboro stood clean and ready to fill.

He knew how to buy sugar in bulk without getting reported and he had a couple of migrant crew bosses waiting to buy whenever he was ready to sell.

Best of all, he'd figured out a way to keep the smell of fermenting mash from giving him away. That's how most ALE officers claimed they stumbled over a lot of stills, just following their noses. In his personal opinion, that was a bunch of bull. Oh, maybe once in a blue moon, it'd happen like that. Most times, though, it was somebody talking out of turn or talking for bounty money. All the same, for that one chance in a hundred, he meant not to be found by any smells.

But this rain! The dirt floor was turning into a mudpie and water was seeping down the concrete block walls. And now the weatherman was saying hurricane? Be a hell of a note if he got flooded out before he even got started good.

To Rosa Edwards's relief, she hadn't left it too late. The Freeman children were just coming out to the carport when she got there. She pulled her car in beside Clara's and hopped out, leaving the motor running. "Your mama inside?"

"Yes, ma'am," said Lashanda.

"We're on our way to school," Stan warned her.

"It's okay," said Rosa. "I won't make y'all late."

She darted on into the house just as Clara came down the hall with her purse in one hand and car keys in the other.

"Rosa! Good morning." She tilted her head in concern. "Is something wrong?"

"No, no, and I know you're in a hurry. I got one quick little favor to ask you though."

"It'll have to be real quick," Clara said, glancing at the kitchen clock. "I forgot how rain slows everything down."

Rosa handed her the white envelope she carried. Humidity made the paper limp, but it was sealed with Scotch tape.

"Would you keep this for me?"

The envelope wasn't thick. No more than a single sheet of paper inside. Clara turned it in her hand and looked at Rosa inquiringly.

"I can't tell you what it is," said Rosa. "But would you just hold on to it for me till I ask for it back? Keep it somewhere safe?"

"Sure," said Clara and tucked it in her purse as she shepherded Rosa toward the door. "I'll keep it right here next to my billfold."

"Thanks," Rosa said, heading for her own shabby car which waited with the motor still running. "See you tonight."

Then she was gone before Clara remembered to tell her that prayer meeting was going to be cancelled.

"Millard King? Yes, I know him," said the librarian. "Well, not *know* him, but I know who he is. Why?"

Deputy Mayleen Richards smiled encouragingly. "He said you passed him out on the track at the Dobbs middle school Saturday afternoon."

Peggy Lasater wrinkled her forehead in an effort to remember.

"He said you were wearing red shorts and a white shirt."

"Did he happen to mention that I was also wearing a Walkman?"

Richards checked her notes. "No Walkman."

"People think if you're a librarian, you spend your days reading. They should see all the shelving and cataloging we do. When I run? That's when I get to read."

"Read?"

The librarian nodded. "Books on tape. I did run Saturday afternoon, but I was too absorbed in the last Charlotte MacLeod to notice anything except where I was putting my feet. Sorry."

Clara Freeman left Cotton Grove and drove south on Old 48, a narrow winding road that follows the meanders of Possum Creek. With headlights and wipers both on high, she drove cautiously through the heavy rain. Where the road dipped, deep puddles had formed. They sent up broad wings of water on either side of her Civic as she plowed through.

Once beyond the city limits, there were few cars on the road and she was able to relax a bit and to open her window a tiny crack. Not enough to let the rain in, but enough to keep the windshield from fogging up so badly.

She had dropped the children off at school, taken Brother Wilkins to the eye clinic, picked up the dry cleaning, waited for Brother Wilkins to come out of the clinic, taken him to the Winn-Dixie with her while she shopped for Sister Grace, then helped him into the house with his few bags of groceries. ("Bless you, child," he'd said. "I'm gonna pray God sends you help in your old age like He sent you to help us.")

She would deliver Sister Grace's things and then it would be time for lunch. After lunch — ?

Her mind momentarily blanked on what came next on the list.

As Ralph's wife — no, as the *minister's* wife — she had cheerfully put her services at the beck and call of his congregation and she'd always made lists to organize her days. But since finding those condoms in his desk on Sunday, she tried to pack her days even fuller so she wouldn't have time to brood on how his betrayal undermined the very foundation on which she'd built her life.

Her hands gripped the steering wheel so fiercely that her knuckles gleamed through the tight skin.

How? she asked herself for the thousandth time since she'd found those condoms. How *could* he have done this dreadful, stupid thing? Did every man, from the President of the United States of America right down to her own husband, put sex before honor? Make themselves slaves of their malehood, shackle their God-given free will to their gonads?

At least Ralph didn't try to excuse himself by saying, "The woman tempted me so I sinned." No, he'd rightfully taken the blame on himself. And when he came back home Sunday night and lay down beside her in the darkness, she'd asked two questions. "Does she go to our church?"

"No," he'd answered.

"Is she white?"

"No, Clara."

That was all she'd wanted to know, but he had a question of his own. "Do you want a divorce?"

Her heart leaped up and she'd let Satan tempt her for a moment.

To be free of him always wanting what she didn't have in her to give? To go back to her father's house? To sleep alone in a narrow bed?

Then she remembered being a daughter in her father's house, a minister's daughter, not a minister's wife. Abiding by rules, not making them. Having to ask, not tell.

As a wife, she had the power to do God's work.

As a daughter? A divorced woman with a failed marriage?

Her father would do his duty by her, however much he might disapprove of her decision. His congregation would be kind.

But respect? Position?

"No," she'd said. "No, I don't want a divorce. All I want is your promise that you'll never go to her again."

"As God is my strength," he told her.

She had turned to him then, ready to give her body as a reward for his vow. He had not pushed her away, merely patted her shoulder as if she were Lashanda or Stanley. In that moment, she realized that he might never again reach for her in the night, and part of her was glad.

Another part felt suddenly bereft.

That sense of loss still clung to her this morning even though she knew that she'd acted as God would have her. She had been grievously wronged, yet she had risen above his sin. She had forgiven him. So why should *she* feel this inner need for forgiveness?

With relief, she reached the dead end of the unpaved road where Sister Thomas lived and hurried inside with the groceries and supplies.

She fed Sister Thomas's cat, changed the sheets on the bed and straightened up the kitchen, but when the old woman invited her to stay for lunch, she excused herself and ran through the rain back to her car.

In just the hour that she'd been inside, the rutted clay roadbed had turned into a slippery, treacherous surface that scared her as the tires lost traction and kept skewing toward the deep ditches. She was perspiring freely by the time she'd driven the quarter-mile back to the hardtop.

Pulling out onto the paved road, she recklessly lowered her window and let the cool rain blow in her face. She took deep breaths of the humid air that did nothing to dislodge the weight that seemed to have settled on her heart since Sunday night.

That's when she noticed the lights of a car behind her. Even though it was noon, the sky was black and the dazzle of lights on her rain-smeared rear window made it impossible for her to distinguish make or driver. Dark and late-model were all she could tell about the car as it rushed up behind her.

She moved over to the right as far as possible. If he was in that big a hurry, maybe he'd go ahead and pass even though there were double yellow lines on this twisty stretch.

A second later, her head jerked and she felt her car being bumped from behind.

What the — ?

Another glance in the rearview mirror. He'd done it deliberately! And now he was so close that the headlights were blanked out by the rear of her own car.

She could clearly see the white man behind the steering wheel.

Fear grabbed her and she stepped on the accelerator.

He bumped her again.

It was her worst nightmare unfolding in daylight.

Her dress was getting soaked, but she was too terrified to think of raising the window. Instead, she floored the gas pedal and the Civic leaped forward.

Almost instantly, he caught up with her.

The road curved sharply and she nearly lost control as the car fishtailed on the wet pavement.

Then he pulled even with her and they raced through the rain, neck and neck along the deserted road and through another lazy S-curve that swept down to an old wooden bridge over Possum Creek. With so much rain, the creek had overflowed its banks and was almost level with the narrow bridge.

Again Clara pulled to the right to give him room to pass.

At that instant, he bumped her so hard from the side that her air bag inflated. She automatically braked, but it was too late. The Civic was airborne and momentum carried it straight into the creek. By the time it hit the water, the air bag had deflated and Clara's head cracked hard against the windshield, sending her into darkness.

As the car sank deeper, muddy creek water flooded through the open window.

Just as he was thinking about lunch, Dwight Bryant looked up to see Deputy Richards hovering near his door and he motioned her in.

"I spoke to the librarian that Millard King said was jogging when he was. She was listening to a book on her Walkman and couldn't say who else was out there."

"Too bad. But King said he thought one of the men was a doctor. Try calling around to see if any of them were jogging."

"Yes, sir. And remember that jewelry store manager who bought the other two silver pens?"

"New Orleans, right? You talked to her?"

"Yes, sir, but no help there. She gave those two pens to her granddaughters. They're in high school in New Mexico and still have them so far as she knows."

Dwight frowned. "I knew it wasn't going to be that easy."

"No, sir," said Mayleen Richards. "I'll start calling the doctors."

When his phone rang promptly at six p.m., he was momentarily startled, but he collected himself in the next instant and his voice was calm. "Hello?"

"It's me," said the woman.

The same woman who'd called this morning.

The woman he'd sent crashing into the creek at noon.

Wasn't it?

"You got the ten thousand?"

"Who is this?" he croaked.

"You know who it is," she answered impatiently. "You got the money or do I go to the police?"

"How do I know you won't anyhow?"

" 'Cause I'm giving you my word and I ain't never broke my word yet."

Like I'd trust you far as I could throw you, he thought angrily.

But he willed himself to calmness. He was an educated white man, he told himself, and she was a stupid black bitch. He'd already killed one nigger woman today. He could certainly kill another.

"I've got the money," he lied. "Where do you want to meet?"

"We ain't gonna meet." Tersely, she named the Dobbs Public Library, told him to put the money inside a white plastic bag, and described where he was to leave the packet in precisely forty-five minutes. "I'll be watching. You leave it and just walk on out the front door, 'cause I see your face I'm gonna start screaming the walls down."

That didn't give him much time to fashion a packet that looked like money, wrapped tightly in a plastic bag and wound around with duct tape. She might duck into the ladies' room, but she'd never get into this packet without a knife or scissors. Satisfied, he put the packet into a white plastic bag as instructed, drove to the library, left it on the floor beside the specified chair, and walked out without looking back.

Once outside though, he raced around the corner, through the alley and back to his car that he'd left parked well down the block. A few minutes later, through his rain-streaked windshield, he saw a black woman emerge from the library with her large handbag clutched to her chest. From this distance, she looked only vaguely like the Freeman woman he'd been following all week. Not that he'd paid all that much attention. It wasn't the woman he'd followed, so much as the car.

But who the hell was this woman?

Whoever she was, she hurried through the rain to a junker car that looked like it was on its last legs. This was the tricky part. Did she have something in the car to cut open the packet? And if she did, would she go straight to the police or would she try to call him again?

Neither, he realized as she headed out of town toward Cotton Grove. Dobbs's rush hour was nothing compared to Raleigh's, but he was able to keep one or two cars back as they drove westward.

Stupid bitch.

The weather station's announcer was

going crazy with excitement as Fran appeared to draw a bead on the Carolinas. Stan dutifully noted the huge storm's position — it was something to do to pass the time — but his head wasn't into his science project this evening.

Not with Mama missing.

It wasn't unusual to come home and find her not there.

It *was* unusual to get a call from Lashanda's Brownie leader asking if Mrs. Freeman had forgotten to pick her up.

If it hadn't been raining so hard, he'd have ridden his bicycle over to get her himself. As it was, he'd called his dad.

"I'm on my way, son, but how about you phone over to Sister Edwards's house and see if Mama's there?"

"Sorry, honey," Miss Rosa had said. "I haven't talked to her since this morning."

He remembered Mrs. Thomas's grocery list and called there, but with no better results. By the time Dad's car rolled into the yard with Lashanda, Stan was starting to get worried.

Now it was heading for dark and still no news of Mama.

As word spread through their church, the phone rang frequently, all with the same soft questions: "Sister Clara home yet? Well now, don't you children fret. I'm sure she'll turn up just fine."

When Lashanda's best friend, Angela Herbert, arrived with her mother shortly before seven, Stan had protested. "We don't need a babysitter. I'm almost twelve years old, Dad. I can take care of Lashanda."

"I know you can, son, but your sister's only seven and having a friend here will make it easier on her."

"Then let me come with you," he'd pleaded.

"It would help me more to know you're here answering the phone in case Mama calls," his father said.

Unhappily, Stan watched his father leave through the rain. He sure hoped Mama was somewhere safe and dry.

When the junker car pulled into the yard of a shabby little house at the end of the road, he realized that this was where he'd seen the driver of the Honda Civic drop someone off yesterday morning.

It was instantly clear to him that he'd made a colossal mistake, but instead of remorse, he felt only anger at the woman who was now entering this house without a backward glance. How could he have known? Not his fault that two different women were both driving the same car.

The road curved behind a thick clump of sassafras and wild cherry trees and he pulled his car up close to them, trusting to twilight, the rain and the house's isolation to help him.

Inside, he saw the woman sawing at his packet with a paring knife. The screen door was hooked, but he put his fist right through the rusted mesh and flipped up the hook.

Rosa Edwards turned with a start and screamed as he burst into the room. She held the puny little knife before her, but he backhanded her so hard that the knife went flying and she fell heavily against the table.

He hit her again and blood gushed from her split lips.

"You better not!" she whimpered, scrabbling across the floor as she tried to get away. "I wrote it down. Somebody's got the paper, too!"

"Who?" he snarled and kicked her hard in the stomach.

"I don't get it back, she'll read it!" Her words came raggedly as she gasped for air. "She'll know you the one done it."

Enraged, he grabbed her by the hair and

half-lifted her from the floor as he punched her in the face again. "Who, you bitch? Who you give it to?"

"I ain't telling!" she sobbed.

"Oh yes, you will! Yes, you damn well will."

Still holding her by the hair, he dragged her over to the kitchen counter and started opening drawers till he found a butcher knife.

"You tell me where that paper is or I'm gonna start cutting off fingers, one finger at a time, and then I'm gonna work on your tits. You hear me?"

Desperately, she struggled against him, but he grabbed her arm and twisted it behind her so viciously that she heard the bone snap.

Chapter 12

The twisting tornado is confined to a narrow track and it has no long-drawn-out horrors. Its climax is reached in a moment. The hurricane, however, grows and grows.

It was nearly five before I adjourned court on Wednesday after hearing a silly case that took longer than any of the combatants (and I use the term advisedly) expected. Reid Stephenson was representing a young man who seemed to think he could race his motorcycle engine in front of his ex-girlfriend's house in the middle of the night as long as he didn't actually speak to her or threaten her or come onto her property or get within thirty feet of her as an earlier judgment had enjoined him from doing.

Reid tried to argue that it was only when the young woman came to her window to yell obscenities that the thirty-foot prohibition was violated. In other words, his client got there first and it was the girlfriend who chose to step outside her perimeter. Long-suffering neighbors who called the police wanted a larger perimeter around both of them. I decided they had a point and told the young man he might have obeyed the letter of the law, but I was going to let him sit in jail for three days and think about the spirit.

Despite my ruling, Reid came up to me as I was leaving the courtroom and said, "So how 'bout I pick you up around eight?"

"You're really serious about going to Steve's this evening?"

"Well, sure I am," he said. "Good barbecue? A chance to see the boys, catch up with them?"

Reid was Mother's first cousin, so he's known my brothers all his life, but being a lot younger and growing up in town to boot, it's not like as if they were close or anything, although he used to trail along when his father came out to the farm to hunt or fish.

When Reid passed the bar, Brix Jr. cut him a piece of the firm and retired to fish and play golf full-time. That's when Daddy switched over to John Claude for all his legal needs. Out of loyalty, most of the boys gave me their business while I was in practice there and they still use Lee and Stephenson. They'll even turn to Reid in an emergency — when the kids get in trouble and John Claude's out of town — but like Daddy, they feel safer with John Claude.

In short, Reid does not have a particularly warm and fuzzy ongoing relationship with my brothers, so why this sudden urge to (as Haywood would say) fellowship with them when rain was falling and a hurricane was heading toward our coastline?

Come eight o'clock though, there he was, rapping on my side door. I'd left my two-car garage open so he could drive in out of the rain. He still had on his gray suit but he held a hanger in one hand, slacks and knit shirt in the other.

"Didn't have time to change," he said. "Borrow your bedroom?"

Since I'd sort of flung things around when I went from dress and pantyhose to jeans and sneakers, I pointed him to the guest room instead. While he changed, I neatened my bedroom, hung up clothes and straightened all the surfaces. Maidie's promised to find me someone to do the heavy scrubbing and vacuuming one morning a week, but she hasn't gotten to it yet.

When Reid came out, I handed him my guitar case and went around locking doors, something he watched with amusement.

"You don't need to worry about burglars out here in the middle of Knott land, do you?"

"I'm not so worried about burglars as I am about Knotts," I said lightly.

Half my brothers think nothing of opening an unlocked door and sometimes they're just a little too curious about my personal business. Seth and Maidie are the only ones I trust with a key, which is why I'm trying to get in the habit of locking up every time I leave. I pulled the side door closed behind us and made sure it was securely latched.

"What happened to your fender?" I asked as I circled the front of Reid's black BMW.

It had a serious dent just behind the right headlight.

"Damned if I know," he said. "I found it like that after court yesterday. Two days out of the shop and somebody backs into me. Didn't even have the courtesy to leave me his name."

Considering a courthouse parking lot's clientele, this did not exactly surprise me. What did surprise was that he wasn't bitching about it louder. Reid's as car proud as my nephews and with a five-hundred deductible, every little ding comes out of his pocket.

Rain was falling heavily again and my rutted drive had washed out in a couple of places so that we had to go slower than usual to ease over the humps. We didn't get to Steve's till almost eight-thirty.

Despite the pounds of barbecue I'd eaten in the last month, that tangy smell of vinegar and smoked pork did make me hungry. We sat down at a long wooden table where Haywood and Isabel were finishing up and we both ordered the usual: pig, cole slaw, spiced apples and hush-puppies. We even split a side order of fried chicken livers. (Yeah, yeah, we've both heard all the horror stories of cholesterol and mercury in organ meat, but Miss Ila, Steve's seventy-year-old cook, knows how to make them crispy on the outside and melt-in-your-mouth-moist on the inside and neither of us can believe something that good can do lasting hurt if you don't indulge too often.)

Except for Steve, Miss Ila and a dishwasher, we four were the only ones in the place till Andrew's Ruth and Zach's Lee and Emma came dripping in from choir practice a few minutes later and ordered a helping of banana pudding with three spoons.

"We just came by to tell y'all we can't stay," said Ruth, pushing back her damp hair. "Mom's worried about the roads flooding."

"The water was almost hubcap-deep at Pleasants Crossroads," said Lee, "but that ol' four-by-four's better'n a duck. We won't have any trouble getting home."

All the usual customers had scattered earlier and it was clear that the rest of our families were staying home, battening down miscellaneous hatches in case we got any of Fran in the next twenty-four hours. Aunt Sister had already called to say that none of her crowd would be coming. When the kids left, Miss Ila and her helper were right in behind them. Steve put the CLOSED sign up, but we didn't reach for our instruments. Instead, we talked about Fran and what more rain would do to our already-saturated area, amusing each other with worst-case scenarios in half-serious tones, the way you will when you're fairly confident that any actual disaster will bypass you. Hurricanes do hit our coast with monotonous regularity, but this far inland, we seldom get much fallout beyond some heavy downpours.

Crabtree Valley Mall was built on a flood plain and it does indeed flood every three or four years. (The local TV stations love to film all the new cars bobbing around the sales lots like corks on a fish pond.)

Bottomland crops may drown when the creeksoverflow, a few trees go down and mildew is a constant annoyance, but most storms blow out before they reach us.

"Don't forget Hazel," said Isabel.

As if.

Hazel slammed through here in the mid-fifties before Reid and I were born, but we've been hearing about it every hurricane season since we were old enough to know what a hurricane was. Each year, I have to listen to tales of porches torn off houses, doing without electricity for several days, and about the millions of dollars' worth of damage it did. Down in the woods, there are still huge trees that blew over then but didn't die. Now, all along the leaning trunks, limbs have grown up vertically to form trees on their own.

"Hazel knocked that 'un down," a brother will tell me as he launches into stream-of-consciousness memories of that storm.

"It hit here in the middle of the day while we was still in school," said Haywood, warming to his tale like the Ancient Mariner.

"Back then, they didn't close school for every little raindrop nor snowflake neither," said Isabel, singing backup.

"They should've that day though. Remember how the sky got black and the wind come up?"

"And little children were crying?"

"Blew past in a hurry, but even the principal was worried and he called the county superintendent and they turned us out soon as it was past."

"Trees and light poles down across the road," said Isabel. "Our school bus had to go way outten the way to get us all home and we younguns had to walk in from the hardtop almost half a mile on that muddy road."

"Daddy and Mama Sue —"

Haywood was interrupted by a sharp rap on the restaurant's front door.

We looked over to see a tall dark figure standing in the rain.

Steve signalled that he was closed, but the man rapped again.

The glass was fogged up too much to see exactly who it was. I was nearest the door and as much to end Haywood's remembrances of Hazel as anything else, I went and opened it to find Ralph Freeman.

He was soaking wet and obviously worried, although he managed one of those bone-warming smiles the instant he recognized me.

"Come on in," I said. "Steve, Haywood, Reid — y'all know Reverend Freeman, don't you? Preaches at Balm of Gilead?"

They made welcoming sounds, but Ralph didn't advance past the entryway.

"Sorry to bother you," he said, dripping on the welcome mat, "but it's my wife. She was out this way today, visiting Mrs. Grace Thomas, and I was wondering if any of y'all saw her? White Honda Civic? Sister Thomas says my wife left her house a little after twelve and nobody's seen her since."

"Grace Thomas," said Haywood. "She live on that road off Old Forty-eight, right before Jones Chapel?"

"That's right," Ralph said, turning to him eagerly. "Did you see her?"

Haywood shook his head. "Naw. Sorry."

The others were shaking their heads, too.

"I just don't know where she could be,"

said Ralph. "I thought maybe she'd had a flat tire. Or with all this rain, these deep puddles, she might've drowned out the engine. But I've been up and down almost every road between here and Cotton Grove."

"I'll call around," said Haywood, heading for the phone. "See if any of the family's seen her car."

"Did you call the sheriff's department?" I asked.

"They said she's not been gone long enough for them to do anything official, but they did say they'd keep an eye out for the car."

"Highway patrol?" Reid suggested.

"Same thing," he answered dispiritedly. "And I've called all the hospitals."

"Now don't you go thinking the worst," Isabel comforted. "She could've slid into a ditch and she's either waiting for someone to find her or she's holed up in somebody's house that doesn't have a telephone."

Ralph looked dubious. "I doubt that. She doesn't know anybody else out this way and she wouldn't walk up to a stranger's house."

A tactful way to put it. Knowing that Mrs. Freeman disliked whites almost as much as certain whites dislike blacks, I figured he was right. She probably wouldn't want to chance it with any of us.

Nor was Ralph much comforted by Isabel's suggestion that she could be waiting out the rain in the car somewhere. Not when we were due for a whole lot more if Fran kicked in as weathermen were predicting.

Haywood came back from the telephone shaking his head. "Everybody's sticking close to home and ain't seen no cars in the ditch or nothing. Sorry, Preacher. But we'll surely keep our eyes peeled going home. Which ought to be about now, don't you reckon, Bel?" he asked.

She nodded and came heavily to her feet. She's only about half Haywood's size, but since he's just over six feet tall and just under three hundred pounds, that still makes her a hefty woman by anybody's standards.

"Such a shame we couldn't do any picking and singing tonight," she lamented, reaching for her banjo case. "Maybe next week we'll have more folks to come. You know, we might need to start us a phone tree to turn us out better." As she passed Ralph, she said, "I sure hope Miz Freeman makes it home safe. This is real bad weather to get stuck off somewhere."

We all said goodnight to Steve, who locked up behind us and turned off the lights on his way through the restaurant to the rear door that's a shortcut to his house out back.

Haywood held an umbrella over Isabel as they splashed out to their car. Like the southern gentleman he aspires to become, Reid told me to stay under the porch while he brought the car over.

Ralph Freeman stood beside me staring out at the rain indecisively. His face held the same hopeless misery I'd seen on Cyl's face last night, and to my horror, instead of some innocuous platitude about hoping everything turned out okay, I heard myself say, "Did y'all have a fight? Is she doing this deliberately? Punishing you for Cyl?"

"Cyl?" The worry lines between his eyes deepened. "You mean Ms. DeGraffen-ried?"

I touched his arm. "You don't have to pretend, Ralph. I know about you two."

"You do?" He looked at me warily. "How? She tell you?"

"Only after I guessed," I said and told him how I'd put two and two together last night.

"How is she?" His need was so great that it was almost as if he didn't care that I knew so long as I could tell him about Cyl.

"She's really hurting."

His broad shoulders slumped even more if that was possible.

Reid pulled in beside the single porch step. I held up two fingers and he cut his lights to show that he'd wait with his motor running till I finished talking.

Ralph said, "You must think I'm the world's biggest hypocrite."

"It's not for me to judge," I answered primly.

"No?" He gave me such an ironic lift of his eyebrow that I had to smile.

"You know what I mean. I've got too much glass in my own house for me to go around looking for stones in my neighbors' eyes."

That didn't come out quite the way I intended, although Haywood would surely have understood my mangled metaphors.

"Where are your children?" I asked pointedly.

"Home. The wife of one of our deacons is with them. And to answer your first question, Clara might do something like this to me, but she'd never do it to them. She was supposed to pick Lashanda up from her Brownie meeting after school, but she didn't. I can't understand it."

"Friends?" I said. "Family?"

"All back in Warrenton except for her prayer partner. Rosa's the only one Clara's really taken to since we moved here. Rosa Edwards. I called her right off, but she hasn't seen Clara since first thing this morning. I don't know where else to look, who else to call."

"Maybe you just ought to go on home," I said. "Be with the children. That's where she'd call, wouldn't she?"

He nodded. "She'll know they're worried and she'll want them to know she's all right, soon as possible."

"Want me to speak to Dwight Bryant? He could probably put on a couple of extra patrol cars."

"Would you? I'd appreciate that." He hesitated. "You wouldn't have to tell him about Cyl and me, would you?"

"Of course not."

"Thanks, Deborah."

"No problem," I said.

He took a deep breath and stepped out bareheaded into the rain. Reid pushed open the passenger door and I slid inside.

As we headed back down 48, Reid said, "What was that all about?"

"His wife. He's really worried about her."

With Ralph's red taillights shining up ahead, we rode in a silence broken only by the windshield wipers on wet glass, till Reid turned off the highway onto the road that led to my house. I found myself automatically checking the ditches on both sides, half-expecting to see Clara Freeman's car.

When we got to my house, I pushed the remote and once more the garage door swung up so that Reid could drive in.

"Any chance of a cup of coffee?" he asked.

"Sure," I replied. "Just let me call Dwight first."

I could have called from the kitchen, of course; instead, I went straight to the phone beside my bed. Sometimes Dwight'll give me a hard time for meddling. Tonight he listened as I stated the case against Clara Freeman just taking off without a thought for her children.

"Ralph's afraid she's had a wreck or something and if she has, you know the quicker she gets help, the better it'll be," I urged. "Do you really have to wait twenty-four hours?"

"Okay, okay," he said. "I'll shift all the patrols over to that sector till they've cov-

230

ered all the roads. If she's out there, they'll find her."

Reid was aimlessly opening cabinet doors when I got back to the kitchen.

"Coffee's in the refrigerator," I told him.

"Of course. The one place I didn't look."

He put two filters in the basket — "Cuts the caffeine and acids" — scooped in the ground coffee and flicked the switch.

"Does that weather board I gave you work okay?"

"Sure," I said, though truth to tell, I'd barely glanced at it since he hung it up.

"Let's see how low the pressure is right now with all this rain."

He headed for my bedroom and I trailed along at his heels. Did I mention that all good lawyers are actors? Reid was giving a charming performance at the moment — burbling about how his dad still checks the barometer every morning even though he can now look out the window overlooking the ninth green and see for himself whether it's a good day for golf.

" 'Course with Dad, any day it's not sleeting is a good day for golf."

Once inside my bedroom, he went right over to the dials and started reading them off. I just leaned against the door-

231

jamb and watched him.

He turned around. "Aren't you interested?"

"Oh, I'm interested all right," I said
wickedly. "Since you haven't been able to
get back here alone, what did you plan to
do? Slide it under my bed as soon as I
came over to look? Hope I'd think it rolled
there by accident?"

"Huh?"

A textbook look of puzzled innocence
spread across his face.

"Considering that it got you off the hook
with Dwight, I really think you should have
given me something nicer for my wall than
a twenty-dollar weather center."

He gave a sheepish grin, his first honest
expression of the night. "Wal-Mart doesn't
offer a lot of choice. It was this or a sun-
burst clock or a bad knockoff of a Bob
Timberlake painting."

Overall, I had to agree with his decision.
Nevertheless, I held out my hand and he
reached into his pocket and pulled out the
sterling silver pen that he'd lifted from the
pencil mug beside my phone on Monday.

"When did you miss it?" he asked,
turning the gleaming shaft in his fingers.

"While you were changing clothes
tonight, I tidied up in here."

"Well, damn! You mean I was that close to getting away with it?"

"Not really. I knew you were up to something, I just hadn't figured out what. You hate gospel music, remember?"

He shrugged. "I was hoping you wouldn't."

"No more games," I said sternly. "How did your pen get under Lynn Bullock's body?"

"I don't know, Deborah, and that's the God-honest truth. She borrowed it the last time we were together and didn't give it back and, well, it seemed a little petty to make a big point about it since I didn't want to see her again anyhow."

"So why didn't you just tell Dwight?"

"Oh, sure. My pen under the body of a woman whose neck I'd threatened to wring?"

"What?"

"I didn't mean it," he said hastily. "You know how you say things — 'I'll kill him,' 'I'm going to clean his clock'? It's just talk. But I was so mad when I saw what she'd done to my car. Hot as it's been? And with the windows rolled up? I had to go buy a pair of rubber gloves just to drive it to the shop. I was so pissed, I kept saying that I was going to wring the little bitch's neck.

233

Everybody at the shop just laughed at me, they didn't have a clue who I was talking about, but Will was there and I'm pretty sure he knew because he gave me a wink and said he'd swear it was justifiable homicide."

If my brother had known Lynn Bullock was the woman who'd done something like that to Reid's car, he certainly would have mentioned it Sunday night when we were talking about her death. Will's a consummate con man though, and he can be incredibly sneaky when he puts his mind to it. He has a way of pretending he knows more about things than he does, hoping to bluff you into telling him what you assume he already knows.

"Don't you see? If Dwight knew it was my pen, he'd go digging around and find out —"

"And find out what?" I asked. Then it hit me. "Wait a minute! You had two dates with her last Christmas and she only lately fouled your car? When?"

"Tuesday, a week ago," he admitted.

"Why?" I asked, even though that mulish look on his face gave me the answer. "Oh for God's sake, Reid! Tell me you didn't. You said she wasn't your type."

"Well, she wasn't," he said sulkily. "All

the same, for all her snob talk, there was something — I don't know — vulnerable? Did I tell you what she said about Dad coming out to her grandfather's place when she was a little girl?"

"No."

"She was just a kid when it happened, but she never forgot. Dad had gone out to coach her grandfather for a court appearance. She talked about Dad's fingernails. How clean and even they were."

Reid looked down at his own neatly manicured nails and I had a sudden mental image of my daddy's hands, the nails split and stained with country work.

"What was her grandfather charged with?"

"I looked it up in the files." Reid gave me a lopsided grin. "Let's put it this way. Your dad was paying my dad's bill. *And* he paid her grandfather's fine and court costs."

"*What?*"

"Oh, come on, Deb'rah. Everybody knows Mr. Kezzie made his money in bootleg whiskey."

"When he was younger, yes," I agreed, "but he gave all that up before I was born and Lynn Bullock was younger than me."

"Whiskey's the only thing your daddy's

ever lied to me about," Mother once told me. "The only thing I *know* he lied about anyhow."

I looked at Reid sharply. "Is he still mixed up in it?"

"Old as he is? I doubt it," said Reid. " 'Course, a lot of people still think he is, and it probably amuses him to let them. I'm sure you'd've heard about it, if he were."

"True," I said, relieved. Dwight or Terry or certainly Ed Gardner, who works ATF, would have put a bug in my ear if he were still active. One thing a judge doesn't need is to have her daddy hauled in for making moonshine.

"Anyhow," said Reid, "Lynn Bullock was a damn good lay. I'm not seeing anybody special these days, so I thought what the hell, why not give her another call?"

"Only her memory being better than yours, she was still ticked that you'd dumped her after the second night and it really steamed her when you called out of the blue with nothing on your mind but sex?"

"Something like that. Look, Deborah, you've got to help me. Don't tell Dwight it was your pen I showed him. Okay?"

"You're crazy. I'm a judge. An officer of

the court. I can't *not* tell him. So she smeared dog dirt inside your car. Big deal. And you vented at the garage. Hyperbole. You tell him who you were with before you got to the ball field, she confirms it and —"

There was that look again. "No who?"

"No who," he said.

"You're not being noble, are you?" I asked suspiciously. "Saving somebody's reputation?"

"The only reputation I was saving was mine. Everybody thinks I get laid six days a week and twice on Sundays. Truth is, I'm damn near a virgin these days. I went to the office Saturday morning, got sleepy after lunch, flaked out upstairs and almost slept through the game."

I looked at him. I may have eleven older brothers, but he's the nearest thing to a kid brother I'd ever had. His handsome face was an open book.

Or was it?

"Oh come on, Deborah. I did *not* kill Lynn Bullock."

"*You know he couldn't,*" whispered my internal preacher.

"*Irrelevant!*" snapped the pragmatist from the other side of my head. "*You withhold something like this from Dwight and you could find yourself facing an ethics review.* "

Reid still held my pen in his hand.

"If I'd been a little smarter, I'd have found a way to put this back and you wouldn't have known the difference. All you have to do is forget the last few minutes ever happened."

He walked over to my telephone and dropped the pen into my pencil mug.

"See?"

"Reid —"

"Please, Deborah. All I'm asking is that you wait about talking to Dwight. Give him a chance to find Lynn's real killer. Or —" He gave me a sharp, considering look. "Maybe we could find him first."

"We?"

"Why not? We're both professionals. Taking depositions is what we do. And people talk to civilians like us quicker than they'll talk to Dwight. We just ask a few questions around town, listen hard to all the gossip and figure it out. What do you say?"

His eager, almost adolescent expression suddenly reminded me of Mickey Rooney in those old movies Dwight and I sometimes watch.

I didn't feel one bit like Judy Garland though and I sure as hell didn't want to try

238

putting on a show in the barn.

"How hard can it be for us to figure out who was balling her?" Reid wheedled, as he followed me out to the kitchen. "She didn't do it in the middle of Main Street or in her own house, even, but she sure wasn't the most discreet woman I ever slept with."

"Do you suppose Jason knew?" I asked, pouring us a cup of the freshly brewed coffee.

"Had to, you'd think." Reid reached into my refrigerator for milk and kept dribbling it in until his coffee was more *au lait* than *café*. "Unless he's one of those husbands who makes a point of not knowing? He's such a grind though, maybe not."

"Grind? He was playing ball Saturday."

"Grind," Reid said firmly. "He and Millard King. Birds of a feather. And not just because they humped the same woman."

"How's that?"

"Both of them are ambitious as hell and both of 'em have at least two reasons for everything they do. Like playing ball. That's an appropriate 'guy' activity. Makes you seem human. Puts you right out there to bond with your peer group. Good social contacts. Like the way you moved your membership over to First Baptist in

Dobbs," he added shrewdly.

"See?" said the preacher, who's always been embarrassed by that cynical act.

The pragmatist shrugged.

"Before it's over, you're going to see King and Bullock both on a statewide ballot," said Reid. "Just remember that you heard it here first."

"Elective office?"

"Why else do you think King's so hot to marry one of the homeliest gals that ever wore lipstick? Because she's connected on both sides of her family to some political heavy hitters, that's why. And in this state, you still need a ladywife to do the whole white-glove bit. If Lynn Bullock threatened to make a scandal, she could've scared the little debutante off. Soured things with her daddy the Justice."

His venom surprised me. "What's Millard King ever done to you?"

"Nothing really. Just sometimes I get a shade tired of the deserving poor."

"Come again?"

"All these up-by-their-bootstrap people, who keep reminding you that you were born with a silver spoon in your mouth while they had to work for everything they got," he said scornfully. "As if you're worth shit because your parents and your grand-

240

parents could read and write, while they're the *true* yeoman nobility who really deserve it. And all the time they're sneering, they're out there busting their balls to have what they think you're born to. As if money's all it takes."

"Why, Reid Stephenson! You really *are* a snob."

"If not apologizing for who and what my parents are and what they gave me makes me a snob, then guilty as charged," he said as his scowl dissolved into one of those roguish smiles. "But I'm not guilty of murder."

"You're the one without an alibi though."

I drained the last of my coffee and as he took my mug to pour me another cup of the rich dark brew, we mulled over the other men known to be in Lynn Bullock's life.

"She died between five-fifteen and eight, give or take a few minutes," I said. "Dwight and I got to the ball field around four-thirty. Jason Bullock was right behind me when she called at five and after the game, he went straight from the field to the pizza place with us. We even followed him back to Cotton Grove."

"He may be out of it," said Reid, "but

what about Millard King?"

"He told Dwight that he was there jogging for at least an hour, but I didn't notice him till he was coming off the track around six o'clock. I suppose he could have cut through the trees and jogged over from the Orchid Motel. It's on this side of the bypass and less than a quarter-mile as the crow flies."

"Or the jogger jogs," said Reid, brightening up a bit.

"Courthouse gossip says that she was with Brandon Frazier for a while."

"Yeah, I heard that, too, but so what? Frazier doesn't have a wife or anybody special and he doesn't act like someone planning to run for political office."

"Frazier and King. Not much of a pool," I observed.

"And neither of them threatened to wring her neck," Reid said glumly. "There has to be somebody else, somebody we haven't heard about yet."

"Maybe we're going at this the wrong way," I said. "Maybe it's not who she slept with, but who she didn't. Like Dr. Jeremy Potts."

"Who?"

So I told him about young Dr. Potts, who would have walked away from his marriage with no strings attached to his income had it not been for Lynn Bullock's shrewd advice to his wife and Jason Bullock's equally shrewd representation.

"Oh, yeah, I heard about that. A professional degree as marital property. Good thing I made Dotty settle out of court."

(Tough talk, but Dotty herself told me that Reid was voluntarily paying twenty percent of his income for young Tip's support.

("I'm socking it all away in mutual funds for his education," she'd said complacently.

(Like most hotshot real estate agents in this part of the state, Dotty's doing very well for herself these days.)

"Did you hear that she's getting married again?" Reid asked abruptly.

"Who? Felicia Potts?"

"Dotty."

Most of the time, Reid kept the torch he carried for his ex-wife well hidden under his Casanova cloak, but every once in a while, I caught a glimpse of it. She was the love of his life and he'd screwed it up by screwing around.

I reached out and squeezed his arm. "Maybe I'll call Amy," I said, offering what comfort I could. "See if she's heard anything about Dr. Potts."

Against my better judgment and only because it would be his word against mine if this ever came to Dwight's attention, it seemed I had agreed to keep quiet about my pen for the time being.

And now, God help me, I was even volunteering to ask a few questions on my own. And yeah, part of it might be to help Reid, but part of my very nature is a basic need to find the truth and bring the facts to judgment.

My internal preacher was not fooled by such high-flown rationalizations.

"You'd risk your career for curiosity? Curiosity killed the cat."

"But no cat ever caught a rat without it," said the pragmatist.

Chapter 13

The people of the North might differ radically from the people of the South in many ways, but in the presence of such a dreadful visitation of nature, involving suffering and death, the brotherhood of man asserts itself and all things else are forgotten.

After Reid left, I watched the late news. The situation in Iraq might be occupying the rest of the country's TV screens, but here in central North Carolina, most of the newscast was given over to Hurricane Fran which seemed to be heading straight toward Wilmington. It was packing winds of 130 miles per hour and forecasters were saying it could push in a wall of water twenty feet high. The sheer size of the storm — more than five hundred miles across — guaranteed that we were going to feel its effects here in the Triangle.

All along the coast, people were nailing sheets of plywood over their windows and getting their boats out of the water. Portland and Avery were congratulating themselves for bringing their boat back to Dobbs.

Skycams showed us thick lines of headlights heading inland through the rainy night as coastal residents from Myrtle Beach to Manteo sought higher ground. Channel 11's Miriam Thomas and Larry Stogner spoke of ordered evacuations in both South Carolina and Ocracoke, which is linked to the mainland only by ferries. New Hanover County had ordered a voluntary evacuation of all beach communities, including Wrightsville Beach where some of my Wilmington colleagues live; while Brunswick County was taking no chances. Evacuation was mandatory on all the barrier islands.

Reporter Greg Barnes showed motels filling up fast and shelters that were opening in schools and fire stations around Fayetteville to help handle the evacuees.

Even Don Ross, WTVD's color man, was unusually serious as he reported on local grocery stores that were already experiencing a run on batteries and canned goods. Eric Curry's camera panned over empty bread shelves and depleted milk cases.

I tried to call Kidd, but all I got was his answering machine.

It was nearly midnight but I wasn't a bit sleepy. Instead, I switched off the television and roamed around the house restlessly. I had candles and a stash of batteries for my radio, a half a loaf of bread and a fresh quart of milk. I should be okay, but the dire predictions left me uneasy.

The rain had finally stopped and I went out to put all the porch and lawn chairs into my garage. The night should have been quiet except for frogs and crickets, yet male voices floated faintly on the soggy warm air and sirens seemed to be converging from different directions. I was about to get my car out and go see what was happening, when headlights appeared on the lane that runs from Andrew's house to mine and connects with a homemade bridge across Possum Creek.

The truck slowed to a stop as it drew near me and I saw Andrew behind the wheel with his son, A.K. Just topping the rise a few yards behind was Robert on the farm's biggest tractor.

I ran over to meet them. "What's happening?"

"Rescue squad's been called out," said Andrew. "A car's gone in the creek and they want us to help get it out."

"Oh, no!" Without being invited, I ran around to the passenger side, pulled open the door and shoved in next to A.K.

"You know who it is?" he asked as his dad put it in gear for the creek. The tractor lights behind us lit up the cab.

"I hope not," I answered. "But you know Ralph Freeman, the preacher at Balm of Gilead? His wife was out this way today visiting one of their church members and she never came home."

"That don't sound good," said Andrew. "No, sir, that don't sound good at all."

We came out onto the hardtop just south of the creek, where it bends at the bridge before the turn-in to the homeplace.

The curve was lit up like a carnival. Flashing lights of red, yellow, and blue bounced against the low-lying clouds and were reflected back in ghastly hues. Three patrol cars, a fire truck, and a rescue truck had their spotlights aimed down toward the muddy water that rushed under the bridge. The creek had flooded its channel and was as high as I'd ever seen it.

Men were out there in it up to their necks, working around the door of a white car whose top projected only a few inches above the turbulent waters. I recognized Donny Turner and Rudy Peacock from the West Colleton volunteer fire department — both were too big to miss — and skinny little Skeeter Collins from the Cotton Grove rescue squad. Five or six other dark and indistinguishable figures milled around in the water and I heard someone yell, "Damn! Is that a cottonmouth?"

"Fuck the cottonmouth and hand me the damn collar!" cried Skeeter.

By the glare of the spotlights, I saw the men relay a cervical collar to him without letting the water touch it. Skeeter's head disappeared inside the car.

"That's a good sign, ain't — *isn't* it?" asked A.K. "They don't put collars on dead people, do they?"

"I don't know," I said, wondering how they could possibly remove Clara Freeman — if it *was* Clara Freeman — from the car without drowning her in the process.

"Watch it, boys!" Skeeter shouted. "I felt it start to shift."

"Get that tractor in here," said the fire chief. "We need to get a chain or something on this car."

Robert backed his big John Deere down through the bushes at the water's edge. There was a winch above the drawbar and someone grabbed the hook and waded into the water with it. Robert let the cable feed out slowly as the man hauled the hook over toward the car where other hands reached for it. There was a confused splashing around the end of the car and several strangled coughs as men came up gasping for air before the hook was securely attached to the back undercarriage.

There were also enough strangled curses to make me glad I was a woman on the shore instead of a man out there in the middle of a muddy, moccasin-infested creek. (We may be technically equal these days but that doesn't mean we jump into every activity with equal enthusiasm.)

Finally, a vaguely familiar voice called, "Put some tension on it, but for God's sake, go easy!"

That's when I recognized that the man who'd carried the hook out to the car was Jason Bullock. I'd heard that he'd joined a lot of civic organizations like the volunteer fire department, but this was the first time I'd seen him since the night of our post-game pizza over in Dobbs.

With the tractor in its lowest gear and half a dozen men doing what they could to support the car upright, Robert kept the cable taut as he slowly pulled until the Honda was on solid ground. Water was still waist-high where the men now stood on what was normally the creekbank, but at least there was no immediate danger of losing the car and the person inside. A lightweight molded plastic stretcher board was passed from the rescue truck and soon they had a recumbent form strapped onto it.

When they came ashore, I saw that it was indeed Clara Freeman, unconscious and with all her vital signs erratic, but alive.

Dwight had arrived by then. As they loaded Mrs. Freeman into the ambulance, he turned to me with a lopsided smile. "Sometimes I'm glad I listen to you. If she'd spent the night out there . . ."

"Another two inches and her nose would have been in the water," said a dripping Jason Bullock as we watched the ambulance speed away with lights flashing and siren wailing. "Anybody call her husband yet? He ought to be told."

My heart went out to him in his empathy for Ralph Freeman and I knew he was probably remembering his own tense hours of worry before Dwight came and told him the worst a husband can hear.

"The dispatcher's calling him right now," Dwight said. "She'll tell him to meet the ambulance at Dobbs Memorial."

I put out my hand to Jason and told him how sorry I was for his own loss. He thanked me, then looked at Dwight. "I've tried not to bug you, Bryant, but do you have anything yet?"

"Sorry. We have a few leads, but nothing solid. But maybe you could come by the office tomorrow and let's talk again? Go over a few possibilities?"

"Sure."

We stood there on the side of the road and watched as the excitement wound down and the volunteers packed it in. The fire truck trundled across the bridge, back toward Cotton Grove, the extra patrol cars headed off to their usual sectors, and the remaining deputy showed Dwight the sketch he'd made to explain how Clara Freeman wound up in Possum Creek.

"We'll check again tomorrow in the daylight, but we couldn't see skid marks. Looks like she came flying down the slope, misjudged the curve and drove straight off the road without touching the brakes, going so fast, she just sailed into the creek."

I was craning over Dwight's shoulder, but Jason stared back up the slope that was now washed in light by Robert's tractor lights.

"You reckon she might've blacked out? Or the gas pedal stuck?"

"With a stuck accelerator, she'd have been standing on her brakes," said Dwight.

"And if she was blacked out," said the deputy, "she wouldn't've been going fast enough to skip the bank."

"Hey, Deb'rah," Andrew called. "You ready to go?"

It was getting late and he had a couple of bulk barns loaded with curing tobacco to see to.

"Go on ahead," I called back. "I'll ride with Robert."

All this time, local traffic had come and gone sporadically on this back road. When we first arrived, it was one-lane, directed by a trooper who kept the rubberneckers moving. This late, long past midnight, in a community that was still mostly farmers and early-rising blue-collar workers, the road was practically deserted. Nevertheless, an occasional car came by and slowed to ask whether everything was under control. If they knew Dwight or recognized Robert's tractor, the driver would even get out of his vehicle and come over to gawk at Clara Freeman's drowned car.

My brother Robert had finished pulling it up onto the shoulder of the road and water streamed from the open doors. I walked over to have a look myself while Dwight and his deputy finished conferring and Jason was right behind me when an oncoming car slowed, stopped, and a man came toward us.

"Evening, Judge," said Millard King. "That's not your car, is it? You all right?"

I sensed Jason Bullock stiffening behind me and I knew that King hadn't immediately realized who was standing there with me. In the half-light cast by reflected headlights, I saw recognition spread across his face when he came closer.

"Bullock." His voice was neutral as he nodded to Jason.

"King." Jason's voice was equally neutral, but I finally had an answer to whether or not he knew his wife had been sleeping around.

And with whom.

Like a nervous hostess smoothing over an awkward social lapse, I found myself chattering about the accident, about Jason's part in helping to rescue Clara Freeman and how lucky she was to have been found before drowning.

"You live around here?" Jason Bullock asked bluntly.

Now that he mentioned it, what *was* Millard King doing on this back road at this hour?

"Just down in Makely," he answered easily. "But my brother lives over in Fuquay, so I'm up and down this road a lot. You say she went in this afternoon sometime? I sure didn't notice when I came through around eight. 'Course, it was still raining then."

"Oh look!" I said. "There's Lashanda's baby doll."

I went over and pulled a soggy brown rubber doll from the car. As I did, I saw something lumpy on the floor beneath the steering wheel. Clara Freeman's pocketbook. I gathered it up, too, thinking that I'd carry it to the hospital with me tomorrow morning.

The two men circled the car.

"It's amazing," said King. "The car doesn't seem to have a scratch on it."

"Dry it out and it should be good as new," agreed Bullock.

My brother Robert came over, put the car in neutral and closed the doors. "What you planning to do with the car, Dwight?

Want me to tow it over to Jimmy White's garage?"

"Would you mind?"

"Naw, but he ain't gonna be up this time of night."

"That's okay. I'll call him first thing tomorrow."

As I climbed up to the glassed-in cab of the big tractor with Robert, I saw King and Bullock walk to their separate cars. I guess they didn't have much to say to each other.

Not tonight anyhow.

Jimmy's garage was only a couple of miles away and the car pulled easily, so we were there in ten minutes. Not surprisingly, the building was dark and silent, as was Jimmy's house out back, behind a thick row of Leland cypresses.

I helped Robert unhitch the car. We left the key in the ignition switch, although I did detach it from Clara's keyring. When we climbed back into the tractor cab, I stuck the keyring in Clara's soggy handbag and tucked it back under the tractor seat so I could hold on.

Now that we weren't towing the car, Robert put it in gear and soon we were jouncing briskly across rutted dirt lanes. The tractor is air-conditioned and has an

AM/FM radio, but Robert keeps the tape deck loaded with Patsy, Hank and George.

"Ain't no country music on the radio no more," he said. "Hell of a note when country stations don't play nothing but Garth Brooks and Dixie Chicks and think that's country."

We rode through the night harmonizing along with Ernest Tubbs and Loretta Lynn on "Sweet Thang," a song that used to really crack me up when I was six.

Chapter 14

"Prepare for the worst, which is yet to come," were the only consoling words of the weather bureau officials.

The calls started at daybreak.

"You got you plenty of batteries laid in?" asked Robert.

"Batteries?" I asked groggily.

"They're saying we're definitely gonna get us some of that hurricane. You want to make sure your flashlight works when the lights go off."

"We got an extra kerosene lantern," said his wife Doris, who was on their extension phone. "How 'bout I send Robert over with it?"

Less than ninety seconds after they rang off, it was Haywood and Isabel.

"Don't forget to bring in all your porch chairs," said Haywood.

"And fill some milk jugs with clean

258

water," said Isabel.

"Water?" I yawned.

"If the power goes, so does your water pump."

Seth and Minnie were also solicitous of my water supply.

"I've already got both bathtubs filled," Minnie said. "This hot weather, you want to be able to flush if the electricity goes out."

I hadn't lost power since I moved into my new house the end of July, but it wasn't unusual when I was growing up out here in the country. It seldom stayed off more than a couple of days and since we heated with woodstoves that could double as cookstoves, no electricity wasn't much of a hardship in the winter. More like going camping in your house. Especially since it was usually caused by an ice storm that had closed school anyhow, so that you got to stay home and go sliding during the day, then come in to hot chocolate and a warm and cozy candlelit evening of talking or making music around the stove.

Summer was a little worse. We never had air-conditioning so we didn't expect to stay cool even when the electricity was on, but running out of ice for our tea and soft drinks was a problem. And two days were about as long as you could trust food from the refrigerator in hot weather.

I emptied the ice bin into a plastic bag so that my icemaker would make a fresh batch. And I dutifully filled my tub, kettle, and a couple of pots with water since I had no empty plastic jugs on hand.

Daddy drove through the yard with my newspaper and said I ought to come over and stay at the homeplace till the hurricane had passed.

I pointed out that my new house had steel framing and was guaranteed to hold up under winds of a hundred and seventy miles an hour, "So maybe you should spend the night with me."

"Mine's stood solid through a hundred years of storms and Hazel, too, and it ain't never even lost a piece of tin." The mention of tin must have reminded him of the house trailer Herman's son Reese was renting from Seth because he added, "Reese is gonna come. And Maidie and Cletus."

Now a hurricane party was a tempting thought and I told him I'd let him know.

After he left and before someone else could tie up my line, I picked up the phone to call Kidd even though he was probably already gone. And then I put it back down again, more than a little annoyed. After all, shouldn't he be worried about me? The way Fran was lining up, Colleton County was just as likely to get hit as New Bern. Couldn't he find a spare minute to see if I was okay?

No?

Then he could damn well wonder.

With all the distractions, I was halfway to Dobbs before I remembered Clara Freeman's purse and Lashanda's doll. No time to go back for them if I wanted to check past the hospital before going to court.

At Dobbs Memorial, it was only a few minutes past eight but the intensive care unit's waiting room was jammed with Balm of Gilead members. A couple of Ralph Freeman's colleagues from the middle school where he taught were there, along with some ministers from nearby churches. I greeted those I recognized and learned that Clara Freeman was in critical but stable condition. They had operated on her early this morning to relieve the pressure on her brain but it was too soon to make predictions, although Ralph was with the surgeon now.

Mingled with the hospital smells of antiseptics and floor wax were the appetizing aromas of hot coffee and fast-food break-fast meals — sausage biscuits from Hardee's, Egg McMuffins, and Krispy Kreme doughnuts — nourishment for people who'd evidently been here since Mrs. Freeman was brought in last night.

Stan and his little sister were seated against the far wall and I went over to them.

"Stan, Lashanda, I'm so sorry about your mother."

"Thank you, Miss Deborah," the boy said.

Before he could say anything else, the large elderly man who sat beside him said, "Stanley, will you introduce this lady to me?"

It may have been couched as a request, but the tone sounded awfully like an order to me.

"Yes, sir. This is Judge Deborah Knott," he said with touching formality. "Miss Deborah, this is my grandfather, the Reverend James McElroy Gaithers."

"Judge?" He looked faintly disapproving. Because I was a judge? (*"I suffer not a woman to teach, nor to usurp authority over the man."*) Or because I was white? (*"He shall separate them one from another."*)

"Yes, sir," I said. "District Court. And

262

you're Mrs. Freeman's father?"

"I am."

There are many preachers who prefer the Old Testament to the New and the Reverend James McElroy Gaithers was clearly one of them. For him, I was pretty sure that the dominant element of the Trinity would be God the stern father of retribution, not Jesus the forgiving son.

"You're from Warrenton, I believe?"

He nodded magisterially.

"It's a sad thing that brings you down here," I commiserated. "I'm really sorry."

"My daughter is in the hands of the Lord," he said. "His will shall be done."

At the old man's words, Stan looked stricken and little Lashanda simply looked miserable. Was there no one to rescue the children from this Jeremiah and give them true comfort? Where was Clara Freeman's good friend that Ralph had mentioned last night? Rosa Somebody? Surely she was somewhere in this crowd and with a hint dropped into her ear, maybe she would —

Stan's face suddenly brightened at the sight of someone behind me and I turned to see Cyl DeGraffenried.

I had to hand it to her. For a woman who was falling apart the last time I saw her, she was in complete control now, poised and professional in a crisp hunter green linen suit with soft white silk blouse and matching low-heeled pumps. Her hair fell in artful perfection around her lovely face and pearls gleamed coolly at her throat and earlobes.

She spoke to Stan and Lashanda, was introduced to their grandfather, immediately sized up the situation and said to him in solicitous female tones, "I know you'll want to speak privately with the doctor when he comes, so why don't the Judge and I take your grandchildren out for some fresh air and breakfast?"

Both children immediately stood up as Cyl looked at me brightly. "Deborah?"

"Sure," I said, trying not to look as taken aback as I actually was.

My court session was technically due to start at nine, but by the time most ADAs finish working out their plea bargains and stipulations, things seldom get moving much before nine-thirty or a quarter till ten, so we had more than an hour to give the children.

Reverend Gaithers started to object but Cyl blithely chose to misunderstand him. "No, no, you do *not* have to thank us. It's no trouble at all. We haven't had breakfast yet either, have we, Deborah?"

We made our getaway through the swinging doors and came face-to-face with Ralph Freeman and a doctor in surgical scrubs.

Ralph looked at us in confusion and Cyl seemed suddenly out of words herself.

"Daddy!" cried Lashanda and bounded into his arms.

"Is Mama going to be all right?" asked Stan.

"Dr. Potts thinks so," Ralph said, swinging his daughter up to hug her as he nodded toward his companion.

Having only seen a man in a suit and tie when I was deciding on his divorce settlement, I hadn't immediately recognized Dr. Jeremy Potts. He knew me though, and gave a sour tilt of the head.

"We were just coming in so Dr. Potts can explain to Clara's father." He kissed Lashanda and stood her back on her own feet. "Thanks, Deborah, for getting extra patrol cars out to look for her. Somebody said you helped pull her out?"

The children stared at me, wide-eyed.

"Not me, my brother Robert. His tractor. With a lot of help from the fire and rescue squads. I just did the heavy looking on." I smiled down at Lashanda. "I saved your doll though. Oh, and your wife's purse and keys," I told Ralph. "I forgot to bring them in with me, but I'll get them to you as soon as I can."

"No hurry," he said. "I'm afraid she's not going to be driving any time soon."

He was now under control enough to speak directly to Cyl. "Where are y'all off to?"

Stan spoke up. "Miss Cyl and Miss Deborah's taking us out to breakfast."

"If that's okay with you?" Cyl managed to add. "We thought they could use a break from the waiting room."

"That's very kind of y'all."

He looked at her as if he didn't want to stop looking and my heart broke for them, but Dr. Potts cleared his throat and said, "Mr. Freeman?"

"Sorry, Doctor. I guess I'm holding you up."

The two men went on into the waiting room and we drove over to the north end of Main Street in Cyl's car. The air was thick with humidity and the sky was full of low gray clouds. There wasn't much wind here on the ground, but overhead, those clouds scudded eerily past like frantic dirty sheep scattering before wolves we couldn't yet see.

★ ★ ★

The Coffee Pot has a long counter where hungry folks in a hurry perch, a big round table with ashtrays for retirees who are more interested in gossip than food, and four non-smoking booths in back for those who want a little privacy.

We took a booth and Ava Dupree came straight over with a menu, her pale blue eyes bright with curiosity. My brother Herman's electrical shop is right next door and we often meet here for coffee. Ava greeted Cyl by name, too, but she didn't recognize the children and she's not shy about asking personal questions.

"Freeman? Oh, yeah, your mama's the one that went and run off the road into Possum Creek last night, ain't she? I heard 'em talking about it first thing this morning. She's gonna be okay, ain't she?"

"We sure could use some orange juice here, Ava," I said pointedly.

"And how about some blueberry pancakes, bacon, milk and coffee?" said Cyl. "That okay with y'all?"

Next to me, Stan nodded agreement and Lashanda, seated beside Cyl, smiled shyly. Blue barrettes in the shape of little bluebirds were clipped to the ends of all her braids.

Stan knew Cyl because she'd given him a lift home from my Fourth of July pig-picking last month and from seeing her at the ball field, but she was a stranger to the little girl.

Not for long though.

"Somebody just lost a tooth," Cyl said. "Was the Tooth Fairy good to you?"

"I thought she wasn't," the child replied, " 'cause guess what? My tooth was still in the glass this morning when I woke up! But Stan said it was because too many people were in the house awake last night and maybe she got afraid."

"Shandy!" An awkward, bony pre-adolescent, eleven-year-old Stan looked so exceedingly self-conscious that I could almost swear he was blushing, but his little sister was oblivious.

"And guess what? When I came back from brushing my teeth, my tooth was gone and guess what was in the water?"

She drew her hand out of her pocket and proudly showed us two shiny quarters.

"Hey, that's really cool," Cyl said, smiling at Stan. "She never left me more than a dime."

"Inflation." Stan grinned.

By the time our pancakes arrived, she had charmed them both. Stan told us about a school science project he was working on — how he'd been documenting Fran's path from the time she was nothing more than a tropical depression off the coast of Africa till whatever happened in the next twenty-four hours. I learned things about hurricanes I'd never given much thought to before.

"They're saying it's going to be one of the really big ones!" He gestured so excitedly as he described the spiraling bands of storms around the eye that the plastic syrup dispenser went flying and he had to get up and chase it down.

Lashanda looked less than thrilled by the approaching storm and moved closer to Cyl till she was tucked up almost under Cyl's arm. "I wish we could spend the night at your house."

Cyl put her arm around the child and gave a little squeeze. "I wish you could, too, baby."

"Shandy!" said her brother.

"Grandfather scares me." A tear slid down her cheek. "And Mama's not coming home tonight and if Daddy stays with her and we get tornadoes —"

Her lip quivered.

"What about your mother's friend?" I asked. "Someone named Rosa?"

"Miss Rosa hasn't come yet," said Stan. "She must've worked last night 'cause we couldn't get her on the phone either."

Not much of a best friend, I thought, thinking how I'd react if something like this happened to Portland or Morgan or Dixie or two or three other close friends.

"And you just might have just a little more freedom to come and go when you like," the preacher reminded me. "You don't know what obstacles of job or children might be keeping her away."

"Don't worry," Cyl told Lashanda. "Things will work out."

She wet a napkin in a glass of water and gently wiped the little girl's sticky lips.

When we delivered the children back to the ICU waiting room, Ralph immediately came over and thanked us again.

"How is Mrs. Freeman really?" Cyl asked when Stan and Lashanda spotted friends of their own age and moved away from us.

"Really?" Ralph shook his head, clearly weary from lack of sleep and a deep sadness. "Dr. Potts can't say. She should have regained consciousness by now, but she hasn't. There are broken ribs, bruised windpipe from the seat belt — thank God she was wearing it! Those things are relatively superficial. But the concussion . . . and of course, the longer she's in a coma, the worse the prospects. Maybe by lunchtime we'll know better."

The mention of lunchtime made me look at my watch. Ten after nine.

I squeezed Ralph's hand. "We have to go now, but we'll be praying for her."

"You'll come back?"

"Yes," said Cyl.

She was silent in the elevator down and as we walked out through the parking lot, I said, "You okay?"

"I'm holding it together." She gave me an unhappy smile. "For the moment anyhow."

"See you at the courthouse, then." I headed for my car a few spaces past hers, then stopped short. "Oh, damn!"

"What?" asked Cyl.

"Somebody's popped the lock on my trunk again." I was totally exasperated. This was the second time in a year. "What the hell do they think I carry?"

"They take anything?" she asked, peering over my shoulder.

My briefcase was still there. So were my robe and the heavy locked toolbox where I stash wrenches, screwdrivers, pliers, extra windshield wipers and the registered .38 Daddy gave me when I told him I was going to keep on driving deserted roads at night and that I didn't need a man to protect me. Things had been stirred and the roll of paper towels was tangled in my robe, but I couldn't see that anything was missing.

I transferred robe and briefcase to the front seat and wired the trunk lid down. It irked me that I was going to have to spend my morning break filing another police complaint so I could prove to the insurance company that the damage really happened.

Court was disjointed that morning, complicated by a bunch of no-shows and motions to recalendar due to the weather. With Fran expected to come ashore tonight somewhere between Myrtle Beach and Wilmington, everyone seemed to have trouble concentrating and by the time I gave up and adjourned for the day at one p.m., the wind had picked up and it was raining hard again.

Frankly, I was getting more than a little tired of both the anticipation and the rain, too.

"Enough already!" I grumbled to Luther

Parker, with whom I share a connecting bathroom. "Let's just have a good blow and get it over with and get back to sunshine."

"Hope it's that easy," he said.

Everything smelled musty and felt damp. I almost slipped off my shoes and wiggled my stockinged toes just to make sure they weren't starting to grow little webs.

At the midmorning break, when I reported my jimmied trunk to the Dobbs town police, I'd cut through the Sheriff's Department to gripe about it to Dwight, but his office was empty.

He was there at one-fifteen, though, munching a hamburger at his desk. I started through the door of his office singing my song of woe, then stopped when I saw Terry Wilson sitting at the other end of the desk with his own hamburger and drink can.

"What's happened, Terry?" There's only a short list of things to bring an SBI agent out during working hours. "Dwight? Somebody get killed?"

"Yeah. One of the maids out at the Orchid Motel," Dwight said. "Lived in Cotton Grove. A neighbor found her around five this morning. Somebody sliced her up pretty bad last night. Knocked her around first, then cut off one of her fingers slick as a surgeon would. While she was still alive. Blood everywhere."

I watched as Terry squirted a tinfoil packet of ketchup on his french fries. I guess you get anesthetized after a while.

"Is her death related to Lynn Bullock's?"

"Be a right big coincidence if it isn't," said Terry, who's as tolerant of my questions as Dwight.

"You get any hint of it when you interviewed her?" I asked Dwight.

"The thing is, we never did," he admitted with a huge sigh of regret. "She got off work before the Bullock woman checked in and didn't come back on duty till the next day, long after the killing took place. Didn't seem to be any urgency about talking with her. Sloppy."

"Don't beat up on yourself," said Terry, as I opened Dwight's little refrigerator and helped myself to one of the cold drinks inside. "You and your people were all over that motel. If Rosa Edwards knew something about the murder, she should've —"

"Rosa Edwards?" I asked, popping the top of a Diet Pepsi. "That's who got killed?"

"Yeah," said Dwight. "You know her?"

I shook my head. "No, but Ralph

Freeman said she was his wife's closest friend here." I stared at them, struck by a sudden thought. "What if it's nothing to do with Lynn Bullock? What if it's about how Clara Freeman wound up in Possum Creek without leaving any skid marks on the pavement?"

Dwight reached for his Rolodex and started dialing. "Jimmy? You done anything yet with that Honda Civic Robert Knott pulled out of the creek last night? . . . Good. Don't touch it. I'm sending a crew out to examine it."

Chapter 15

But when their hearts are really touched they drop everything and rush to the rescue of the afflicted.

Cyl stuck her head in my office as I was sliding my feet into a pair of sandals so old that it wouldn't matter if they got soaked. I saw that she, too, had changed from those expensive dark green heels to scuffed black flats that had seen better days. Fran was still out in the Atlantic, just off the coast of Wilmington, but so huge that her leading edge was already spilling into the Triangle area. We were in for a night of high wind and heavy rain whether or not the hurricane actually came inland.

Cyl had heard about Rosa Edwards's murder, but she hadn't connected it to Clara Freeman until I told her of their friendship. Instantly, her thoughts flew to Stan and Lashanda. Their mother was in a coma, her closest friend had been brutally butchered and a big storm was on the way. Anything that touched Ralph Freeman was going to touch her but she did seem genuinely distressed for the children, who might have to stay alone with their stern-faced grandfather.

"I could take them to my grandmother's, but she's already gone to my uncle's house in Durham."

"I'm sure some kind family from the church will take them in," I soothed.

I was anxious to head back to the farm, but Cyl asked if I'd go with her to the hospital and I couldn't turn her down since it was only the second time she'd ever asked me for a favor.

The sky was dark as we drove in tandem to the hospital on the northwest side of Dobbs and the ICU waiting room was nearly empty except for the children, the Reverend James McElroy Gaithers, and a couple of church people who were clearly torn between a wish to comfort and an even more sincere wish to get home under shelter before the wind got too heavy.

Lashanda was sitting on Ralph's lap and her eyes lit up as we came through the door. Heaven help him, so did Ralph's. His father-in-law gave a stately nod that acknowledged our acquaintance.

"You sure you kids don't want to come home with Crystal and me?" I heard one of the women coax as we joined them.

Lashanda sank deeper into her father's arms and Ralph said, "Thank you, Sister Garrett, but they'll be fine here. I already spoke to one of the staff about some blankets and pillows. They can stretch out here on the couches."

Impulsively, I excused myself and went and found a telephone.

Daddy doesn't like talking on the phone and he answered with his usual abrupt, "Yeah?"

I quickly explained the situation.

"Bring 'em on here," he said, before I could ask. "I'll tell Maidie. And, Deb'rah?"

"Sir?"

"Don't y'all dilly-dally around. They's gonna be tree limbs down in the road 'fore long, so come on now, you hear?"

I heard.

When I got back, Cyl was extending her own invitation to the children.

"I've got a better idea," I told her brightly. "My daddy just invited you and Stan and Lashanda to his hurricane party."

"Hurricane party?" asked Lashanda. The bluebird barrettes on her braids brushed her cheeks as she uncurled a bit from Ralph's protective arms. "What's that?"

"That's where we have like a pajama party and while the wind's blowing and the rain's coming down, we're snug inside with candles and lanterns. We'll sit up half the night, make popcorn and sing and tell stories —"

The Reverend Gaithers cleared his throat.

"— but mostly we'll just laugh at any old storm that tries to scare us," I finished hastily. "And Stan can take notes for his science project and tell us what's happening."

"Can we, Daddy?"

For the first time since we'd come back, the little girl seemed animated instead of tired and apprehensive. Even Stan looked interested.

"Please?" I appealed to Ralph. "You've been out to the farm. It's not all that far from Cotton Grove so you could easily swing by if you should go home tomorrow morning."

"We-ell," said Ralph. "You sure it's not too much trouble."

"No trouble at all," I assured him. "There's plenty of room for you, too, Reverend Gaithers, if you'd care to come," I added.

"Thank you," he said gravely, "but I will keep the vigil for my daughter here."

The brightness faded from Stan's face. "I guess I better stay, too."

"No," said the older man, showing more compassion than I'd credited him with. "You go and look after your sister, Stanley. Your father and I will do the praying tonight."

"You'll come, too, Miss Cyl?" Stan asked as Lashanda slid off Ralph's lap and took Cyl's hand.

Confused, Cyl started to murmur about not having the right clothes, but I quickly scotched that. "I have everything you need, even an extra toothbrush. Come on. It'll be fun."

She might have hesitated longer, but one of Bo Poole's deputies, Mayleen Richards, entered the waiting room and we both knew that she'd probably come to question Ralph about Rosa Edwards's death. The children didn't seem to know about it yet and Cyl and I were in instant silent agreement that this was no time to hit them with another shock.

"Sure," said Cyl. "Let's go."

Downstairs, we agreed to split up. Cyl would drive Stan and Lashanda to Cotton Grove for their over-night things while I stopped by Jimmy White's to see what he could do about my trunk lock, then we'd meet at the homeplace. Maidie was active in the same church as Cyl's grandmother, so Cyl would see at least one familiar face if they got there before I did.

Even though it wasn't yet three o'clock, the road home was busier than usual. A lot of places must have let their employees go home early. Rain was falling quite heavily now and wind gusts buffeted my car, giving me pleasant little bursts of adrenaline each time I had to correct the steering. It was both scary and exhilarating. Like riding a horse you're not too sure of.

When I reached Jimmy's garage and pulled into his drive, the county's crime scene van blocked the entrance to the garage itself and Dwight's car was there, too.

They had pushed Clara Freeman's Civic inside and found what we hadn't noticed the night before: a small dent in her left rear fender and a smear of black paint ground into that dent. It might just be enough.

"*If* we can find a black car to match it with," Dwight said with unwonted pessimism. "And you want to hear something cute? I stopped by the Orchid Motel on my way out of Dobbs and Marie O'Day said she was just about to call me. They'd heard about Edwards's death and one of the maids finally thought to mention that she came back to the motel late Saturday afternoon. Guess what car she was driving?"

"This one here?"

"You got it," he said glumly. "Rosa Edwards might still be alive if we'd talked to her."

"Or not," I said, patting his shoulder as if he were Reese or A.K. "If she was the talking kind, she had four days to come to you."

It would have been interesting to bat around theories, but we all were getting antsy. Jimmy promised to get to my trunk lock by the first of the week, but right now he wanted to close down the garage. Dwight had a few loose ends of his own to see to before the storm got worse. The crime scene van was already on its way back to Dobbs.

I hurried on home to change clothes and pick up some overnight things for Cyl and me. As I was hunting for the extra toothbrushes I'd stashed in my linen closet, Robert stopped by with a kerosene lantern, Lashanda's doll and Clara Freeman's purse, which were still soggy and starting to mildew after such a hot day in the airless cab of his tractor. I gave him a hug for the lantern and thanks for remembering the doll and purse.

"I'm real glad you and Reese're going to Daddy's," he said, hugging me back. "It's not gonna be anything like Hazel, but it don't pay to take risks."

I tried to stick up for my house's steel framing, but he just laughed and drove on off toward his own place.

I took the things inside and put them on my kitchen counter. The mildew wiped right off Lashanda's rubber doll and Clara's brown plastic purse. I rinsed out the doll's dress and underpants and threw them in the dryer. Next, I unloaded the purse and propped it open, then spread the contents across the countertop so they'd dry and air out — keys, lipstick, comb, nail file, a damp notepad with a list of items crossed off, a couple of envelopes. One was plain and sealed with Scotch tape. The other looked like a bill from Carolina Power and Light. I threw away a couple of sodden tissues and a half-melted roll of breath mints.

Along with the usual cards and paper money in the wallet, there were pictures of Stan and Lashanda and a studio picture of Clara and Ralph with the two kids. I looked at that one long and hard. In her neat blue dress with a chaste white collar, she was no-where near as beautiful as Cyl, but there was something wistful in her eyes and I wondered if Ralph had been unfaithful to her before or was Cyl an aberration waiting to happen? I tried to imagine Cyl into this picture if Clara didn't make it. Cyl as a preacher's wife? As stepmother to these two children? Cyl DeGraffenried of the sophisticated haircut, the elegant understated clothes, the competitive career woman?

There'd be a lot of hard adjusting all around.

I put down paper towels and spread the pictures and cards to dry as I switched on the radio. Bulletins were coming thick and fast on WPTF. Fran was definitely coming ashore around eight o'clock at Bald Head Island at the mouth of the Cape Fear River.

Rain was falling hard in long windblown sheets that almost obscured the pond as it lashed at my windows. I went around making a final check and had just latched the last window when the phone rang.

"Your people are here," said Daddy. "Why ain't you?"

"On my way," I told him and dashed out into the rain with my duffle bag crammed with enough clothes and toiletries to last a week.

Chapter 16

Here are all the terrible phenomena of the West Indian hurricane — the tremendous wind, the thrashing sea, the lightning, the bellowing thunder, and the drowning rain that seems to be dashed from mighty tanks with the force of Titans.

We spent the next hour settling in. Since the quickest way to get people past their initial awkwardness is to give them something to do, Maidie and I soon had Lashanda and Stan racing up and down the stairs, bringing down pillows, quilts and blankets. Here at the homeplace, kitchen and den flow into each other and Daddy and Cletus sat at the kitchen table to keep from getting run over.

There were enough bedrooms in this old house for everyone to have a choice, but who ever heard of going off to separate rooms during a hurricane party?

The den couch opens into a bed that I claimed for Cyl and me, and there were a couple of recliner chairs as well. We made thick pallets for the children right on the area rugs that dot the worn linoleum floor.

Both Blue and Ladybelle had been turned in and Ladybelle immediately went over and started pushing at Lashanda's hand with her head.

"She wants you to scratch behind her ears," Daddy told her.

Half-apprehensively — the hound was almost as tall as she was — Lashanda reached out and scratched. Ladybelle gave a sigh of pure pleasure and sank down at the little girl's feet.

Daddy's television was tuned to the weather channel and Stan sat on the floor in front of it, entranced by the colored graphics that covered the screen.

"So *that's* what he looks like," he murmured when a black forecaster started explaining for the umpteenth time how the Saffir-Simpson scale rated hurricanes. "I wondered."

"You don't have cable?" Cyl asked, stuffing pillows into cotton pillowcases that Maidie had ironed to crisp perfection.

"We don't have television at all," said Lashanda, abandoning Ladybelle so that she could help Cyl.

Stan looked embarrassed. "Mama doesn't believe in it. But I can pick up this channel on my shortwave. That's how I know that guy's voice."

I wasn't as shocked as some people might be. Like a lot of members in her fundamentalist church, my sister-in-law Nadine doesn't, quote, believe in television either, but Herman's overruled her on that from the beginning. And as soon as cable came to Dobbs, he signed up for it. Now that the population's getting dense enough to make it economically feasible, cable's finally reached our end of the county, too, but Daddy and the boys have had satellite dishes for years.

All the same, even though I could understand where Clara Freeman was coming from — especially after meeting her father — it did make me wonder how much slack she cut her children.

Or her husband.

"They's crayons in the children's drawer," Maidie reminded me on one of her trips through the den, when she realized Stan was trying to copy some of the color graphics of the storm.

The television sat atop an enormous old turn-of-the-century sideboard. Mother had turned the bottom drawer into a catchall for games and toys as soon as the first grandchild was born. And yes, it was now being used for great-grandchildren, so it still held a big Tupperware bowl full of broken crayons of all colors. Some of them had probably been there since Reese was a baby. Stan seized upon them and one of his blank weather maps soon sported an amorphous gray storm with a dark red blotch in the center.

All this time, the house had been filling with delicious aromas. For Maidie, picnics and parties always mean fried chicken and she had the meaty parts of at least four chickens bubbling away in three large black iron frying pans. There was a bowl of potato salad in the refrigerator, a big pot of newly picked butter beans on the spare burner, and Maidie set Cletus to slicing a half-dozen fresh-off-the-vine tomatoes while she got out her bread tray.

"You've already cooked enough for an army," I said as Cyl and Lashanda and I set the table. "Don't tell me you're going to make biscuits, too?"

"Well, you know how Reese eats." She was already mixing shortening into a mound of self-rising flour. "And that Stan looks like he could stand some fattening."

Lashanda giggled, her little blue barrettes jiggling with each movement. "And you know what? Mama says he eats like he's got a tapeworm."

I had to smile, too. You don't grow up in a houseful of adolescent boys without hearing that phrase a time or twenty.

Following his nose, Reese blew in through the back door a few minutes later, carrying a full ice chest as if it weighed no more than a five-pound bag of sugar. Like his father Herman, Reese is also a twin, but he's built like all the other Knott men: six feet tall, sandy brown hair, clear blue eyes. No movie stars in the whole lot, but no trouble getting women either.

"Something sure smells fit to eat in this house," he said, buttering Maidie before he was even through the door good.

He spotted Cyl and Lashanda, did a double take and then squatted down so he'd be level with the child. "Well, well, well! Who's this pretty little thing we got here?"

His words were for Lashanda, but his eyes were all over Cyl, who had changed into the jeans and T-shirt I'd brought her. Both were a trifle snug on me, but she had room to spare in all the right places.

"Behave yourself, Reese," I scolded and

introduced him to our guests.

"Oh, yeah, Uncle Robert told me about Miz Freeman. I'm real sorry." He straightened up and looked at Cyl and me. "If y'all'll give me your keys, I'll go move your cars."

"Why?" I asked. "We're not blocking you, are we?"

"No, but they're right under those big oaks and the way this wind's blowing, you might be better off out in the open."

We immediately handed them over. By the time he came back, soaked to the skin, we were putting the food on the table. He quickly changed into some of Daddy's clothes and put his own in the dryer.

Daddy likes to pray about as much as he likes talking on the telephone, but with Maidie and the children sitting there with bowed heads, the rest of us followed their example and he offered up his usual, "For what we are about to receive, O Lord, make us truly thankful. Amen."

"Amen," we said and passed the bowls and platters.

The biscuits were hot and flaky. The chicken was crisp on the outside, tender and juicy on the inside — ambrosia from the southern part of heaven.

Stan was a little more polite about it

than Reese, but both ate as if it was their first meal in three days.

"Did you know that Edwards woman that got killed in Cotton Grove last night?" Reese asked Maidie as he spooned a third helping of potato salad onto his plate.

I was sitting next to him and I gave his thigh a sharp nudge.

"Let's don't talk about that right now," I said warningly.

Luckily, Lashanda had been distracted by Ladybelle, who knows better than to beg food from any of us, but couldn't be prevented from sitting near any newcomer in the hope that she might not know the rules. Stan had heard though, and his eyes widened. He turned to Cyl, who sat on the other side of him, and she nodded gravely.

Suddenly he didn't seem to be hungry any more and when he asked to be excused so he could go check on what Fran was doing, Cyl went with him.

Reese and Maidie picked up that something was going on and they kept Lashanda laughing and talking and plied with honey for her biscuit till Cyl came back to the table.

We were more than halfway through the dishes when the power went off, plunging us into darkness deeper than most of us had seen since the last power outage. What with security lights and even streetlights popping up all over the area, we don't get much true darkness anymore. Daddy had a flashlight to hand and once the candles and lanterns had been lit, Maidie insisted we go ahead and finish washing up while the water system still had enough pressure to do the job.

Power failure rules immediately went into effect: boys in the upstairs bathroom, girls in the downstairs and no flushing unless absolutely necessary, using water dipped from the full tubs.

Daddy and Cletus had moved into the den recliners and were regaling Stan with well-worn memories of Hurricane Hazel. Maidie's only about fifteen years older than me, so her memories of Hazel are pretty vague, but Cletus has another six or eight years on her and can match Daddy tree for fallen tree.

The candlelight soon took Daddy even further back, back before electricity came to this area.

"We didn't even have radio when I was a little fellow," he reminisced. "I was near-bout grown 'fore I heared it the first time. Seventy-five years ago, they was no weather satellites and the weather bureau did a lot of its predicting by what ships out at sea telegraphed to shore about the weather where they was. Way back here in the woods, we didn't know it was hurricanes stomping around out off the coast yonder. Old-timers used to call 'em August blows, 'cause most years, come late August, we'd get days and days of wind out of the northeast and sometimes we'd get a bunch of rain with it. A lot of times though, the sky'd be just as blue as you please, and that wind a-blowing."

As he spoke, the wind was blowing again, rattling the old wooden windows in their loose-fitting casements, and Lashanda tugged at my shirt. "Did you bring my baby doll, Miss Deborah?"

It was the first time I'd thought of it since I put the damp doll dress in my dryer. "Oh, honey, I'm so sorry. I went and left it at my house."

"Is that far away?" she asked plaintively.

"Not too far," I said brightly. "Why don't I just run over and get it for you."

"Here now," said Daddy. "I don't think that's a real smart idea. Wind catch hold of that little car of your'n and no telling where you'll fetch up."

"I'll carry her in my truck," said Reese,

who seemed to have taken a shine to the child. "It's heavy enough. We won't be more'n a minute."

Before Daddy could order us not to go, Reese and I had grabbed flashlights and were out the back door, dashing across the yard to his truck. Umbrellas were useless in this wind and neither of us bothered with one. The ground was soft and soggy and squished with each running step I took. Reese's white truck has such over-sized tires that I almost needed a step-ladder to swing up into the cab. There was a time when he wouldn't have let my wet clothes and muddy shoes into his truck. But that was before a deer tore the living bejeesus out of his beautiful leather seat covers and headliner last fall. Vinyl replacements were all he could afford and nowadays he's not quite as particular about water and dirt.

"We better not try going through the woods," Reese said, throwing the truck into four-wheel drive before we were even out of the yard.

Instead, he took the long way, through drag rows and lanes that bordered the fields. It was an exciting ride. Treetops were whipping in the wind, rain was coming down in buckets, and green leaves and pine needles were hurled so thickly against the windshield, the wipers almost couldn't handle them.

"Aren't you scared?" Reese asked, almost shouting to be heard above the rain pounding on the cab roof as we skidded through a cut in the woods that was almost blocked by a large pine limb.

I just laughed, feeling more alive than I had in ages. This was more exhilarating than a roller coaster.

As we turned out into the next field and followed the lane that runs alongside the pond, we saw car lights suddenly come on at the back of my house. We thought it might be one of the family, but instead of waiting for us or coming to meet us, it sped away down my driveway toward the road. By the time we got up to the house, the taillights were long gone, but the glare of Reese's lights showed that the door of my house was standing wide open. The window beside it had been smashed so that someone could reach inside and unlock the door.

Wind and rain were howling through the rooms. We slammed the door, then Reese headed through the kitchen to the garage for a tarp to nail over the window. When he brought it back, it was like hanging on to a sail even though my porch is roofed and screened. I had to pull the tarp taut and hold the flashlight steady, too, so he could see to nail.

As soon as that was taken care of, Reese lit the kerosene lamp on my kitchen counter and we shone our flashlights through the rest of the house to see what had been taken. Wind funnelling through the open door had scattered stuff, but no real damage had been done and I couldn't immediately see that the house had been seriously tossed. My few bits of real jewelry were untouched in the case on my dresser and all of Mother's sterling silver seemed to be occupying their proper compartments in the flannel-lined drawers.

The cards, pictures and bills from Clara Freeman's wallet had blown onto the floor, yet all were still there, including a five and two tens.

"We must've scared him off 'fore he could grab anything," said Reese.

I finished laying Clara's things back on fresh dry paper towels, then shone my light around the floor for items I might have missed.

"What you looking for?" asked my nephew.

"There were two envelopes," I said. "Here's the light bill, but the other one —"

I widened my search over every square inch of the area, to no avail. The damp envelope that had been sealed with Scotch tape was definitely gone.

At that instant, it was as if a flashbulb suddenly exploded in my head. *This* was why my car had been broken into? Looking for Clara Freeman's purse and the envelope? What could have been in it? And more importantly, who knew I had it?

Millard King had been there with Jason Bullock and me when I fished it out of the car. And at the hospital this morning, Dr. Jeremy Potts was standing beside Ralph Freeman when I said I had Lashanda's doll and Clara's purse.

"But not Brandon Frazier," whispered the preacher.

"And not Reid," said his headmate.

Until that moment of giddy relief, I hadn't realized how much I'd been subconsciously worrying about that dent in the right front fender of Reid's black BMW.

I was uneasy about leaving my house unprotected, but Reese wasn't about to let me stay.

"Granddaddy'll have my hide if I come

back without you," he said.

I stuck the doll and its clothes into a plastic bag so it wouldn't get wet and we drove down my long rutted driveway just to make sure the intruder was well and truly gone. Normally, our sandy soil slurps up water like a sponge. Tonight, the wheel ruts were overflowing channels. Just as we paused before pulling onto the hardtop, the big wisteria-covered pine tree beside my mailbox crashed down across the driveway behind us, rocking the truck as its lower limb swiped the tailgate. Two seconds earlier and we'd have been smashed beneath it.

"Holy shit!" Reese yelped and floored the accelerator.

"Watch out!" I shrieked and he almost put us in the ditch when he swerved to miss a limb lying in our lane. "Dammit, Reese, if you can't handle the speed, slow down!"

He did, but he was still shaking his head at two close calls.

"Well, one thing about it," he said sheepishly. "You don't have to worry about that guy coming back tonight. Nobody's gonna get through your lane without a chain saw or a bulldozer."

It was a short wild ride back to the

homeplace. Along the way, I cautioned him not to talk about the break-in to Lashanda. "She's handling the storm and what's happened to her mother pretty good, but too much more might set her off."

"She knew the Edwards woman?" he asked.

"Her mother's best friend," I told him.

As we pulled up to the back porch, I was surprised to see Dwight's patrol car.

"I was about to send Dwight looking for you," Daddy said when Reese and I were back inside and I had handed Lashanda her doll.

"What're you doing out in this weather?" I asked him curiously.

Dwight shrugged. "This and that. And by the time I was ready to head back to Dobbs, I realized I might better stay the night out here at Mother's. Just thought I'd check on y'all since it's on my way."

I walked out to the shadowy kitchen with him and we paused at the doorway. In low tones, I told him about the intruder at my house, about the missing envelope and who knew I had Clara Freeman's purse, ending with my theory that that's why my trunk was popped.

"Dr. Jeremy Potts was standing right there when I told Ralph Freeman I'd forgotten to bring the purse in with me. I meant into Dobbs. If it *is* Potts, he might've thought I meant in from the car."

"Potts?" Dwight asked blankly. "What's he got to do with the price of eggs?"

I gave him a quick rundown on the Potts divorce and how Lynn Bullock found the argument that let Jason vacuum the good doctor's assets. "And Amy said he was downright gloating when he contributed to her memorial fund yesterday."

"Millard King did say he thought there was a doctor out on the running track with him," Dwight mused. "Maybe I'd better have a talk with Potts. And I'll definitely send someone out tomorrow to dust your kitchen and that purse."

He glanced over my shoulder to the cozy candlelit scene in the den.

Cyl and Stan were lounging at opposite ends of the opened couch with his battery-powered radio turned low to catch the latest storm updates. Reese sat on the floor nearby, absently strumming soft chords on my guitar. Maidie was crocheting almost by touch alone in one of the wooden rockers. Candles threw exaggerated shadows on the wall and Daddy and Cletus were amusing Lashanda by making shadow birds and animals with their hands. Some of their creations took all four hands and were quite complicated.

"Almost wish I was staying," Dwight said wistfully as he opened the door and stepped onto the porch.

The door was on the leeward side of the wind, and I walked out onto the porch with him. Between candles and kerosene lanterns, the house was starting to get too warm and stuffy and I was so glad for the fresh air that I continued to stand there with rainwater cascading off the porch roof while Dwight dashed out to his cruiser and drove away.

And I was still standing there three minutes later when the cruiser returned.

"This should teach me to be careful what I ask for," Dwight said wryly when he rejoined me on the porch. He dried his face on the shoulder of his wet sports shirt. "Two of Mr. Kezzie's pecan trees are laying across the lane and I can't get out. Use your phone?"

"If it's still working."

It was. First he called Miss Emily to say he wouldn't be coming after all. Too late. She'd left a message for him on her answering machine that Rob and Kate had

We hope you have enjoyed this Large Print book. Other Thorndike Press or Chivers Press Large Print books are available at your library or directly from the publishers.

For more information about current and upcoming titles, please call or write, without obligation, to:

Thorndike Press
P.O. Box 159
Thorndike, Maine 04986 USA
Tel. (800) 223-1244
        (800) 223-6121

OR

Chivers Press Limited
Windsor Bridge Road
Bath BA2 3AX
England
Tel. (0225) 335336

All our Large Print titles are designed for easy reading, and all our books are made to last.

moment and get back again, but how would anybody know where she was unless they'd spent the morning trailing her? Reid and Millard King were both roaming in and out of my courtroom all morning. Even Brandon Frazier came up during the lunch break to get me to sign a pleading, so unless Dr. Potts —"

"Wait, wait, wait!" Cyl protested. "Brandon Frazier? Millard King? Reid Stephenson? Your cousin? What do they have to do with the wreck or last night's murder?"

We'd forgotten that she wasn't up to speed on this.

"Rosa Edwards worked at the Orchid Motel. We think she saw Lynn Bullock's killer, and each of those three men slept with Lynn Bullock in the last few months," I said bluntly.

"Really?" Despite her own situation, Cyl frowned in distaste. All the men were familiar courthouse regulars, but she hadn't known Jason Bullock's wife. "Was she such a fox?" Cyl asked curiously. "Or such a slut?"

Dwight and I both shrugged. "Some of both probably," I said.

Interrupting each other, he and I almost did a probable cause on each man and how

none of them had a watertight alibi for the time of death — between five and eight on Saturday evening. As rain pounded against the window glass, we discussed Millard King's desire for future elective office, Reid's late arrival and early departure from the field, Brandon Frazier's frank admissions, and the tie tack that probably belonged to Millard King. (I busied myself tidying the table while Dwight told her about the silver pen.)

"What about her husband — Jason Bullock? Did you eliminate him?"

I explained how I was there when Lynn Bullock called, pretending to be a hundred miles away and how he'd been at the field during the relevant times.

"She was registered under her maiden name, and some man called the motel switchboard before she checked in and again just a few minutes after she talked to Jason. Asked for her by the name she was using, too."

"Might as well tell her about Jeremy Potts, too," said Dwight. "Deborah thinks —"

At that moment, we were startled when the back door opened with a loud squeak and something dark and shiny walked in from the storm. In the flickering candle-

light, it gave the three of us a start till we realized it was Cletus, wearing a large black plastic garbage bag for a rain poncho.

"I thought you went up to bed," I said.

"Naw, I got to worrying about how the house was faring down there. Went out the side door. They's a tree down across the path now, so I had to come back in this way." He pulled off the bag and left it to drip in the sink before heading back upstairs. "You young folks oughta get a little rest. Be morning soon."

Physically, we were all tired but were too keyed up to call it a night just yet. And Cyl wanted to know about Jeremy Potts. Once again, I found myself describing that acrimonious divorce and Lynn Bullock's part in it.

I finished up by reminding her that she was there at the hospital when I told Ralph that I had his wife's handbag. "And less than forty-five minutes later, somebody popped the lock on my car trunk."

"Looking for her purse? But why?" Cyl asked. "And why would anybody hurt Ralph's wife if this Rosa Edwards was the one who could put him at the motel?"

"Maybe he was afraid Rosa had talked to her good friend Clara," I said. "I don't know."

"We do know that she was driving Mrs. Freeman's car last Saturday," Dwight reminded me.

"So maybe he thought she was the one who'd seen him."

"*If* anyone saw him," Cyl said, sounding like a skeptical prosecutor. "Coincidences do happen and —"

Yawning widely, Stan came out to the kitchen. "They say the eye just collapsed over Garner a few minutes ago. I guess it's pretty much over."

His own eyes were looking at the chicken with such interest that I got him a paper plate, napkins, and a big glass of milk to go with it. He wasn't interested in a tomato sandwich, "but if there's any of that potato salad left?"

There was.

When his plate was full, Stan looked around the table. "Miss Cyl told me about Miss Rosa getting killed. Is that what y'all were talking about?"

We admitted we were.

"When did you last see her?" I asked.

"Deborah!" Cyl protested. "He's a minor."

"And if Ralph were here, do you think he'd object to Stan telling us that?"

"It's okay, Miss Cyl," said Stan, using his

310

paper napkin to wipe milk from his upper lip. "She came over to the house yesterday morning just as Mama was fixing to drive us to school. Shandy and I were already in the car, but Mama was still in the house and Miss Rosa just went on in. Said she had to speak to Mama about something."

"Did she say what about?" asked Dwight.

"No, sir. And Mama didn't say, either. They both came out together and Miss Rosa drove off and then Mama took us to school. That's the last time we saw her. I tried to call her when Mama went missing, but she never answered her phone. I guess she was working then?"

"Do you know where she works?" I interjected curiously.

He shook his head. "I think she's a housekeeper somewhere in Dobbs. One of the motels?"

Dwight gave me one of his do-you-mind? looks. "And all she said was that she had to speak to your mother? Those were her exact words? Nothing about why?"

Stan nibbled thoughtfully on the drumstick he held, then shook his head. "I'm sorry, no."

"Stan," I said slowly. "There was an envelope in your mother's purse and —"

"Hey, right!" His face brightened. "I forgot. When Miss Rosa went in the house, she was carrying a white envelope. And when she came back out, she wasn't. She must've given it to Mama. Did you open it? What was in it?"

"I didn't open it. Someone burgled my house tonight and took it."

"What?"

Cyl and Stan were both looking at me in disbelief.

"That's why Reese and I were so long getting back with Lashanda's doll," I said and told them about the broken window and fleeing taillights.

Cyl shook her head. "Girl, you do stay in the middle of things, don't you?"

"That's why Miss Rosa got killed, wasn't it?" asked Stan, making the same leap I'd made but not for the same reasons. If Lynn Bullock's murder over in Dobbs had even registered on him, it was clear he didn't connect it to Rosa Edwards. "She had something somebody wanted and she gave it to Mama to hold for her? And then when Mama disappeared, they must've thought Miss Rosa was lying about not being able to get it back?"

He yawned again. "I wonder if she told Mama what it was?" Suddenly he looked

very young. "I sure hope she wakes up tomorrow."

"Today," said Cyl. "And you'd better get some sleep."

"You okay on that pallet?" I asked. "Or would you rather try one of the recliners?"

"The floor's fine," he said with yet another wide yawn that made me yawn, too.

Cyl and Dwight were smothering yawns of their own as Stan said goodnight and went to lie down in the den.

I opened the back door to let in some fresh air. It was only marginally cooler than the air inside and heavy with moisture. Rain still pounded the tin roof and fell as if it meant to go on falling forever.

Dwight's face was grim as he joined me by the doorway.

"It was her insurance policy, wasn't it?" I said.

"Probably."

"She told him she'd written it down and given it to someone to hold," Cyl said softly from behind us. "That's why he cut her so badly. And kept cutting till she told him who."

"Then killed her because he thought he'd already killed the who and sunk her purse," I said. "I wonder if Millard King

313

really was visiting his brother in Fuquay last night or was he hanging around Possum Creek waiting to see if he could get to Clara Freeman's car before anyone else did?"

"If he was, it must've scared the hell out of him when you grabbed her purse," said Dwight with a wry smile.

"Unless it was Dr. Jeremy Potts," said Cyl. "Surgeons don't mind blood, do they?"

After Dwight went off to bed in my old corner room upstairs, Cyl and I changed into gym shorts and baggy T-shirts for sleeping. I turned the lantern wick down real low, then went around blowing out all the candles.

Stan had crawled under the sheet next to his little sister's feet and both children were breathing deeply.

I crawled onto my side of the couch. It felt wonderful to lie down.

I watched as Cyl untangled the top of the sheet from Lashanda's arm and moved Ladybelle away from her face, then came and stretched out beside me.

"They're really nice kids, aren't they?" she sighed.

"You're going to make a terrific mother

someday," I told her.

"But not their mother." A great sadness was in her voice.

"They have a mother, Cyl."

"You think I don't know that?"

"But you can't help wishing — ?"

"That they were mine?" She turned to me with a low moan. "Oh, God, Deborah, I'm such a horrible person!"

"No, you're not," I said, trying to comfort her. "You didn't mean to fall in love with Ralph. You didn't set out to snare him or anything. It just happened."

"That's not what I mean."

"What then?"

She was silent for a long moment and when she finally did speak, her voice was so hushed I had to strain to hear her.

"When I heard that she was hurt — in a coma — I thought, What if she never wakes up? What if she just goes ahead and dies?" She looked at me and her eyes were dark pools of despair in the dim light. "What kind of a monster could wish for something like that?"

"You're no monster," I said. "You're only human."

"I thought that . . . in the end, he'd choose love," she whispered. "Our love. But now she's hurt so bad. It could take

her months, years, to recover. He'll never leave her like that. He couldn't do it to his children."

Tears spilled down her cheeks.

"And neither could I."

"What will you do?"

She shook her head helplessly. "All I know is that I can't stay here. I can give him up, but not if I stay here."

She began to cry and her muffled sobs tore at my heart.

I felt movement at the end of the couch, then Lashanda was there between us on the sofa bed. She patted Cyl's cheek tenderly.

"Don't cry, Miss Cyl. It'll soon be morning."

Chapter 17

Is it at all wonderful that, after the strain was over and all danger gone, reason should finally be unseated and men and women break into the unmeaning gayety of the maniac?

We awoke on Friday morning to sunshine, dead still mugginess and the sound of chain saws and tractors. Trees were down all around the house. We'd had so much rain these last few weeks and the ground was so saturated that roots had pulled right out of the earth in Fran's high sustained winds. The children were already outdoors and Cyl and I got a cup of coffee and went out to survey the damage more closely. Lashanda immediately ran to greet us.

Mother's magnolias still stood tall and proud, although one had been skinned the full length of its trunk when a neighboring pine fell over.

"We'll prune it up. See if we can save it," said my brother Seth, giving me a sweaty morning hug.

His mother, Daddy's first wife, hadn't found the time to worry about landscaping, so it was my mother who planted azaleas and dogwoods and magnolias with the help of her stepsons who came to love her as their own. Seth could remember the first year the magnolias bloomed and how their fragrance drifted through the bedroom windows at night, bewitching their dreams.

He, Robert and Haywood were there to help Daddy clear the drive so we could get in and out. The tree across the porch looked awful, but the actual damage was minimal and would have to wait in line since there was worse to be taken care of on the farm.

Reese's place was the hardest hit. Two sixty-foot pines had crashed down on the trailer he was renting from Seth and everything he owned was either smashed or waterlogged. Seth had insurance on the trailer itself, but Reese had nothing on the contents. "First my truck, now my trailer," he said gloomily.

He'd already been over to the wreckage this morning and the back of his pickup

was loaded with wet clothes, tapes and CDs, and other odds and ends that were salvageable. Daddy'd told him to come stay at the homeplace till he could figure out what he wanted to do.

Andrew and April were hard hit, too. A huge oak had taken out the whole northwest side of their house, shearing off the kitchen and dining room wall.

"You know April, though," said Seth with a grin. "She's already talking about how she's been wanting to get more light into that part of the house and now the insurance money will help her do it."

(April moves walls in that house like other women move furniture.)

In addition to Reese's trailer, Seth was mourning four mature pecans. Haywood said he had nineteen trees down in his yard, but none of them hit the house. Robert hadn't counted his downed trees, "but the yard's full of 'em," and they said that the farm's biggest potato house had lost three sheets of tin off the roof.

("I've heard of being three sheets in the wind," Haywood chuckled, "but I didn't know they was talking about tin sheets.")

Other than a little water damage, most of the other houses on the farm, including my own, were pretty much unscathed.

The roads were blocked all around, they said, but neighbors were out, working on getting at least one lane cleared.

Power was still off and phones were out over most of the county. Even cell phones were spotty, depending on which company you were with. Dwight had already used his car radio to send word to Ralph Freeman at the hospital that Stan and Lashanda were fine, and word had come back that Ralph would try to get home to Cotton Grove by mid-morning to meet them there.

I managed to get through to Aunt Zell on my cell phone, even though it was staticky and other voices kept fading in and out. She said most of Dobbs was without power but the phones were still working. She'd been worried since she hadn't heard from any of us. I assured her that we were all physically fine.

"What about y'all?" I asked. "Everything okay there?"

"Not exactly," she admitted. "Your Uncle Ash put our new Lincoln in the garage last night and left the old one sitting in the drive. You remember that big elm out by the edge of the yard? It totalled the garage and our new car both. Not a scratch on the old one. Ash is so provoked."

I could imagine.

"And Portland called this morning. Remember how she and Avery fetched their boat home to get it out of harm's way?"

I had to laugh. "Don't tell me."

"Yep. A pine tree cut it right half in two."

Lashanda followed us around the yard, chattering sixty to the dozen, but Stan stayed busy helping the menfolks till Maidie called us in for sausage and griddle cakes.

There was no school, of course, and no court either, for that matter. Seth had brought over a battery-powered radio for Daddy and we listened open-mouthed to the reports coming in from around the area. Fran never made it beyond a category 3 storm, but it had moved across the state so slowly that it did much more damage than a stronger, faster-moving hurricane would have. Even more than legendary Hazel, they were saying. Most of the problems seemed to have been caused by trees falling on cars, houses and power lines. And there was quite a bit of flooding in low-lying areas.

"You'll probably have the most dramatic science project in your class," Cyl told Stan.

"Sounds like an A to me, too," I said.

"Maybe," he said, not meeting our eyes.

Andrew and A.K arrived with news that at least one lane of Highway 48 was clear in either direction and that they'd also heard it was possible to drive to Cotton Grove on Old 48.

"Reckon I'll be going then," said Dwight. "If Stan and Lashanda are ready to go, I can drop them off."

Stan immediately put down his fork and stood up, but I said, "That's okay. Cyl and I'll take them. Ralph's probably not home yet and Stan needs to get all his notes and books together, so we won't hold you up."

He and my brothers, Daddy and Cletus went back outside. Maidie was putting together the scraps of breakfast ham to take down to the caged hunting beagles.

"Why don't you let Lashanda help you?" I asked with a meaningful cut of my eyes that Maidie read like a book.

As soon as Cyl and I were alone with Stan, I said, "What's wrong?"

"Nothing," he answered sullenly. At eleven, almost twelve, he might have a man's height, but he was still a boy, a boy who wanted to play it cool, yet was still too inexperienced not to show his raw emotions. He pushed away from the table and

walked into the den area to gather up his things.

Cyl shot me an apprehensive glance as we followed him in and began folding up the bedclothes.

"Did you hear us talking last night?" I asked him bluntly.

"What if I did?" he said, his back to us.

"Did you understand what you heard?"

Angry and confused, he turned on Cyl. "I liked you! I thought you were our friend."

"I liked you too, Stan," she said sadly. "I still do."

"But you — ? With my dad? While Mama's lying there hurt?"

"What happened was before she was hurt," Cyl said.

"But you want her dead!"

Cyl shook her head. "No, I don't."

"If you heard us talking," I said, "then you heard that it's over. Almost before it began. Stan — ?"

He didn't want to listen and when Cyl put her hand out to him, he backed away from her.

"I know you're upset about your mom," she said. "Mad at me and mad at your dad, and I can't blame you for that. I'm not even going to try and ask you to

understand, but —"

"Good!" he said hotly. "Because I don't. And don't try saying it's because I'm too young either!"

"I wasn't." She finished folding a quilt, laid it on the growing stack I'd begun, and took a deep breath. "What happened between your father and me happened. It can't ever be undone, but it *is* over. Finished. It doesn't have to affect you and your sister unless you let it fester. What I'm asking is that you keep it between your father and me. Talk to him if you need to talk about it, but don't bring anybody else into it. Especially your mom."

"Yeah, I just bet you don't want her to know!" he said angrily. "But she has a right to. She *needs* to!"

"No, she doesn't."

"But —"

"You said you don't want to be treated like a child, Stan."

"I don't."

"Then you're going to have to think before you speak. And you're going to have to realize that the hardest thing about being grown up is keeping hurtful things to yourself. You think you can get rid of a hurt like this by giving it to your mother?" She shook her head sadly. "It doesn't work

like that, Stan. You won't divide the hurt you're feeling, you'll only double it. Do you really want to do that to her?"

Anguish mingled with resentment in the boy's eyes.

"No, ma'am," he said at last.

Cyl and I drove Stan and Lashanda back to Cotton Grove in mid-morning. Angry and confused as he was, he was still young enough to be as distracted as his little sister by all the devastation. And it truly was amazing. Andrew and A.K. had been told that it was possible to drive Old 48 into town, and it was. But only because we kept detouring and backtracking. We had heard reports of tornadoes in the night and now we could see where small ones might have touched down: swaths of woodlands where treetops had been twisted off still-standing trunks.

Trunks and limbs were everywhere. Power poles were down. Every fifth house seemed to have a big leafy tree on it somewhere, mostly on the roof, but also through windows and across porches and cars. Yet, considering the number of trees that had fallen, it was amazing how many did *not* hit houses. I had to drive slowly because the roads were often single lanes

and clogged with other drivers who were out to survey the damage before tackling their own.

As we entered town, an almost festive air hung over the streets. Everyone seemed to be out sightseeing along the sidewalks and the mood was one of good-natured excitement. Children clambered on fallen tree trunks, chattering and pointing. Neighbors called out to other neighbors who drove past with rolled-down windows despite the hot and muggy day. Part of it was amazement at so much destruction, another part had to be relief that the destruction wasn't worse. As we crept along at a snail's pace, I did my own share of exchanging news.

"Hey, there, Deb'rah," folks would call. "Mr. Kezzie okay?"

"He's fine," I'd call back. "Y'all come through it all right? Anybody have power yet?"

"Not on this side of town. Heared it's back on from North Main to the town limits, though."

More detours through parts of Cotton Grove I hadn't visited in ages, more waits for our turn to pass through the single open lanes.

"Isn't that Jason Bullock?" asked Cyl as we were routed down an unfamiliar street.

I followed her pointing finger and there he was, coming along the driveway of a nondescript house and carrying a chain saw and gas can.

He saw us at the same time and walked over to my open window. His blue T-shirt was drenched with perspiration, flecks of sawdust sprinkled his brown hair and I smelled the strong odor of gasoline from his chain saw.

"Ms. DeGraffenried, Judge. This is really something, isn't it?"

"That your house?" I asked. "Doesn't look like you had much damage."

He laughed. "Look a little closer. See that brush pile? I just finished cutting it off my car. You can't see it from here, but the top's got a dent the size of a fish pond and the side's smashed in. Still, I was luckier than Mrs. Wesley down there." He gestured to a house half a block further on, where an enormous oak had pulled out of the ground and crushed the front of a shabby old two-story frame house that had seen better days. "She's eighty-three and her only relative's the seventy-year-old niece who lives with her. Some of the neighbors and I are fixing to clear their yard for them."

By this time, Lashanda had slipped out

of her seat belt and was kneeling on the backseat with her forearms on the back of my seat and her small face next to mine.

"Hey, there," she said.

Jason smiled down at her, then said to Cyl, "These aren't your children, are they?"

She shook her head. "No."

"Actually, though, you need to meet them," I said. "Lashanda, Stan, this is Mr. Bullock. He's one of the men from the rescue squad that pulled your mother out of the creek night before last."

Before he or Stan could respond, Lashanda said, "Do you have a little girl, too?"

"Nope, I'm afraid not," said Jason.

As the cars ahead of me began to move, we said goodbye and he stood back, so we could drive on.

From the backseat, I heard Stan say, "You know him?"

"Not really. Can you do my seat belt? I can't click it."

"Then how come you thought he had a daughter?"

" 'Cause when Mama comes to pick me up at school, he's there, too."

Despite the heat, a chill went down my spine at the child's words. Making my

voice as casual as I could, I said, "You've seen him at your school, honey?"

"Yes'm, and guess what? When we stop for groceries and stuff, he goes to the same places."

Cyl glanced at me curiously and then her eyes widened as she picked up on what I was thinking.

Goes to the same places? Childless, white Jason Bullock "goes to the same places" as Clara Freeman, a black mother?

My mind raced across the events of the last week, fitting one fact with another as everything spun like the wheels of a slot machine planning to come up cherries straight across. Unfortunately, it was another four minutes to the Freeman house and I couldn't say a word to Cyl.

Ralph and his father-in-law were getting out of the car when we drove up. A chinaball tree had blown down near the carport, just missing one of the support posts, but that seemed to be the only damage here.

By the set of his chin, I saw that Stan meant to step between Cyl and his father so I quickly loaded him down with his and Lashanda's overnight backpacks and asked where he wanted his radio as I carried it up to the side door. Too well-mannered to dig

in his heels, he reluctantly followed Lashanda and me up the drive. I greeted a weary Reverend Gaithers with burbling cheerfulness, asked about Clara, and said how much we'd enjoyed having the two kids. All this so that Cyl could have one very quick, if very public, moment with Ralph.

"She's doing better," said the old man. "I really do believe the good Lord's going to spare her. She opened her eyes this morning for a few minutes. I don't know if she knew me, but when I squeezed her hand, she squeezed mine back."

As we stood talking, the kids went on into the house and began opening all the windows, not that there was any breeze to mitigate the smothering, humidity-drenched heat. A chain saw three doors down made it difficult to understand each other and when it paused, I heard the siren of a rescue vehicle rushing somewhere several streets over. Ralph came up the drive and it was hard to meet his eyes as I told him I was glad to hear that his wife seemed to be coming out of her coma.

"Did you tell him Stan knows?" I asked Cyl as we drove away.

She nodded. "I'd give anything to take that knowledge away from him."

"Ralph? Or Stan?"

"Stan."

I started to speak, but she said, "I don't want to talk about it anymore, okay?"

"Okay." I paused at the stop sign, trying to remember precisely how we'd come. "Jason Bullock's car is black," I said.

"I noticed."

"Want to bet he's already lined up a body shop to get the dents banged out and repainted?"

"No bets." She sighed and I wondered if that sigh was for Ralph or Jason.

Either way, I reached over and squeezed her hand.

"I guess I don't have all the facts straight," Cyl said gamely, trying to match my interest in Lynn Bullock's murder. "How could Jason be at the motel killing his wife at the very same time he's at the ball field playing ball?"

I'd already figured it out.

"Remember last night?" I told her. "How we thought Cletus was upstairs asleep? If anybody'd asked me to alibi him, I'd have taken my oath he was there all the time, wouldn't you?"

"I guess."

"Well, it's the same with Jason Bullock. I heard him get a call from his wife around

five and he was there for pregame pictures around six-thirty. He wandered down for a Coke, and I saw him talking to people on his way to the rest area, but he could have slipped away for a half-hour and who would notice? I wonder if he got a little too cute, though?"

"How do you mean?"

"The switchboard says a man called the motel twice — right before she checked in and again after she called Jason. If he got cocky and made those calls from his cell phone, there'll be a record of it on his bill. Reid, Millard King, and Brandon Frazier all say she wouldn't give them the time of day anymore. Maybe she really had quit messing around with other men."

Cyl nodded thoughtfully. "So she went to that motel expecting Jason to join her for a romantic tryst after his ball game, perhaps trying to put the spark back into their marriage?"

Our line of work made us familiar with the sexual games some couples play.

"And Jason used it to set up her death. Reid says he's ambitious, and he's certainly bright enough to see how a woman like Lynn could hold him back. The way she dressed, the way she'd slept with half the bar in Colleton County? He could divorce

her, but then he'd be in the same spot as Dr. Jeremy Potts. Everybody knows Lynn put him through law school. He wouldn't want to pay alimony the rest of his life based on his enhanced income potential, now would he?"

"But Rosa Edwards saw him and he came after her," said Cyl.

"Only first, he came after an African-American woman driving a white Honda Civic," I said.

Cyl's lovely mobile face froze as the implications of my words sank in.

"Of course," she said bitterly. "He didn't run Clara Freeman into the creek, it was the car and whatever black woman happened to be driving that car. We probably all look alike to him."

The street ahead led straight out of town and seemed to be clear as far as I could see. Nevertheless, I turned left, retracing our trek through town.

"Why are we going this way?" asked Cyl.

"Because I want another look at Jason Bullock's car. It seems to me that that was an awfully small tree to have done that much damage. Maybe he helped it along with a sledgehammer or something."

"And you want to play detective? No. Call the Sheriff's Department. Let Dwight

Bryant handle it. I mean it, Deborah. I want to go home."

"It won't take but a minute," I soothed.

But as we turned into Jason's street, we immediately ran into a solid wall of cars and people, all focused on the rescue truck halfway down the block.

"Oh, Lord," said Cyl. "That's where they were going to cut up a tree. Did that old woman have a heart attack or somebody get hurt?"

With the crowd watching whatever fresh disaster was unfolding, it seemed like a good time to slip over and take a closer look at Jason's car. Accordingly, I copied several other vehicles and parked diagonally with two wheels on the pavement and the other two on someone's front lawn.

"Be right back," I told Cyl, who grabbed at a nearby woman's arm, to ask what was going on. I saw men running with shovels from all over and I hesitated, finally registering the naked horror that hung palpably in the air.

A man I recognized by face though not by name was backing out of the crowd. He was built like a bear with thick neck and brawny arms and he was covered with sawdust and a cold sweat. His eyes were glazed, his face was greenish white. I

couldn't tell if he was in shock or about to throw up.

"What happened?" I asked.

"Oh, God! I didn't know he was down there. I didn't know!"

"Know what?" I asked again.

"The stump just stood back up."

I couldn't make sense of his words, but someone who knew him hurried out of the crowd and put his arm around the man and told me to leave him alone. "Come away, Fred. It's not your fault. The damn fool shouldn't have been down there."

If Fred couldn't talk, there were others almost hysterical at witnessing such a ghastly accident. A hundred-year-old oak had pulled halfway out of the ground, they said, leaving behind a huge root hole, several feet across and three or four feet deep. A neighbor had gone into the hole and was bending down to cut through the roots that were still in the ground just as another neighbor — the man they called Fred — finished cutting through the trunk's three-foot diameter.

Released from the weight of those heavy, leaf-laden branches, the thick stump and enormous root ball suddenly flipped back into the hole, completely burying the man who was there. A dozen men were digging

with shovels and picks, others were trying to hitch ropes and chains from the stump to a team of pickup trucks. They had sent for a bulldozer that was even now lumbering down the street, but everyone knew it was too late the instant the stump righted itself.

"That poor bastard!" said one of the men. "First his wife and now him."

"Such a good man," said an elderly white woman with tears running down her face. "He was always looking to help others."

Before I could ask the final question, Cyl pulled me away.

"It's Jason Bullock," she said.

Chapter 18

Most of these storms describe a parabola, with the westward arch touching the Atlantic Coast, after which the track is northeastward, finally disappearing with the storm itself in the north Atlantic.

With Jason Bullock dead, there was no way to know whether Cyl and I were right about his reasons for killing his wife — anger over Lynn's affairs, political aspirations, or a simple wish to be free of her without paying the price of divorce. The important thing was that once Dwight's people concentrated on him, there was plenty of proof that he had indeed done it.

I was right about his cell phone bills. He'd called the Orchid Motel from the ball ꞏice, trying to make it look as if knew she was there. We still jogged over to the motel

or drove. No witness has come forward to say they saw him do either, but there's at least a half-hour gap when none of us can say positively that he was at the field.

They haven't found the envelope Rosa Edwards gave Clara Freeman, but the bloody clothes he'd worn when he butchered her were in a garbage bag at the bottom of his trash barrel, so we're pretty sure he's the one who stole the envelope from my house. And as soon as Clara Freeman was well enough for Dwight to interview her, she described Jason's car and identified his picture as the white man who ran her off the road.

When Reid eventually heard that Millard King's tie tack had also been found in Lynn's motel room, he theorized that she must have had a cache of souvenirs and that Jason had planted them to implicate the men who had slept with his wife. He was real proud of his theory and ready to run tell it to Dwight until I reminded him why this would not be a good idea.

"But I could get my pen back," he argued.

"Forget it," I snarled.

Dwight beat up on himself when other facts were in. "Last time I lawyer about anything," he

"That night I went to tell him about his wife? If you could've seen it — table set for two, salad wilting in the bowl, steaks drying up on the drainboard — and just the right mixture of shock and anger. He played me like a goddamned violin."

"Or a jury," I said cynically.

Five hot and sweaty days later, power was still out over the rural parts of Colleton County, although phone service had been restored in less than forty-eight hours. Eighteen states had sent crews to help restore North Carolina's electricity but over five thousand poles were down and at least three thousand miles of wires and cables needed to be replaced.

Every day reminded us all over again just how much we relied on electricity in ways we didn't even realize. My family could be smug about cooking with propane gas but in this heat, we were having trouble keeping food fresh in our picnic coolers without a ready supply of ice. Robert, Andrew and Haywood had portable gas-run generators and were sharing them with Daddy and Seth every eight hours so that nobody lost a freezer chest full of meat and vegetables, but all the gasoline pumps at the local crossroads stations worked by

electricity and for the first couple of days, lines were long at the few in-town stations that hadn't lost power.

We had to recharge our portable phones at work, tell time by wristwatches, prise open windows that had been painted shut after the advent of year-round "climate control," and swelter through long smothery nights without even a ceiling fan to stir a breeze. We had to think before flushing toilets and forget about showers. Candlelight lost its romantic novelty after two days and there was a lot of grumbling about spending the evenings without any electronic entertainments.

I cleaned out my refrigerator before it started smelling and put trays of baking soda on the shelves so that stale odors wouldn't build up. Some of my perishables went to Aunt Zell's refrigerator over in Dobbs. I started a compost pile with the rest.

Dobbs had gone without power a mere thirty-six hours, but our courts were still on half-session.

On Thursday morning, I heard a probable cause against a Norwood Love from down near Makely, who was represented by my cousin John Claude Lee. During the storm, the back of young Mr. Love's hog

pen collapsed, revealing an underground chamber beneath the barn it abutted — a chamber full of large plastic barrels and a stainless steel cooker, all set to start making bootleg whiskey.

According to the agent who testified that morning, it did not appear that the still had ever been in operation, but mere possession of such equipment is against the law. I agreed that there was indeed probable cause and set a trial date. Since Mr. Love had no record, though, I released him without bail.

Afterwards, I visited with Aunt Zell to pick up a couple of loads of laundry that she'd done for Daddy and Maidie and me.

"If Kidd wants to come up this weekend, he can stay here," she offered, knowing how long it'd been.

I thanked her, but said I doubted he could get away.

Truth is, I wasn't sure if he wanted to get away.

We'd spoken a couple of times. I called him that first day to say I was all right, in case he was worried, and to hear how he was. What he was, was . . . shall we say, occupied?

The storm surge at New Bern was more than nine feet and it had flooded his

341

daughter Amber and his ex-wife out of their house. Last time I phoned, they were both staying with Kidd, whose cabin was on higher ground. So maybe that was the reason he didn't sound anxious to come to me, and it was certainly the reason I couldn't go to him.

When I stopped past the homeplace to give Maidie the folded laundry, I was surprised to see Daddy standing by an unfamiliar pickup.

It was an awkward moment as Norwood Love and I recognized each other from morning court. He murmured a soft, "Sorry, ma'am," then cranked his truck and drove off.

"How do you know him?" I asked Daddy.

"I know a lot of people, shug," he said.

"Did he tell you he's waiting trial for owning moonshining equipment?"

"Yeah, he told me." He gave a rueful shake of his head. "Reckon that's why he come to me. Thought maybe I'd understand quicker than most folks how come he needs extra work. I said I'd hire him to clear out some of them trees blocking the lanes. Your brothers got so much on their plates, we can use another pair of hands."

Daddy doesn't often touch on his own

past history of moonshining and he's certainly never discussed it with me even though I've heard a lot of the stories from my brothers and a few others from SBI and ATF agents. As I've gotten older and heard more, I have to say that not all of the stories have been warm and funny. Some have a violent edge that makes me uneasy to think about.

There wasn't a breath of wind blowing when I got back to my house and the air was so steamy that I planned to jump into the pond as soon as I arrived.

Cyl was waiting for me on the porch. It was the first time I'd seen her looking halfway like herself since the storm, but then she lived in Garner where there was hot and cold running water, air-conditioning and hair dryers.

"Want to go skinny-dipping?" I said as soon as I got out of the car.

"Not really."

There was something different about her.

"What's up?" I asked.

"I just came from my grandmother's and I wanted you to be the second to know."

"Know what?" I asked with apprehension.

"That I gave Doug Woodall my notice at noon today. I flew up to Washington yesterday to interview with McLean, Applebee and Shaw and they made me a very generous offer."

The name was vaguely familiar.

"They're one of the most effective black lobbyist firms in Washington," she said. "I'll be going back up this weekend to look for an apartment."

"Oh, Cyl," I said, "are you sure?"

"I'm sure," she said firmly. "I just wanted to thank you for being there when I really needed a friend."

My eyes filled with tears. It's in the genes. Half my family can't watch a Hallmark commercial without crying.

She was crisp and cool, I was hot and sweaty, but I hugged her anyhow. "I'm really going to miss you, girl."

"No, you won't. I'll be back to visit Grandma and you can come visit me. I'm hoping to find a place in Georgetown. Think of us in all those great shops and restaurants."

"Yeah," I said glumly.

"It's the only way I can deal with it," she said quietly and this time, she hugged me.

After Cyl left, I changed clothes, then

got out the pane of glass and glazing putty I'd bought a couple of days ago and began repairing my broken window. Different brothers had offered to do it, but they're still working on bigger repairs. At least I don't have tall trees around my house to fall on anything. And maybe I ought to reconsider where I want to plant them. Dwight's right: it'll take twenty years to grow them tall enough to do any damage, but I'll probably still be here — alone — twenty years from now. Certainly doesn't look as if I'll be setting up housekeeping in New Bern any time soon.

I'm probably not cut out to be anybody's stepmom.

Unlike Cyl, who would have been terrific under different circumstances.

I hadn't seen Ralph Freeman since the day after the storm, but I heard that Clara was making a pretty good recovery, all things considered, and would probably be home before the weekend although Amy says she's going to need a lot of physical therapy in the next few months.

Reese came by for a swim just as I was ready to jump in myself. He said that a power crew from Virginia was working its way out from Cotton Grove.

"The way they're moving, we might get

our lights back by midnight."

"And not a minute too soon," I said fervently as I floated on my back and let the warm water relax me.

"I'll tell you one good thing about Fran, though," he said, drifting along beside me.

"Yeah?"

"We're not gonna have to listen to any more Hazel stories any time soon, are we?"

I laughed. "And fifty years from now, if I catch you telling Fran stories to your grandbabies, I'll punch you hard."

Darkness fell much as it did a hundred years ago, quietly and utterly. The night sky was radiant with stars undimmed by electric yard lights or the streetlights going in across the creek where a new housing development's being built. Fireflies glowed with flicks of soft golden yellow while crickets sang to the stars.

It was the dark of the moon, yet the countryside seemed luminous to me. I blew out my candles and walked out to the pond, then skirted the edge and followed the rutted lane that was a double line of white sand against the darker grass.

Near the end of the pond, I smelled smoke and followed my nose till I saw fire reflected off bushes beyond the cut in the

undergrowth. As I passed through the cut into the open field, I saw Daddy burning a brush pile and I couldn't help but smile. Other men burn brush in the daytime but Daddy's always done his burning at night. I watched him stir the flaming branches with his pitchfork. Sparks jetted thirty feet upwards like a fiery fountain against the velvet darkness.

Blue and Ladybelle came out to greet me, and as I walked into the circle of light, Daddy said, "Looks like roman candles, don't it?"

For the next half hour, we circled the fire, pushing the longer branches in as their twiggy tops burned away. It was hot, sweaty work, but the flames kept our clothes dry. The smell of green leaves burning was unbearably nostalgic. Most of the time, I'm an adult, able to bear what has to be borne with an adult's stoicism. But there are times when I miss Mother so much it's like a physical hurt that's never healed. She used to love bonfires, too.

Eventually, as the fire settled down, we sat on a nearby fallen log, talking of nothing important, watching the fire burn lower.

Without really thinking, I said, "You

paying John Claude to represent the Love boy?"

He didn't answer.

"You're still messing with whiskey, aren't you?"

There was such a long silence that I was almost afraid that I'd made him really mad. On the other hand, if he *is* still bootlegging, it threatens my professional reputation.

At last he said, "Your mama never understood why I couldn't leave it alone. She thought it was the whiskey itself, but it won't. You never seen me drunk, did you?"

"No, sir."

"No, it won't the whiskey. And after a while, it won't even the money."

Another silence.

"What, then?" I asked.

"I guess you might say it was the excitement. Running the risks. Knowing what I could lose if I got caught. That's something your mama never rightly understood."

He turned and looked at me a long level moment by the dying fire. "You understand though, don't you, shug?"

Now it was my turn to sit silently.

He nodded and poked the fire again. Another burst of bright sparks gushed

upward in swirls of red and gold against the night sky.

Through the ravaged trees to the north, an answering glow suddenly appeared, a brilliant whiteness against the treetops.

It was the floodlights of a power crew working its way into the dark countryside.

insisted she spend the night with them and that he should come, too. Rob is Dwight's younger brother and lives just down the road from their mother in a big old farmhouse that Kate inherited from her first husband.

He dialled their number and had just explained about Daddy's pecan trees when the phone went dead in his ear.

Which meant he had to struggle back out to his cruiser to radio the departmental dispatcher and let them know his location.

I had thought the rain was coming down as hard as it could possibly fall, but suddenly it was as if all the firehoses of heaven were pouring down on the backyard. Even in such utter darkness, the cruiser's interior light was only a faint glow through the heavy sheets of water and Dwight was wetter than if he'd gone into the pond fully dressed.

"You people keep going in and out and Mr. Kezzie ain't gonna have no clothes left," Maidie grumbled as she fetched dry pants and shirt.

When I invited the Freeman kids to come to a hurricane party, I'd expected a mildly exciting storm. Fran would come ashore, I thought, and immediately collapse — lots of rain, a little wind, a brief power outage so we could have candles, maybe even a few dead twigs to clatter down across the old tin roof.

I did *not* expect the eye to come marching up I-40 straight through Colleton County, wreaking as much damage as Sherman's march through Georgia. Yet, as Stan's radio made clear, that was exactly what was happening.

The storm hit Wilmington around nine, packing winds of a hundred and five miles per hour, and barely faltered as it moved across land on a north-by-northwest heading. By midnight, rain seemed to be coming down horizontally. It kept us busy stuffing newspapers and towels around door and window sills on the northeast side of the house.

"Good thing your mama never wanted wall-to-wall carpet," Daddy told me.

The house creaked like a ship at sea, then shuddered as a tree crashed onto the porch. We grabbed our flashlights, peered through the front windows and found the porch completely covered with the leaf-heavy top of an oak. At least two support posts had collapsed under the weight. Lashanda's eyes were wide with apprehension and she attached herself firmly to Cyl's side.

Dwight, Reese and Stan went up to the attic to check on the gable vents and Reese came back immediately for hammer, nails, and large plastic garbage bags.

"Rain's coming in through that northeast vent like somebody's standing outside with a hose aimed straight at it," he said. "We're going to try to plug it up."

"How's the roof?" asked Daddy.

"So far, it seems to be holding."

There was no guitar or fiddle for us that night, though at one point, Reese did manage to distract Lashanda with train sounds on his harmonica.

WPTF ("We Protect The Family") was tracking the storm the old-fashioned way as people along the route called in to the AM radio station with reports of trees down, possible tornadoes, wind and rain damage, and barometric pressure all the way down to 48.4 inches.

Around two, the wind finally slacked off enough to be noticeable. Lashanda had fallen asleep with one arm around Ladybelle and the other hugging her doll. Reese, too, was snoring on a pallet in the corner.

Daddy stood up stiffly and said, "Well, if that's the worst it's gonna do, I reckon I'll go lay down and get a little rest."

Maidie and Cletus followed him upstairs to real beds.

Stan lay on his pallet, fighting to stay awake enough to jot notes from the radio reports.

Cyl, Dwight and I went out to the kitchen where I boiled water for coffee. (With the power going off so often, a lot of us have our own LP tanks and cook with gas.) Dwight was hungry again, so I set out leftover fried chicken and the fixings for tomato sandwiches.

While he ate and Cyl and I drank coffee, we talked about the two killings — Lynn Bullock and Rosa Edwards — and whether Clara Freeman's wreck had anything to do with either of them.

"Which happened first?" I asked, trying to make sense of it. "The wreck or the Edwards killing?"

"If she went into Possum Creek immediately after leaving Miz Thomas, then that was first," said Dwight, "because Rosa Edwards worked her regular shift yesterday."

I tried doing a timetable. "So say Clara Freeman crashed her car around noon. It probably wouldn't take an hour to zoom out here from Dobbs at the precise

Also by Margaret Maron
in Large Print:

Home Fires
Killer Market
Up Jumps the Devil
Southern Discomfort
Bootlegger's Daughter
Fugitive Colors

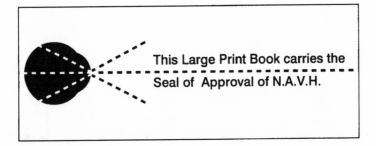

STORM TRACK